W9-BUT-522

NEST

Center Point
Large Print

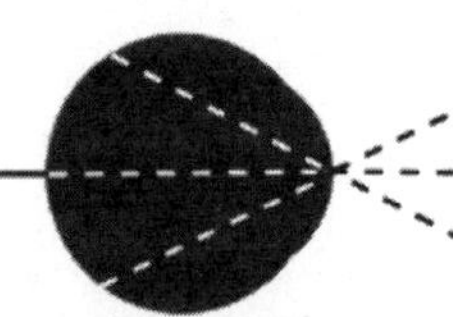

This Large Print Book carries the
Seal of Approval of N.A.V.H.

NEST

TERRY GOODKIND

CENTER POINT LARGE PRINT
THORNDIKE, MAINE

This Center Point Large Print edition
is published in the year 2017 by arrangement with
Skyhorse Publishing.

The text of this Large Print edition is unabridged.
In other aspects, this book may vary
from the original edition.
Printed in the United States of America
on permanent paper.
Set in 16-point Times New Roman type.

ISBN: 978-1-68324-331-1

Library of Congress Cataloging-in-Publication Data

Names: Goodkind, Terry, author.
Title: Nest / Terry Goodkind.
Description: Center Point Large Print edition. | Thorndike, Maine :
Center Point Large Print, 2017.
Identifiers: LCCN 2017000936 | ISBN 9781683243311
(hardcover : alk. paper)
Subjects: LCSH: Murder—Investigation—Fiction. | Psychic ability—
Fiction. | Large type books. | GSAFD: Mystery fiction.
Classification: LCC PS3557.O5826 N47 2017 | DDC 813/.54—dc23
LC record available at https://lccn.loc.gov/2017000936

To Jeri, the love of my life,
for her unwavering support and for
waiting so patiently for this very special book
to finally be brought to life.

NEST

CHAPTER ONE

For the past three weeks, John Allen Bishop had been keeping the devil chained in the basement. What, exactly, the devil had been doing in Chicago John didn't know and the devil wasn't saying. What John did know was that over the past several days the situation had been getting increasingly worrisome.

At first, the threats yelled up from the basement had been the most vile things imaginable—things that John would have expected to hear from the devil. But in the last few days something had changed. In those long, hushed moments as the sun went down and the world went still, John had found himself shuffling closer to the basement door, carefully leaning in, stretching his neck to put his ear close to the narrow crack in the door that led to the darkness down below.

That was when he had first heard the whispers.

Since the floor squeaked, the devil knew whenever John was in the kitchen, near the top of the stairs. When John put his ear close to the crack in the door, the devil always greeted him by name. Sometimes the devil chuckled softly to himself. The whispered promises never failed to make John's mouth go dry.

But now the menace in the basement had

inexplicably fallen silent. The silence worried him more than the whispers had.

He paced from the refrigerator to the sink and back, debating what to do. He didn't relish the thought of going down there again. The chain was strong enough, he was sure of that, and he knew how far it could reach. He knew to the inch. Still, he didn't want to go down there any sooner than he had to.

As he paced, the fluorescent light hummed above a sink full of disorderly stacks of dirty dishes. A clump of crusted forks waiting to be washed stuck up from a cracked green plastic tumbler. Ordinarily, John prided himself on being tidy, but with the dire turn of events he certainly didn't think he could be blamed for ignoring the dishes.

The dishes would just have to wait; the devil was more important.

John turned away from the mess in the sink and paced back toward the refrigerator, following the same track he'd been walking for the past hour as regret kept building, bringing on the familiar weight of indecision. He didn't know how he had ever gotten such a crazy idea in the first place.

He hadn't thought it through. He realized that now. He should have thought it through. People always told him to think things through.

But what else could he have done? It had been

so unexpected. He had to do something. The devil knew things—too many things.

It had seemed simple at first. Chain up the devil; the world would be safe.

Kate would be safe.

It was turning out to be not so simple.

John told himself that he should go down and bash in the devil's head. He knew he should. There were tools in the basement—beyond the reach of the chain, of course. There was a sledgehammer that could do the ghastly job.

But John didn't have that much courage. He should have done it in the beginning, when the devil had been unconscious, but he hadn't had the courage then, either. Even as he tried to summon the courage to do what needed doing, he knew that his chance had passed.

John wondered if he should call Detective Janek. From time to time she would come to see him, to show him the pictures. She was nice. He liked helping her.

He glanced over at the phone on the wall in the hallway. Detective Janek's card was sitting on the top of the phone, leaning against the wall. She had left it there one day when she'd told him that he could call her anytime, day or night.

He wondered if maybe he should do that now.

John didn't like to use the phone, though. He didn't like to call people. He got confused on the phone.

He feared that this was different from the times she'd come to see him. He feared that this time she might not believe him.

He might even get into trouble.

Fear and doubt welled up. What if he lost his job?

His sister had helped him get his job. She'd told him that he could do it, told him to do his best. It was the first job that he'd ever had. He liked his job of fitting the colorful plastic pieces together, but mostly he liked that it made him independent. Having his job meant he could pay the bills and take care of himself.

Kate helped him when he got confused, but he could do most things on his own. She said that she was proud of him, of how well he was doing.

He liked being on his own. He didn't want to lose his job. He didn't want Kate to be disappointed in him.

John didn't ever tell his sister about Detective Janek. He didn't want her to be afraid. It was the only way he could protect her.

He knew that it was wrong to chain people in the basement, of course, but this wasn't a regular person. This was the devil.

Still, he feared that even Detective Janek might not believe him.

He suddenly wondered if he might even be put in jail.

John wiped his sweaty palms on his pant legs.

He swallowed in terror at what might happen to him if he was arrested. The very thought of going to jail and having to look into the eyes of all those men nearly made his knees give out.

His attention was snatched by his own shadow falling across the refrigerator. He drew his collar tight at his throat and told himself that he had things under control. He just had to keep them that way, that was all.

It was getting late and he knew that he needed to get down there. He didn't like taking food down to the basement, but John just didn't have it in him to kill, either by a quick blow or by slow starvation. He couldn't stand it when people hurt, even if the hurt was hunger.

Distantly, through the tumbling fragments of thoughts pulling him this way and that, it seemed that there was something not right about the refrigerator. Something different.

In the dim light he surveyed the newspaper clippings that he had carefully cut out and taped to the door. They were all still there. John hated the stark look of the white refrigerator, so he frequently taped items that interested him on the blank door, after he had carefully folded over the pointed corners. He didn't like sharp points.

He changed the clippings often, whenever something new caught his eye. It didn't have to be anything especially meaningful. Pictures of animals, headlines about holidays, or sometimes even just a single word that was pleasing—anything to cover the nakedness of the refrigerator.

There were photos as well, their corners also carefully bent over, stuck on the refrigerator door with word magnets. He smiled back at his sister smiling out at him from a sunny beach, from behind the wheel of her first car, from the couch in his living room.

He scanned the newspaper headlines about parades and holidays and sunny forecasts, looking for something new, something that might have changed. Some word. Some sign.

Then, he spotted what wasn't right.

There were dozens of little magnets attached to the door. They'd been a birthday gift from his sister. Each magnet was a white word on a black background. He liked to arrange the words so that they rhymed, or so that they said something cheerful. The words stuck to the white metal door always seemed welcoming, offering a friendly greeting when he came home and went to get himself something to eat—or, like now, when he went to get the devil something to eat.

The last message he'd made from arranging the magnets was still there: A CASTLE KEEPS YOU SAFE.

He'd made the saying with the magnets some time ago, after he had heard that a man's home was his castle. Except for going to work and the store, John didn't like going out. He liked to be inside. Safe. Home was safe. Home was his castle.

Chaining up the devil was the most daring thing John had ever done in his whole life.

But now the little magnets that he had so carefully arranged into A CASTLE KEEPS YOU SAFE were no longer in a line by themselves the way they had been.

All the spare words that had been pushed off to the right side were now arranged into a circle, leaving a cleared, round, white patch near the refrigerator door's handle. A CASTLE KEEPS YOU SAFE sat in the middle of that circle.

But now there were new words arranged in a neat line below, as if in answer.

The new words said NOT ANY MORE.

CHAPTER TWO

John leaned closer and peered at the new words.

NOT ANY MORE.

He hadn't put those words there.

He glanced over at the basement door. It was a thick, six-panel pine door. Here and there, faded blue peeked through the peeling cream-colored paint. John remembered happy times playing on the floor in the kitchen when that door had been all blue.

The door was open a little, at the top corner, because it was warped and wouldn't close properly.

The door had a lock, but John didn't have a key for it. It was one of those old-fashioned keyholes, like he'd seen in cartoons and the movies. When he had been little, John used to peer through the keyhole and pretend that he was a spy watching for danger. Now, he knew what sort of danger waited on the other side of that door.

Through the slit of the partially open door he could see inky blackness. The devil down below in that darkness was silent. Not even a whisper came up from the basement. John wondered if that was a good thing or not. He stood still as stone, leaning in, listening.

John reconsidered calling the police. He glanced

again at the card that Detective Janek had set on the top of his wall phone, after she had carefully folded over the corners so the points wouldn't scare him.

She had always been nice to him, always believed him, but he wondered if she would believe him this time. If Detective Janek went down in the basement and saw him, if she just looked into his eyes, wouldn't she know?

John had looked into the devil's eyes. John knew.

As he stood motionless, watching the sliver of blackness from below, he realized that his castle wasn't as safe as he had thought it was.

That was what the words on the refrigerator meant. This place wasn't safe anymore. Not since the devil had come into it.

John stole another glance at the aqua-colored phone hanging on the floral-papered wall at the side of the stairwell leading upstairs, just around the corner from the basement door. Maybe he should call Detective Janek. The police would want to know that the devil was in Chicago.

Or maybe he should call his sister.

The devil knew her name. She ought to know that—that the devil knew her name.

He should call Kate and tell her. He wanted her to be safe.

If he called her she might know what to do. The police might not listen to him, might not believe him, but Kate would believe him this time. She had to.

All at once, the solution seemed clear. He would call his sister and tell her everything, tell her what had happened, tell her that the devil knew her name, too, just like he'd known John's name. She would know what to do.

Springing into action, John hastily pulled all the pictures of his sister off the refrigerator door. The magnets holding them rained down, clattering on the floor. Rather than slow to pick up the magnets, he started stuffing the photos in the front pocket of his work pants. He was worried that the devil might look at Kate's pictures. He didn't think it would be a good idea to let the devil get a look at his sister.

John didn't want evil looking at her.

Once the photos were all tucked safely into his pocket, he hurried into the hallway to call her.

Just as he reached for the receiver, the phone rang.

His heart pounding out of control, John snatched up the handpiece and put it to his ear, listening. He feared that it might be the devil calling him from the basement.

"Hi, Johnny. It's me."

John felt a wave of giddy relief wash through him at hearing his sister's familiar, cheerful voice. He clutched the tangled cord with his other hand as he sagged against the wall.

"Hi, Kate," he said in an expectant pant.

He glanced toward the slit of darkness under the basement door.

"I'm back from my trip a day early and the driver is about to drop me at home."

"Uh-huh."

"What's the matter? You sound winded. Did you just run up the front steps?"

John needed to tell her about the devil. Kate would know what to do. She was smart. His sister always knew what to do. She always helped him. He missed her. Right at that moment he missed her more than anything in the world. He cupped the phone close with both hands so that the devil couldn't hear.

"Uh . . . no."

"Hey, listen," she said, not pressing. She was the only one who didn't get impatient and press him. "I got a call from a lawyer."

John blinked. "A lawyer?"

"Yeah. Remember Mom's half brother who lived out west—Everett—remember him?"

John wasn't sure he did. With all the things racing through his mind as he stared at the basement door, it was hard to think.

"Uh . . ."

She breathed a lighthearted laugh. "Me neither, really. We went there, once—to his trailer out in that little town in the desert. He wasn't the friendliest guy. You were little at the time. I wouldn't expect you to remember him. I hardly remember him myself. Anyway, I'm afraid he died."

John turned his eyes from the dark slit. "Died?"

"Yeah. The lawyer said it was about three weeks ago—"

"Three weeks?"

"Yeah, three, well, almost four weeks ago."

John wiped a tear from his cheek as he listened to her breathing for a moment before she went on.

"I know how it bothers you when people die, John, but he was really old. Don't be too sad. He never left that place of his and I bet it was because he loved it just like you love your house. I bet he had a good life there, a good long life."

"What did he die of?"

There was a long moment of silence before she said, "He was old, John."

She didn't want to tell him. He knew that sometimes Kate didn't want to tell him things, so she would say something simple.

"Anyway, the lawyer said that we're the only relatives and Everett left his place to us. He doesn't think the estate is worth a great deal but it belongs to you and me, now. I'm going to have to go out there and handle it. I guess I'll have to see about selling the place or something."

John glanced back at the basement door. He needed to tell her before anything else happened. He swallowed as he gathered his courage, determined to tell her the whole story from the beginning.

"I went to the cemetery," he blurted out.

"You did?" She paused, seeming surprised. "Alone?"

John nodded and all of a sudden started talking faster, trying to get it out all at once. "I went to the store and bought flowers and then put them on Mom and Pop's grave, by the headstones—like you showed me—in the vase the way the cemetery people like it done. I put your name on the card, too."

"That's so sweet." Her voice had turned soft. "Thanks. I bet Mom and Pop liked the flowers." She cleared her throat. "When did you go to the cemetery?"

He'd never gone there alone before. John wiped the back of his hand across his nose, trying not to cry. "Three weeks ago." He felt another tear run down his cheek. He had to tell her. She would know what to do. "I—I—I was there, and someone was watching me—and then when I got home I—"

The basement light snapped on.

John froze.

He stood motionless, staring wide-eyed at the slit of light stabbing up from below the door.

"John, it was probably just someone else putting flowers on a grave," his sister said in his ear.

He couldn't make himself talk. In his head, he

was screaming *Tell her, hurry, tell her,* but he couldn't make the words come out. His voice wouldn't work. He was afraid to make a sound.

And then something else came up from beyond the doorway—a low voice speaking his name. His whole name, the way people used to do when he was little and he'd gotten himself into trouble.

"John Allen Bishop."

He watched the shafts of light from below shifting lighter, darker, and lighter again.

"John?" Kate asked. "Is there someone there in the house with you?"

He desperately wanted Kate's help. But what if the devil could get to her through the phone? He didn't want danger coming near his sister.

The hiss of a voice from below called his name again—but just the first part—then again, coming closer, moving up the stairs. The door creaked as it started to open.

"John? What's that sound? Do you have company? John?"

"Run, Kate!" he screamed into the receiver. "Run!"

John slammed the phone back on the hook so that the devil couldn't get to her through the phone lines. He raced for the front door as fast as his crooked legs would carry him.

He nearly made it.

A great weight slammed into him from behind, smashing him face-first into the door. He rebounded only to have a powerful hand grab his shirt and spin him around. The impact had dazed him. His nose felt like it had been hit with a baseball bat. He felt warm blood running down his face, dripping off his chin. The thought of so much blood gushing out of his nose horrified him.

John looked up and went stiff with terror. The devil had his pitchfork.

His eyes seemed lit from within by pure evil. They were eyes that sought only to see suffering.

His face twisting in rage, the devil roared as he drove his pitchfork down at the floor. The tines of the pitchfork punctured both of John's shoes, severed the bones in his feet, pierced the heavy soles, and stuck solidly in the floorboards.

Even if John had tried to move, he wouldn't have been able to. He was pinned to the floor.

As he stood in stunned terror, the devil slid a hand down into John's pants pocket. He pulled out the photos of Kate. As John trembled, unable to think, the pain keeping him from trying to move, the devil slowly looked at the pictures, one by one, his wicked smile growing wider and wider.

John didn't want the devil to look at Kate. He snatched for the photos. The devil caught John's hand and twisted his fingers back until they snapped with sickening pops, like twigs breaking.

As John screamed in shock and pain, holding his twisted and broken fingers with his good hand, the devil slipped the photos of Kate into his own pocket.

"You've caused me quite a bit of trouble, Johnny boy."

"Leave us alone," John wept. "Please . . ."

Towering over him, the devil peered deeply into John's eyes. "Do you remember my promise, John?"

The shocking pain of his feet impaled by the tines was just starting to register through paralyzing panic and the horrific agony of his ruined fingers.

He remembered the promises. He remembered them all too well. John's helpless sobs grew louder.

"What do you see with those eyes of yours?" the devil asked as he loomed closer yet, as if trying to see some secret hidden in John's eyes. "What do you see, Johnny boy?" he whispered from only an inch away.

John shook uncontrollably. "Nothing!"

"I think you see way too much." A big hand grabbed John's hair at the back of his head. "I'm going to fix that."

And then the devil leaned close, his mouth beside John's ear, and he again whispered his promise.

"I'm going to bring you everlasting darkness."

John shrieked in fright and pain as something terribly long and sickeningly sharp slammed twice up into the core of his body. He couldn't draw the full breath he so desperately needed.

The devil's teeth looked huge as his jaws opened wide, coming for what he wanted. The teeth raked John's face, peeling away his eyelids.

"In the scheme of things," the devil said as he forced a thumb deep into the side of one of John's eye sockets, "this doesn't really matter. After all, the universe, too, is blind."

The distant words made no sense to John as he struggled and screamed in the agony that was only just beginning.

He felt twisting pain and darkness pressing into his eyes.

He hoped that Kate would run, run fast, run far, get away. . . .

CHAPTER THREE

Kate looked up when Detective Sanders called her name. She was in a daze. None of it felt real.

He leaned an arm on the roof of the car, just above the open back door where she sat sideways, despairing because there was nothing she could do. He'd been the one who had met her and taken her aside when she had arrived at John's house.

He was older and a bit overweight, and more comforting than his austere, pockmarked face had at first suggested.

"Miss Bishop," he said in a sympathetic but formal tone, "do you feel up to answering a few questions?"

Kate nodded. "But I'm afraid I don't know anything that could help you find out who could have done this."

A woman detective in a dark suit stood nearby, within earshot, as she scanned the scene lit by all the headlights of police cars. She had only just arrived and hadn't said anything after coming out of the house. She looked to be a few years older than Kate, maybe in her middle thirties. Her posture, her shoulders, the open collar of her stark white shirt, and the cut of her clothes suggested that she took care of herself. Her short brown hair turned inward just below her strong jawline. Her dark eyes scrutinized Kate so closely, so deliberately, that it was beginning to make her feel self-conscious.

Detective Gibson, also in a white shirt, a tie, and a gray jacket similar to the one that Detective Sanders wore, returned from the house to whisper to the woman detective. Like Detective Sanders's, his hair was cut so short it was the next closest thing to being shaved bald. Thick skin bunched up in creases at the back of his bull neck.

Detective Sanders sucked something from between his two front teeth and held up a finger toward Kate to excuse himself for a moment as he stepped away to speak with the others.

All three wore police badges on their belts. Under their jackets, at their sides, Kate saw that they all carried Glock handguns. The detectives all seemed professional in a way that Kate found reassuring, if there could be such a thing in such a situation.

A pair of patrolmen in dark uniforms stood at ease on the porch, flanking the front door, seeing to it that no one without authorization went in. All the activity was quieting down somewhat, now that her brother's body had finally been removed from the house to a coroner's van. She wondered what she would need to do to recover her brother for burial. She supposed she should call the funeral home she had used for her parents. They would likely know what to do.

People carrying cases of equipment came and went. All of the activities and procedures were a confusing mystery to Kate, although they were obviously looking for evidence to try to find the killer. From time to time she'd seen flashes as everything in the house, it seemed, had been photographed.

But even if she didn't know much about their specific jobs, she recognized that they were well orchestrated and methodical as they went about their tasks. No one wandered around in confusion. Everyone but Kate knew what to do.

No one hurried, either. She supposed that there wasn't any point in rushing. There was no one to rescue, no fleeing suspect to chase down and arrest. Besides, this was their daily job. It was just another day at work to them. Kate knew that, for her, it would always stand out as one in a handful of the worst days in her life.

When she'd first arrived she had wanted to go into the house and see her brother. The detectives wouldn't let her. They told her that they needed to do their work first. Detective Sanders told her, in a confidential tone, that it would be better if she didn't see her brother that way, in the house where it had happened. He told her that she would not want that to be her memory of her brother. As much as she'd thought that she wanted to see for herself, his candor as he had looked into her eyes had given her pause and made her realize that he was probably right.

With all the people going in and out, the detectives huddled in hushed discussions, and the technicians carrying equipment, it was hard to imagine the horrific scene in the house. In a way, the unknown only made it worse.

So far the only thing she knew for sure was that her brother was dead. Right from the beginning they'd said that it was murder. The way they said it made it clear that there was no doubt at all about that part of it. Kate couldn't stop her imagination from racing off in every direction. But most of all, she couldn't imagine why anyone would harm her brother.

On the sidewalk to either side of the house, beyond the police tape, the crowds of onlookers had thinned as the night had worn on. When she'd first arrived a lot of people had been milling around outside the house, watching, gossiping, and worrying about what kind of maniac might be loose in the neighborhood.

Once, an odd, uneasy feeling had made her look up. A tall man with disheveled hair, his hands stuffed into the pockets of a light jacket, was just turning away. Even though she didn't catch sight of his face, she could tell by the way he slipped back through the crowd that he had been standing there watching her. It gave her a chill to have strangers staring at her like that. It made her feel naked and vulnerable.

Other people looked away from her when she glanced in their direction. They, too, had been staring at her.

Detectives or uniformed officers had been close by Kate the whole time, saying little, explaining some of the process when she asked questions about suspects, about her brother's body, about what they were doing with it and what she would need to do.

Reporters, cameramen, and news crews holding up lights had talked to a higher-ranking police officer, who basically told them nothing except that the victim was named John Allen Bishop and he had apparently been murdered in his home by an unknown assailant. When they asked about how it had happened, he said the details were being withheld and gave a number for tips.

Impeccably dressed on-air female reporters talked into cameras for the eleven o'clock news, describing it as a grisly scene. Thankfully, the police had kept Kate sheltered from the newspeople, not letting them know she was the victim's sister. Having a reporter with fresh lipstick shove a microphone in her face and ask how she felt when she had learned that her brother had been murdered was about the last thing in the world Kate wanted to have to deal with.

"He didn't suffer, did he?" Kate asked up to Detective Sanders when he finally returned. She wondered if she'd already asked the question, but if she had, she didn't remember his answer. "Did John suffer? Can you at least tell me that?"

Detective Sanders stopped leafing through his notes as he looked down from beside the open car door. "I can't say for sure, Miss Bishop, but I don't believe so. We believe it to have been over quickly."

Kate pulled a crumpled tissue from the pocket of her jeans and worked it in her fingers. He returned to methodically flipping back through his notes. "Miss Bishop, you said that when you were on the phone with him, your brother suddenly yelled at you to run, and then hung up."

Kate nodded. "That's right. I called 911 right away."

"Do you have any idea why he would say such a thing? Why would he say to run? You weren't close to his house."

Kate wiped her nose with the tissue before answering. "With John's mental handicap he wasn't able to understand things the way a normal adult could. Being halfway across the city or even halfway across the country wouldn't have meant anything to him if he was afraid. He viewed the world simplistically, as if everything was immediately around him. He didn't grasp concepts like distance very well."

Detective Sanders gestured with his pen. "So

when he said for you to run, you feel that he might have simply meant that there was someone there, in the house, and so in his way of thinking that person represented a danger to you as well as to him."

"Probably." Kate brushed her black bangs to the side as she glanced up. "He always worried about me."

"And with his mental disability he was still able to hold down a job?" Detective Gibson asked as he stepped up beside Detective Sanders.

"Yes." Kate looked up into the man's unexpressive face. "He worked at the Clarkson Center for Developmental Disability." She gestured over her shoulder. "On Hamilton Street. They provide work that people like John can do. It helps them be self-sufficient. The doctors had recommended that he be allowed to lead as normal a life as possible."

"So you feel he was competent to live alone?" Detective Gibson asked. Despite his formidable looks, he had an agreeable voice. She could tell that he was deliberately trying not to make it sound like an accusation of negligence on her part.

"Yes. Fortunately, he wasn't as profoundly mentally handicapped as some. He was able to take care of himself pretty well. The doctors said that it would be better for him if he did, if he felt responsible for his own life. Having a sense of purpose and control really did help him be happier.

"He took the bus to work and back. He could walk to the store. The people there all know him. He could mostly take care of himself and he liked doing it. He felt comfortable in the limited places he went.

"He wasn't left to fend for himself as much as it might seem. Unless I was out of town for my job I'd come over often to check on him. I drove him laces like to the doctor, or to the dentist, or to go out for a meal. Sometimes I'd take him with me when I shopped for clothes. He liked that. As long as I was with him when he was in a strange environment he felt safe.

"I helped him take care of bills, made sure that he ate properly, made sure he did his chores—things like that. He was slow, but he could do simple things for himself. It was hard on me, emotionally, not to be there all the time, but I think it was right for him to be able to live his own life."

"When was the last time you were here?" Detective Sanders asked without looking up as he wrote in his notebook. "The last time you actually saw him?"

Kate rubbed her fingertips back and forth across her brow. "A little over three weeks ago. I've never been gone for that long before but I had to be in Dallas for my job. I'm an auditor at

KDEX Systems. There were irregularities at our office in Dallas and I had to go down there to look into it. I called John just about every night, though."

"So the reason for your call to him earlier tonight was to let him know that you were back in town?"

"Yes." Kate looked up at the man's waiting face. "Besides checking on him, I had to tell him that a relative—my mother's half brother—had died. I just found out about it earlier today."

"I'm sorry to hear about that, ma'am," Detective Gibson said. "When did he pass away?"

"He died a little over three weeks ago—the twelfth of last month—out in Nevada. He was murdered."

Detective Sanders looked at her over the top of his notebook. "Murdered?"

CHAPTER FOUR

Detective Gibson, a few creases appearing on his brow, asked the same thing. "This uncle of yours was murdered?"

"Yes."

"How was he killed?" Detective Sanders asked.

Kate lifted a hand in a weak gesture. "I'm not sure of the circumstances. An Esmeralda County sheriff, out in Nevada, called to tell me that Everett had been killed in the course of a robbery. It didn't make a lot of sense. Everett didn't have much worth stealing, at least not from what I knew of him."

"Did they say how he was murdered? Any specifics?"

Kate shook her head. "No. Just that he'd been killed in the course of a robbery. I assumed that he'd been shot. But now that you ask, I guess I don't know that for a fact.

"I only met Everett once when I was a girl and don't really know much about him. The sheriff gave me the number of Everett's lawyer and suggested I call him. When I did, the lawyer told me that John and I had been named in Everett's will because we were the only next of kin. I thought Everett would have left his things to a friend, or someone he knew out there, but he didn't. Whatever he has, he left it to us.

"The lawyer said that Everett had long ago made arrangements for his burial—one of those payment plans—so he had already been laid to rest as per his wishes. The lawyer said that John and I now owned the trailer Everett lived in, his pickup, and his personal effects. I'm supposed to go out there and see to them as soon as it's convenient. But now . . ." She gestured helplessly toward the house.

She felt stupid for not having asked such a basic question as how a relative had been murdered. It wasn't like her not to ask questions. In fact, her job was to investigate, ask questions, get to the bottom of things.

But it had been such an unexpected call, and such unexpected news, that she hadn't thought to ask how he had been killed. That, and the sheriff had been rather terse in a way that didn't invite questions. She thought that with a murder on his hands he must have been busy.

With a thumb, Kate smoothed down creases on the leg of her jeans as she watched another man wearing latex gloves carry a black plastic bag out of the house, then slide open the door of a white police van and put the bag inside.

Kate didn't really even know Everett. He was a hermit of sorts and virtually a stranger to her. Needing to handle his estate had seemed like it was going to be a nuisance she really didn't need. After the call it had occurred to her that maybe she could tell the lawyer to simply donate everything to a charity.

Detective Gibson started back toward his car. "I'll go check it out," he said over his shoulder to Detective Sanders. As she watched him walking away, Kate noticed the female detective still standing close, listening, watching her.

"Did your brother have any . . . disagreements with anyone at his job?" Detective Sanders asked.

Kate glanced up at the frown on his pock-marked face. "I don't think so. John always told me about what was happening in his life. He never mentioned anything like that. He was upset a while back because some kids called him names when he was walking home from the bus. Once he told me about it he seemed to feel better. I think he'd forgotten all about it by the next day.

"He liked his job. He always said that the people there were nice. John depended on me to protect him when he was afraid. I think he would have told me if he was having any kind of trouble at work."

With the notepad in one hand and his pen in the other, Detective Sanders hiked up his pants as he eyed a group of men leaving the house with boxes and metal cases. Each person took off blue paper booties and put them in a sack on the porch.

"Miss Bishop, would you be willing to go in with us? They haven't cleaned up anything, except for removing your brother, but it would be a big help if maybe you could explain a few things for us. But if you don't feel comfortable—"

"Is there still . . . blood? Has the blood been cleaned up?"

The woman detective, surveying the darkness and the spectators, turned away and stepped closer to Kate to explain.

"I'm afraid that we have to leave everything as is until the investigation is complete. We can recommend a couple of companies that are licensed and bonded to clean up crime scenes. When the investigation is finished in a few days they can come in and take care of everything for you. They have the proper experience. It's better to let them handle it.

"We'd just like you to take a quick look around, now, if you feel up to it."

The woman put out a hand to steady Kate when she stood, but Kate didn't need the hand.

"I'm Detective Janek, by the way," the woman said as she shook Kate's hand. "I'll go with you if you're willing to go inside and maybe help us answer a few questions."

If she was willing? For hours, Kate had been asking them to let her go in. Instead of reminding them of that fact, she forced a brief smile.

"I'm fine. Really. It's just such a shock. I can't believe that someone would want to hurt John. He was like a kid—you know, innocently happy most of the time. I just can't believe that anyone would want to hurt him." She thought again about her mother's half brother, Everett. "Was John killed in a robbery? Was someone robbing the house and they killed John?"

The detectives shared a look.

Detective Janek leaned in a little. "Listen, Miss Bishop—"

"Please, call me Kate?"

"Miss Bishop" was what people working for KDEX Systems always called her when she showed up unexpectedly from the home office.

Detective Janek smiled. Kate thought it looked genuine. "Kate, we need to tell you about a few things before you hear them in the press. And then after we go inside we'd like you to identify your brother while the coroner's van is still here. It will save you from having to go down to the morgue. But we want you to be prepared, first."

Prepared? Kate swallowed. "All right."

Detective Janek glanced around to check if anyone was close, then looked back to search Kate's eyes. "Whoever did this was pretty sick."

"What do you mean?"

"He . . . removed your brother's eyes."

"Removed his eyes?" Kate blinked. "Why?"

"We haven't determined that. One of them was missing. The other was lying beside the body. It appears to have been partially eaten."

Kate's brain seemed to go blank.

She usually had command of matters that

needed figuring out. She usually knew just what to ask to get to the bottom of things.

But now she couldn't seem to make her mind work. She felt numb with anger at someone hurting John and doing such a thing to him. She knew John's fears well. She tried not to imagine his cries of terror and pain. She felt a hot wave of guilt for not being there to protect him.

"Who could do such a thing?"

"That's what we're going to try to find out," Detective Sanders said.

"Take me in there," Kate said, her anger rising. "Show me what you need me to explain."

Detectives Sanders and Janek shared a look at her determined tone, at the simmering rage it carried.

When they started for the house, Kate followed close on Detective Sanders's heels. Detective Janek stayed protectively at her side. When they reached the steps, they put on blue paper booties and asked Kate to do the same.

On the porch outside, a numbered yellow tag stood beside what looked like a bloody footprint. As she stepped into the living room, where there was more light, she saw a smear of blood at about eye level on the inside of the oak door.

The blood in the living room didn't look the way Kate had imagined it. She thought it would be mostly soaked into the wood floor or dried up. Instead, not far inside the door, there was a horrific, vast pool of it that they had to skirt.

Kate was shocked to see blood splattered everywhere in the living room. Besides what was on the floor, the violence of the attack had left strings and splatters of blood on the walls, the couch, the lampshades, even the drapes.

Some dim, analytical part of her brain said, *So this is what a murder scene looks like.*

Kate saw smeared, bloody footprints in a twisting path. At the far edge of the pool of blood was a crooked smear that looked like it might have been where her brother's arm lay sprawled across the floor. There seemed little doubt that John had tried desperately to get away. He had not gone down easily. He had struggled for his life.

"Why is that up here?" Kate asked, pointing.

A rusty, four-tined garden fork lay on the floor near the pool of blood. A yellow plastic tag with the black number "6" stood beside it. She was beginning to see why they had questions.

"My father used that fork to till a small garden in the backyard," she said. "In the fall he dug potatoes with it."

Kate frowned as she leaned down a little for a better look. "The tines have been sharpened. My father just turned dirt over with it. It was rusty and it wasn't sharp. The tips look like they've been filed."

Before they could answer, Kate pointed to four splintered holes in the pine floor, amid a broad area of blood. "It looks like someone stuck it in the floor, right there."

Detective Sanders nodded. "I'm afraid that the killer used it to pin the deceased's feet to the floor, probably to prevent him from escaping."

Kate's jaw hung in stunned surprise. "Why not just hit him over the head?"

"We don't know the answer to that," Detective Janek said. "Sometimes it's simply an act of blind rage, sometimes they have a reason. When I find him, I'll ask."

By the woman's icy, controlled expression, Kate knew that Detective Janek fully intended to keep that promise.

Kate finally had to break her gaze with the woman to instead look around. By the way blood was splattered everywhere, she thought it looked like an act of blind rage.

"Do you know where the gardening fork was kept?" Detective Sanders asked.

Kate nodded. "In the basement."

He turned to one of the forensic team and waggled his pen down at the floor as he spoke in a low voice. "You can take it, now."

The balding man wearing blue latex gloves squatted down and carefully fed the garden fork into a long cardboard box.

Detective Janek gently took Kate's elbow, turning her away. "What we'd really like to show you is in the basement."

"The basement?" Kate couldn't imagine what was in the basement, but she followed behind Detective Sanders as the man headed in that direction once Detective Janek gave him a nod.

Unlike the living room, the short hall didn't have blood on the walls. Kate paused in the kitchen. Dirty forks and spoons stood up in a green plastic tumbler in the sink.

"John always washed the dishes after using them. I don't remember ever seeing him leave dirty dishes like that. Washing the dishes after he ate was part of his compulsive routine."

"Anything else that you notice out of the ordinary?" Detective Janek asked.

"My pictures," Kate said, gesturing. "John kept pictures of me on the refrigerator. All the corners were folded over. Sometimes he took the photos down and put them in his pocket for safekeeping, otherwise they were there, on the refrigerator."

There were other pictures still there on the refrigerator—one of the bushes in the backyard in full bloom, an old one of their parents—but most of the rest were newspaper clippings.

She looked back at the detectives. "Did John have my pictures with him?"

Detective Sanders shook his head as he started writing a note in his pad. "There weren't any pictures in his pockets."

Kate wondered where they were.

"Those magnets on the floor, then, were what

he used to hold the photos of you on the refrigerator?" Detective Janek asked.

It sounded more like a statement than a question. Kate confirmed it with a nod.

It felt so odd being in the house. She had grown up in the place and had always felt safe there, but now it felt alien. It felt violated. It felt . . . dangerous.

Kate followed the heavyset Detective Sanders across the kitchen and down the plank steps into the musty basement. Detective Janek followed Kate down. Both of the bare-bulb lights were on, casting harsh shadows.

At the bottom, Kate was dumbfounded by what she saw.

"We suspect," Detective Sanders said, choosing his words carefully, "that your brother had some-one chained down here."

A heavy chain was padlocked to a large loop in the concrete floor. The iron ring had once been used as an anchor point to help straighten out a foundation wall. She had been little at the time but she vaguely remembered men working in the basement, and she remembered a chain running through that heavy iron ring.

Broken bits of metal lay at the end of the chain snaked across the floor. To the side, against a foundation wall made of mortared brick, was a wastebasket overflowing with used paper plates. Other plates lay randomly scattered around on the floor as if they had simply been flicked aside. Smears of dried food covered most of them.

"The chain could just reach the toilet and sink in that corner," Detective Sanders said, gesturing with his pen, "but not this other side of the room."

The side of the room out of reach of the chain was stacked with years of dusty, collected junk. There was everything from an old water heater that her father had meant to have hauled out, to boxes of outdoor Christmas decorations, to window screens, to broken chairs. In the corner stood a rake, a hoe, and a variety of shovels. The metal on all of them was rusty.

"The garden fork used to be over there," Kate told them, pointing at the collection of tools standing in the corner. "Just as rusty as the rest of them."

Detective Sanders glanced at the tools and nodded. "It appears that someone was chained down here for a few weeks."

Kate gestured to a screwdriver, pliers, and file on the floor. "He must have used his clothes, maybe his belt, to finally snag some of the tools kept off on the other side of the room and then pull them closer. It looks like he used the tools to break the chain."

"That's our assumption as well," Detective Sanders said.

Kate saw a pile of rusty iron filings. "It looks like he used a file to sharpen the garden fork over there."

Detective Sanders tilted his head around at the dirty paper plates ringing the room. "Have you ever known your brother to do anything like this before?"

"No, never," Kate said without hesitation as she gazed around at the scene. "I can't explain any of this."

"Has your brother ever acted violently?" he asked.

Kate was shaking her head even as he was asking the question. "No," she insisted. "No. It wasn't in his nature. I mean, I know how this looks, but I simply can't imagine John doing such a thing. He was shy. If someone called him names he ran away. He never got in fights. I never once knew him to fight back, even if someone shoved him. The most he would ever do was to sit in his bedroom and brood."

Detective Sanders glanced around again. "It appears that he moved beyond the brooding stage."

Kate lifted her arms in exasperation. "And what?" She let her hands flop down at her sides. "A retarded man with the mind of a child overpowered a homicidal maniac who eats human eyeballs and kept him chained up down here?"

Detective Sanders arched an eyebrow.

"So it would appear."

CHAPTER FIVE

Detective Janek rolled the steel-gray unmarked police car to the curb, put it in park, and shut off the engine. There were still police at John's house, and would be all night. She'd told Kate that the homicide detectives would be back there first thing in the morning to continue collecting evidence, interviewing all the neighbors, and following up on any leads. Detective Janek said she was going home to get a few hours' sleep and had offered to drop Kate off at her house.

Kate knew better. She knew it was not simply a convenient lift home. She knew that it was an opportunity for the homicide detective to have Kate isolated so she could question her informally without making it sound like an interrogation.

In her own job, Kate often made some people nervous. When she showed up it was only because there was trouble and she was there to get to thc bottom of it. The innocent, hardworking people were often more nervous about her questions than the ones causing the problems, so in those cases she tried to frame her questions in a gentle, nonthreatening way.

Kate, though, had no real answers for the detective's gentle questioning, but did her best to be open and honest. She wanted her brother's killer found and brought to justice.

Despite the wide-ranging questions sprinkled in among the small talk, Kate could tell that the woman had something else on her mind.

Kate did, too. She was confused and upset by what she had seen in the basement, but those thoughts were blanketed by the weight of grief. Between her job and spending a great deal of her free time with John, she never really had the chance to develop close friendships, so in an odd way John had not only been her responsibility but her closest friend. Now, she felt all alone in the world.

John had always depended on her. She should have known something was wrong. She should have been there. When she had been little her mother had often talked to her in a serious tone, telling her that John would always have to depend on them to watch over him because he couldn't do it himself. She'd said that was just the way it was. Kate had always known that there was an implied "sometimes life isn't fair and that's just the way it is" at the end of her mother's words. After her parents had died, that left only Kate to watch over her brother.

John had always been a sympathetic ear, never interrupting as she sometimes rambled on about her own problems at work. His problems were usually simple for her to fix. She couldn't help wondering, though, if she had made the wrong choices in the larger life decisions for her brother and if those decisions had resulted in him dying alone and afraid.

Mostly, though, she knew she should have been there for him.

"This is my fault," Kate said as she stared at the meaningless numbers, addresses, and names on the police computer screen mounted between the front seats.

"It's normal for people to feel guilty, to feel there was something they could have done. But this isn't your fault, Kate."

Kate stared at the computer screen without seeing it. "Yes, it is. I could have prevented this."

The detective paused a moment before asking, "What are you talking about?"

Kate finally looked over at the other woman. "My plane came in this afternoon. I was booked to fly back tomorrow night, but my investigation had finished up and by luck I was able to get on a flight back today. I could have picked John up from work, or I could have gone to his house and been there for him when he got home. If I had gone to his house first . . ."

Detective Janek's brow tightened. "With the way you looked after him—and after having been gone for three weeks—why didn't you?"

Kate swallowed. "A woman I know from work is in the hospital. I heard about it when I was out of town. When I got in, the driver from my office who picked me up at the airport let me know that she isn't likely to live the night. John hadn't been expecting me to be back until tomorrow night, so I had the driver take me home to drop off my bags and change before I had him take me to the hospital. I wanted to stop and see her. I wanted to be there to support her family. She has a nice family."

"Oh. I'm awfully sorry to hear that. What's wrong with her?"

Kate's gaze wandered back to the computer screen. "The side of her face is caved in. Her eye socket is crushed. Even if she lives, they say she will be blind in that eye. She has brain damage from bone fragments. Her husband told me that she already had two operations to save her life, but there is only so much the doctors can do. He said that even if she lives, she will never be Wilma again."

"Wilma . . ." Detective Janek's gaze flicked to the computer screen. "How did it happen?"

"A few days ago she went out to lunch and a guy walking past her—right outside our building—suddenly hit her in the face as hard as he could. He was big and powerful. She was small and frail. She went down and hasn't recovered consciousness since. Her children were there at the hospital. The doctors told them all that she isn't likely to make it through the night.

"People at work said that a blurry video of it was posted online. The guys in the video were laughing at the way she went down and giving high fives to the guy who did it."

The detective nodded. "Now I know who you're talking about. I saw the report. It was another case of the knockout game."

Kate shook her head without looking up. "Some game. She might die."

"She wouldn't be the first, nor the last. The videos spread like a disease. We've had a raft of such attacks, as have a number of other cities.

"It's murder in my book, or at least attempted murder, but they rarely get caught; since it's random, they don't have any connection to their victims. Since it's usually not possible to identify the attackers from the videos, there's not much evidence to go on. Even when they do get caught their punishment rarely matches the severity of the harm they do."

"It's hard to believe what the world is coming to."

"I couldn't agree more," Detective Janek said with a sigh. "The law is increasingly viewed with contempt and the police are seen as oppressors for enforcing it." She seemed to catch herself and looked back over at Kate. "So you stopped in to see her, rather than go to see John, first?"

"Yes." Kate looked over into the woman's dark eyes. "The driver was taking me home after I spent some time at the hospital. I was tired from a long day. John hadn't expected me to get in until tomorrow, so I was planning on going to bed early and getting a good night's sleep and then seeing John tomorrow.

"I called him from the car when I was almost home. When I heard him scream for me to run, I immediately called 911 from the car while the driver rushed me to John's house. You all beat me there.

"If I'd done as I'd originally planned and surprised John by picking him up from his job, rather than go to the hospital, then he wouldn't be dead. But I didn't want to take him with me to the hospital. He doesn't like to see people who are hurting."

"You only did what made the most sense."

Kate swallowed at the lump swelling in the back of her throat. "No, I should have taken care of my brother, first. If I had gone to his house I would have found out that something was going on, that there was someone chained in the basement. I would have found out and called the police."

Kate turned away to stare out the window into the darkness. "Wilma was unconscious and didn't even know that I was there. I hadn't seen John in three weeks. I should have seen to him, first, and then this would never have happened. John would have told me if I'd gone to the house. It's my fault he's dead."

"You're wrong, Kate." Detective Janek leaned a little closer. "Listen to me. Someone murdered him. That's who is at fault, not you. The only thing that would be different had you gone there first is that you would have walked into a very bizarre scene—an unexpected scene. You would have been caught unaware and murdered along with your brother. Whatever was happening, his death is not your fault. You need to know that."

Kate offered a brief smile. "I wish I could believe that."

"Someday you will. In the meantime, I'm going to work very hard to find the guy who did this. We have a lot of people to interview. We'll find a lead that takes us to the killer."

"Do you get the names of all the people who were standing around, watching?"

"You bet we do."

Kate stared out the window at nothing. "There was a tall man with messy hair in the crowd. He had his hands in the pockets of a loose-fitting, dark jacket. I think it was a hoodie. You should talk to him."

"Why do you say that? Do you know something about him? Do you know who he is? Has he ever caused trouble for John?"

Kate blinked and looked over at the frowning detective. "What? No—no, I don't know him. I've never seen him before." She shook her head. "I don't even know why I mentioned it."

"Maybe because you know the people in the neighborhood and you didn't recognize him as belonging there?"

Kate suddenly felt foolish and wished she hadn't said something so out-of-the-blue. In fact, she was puzzled as to why she had.

"Maybe that's it. I grew up there and I know most of the people in the neighborhood. I recognized a number of the faces, even if I don't know their names. But the man just seemed . . . I don't know. I don't know why I said anything."

"What did he look like?"

Kate tried to remember any details. "I never saw his face. I only saw him from the back. He was six-one, six-two. Something like that. I couldn't see him very well. He was back where it was dark, so I don't even know what color his hair was. I could just see by the way he was silhouetted in the lights from police cars that his hair was sticking up and messy."

Detective Janek was still frowning, still staring at her. "You didn't see his face at all? Did you make eye contact?"

Kate shook her head again. "No. I guess I'm just so shaken that I'm grasping at straws."

"Did John have a hoodie?"

"Yes. Dark blue. He kept it in the closet to the side of the front door."

The detective pulled out her phone and pressed a couple of keys with her thumb. "It's me," she said after a moment, when someone answered. “You still at the house? Good. Do me a favor. Go inside and check in the closet by the front door. Tell me if there’s a dark blue hoodie in there.”

While she was waiting, Kate asked, “You think the guy took John’s hoodie? Maybe to cover up the blood?”

Before she could answer, the detective still at the house came back on the line and Detective Janek pressed the phone back to her ear. “Okay, thanks,” she said. “See you in the morning.” She slipped the phone back in her pocket. “John’s hoodie is still there.”

“Oh. Okay. Sorry. I shouldn’t be trying to give you leads when I don’t know what I’m even talking about.”

“It’s part of the job. Most leads end up going nowhere, but sometimes they do.” She frowned again. “Are you usually a suspicious person?”

“It’s my job.”

“I thought you were an accountant. You said you were an auditor for KDEX.”

“Not that kind of an auditor,” Kate said. “I’m a security auditor. I get paid to be suspicious.”

“Really.” The detective was staring again. “Are you good at it?”

Feeling self-conscious, Kate shrugged. “I’m told I have a knack for it. I must be good enough—I still have a job.”

“Who are you paid to be suspicious of?”

"KDEX Systems supplies parts for missile guidance systems. It's a pretty sensitive industry, so we're naturally serious about everything we do. We have an electronic security team—that's a whole world unto itself. I don't generally get called in on that kind of issue unless it's an internal breach.

"But there are other threats—thieves trying to steal valuable equipment, corporate spies after sensitive information, people with a grudge against the company who want to cause trouble, that kind of thing. When a bad actor like that slips into the company under the radar, they become my responsibility. I deal with that kind. It's my job to ferret them out."

"Sort of a corporate cop?"

Kate offered a weak smile. "I'm hardly in your league. It's nothing like what you do."

The woman was back to studying Kate's eyes but she didn't say anything.

"Well, it's pretty late," Kate said as she curled her fingers around the door handle. "Thank you for the ride home."

"Kate—"

Kate paused before opening the door. Detective Janek tapped the palm of her hand on the steering wheel.

"What is it?"

Kate couldn't imagine what questions could be left. She'd answered so many already that the detective probably now knew more about her than anyone alive.

The woman stared down at her hand gripping the wheel. Her jaw muscles flexed as she considered.

"I know this isn't a good time, but would it be all right if I came in and we had a private conversation?"

"A private conversation?"

"Yes. A private conversation that's strictly off the record."

Kate cocked her head. "Off the record? What do you mean?"

"I mean just between you and me. Not to be repeated. Not to anyone." She finally looked over and held up her thumb, pointing her first finger as if it were a gun. "If you repeat a word of it, I'll have to shoot you."

The woman dropped her thumb, imitating dropping the hammer of a gun.

Kate frowned, not knowing what to say.

The detective smiled then in a suddenly human way, breaking the tension, and in the sincerity of that smile, Kate saw the woman beneath the cool veneer of authority. "Just kidding. About shooting you, I mean. But it is strictly confidential and I'm asking you to keep it that way."

"It's kind of late, Detective," Kate said as she glanced past the barren trees toward her house. The trees would leaf out soon. It was a beautiful street when the maples all leafed out. The older neighborhood had deep yards and mature landscaping that afforded privacy. "I haven't even unpacked, yet."

"I wouldn't ask if it weren't important," Detective Janek said. She sounded troubled.

Kate stared into the woman's dark eyes a moment. They were intense with resolve, along with something Kate couldn't quite figure out.

Worry, maybe.

Or maybe fear.

"Sure, okay." Kate hooked some of her black hair behind an ear. "I'll make some coffee."

Detective Janek smiled with relief. "AJ. Everyone calls me AJ." She let out a weary sigh. "And coffee would be great."

CHAPTER SIX

Kate unlocked the heavy oak door and let them both in. Her house wasn't large, but it had been built with the kind of care and attention to detail that didn't grace newer homes. The crown moldings were finely detailed and perfectly fitted; the walls were real plaster, the cabinets real wood. It wasn't grand or at all extravagant, but it had the kind of simple honesty that had become all too rare. Without being showy, the place exuded a warmth and charm that Kate had always cherished. It was a comforting retreat from the rest of her life.

On the way to the kitchen she noticed that the message machine on a side table beside the couch was blinking. Everyone who knew her called her on her cell. The only people who ever called on her home phone anymore were salespeople and fund-raisers. That kind of annoying message was about the last thing in the world she wanted to hear right then.

In the small kitchen, Kate flicked on the light switch. While AJ followed her in, looking about, Kate pulled a stainless-steel canister out from under the cabinets against the wall. After she set the coffeepot's filter basket on the white laminate counter and put in a paper filter, she added four scoops of coffee. As she filled the pot with water at the kitchen sink, she watched out of the corner of her eye as the detective studied the family photos on the wall.

"Looks like you get your lustrous black hair from your mother."

Kate saw that she was looking at a twenty-five-year-old photo of her parents standing on the front porch, with Kate and John sitting on the steps at their feet.

"And you have your father's green eyes. It's a rather striking combination."

"We're all products of heredity," Kate said. "It's not like we get to choose."

The woman looked back over her shoulder, momentarily giving Kate an odd, unreadable look. She turned back to the photos on the wall and pointed at one.

"What's this one?"

"It's when I earned my black belt."

The detective made an appreciative expression. "Do you still practice?"

"Healthy body, healthy mind," Kate said. "I find that working out helps relieve stress. Sweating from beating the hell out of a bag is a good way to get rid of frustration."

"So you work out at a gym?"

"Twice a week at a Combat Concepts with an instructor."

When AJ raised an eyebrow, Kate explained.

"My job is to find out who is causing problems. Sometimes it's simply incompetence, but most of the time it's criminal activity of one sort or another. We have security people and I've never had any problems, but you never know. I feel better being prepared.

"The rest of the time I work out at home. I have some simple equipment in the basement. A spinner bike for high-intensity work, weights, jump rope, that kind of thing."

AJ looked back at the photo. "I prefer working out at home, too. My husband is a gym rat, but I don't like strange men leering at me from behind when I'm doing dead lifts."

Kate tilted her head toward the nook. "You've been on your feet a long time. Why don't you have a seat."

The expanse of windows created out of smaller squares of glass in a grid of painted wood mullions looked out over a deep backyard. It made the nook in the kitchen a cheerful, cozy place to have coffee in the morning. With the shrubs and trees all along the property line blocking out other homes, it was like gazing out on her own private sanctuary.

Now, the black abyss out the windows offered no sanctuary, but instead echoed her mood.

AJ set her small business satchel down and then slid it ahead of her into the booth on the far side of the table so she would be facing Kate.

"You aren't crying," the detective observed.

Kate took a deep breath as she pulled a pair of white cups from the upper cabinet. "I probably will, later, when I'm alone. Maybe it just hasn't all quite sunk in yet. It doesn't seem real. I mean, if John had been hit by a car I think it would seem real, but this . . ."

"I understand," AJ said.

"After the things I saw in John's house, maybe it doesn't make enough sense to me to seem real." Kate set the cups on the counter, staring into them for a moment. "Maybe I'm afraid that if I cry, it will become real."

From a young age she had learned to set her own emotions aside when it came to John. He was like a child who needed her help to survive. That was just the way it was. Her responsibilities weren't so bad, and they had their rewards. She had a good life. Maybe being somewhat detached and analytical had become her way of dealing with everything in her life, from John to her job.

AJ nodded as she rested her forearms on the table and interlaced her fingers. "Do you have anyone? It's often easier to handle these kinds of losses if you aren't alone."

"My parents are gone."

"Anyone else? Someone close to you? A special man you care about?"

"No." Kate shrugged one shoulder, uncomfortable with an unexpectedly alien notion at such a time. "I guess I haven't found the right one, yet. I don't know why, but men have always seemed to be intimidated by me."

"Maybe they've seen you taking out your aggression on a punching bag," AJ said.

Kate smiled. "Maybe that's it." She looked up. "Cream or sugar for your coffee?"

Detective Janek was watching her hands again. "Cream, please."

Kate retrieved a small carton of heavy cream from the refrigerator. She smelled it first to make sure it was still good, and then poured some into a small pitcher.

"John was used to the house because he grew up there," she said into the dragging silence, feeling the need to explain. "After my parents passed away it just made sense for him to continue living there. I'd already moved out before my parents both passed away—not a year apart."

She stared at the pitcher a moment, searching for the words. "I just didn't want to go back. I know it probably sounds cruel that I didn't go back there to live with John and watch over him, but he was doing fine on his own, and I was on my own, and I just didn't . . ."

"I understand," AJ said in a sympathetic tone. "John needed to be on his own. You both did."

Kate forced a brief smile along with a nod.

The woman lightened the mood with a change of subject, talking a bit about her husband, Mike, and her little boy, Ryan. Despite how much both AJ's husband and son obviously meant to her, Kate could tell that the woman was killing time, working up to the confidential conversation she'd wanted to have.

Kate asked some simple questions about AJ's son, not really hearing the answers. In her mind's eye she kept seeing her brother's blood on the floor and the chain down in the basement with the dirty paper plates thrown off to the sides. For the life of her, she couldn't come up with an explanation that made any sense.

Kate didn't like it when things didn't make sense. She could deal with problems, but the reasons behind them had to make sense.

When the coffee was ready Kate poured two cups and set them on the table along with spoons, paper napkins, and the pitcher of cream, then slid into the booth opposite the detective.

As Detective Janek poured cream, Kate asked, "So, what does the 'A' in 'AJ' stand for?"

As she looked up from under her brow, a crooked smile twisted the detective's expression. "If I wanted people to know my first name, I wouldn't tell them to call me AJ, now would I?"

By the way she smiled Kate knew the woman had been asked that question countless times before, and because her answer was so quick in coming, Kate knew that for some reason it was not a question the woman enjoyed getting.

“Point taken.”

Kate poured herself a healthy dose of cream when the other woman handed her the pitcher. “So, what’s the big secret you want to talk about?”

AJ wrapped her fingers around the cup and stared into her coffee for a time, watching in silence as the cream swirled around.

“I knew your brother,” she finally said in a quiet voice.

Kate’s hand with the pitcher froze in midair just before she set it on the table. Goose bumps tingled up her arms.

She finally set the pitcher down. “You knew John?”

AJ nodded, still staring into her coffee. “I propped a card up on his phone on the wall in the hallway. It was my personal card. I told him that he could call me anytime, day or night. My cell is always on.”

CHAPTER SEVEN

Kate was bewildered as to why John had never told her about Detective Janek. John told Kate everything.

She suddenly realized how wrong she had been about that.

She knew that her being out of town isolated him somewhat, but there were people at work who could help him if need be, and they had Kate's number. Even though she hadn't seen him in weeks, she called often.

She couldn't imagine her brother not telling her about Detective Janek. But even more, she was completely at a loss that he hadn't given her any hint about having a man chained in the basement. At least, not until the last moments of his life, when he'd told her to run.

"I looked at the phone at John's house," Kate said. "I didn't see any card there."

"I looked too," AJ said. "It was gone. Maybe John put it away somewhere."

"How did you know John and why would you give him your card?"

AJ lifted a hand in a weak gesture. "I wanted him to have it in case he ever . . . needed me."

"Needed you?" Kate leaned in. "Why didn't you say anything at the house? Why didn't you mention this when we were talking with the other detectives?"

AJ let out a deep sigh and finally looked up. "It will take a bit of explaining." The look of iron returned to her eyes. It was a look that Kate did not take lightly. "Like I told you, this is strictly confidential. I'm not kidding, Kate. This has to stay between you and me."

Kate didn't know that she wanted to be bound by such terms without knowing the details, especially since it involved the death of her brother, but she decided not to voice her objections for the moment.

"I'm listening."

AJ turned a little to the side and leafed through the satchel resting on the bench beside her. She finally pulled out a thick brown envelope. "I'd like you to look at some pictures."

Kate thought it an awfully strange change of subject, but she decided to see where the woman was going. "All right."

Detective Janek pulled out a deck of photos, drawing the rubber band off the stack and back onto her wrist. She picked a single picture off the top and placed it on the table without taking her gaze from Kate, as if laying down a tarot card. With great care she slid the photo closer.

"I'd like you to look at each of these men and tell me whatever comes to mind—no matter what it might be. I need you to be honest. Don't be afraid to say whatever you think."

Kate frowned at the strange instructions and then looked down at the first photo sitting before her. It was a head-and-shoulders shot of a middle-aged man with a narrow chin. His dark hair was messed up. It was somewhat like the mug shots Kate had seen on TV, but against a plain background and without any numbers or identification.

"I don't know what I'm supposed to see." Kate looked up. "I don't recognize him. I don't know what it is you want me to say."

Without comment, AJ took back the photo and placed it at the bottom of the deck. The second photo she slid across the table, facing toward Kate, was of a heavyset black man. He had a few days' growth of stubble. His nose was flat and wide, and his eyes were puffy and bloodshot.

"He looks bored," Kate said as she looked up from the photo. Other than the clear intensity, the detective's face was unreadable. "Is that what you want to know?"

"I want you to tell me truthfully whatever thoughts come to mind. Nothing more. This isn't a trick. Don't guess. Just tell me what you see."

Kate wondered if maybe they were photos of men that AJ had reason to believe might be responsible for John's death, and she wanted to know if Kate recognized any of them. With that thought, she gave the woman a nod to go on.

The next dozen or so were unremarkable. When AJ slid the next one across the table, Kate paused and looked closer.

"Tell me what you see, Kate."

Kate's mouth twisted a bit as she squinted down at the man. "He looks like a jerk. You know, like one of those men who would try to charm his way into your pants and then later on you find out he's married. Or that he took money out of your purse." Kate sighed. "Maybe I'm tired and I'm just rambling. I don't really know why I said that. Is that really what you want to hear?"

AJ withdrew the photo. "I want you to tell me what comes to mind. If that's what you think when you look at this man's picture, then that's what I want to know."

The next five photos were similarly unfamiliar and unremarkable. Kate didn't recognize any of them. There didn't seem to be anything noteworthy about any of the men, except that one of them looked drunk and a few looked sleazy. She wished she knew what the detective was getting at or what she wanted Kate to see.

It was late and she was exhausted from the long day, to say nothing of the emotionally draining ordeal of finding out that John had been murdered. There were so many things she was going to need to take care of. She needed to make funeral arrangements. Her boss was going to need to know what had happened in Dallas. Her thoughts were scattering in different directions all at once, making mental notes, making to-do lists.

When AJ slid the next photo across the table and Kate looked into the eyes of the man in the picture, she stopped breathing.

The strength seemed to drain out of her in a frigid rush and she nearly dropped her cup.

Her skin flashed icy cold.

"Tell me what you see, Kate."

Kate finally glanced up. AJ was leaning in, staring right into her eyes.

"I, I . . . I don't know. I've never seen him before."

"That's not what I asked you." One fingernail tapped the photo in front of Kate. "Tell me what you see."

Kate squeezed her trembling fingers tighter around the warm cup in an effort to steady herself. Her mouth felt dry. Her heart raced. She felt a drop of sweat run down the icy skin between her breasts.

She didn't understand what was happening. As she stared into the man's eyes, she could feel the fine hairs at the nape of her neck lifting. She'd never had such a reaction before, especially to a photo of a man she had never seen before.

She was about to say she didn't recognize him when she realized that she didn't know what he looked like. She hadn't looked at his face.

She had only looked into his eyes.

Unable to understand her reaction to a stranger, Kate shoved the photo back across the table as if it were something dangerous, something evil, and then sat back against the booth as she tried to slow her breathing and her heart rate.

"Who is he?" she asked, trying to steady her shaky voice and make it sound normal. She turned away from the detective's dark eyes to look out the windows into the blackness.

AJ waited until Kate looked back at her before answering.

"His name is Edward Lester Herzog."

"I . . . I don't recognize his name, either."

The detective's fixed gaze was unnerving. "He abducted, raped, and murdered three young women over the course of a year. He dismembered the bodies and left the pieces in Dumpsters all over south Chicago. Except the heads. We don't know what he did with the heads. We had to ID them from DNA."

Kate swallowed hard and then took a sip of coffee as an excuse to retreat from the detective's unflinching gaze. "Who are the men in the other photos? Are they killers, too?"

"They're nobodies. A few are street cons. Petty thieves—nothing big. Nothing violent. A couple are photos of normal guys. One is my neighbor. His boy plays with my son."

The way AJ sat quietly observing her made Kate restless.

"I've never seen anyone like that last man before," she finally explained, needing to fill the awful silence. "I've never seen a photo of a killer."

AJ cocked her head. "I showed you the photo before I told you who he was or what he had done. Your reaction to the photo came before I told you he was a killer."

Kate fussed with the top button on her blouse, unable to answer.

"When I look at that photo, do you know what I see?" AJ asked.

Kate shook her head, not trusting her voice right then.

"I see a doughy guy in his early thirties who works at an electronics store selling televisions. I see a nerd who can wire surround sound in his sleep. I see a guy who plays online games half the night, likes fish tacos, and wouldn't have a clue how to change a flat tire.

"When Eddie sold televisions he always collected the name and contact information of the customers. Sometimes the information was needed for delivery, but the salespeople collected the data from every buyer—even when they were taking the purchase with them. It was store policy so they could send out advertising flyers and emails.

"It's surprising how freely people give out such private information. They answer without giving it a second thought.

"That was how Eddie picked his victims.

"When he asked the young women for their contact information, he also asked in the same flat tone if the TV they were buying was for their husband. It flowed right in with the questions about their phone number and address and credit card. It sounded just as boringly official. Each of those three women offhandedly told him no, they each happened to be getting the TV for themselves, for their first apartment.

"They weren't afraid to tell him anything because he looked like a wuss. They probably figured that if they had to they could have beaten the crap out of the dorky sales guy.

"That's all I see when I look at this photo of Eddie Herzog, nothing more. That's all those three young women saw. But you saw something none of them saw.

"Talk to me, Kate. What did you see when you looked at that photo of Edward Lester Herzog?"

Kate wet her lips and swallowed. "I don't know." She struggled to put the swirl of dark emotion into words. "It was his eyes. Something about his eyes." Words had never seemed so utterly inadequate. "I don't know. I've never had a reaction like that before."

"Have you ever seen a photo of a murderer before?"

"Yes."

"Where?"

"On TV, of course. On the news. And I suppose in stories on the internet, or newspapers when I'm waiting at an airport."

AJ shook her head. "That's different. Have you ever seen a man like that in person or have you ever seen a *photo,* printed from a negative, like this one, of a killer?"

Kate's brow twitched. "What do you mean, it's different? A picture is a picture. What difference could it make if I saw a picture on the news or if I saw a photo on my kitchen table?"

AJ ran a thumb under the edge of the open collar of her white shirt. "I wish I had a good answer." She thought a moment, searching for an example. "Try to imagine getting a text saying 'I saw you leaving work today. You have a beautiful smile.' "

"If I didn't know who it came from that would be rather strange and I'd ignore it."

"Sure. But now imagine you're walking down the street after dark on the way to the parking garage and a man stepped out of an alley right front of you. He's dressed in layers of filthy, rotting clothes. He has tangled, greasy gray hair and a beard. He smells of alcohol and it's obvious he hasn't bathed in months. He only has a few teeth. Then he leans toward you, blocking your way. He looks into your eyes while he's grinning with a wild look in his wide eyes. Then he says, 'I saw you leaving work today. You have a beautiful smile.' "

"Now, that would scare the hell out of me."

"Why? It's the same words. What's different?"

Kate thought it was a bizarre comparison. "Context. The words may be the same, but the context is completely different."

AJ's expression tightened with intensity. "I think it might be something a little like that. The text removes many layers from the words. It takes away countless clues and context."

"But this is different. It's a photo of the same person whether it's on the internet or in a photo printed from film."

AJ sighed. "All I can tell you is that I know for certain that it matters. I've come to suspect that maybe an image loses something going through the conversions and steps to put it on TV, in a newspaper, or online. Some kind of tiny clues are lost the farther removed you are from the actual person. The transmission of digital bits of data somehow loses some vital essence of a person that a photo on film is able to capture.

"If you saw Eddie Herzog on TV, or in a newspaper, or in a story online, you wouldn't have had the same reaction as you just did looking at this photo.

"All the images I showed you were shot on film and developed directly from the negative onto photo paper."

Kate shook her head in frustration. "I just don't see what difference that could make."

Elbows resting on the table, AJ opened her hands. "All I can tell you for certain is that there must be something more direct, more pure when the image is on film. Or at least pure enough to capture and preserve in the film that elusive essence that you would have seen in Eddie Herzog's eyes had you encountered him in person. I don't know for sure why it works that way, I just know that it does.

"My own suspicion is that had you seen Eddie Herzog in person your reaction would have been even stronger. Still, the photo was able to convey enough of what you would have seen in real life for you to recognize that quality."

"People in some primitive societies don't like their photo taken because they think it captures their soul," Kate said before she realized she was saying it.

AJ nodded. "I believe that a photo on film preserves some quality that you can see in a person's eyes."

Kate changed the subject to what she really wanted to know. "What were you doing at John's house? How did you know him? Why did you leave your card with him?"

AJ slouched back in the bench. "Do you know how we found out that Edward Lester Herzog had killed those three women?"

"No, how?"

"Your brother told me."

"John?" Kate blinked in surprise. "How would John know?"

"From this photo," she said as she held it up. She put it back in the middle of the rest of the photos, pulled the rubber band off her wrist, and slipped it back around the stack. "I showed John a few dozen photos, like I showed you just now. When he saw that same photo you just looked at—the very same photo of Edward Lester Herzog that upset you—he became hysterical."

Kate knew what the woman was talking about. John could see things in people's eyes. Ever since they had been little John could look into people's eyes and tell if someone was mean, or if they intended him harm. Kate never understood it, or really took it seriously, even though on several occasions John's fears had proven prophetic. Of those times when it had, she'd chalked it up to coincidence and John's general fearful nature.

What she couldn't understand was her own reaction.

A hundred questions were flying through Kate's mind. One in particular floated to the top.

"What did John call that man—that Edward Lester Herzog—when you showed him this photo?"

"John called him 'the devil.' "

Goose bumps ran up Kate's arms.

That was John's name for the kind of man he feared most.

CHAPTER EIGHT

Kate took a sip of coffee, trying to get a grip on what it all meant. Despite the late hour, she knew the coffee wasn't what was going to keep her awake. Her brother's murder, and that photo, were more than enough to do it.

"What were the police doing showing photos of murderers to my brother?"

AJ's gaze turned away at the cutting tone in Kate's voice.

"The police weren't. I was."

"I don't understand."

"The police department is a big bureaucracy. This business"—AJ waggled her stack of photos—"is not politically correct. They don't like anything that even smacks of psychics."

"You think this is some kind of psychic ability?"

"No, as a matter of fact, I don't think that at all. But I do know that for a whole list of reasons the lieutenant would have my badge if he knew about this."

"How many detectives are in on your special procedures?"

AJ slipped the photos back into the envelope and then into her satchel on the seat beside her. "I'm the only one."

Kate wondered what would make AJ act on her

own when she knew it could get her fired. On top of that, Kate felt stupid for not knowing about so many important things that were going on in her brother's life. She couldn't imagine why she'd had no inkling of it from John. She had never known him to keep secrets from her.

"How long has this been going on? How did you get John involved in this? How did you come to ask John to do this in the first place? Why were you—"

AJ held up a hand to ward off the sudden barrage of questions.

"Like I said, it's a long story."

"Start at the beginning."

AJ smiled. "You'd make a good detective."

Just as she did at her job, Kate ignored the diversion, not allowing herself to be led off track. "That wasn't what I asked you. How did you ever start showing photos to my brother in order to identify murderers?"

Unspoken, Kate asked herself how John was able to identify murderers. Equally troubling, how was she?

"It's complicated. It didn't start out that way."

"So how did it start out?" Kate pressed.

AJ pushed her satchel a little to the side to give herself more room as she leaned in. "One of the women on the staff at the Clarkson Center where John worked was robbed one day as she arrived in the back-alley parking lot. When I got there to investigate, one of the forensic team was snapping photos of the surroundings—the parking lot, the place where the woman had parked, the entrance to the center, things like that.

"The woman who had been robbed was pretty shaken and had gone home for the day. Before I could even start interviewing the staff, I got a call to go to a murder scene, so I didn't get back to question the victim until the next day when she returned to work. By then I had the crime-scene photos with me. She told me that she hadn't seen the guy who stuck the gun in her back and couldn't really tell me anything useful about him."

"If she didn't see him, how did she know it was a gun?"

AJ rubbed a thumb up and down the side of her coffee cup as she stared back into the memory. "She said that she knew he had a gun by the way he pushed the weapon at her and the feel of it against her ribs. He told her that he'd shoot her if she did anything to resist. He told her not to move. She didn't. He told her not to turn around. She didn't. He grabbed her purse and ran.

"She was too terrified to turn around and look. Instead, she ran inside. She never saw what he looked like. Until we could come up with some evidence, a description of the guy, or a witness, I knew the case was going nowhere."

"What were you doing investigating a purse

snatching?" Kate asked. "You're a homicide detective. Homicide detectives don't investigate that kind of thing."

"You're right," AJ said. "But about two months before, there was a strikingly similar robbery. A woman parking in an alley parking lot behind her place of work not too far from the Clarkson Center was apparently approached by an assailant, much the same as this woman where John worked. There was no one else around. The guy took her purse. We found it several blocks away in a Dumpster. The woman's wallet was missing.

"Unlike the woman where John works, this woman apparently turned around to confront her assailant."

"How do you know that?" Kate asked.

"Because he shot her in the face."

"So you weren't there to investigate a purse snatching. You were trying to get a lead on a murderer."

AJ nodded. "Like I told you before, we have to follow up every lead we get. Sometimes it's a little thing that's the connection we need to help us find the killer.

"Anyway, when I went back to the Clarkson Center to question the woman, I had the photos with me. I set them down on the table as I talked with her, asking her to point out where it happened, what direction she'd heard the attacker run off in, things like that. While I was asking her questions someone stepped out of the front office and called out her name, saying she had a call from the director of the center. Since there weren't any phones on the work floor, she excused herself for a moment to run to the office to take it.

"John was sitting nearby, working. He leaned over and pointed to a man wearing an apron in the background of one of the photos, not far off at the end of the alley. There were a number of other people in the photo as well—you know, bystanders watching, like at John's house today—but he pointed to one man in particular. He said that was the man who hurt women.

"I asked him if he had been there, if he had been out back and had seen it. He shook his head and went back to work. Even though it looked like the photo had upset him, I thought he was simply a mentally disabled guy who didn't know what he was talking about or that maybe he just wanted to be part of the conversation."

"These were photos?" Kate asked. "Photos on film? You said they had to be real photos. The police don't use digital equipment?"

AJ smiled at the question. "Usually we do. By chance the forensic team had been on a couple of other cases that turned out to be pretty involved. They'd forgotten to charge their extra batteries, so both their digital cameras were dead. The guy who runs the team, Harold Gillen, is older and he keeps his film camera with his equipment as a backup."

"That has to be pretty inefficient. Digital photos are available immediately. They're easier to handle, send, and archive. Why would the police department let him use film?"

AJ shrugged. "I'm sure that sooner or later the department will require digital photos, but at the moment no one pays much attention or cares because our files are filled with older photos and film negatives. Because of that, the lab has developing equipment and scanners to convert photos to digital format when necessary, so for now it's not an issue.

"Since I've gotten photos shot on film from him before, I always suspected that Harold simply liked his older camera better. People would rather use what they are comfortable with. He's going to be retiring this year, so I doubt that he gives a damn if they want him to use digital. For now he simply says the batteries were dead and no one bothers him about it."

Kate gestured across the table toward the satchel AJ had brought with her. "You use Harold Gillen to take those photos for you, don't you? Photos on film? You use him because he's older and about to retire and he doesn't really give a damn about the bureaucracy so he doesn't ask questions or say anything to anyone about what you might be up to."

It wasn't really a question. AJ smiled.

"You're right. But that first time was just chance."

"So what happened with John? How did this start?"

AJ took a sip and set her coffee cup back down. "While I waited for the woman to come back from her phone call, I asked John—just making conversation to be nice—if he hadn't been there, then how did he know that was the guy who had done it. He hesitated and finally said he could tell by his eyes."

Kate nodded. "I've heard him say that about people's eyes."

She wondered at her own reaction to Edward Lester Herzog's eyes. She wondered if that was the same thing John felt. She couldn't imagine how it was possible, or what was going on.

"I didn't think much about it until a few days later when another detective arrested a murder suspect, a local short-order cook. It was also the guy John had pointed out in the photo. The woman he killed probably got a look at him, so he shot her because she would have been able to tell the police that he wore an apron. That would have narrowed their search. The apron identified him. It could be that was why he shot her.

"In that neighborhood an apron made him invisible to most people on the street. They see a cook in an apron, think he's a working man, and discount him as a threat. Killers usually want to look nonthreatening, look invisible. It didn't make him invisible to John, though.

"There are plenty of people who try to identify criminals for the police. Sometimes it's a mentally ill person who gets the killer's name from a voice in their head. Then there are people trying to promote themselves to the press as psychics. They make an educated guess, or a lucky guess. They can be wrong a thousand times, but the one time they say something that turns out to be at least partly true, that's what gets coverage.

"Sometimes I have a feeling myself—a guy just looks guilty. I think any good police officer develops an instinct for when people are lying and when they're guilty. We deal with criminals all the time, so we have a better mental database of patterns in the way guilty people behave. Those feelings aren't reliable, though, and oftentimes I'm wrong.

"But this was different. John wasn't trying to impress me with his ability. He wasn't seeking notoriety. He wasn't making an educated guess. He wasn't making an observation that the guy looked guilty.

"He simply said 'That's the man who hurts women' and then went back to work. There was something eerie about the way he said it that made the hair on the back of my neck stand on end."

CHAPTER NINE

So what happened next?" Kate asked.

AJ turned the cup in her fingers as she collected her thoughts. "Over the next few weeks I couldn't get John's quiet certainty, his sincerity, out of my mind. Something about it, and about him, haunted me. I'm a detective. My life is devoted to investigating. A lot of hard work goes into finding the guilty party. What John had done didn't make any logical sense.

"I decided that I needed to see if I could find a way to explain it. I wanted to prove to myself that I was imagining things, or he was. I wanted to put it to rest as luck or chance or a random coincidence so that I could forget about it.

"I went back to the Clarkson Center with the excuse of following up with the woman after the man had been charged. When we were alone, I asked John if I could stop by his house. He knew I was a police officer, and of course I'm female, so even though I could tell it made him apprehensive to do something so out of the ordinary, he seemed to feel safe with me and agreed.

"That night I came prepared. I showed John a lot of photos. I told him that I just wanted to know his reaction to a variety of people. I wanted to wear him down with pictures of regular people and ones I knew were petty criminals but not violent.

"In the stack I also had a photo of a guy who had just been arrested and charged in a killing spree over in Indiana."

"John picked out that photo," Kate said.

AJ nodded. "The instant John saw the photo of the guy, he flipped out. I had to put it away and then get my arms around him and hold him to calm him down. He was shaking like a leaf."

Kate had often done the same thing herself when John was frightened, so she knew that it would have helped. Kate liked that AJ had done the same.

AJ stared off into her memories moment. "I don't know," she said without looking up, "something happened that night. We kind of bonded a little. I felt a real empathy for him, a sadness at the things he could apparently see that others couldn't. Sadness that he had to live with such fears. He felt safe with me because I believed him. He said that other people didn't believe him, but I did."

Kate felt a flash of guilt, because she had often dismissed John's concerns when he told her about people he said were bad. She would try to tell him that he was just imagining things.

"Even though he was mentally disabled, I felt that maybe he had a special gift, a kind of insight that the rest of us don't have. There was a gentleness about him, a simple sincerity.

"I started to wonder if maybe John might be able to help."

Kate bristled. "Help?"

AJ looked up to meet her gaze.

"Last week I had to tell a young mother that her husband had been murdered in a robbery. The victim had cooperated and handed over the money from the register. There was no reason to bludgeon him to death. It was cold-blooded murder, a complete lack of empathy for the life of another human being. The victim's wife and child are now alone in the world. They were barely making ends meet as it was. What are they going to do now?

"I've had to show mothers and fathers photos of the men who tortured, raped, and murdered their daughters to see if they knew the killer. When I see my own little boy I think of the animals out there and what they do to other children, what they would do to him if given the chance.

"If we catch a killer, then the next victim doesn't die. The next family isn't devastated. That person gets to live their life.

"It was obvious to me that John's murder was a rage killing. The man who did it has likely killed before. He gets off on it. He'll kill again unless he's stopped. Imagine if we could have caught him before he harmed John."

Unable to imagine the things AJ had seen on a regular basis, Kate shifted her gaze to the window, seeking refuge out in the darkness beyond it.

"I told John the truth," AJ said. "I told him that I thought he had a special ability and that maybe he could use it to help me catch bad men before they could hurt people. John was excited by that prospect. He said he didn't like people to get hurt. Even though he was apprehensive, he agreed to help me."

"John didn't ever like anyone to hurt," Kate said quietly as she stared out the window. She looked back. "So you started showing him photos of suspects?"

"Not in the beginning. At first I just came over to visit him to make sure he was comfortable with me and knew he could trust me. A few times I called him the day before and told him that I would bring him dinner the next day. On those days, the days I brought him dinner, I didn't show him photos. I just told him funny stories about my life that I knew he would enjoy hearing. I brought him the photo of the black-and-white cat that was there on his refrigerator. He loved it.

"From the very beginning I knew that I had to protect him from what would happen if anyone else found out, so I impressed upon him that what we did had to be a secret between the two of us. I told him that he didn't ever have to help me if he didn't want to, but if he did he couldn't tell anyone, not even you."

AJ smiled at the memory. "By then I was pretty

sick of hearing all about the great and wonderful Kate."

Kate had to fight back a sob. She wasn't great at all. John had needed her and she hadn't been there for him. She had failed him. She told herself that she could cry later.

"John seemed to grasp that I was being careful to protect him, and that I wanted him to keep it secret in order to keep him safe. He trusted me and kept our secret. At first, I simply wanted to discover what was really going on and the limits of what John could actually do—if he could actually do anything.

"Truth be told, I was really trying to prove him wrong.

"I also needed to find out if whatever it was he was able to do was at all reliable. I was still pretty skeptical. Once in a while I look at someone and know they're guilty. You just get a feeling. But my feelings aren't reliable. I needed to be convinced that John's ability was not only different, but rock-solid reliable.

"So in the beginning I got photos of known felons from solved cases where we had convictions. Of course, John didn't know that the cases had already been solved or that the killers were behind bars. I showed him photos of hundreds of men, even some women, and sprinkled in with those photos were those men who had been convicted of serious crimes.

"John never once got a serious offender wrong. Those photos always upset him.

"He felt uncertain about some of the petty criminals, but even so he was right about them every time. The more serious the crime, the more agitated he became, the more certain he was. He never had any doubts about those and he was never wrong. Not once.

"With murders—the savage, cold-blooded kind—he always went nuts. I had to calm him down after showing him a photo of that kind of killer.

"I remember the night I showed him a photo of a serial killer—Albert Lang, a real psycho. He liked to go after young men who were socially awkward. He tied them up, cut off their clothes, and tortured them for days. Took bites out of them while they were still alive and helpless."

AJ leaned in, her brows drawing together until there were deep vertical creases between them. "Do you have any idea how much force it takes to actually rip off a mouthful of living human flesh, muscle, and sinew with your teeth? Sounds easier than it actually is. Can you imagine having duct tape over your mouth, wrapped around your head a half dozen times, your hands and feet tied to a bed, choking on your own screams and spit as his teeth pulled, twisted, and tore bites out of you? Every agonizing moment must have lasted an eternity."

AJ shook her head as she sat back. Her fierce expression eased, but the knuckles of her fisted hand were white. Kate could see a deep hunger for vengeance in the woman's eyes.

"John cried for two hours when I showed him Albert Lang's photo," she finally said, her voice softer. "I held him and told him that it was all right, that the man was already in prison. I assured John that he was safe, Kate was safe, and Albert Lang couldn't ever hurt anyone else again.

"I told John that his home was his castle and he was safe in his castle. That finally made him smile."

Kate rubbed the goose bumps on her arms as she imagined the terror of Albert Lang's victims. It was easy to imagine John's terror. She had no trouble understanding why Detective Janek wanted to do whatever she could to stop that kind of evil.

"So, you just showed John pictures of convicted people?"

"At first," AJ said, finally looking back at Kate. "After a while I showed him pictures of people I suspected. Once John picked someone out in a photo, I would investigate them to see if I could build a solid case. I never used John's name or involved him in any way, I swear. And I never used the information from John as an excuse to arrest someone. I had to be convinced by the evidence that I had a case against them.

"At first I had been trying to disprove John's ability—that's when by chance I first learned that it had to be a photo printed from a negative. I found myself using John to give me a direction where I might not have looked, or to back up my own suspicions.

"A few times John helped me identify a murderer—simple cases, like men who had murdered their wives. It's usually the husband or boyfriend when a woman is murdered. Most victims know their killer. That kind of killer is usually pretty sloppy and they leave lots of evidence. We usually had strong suspicions to begin with and were already building a case before I showed John the photos. John's ability at first became a way to reassure myself that I had the right guy.

"I always had several stacks of photos, and lots of extra photos to fill out the stacks. I didn't want to show John only one man for fear he might think I was suggesting he react to that particular photo. I always showed him a whole stack, sometimes several stacks.

"One of the men in the extra photos on that particular day just so happened to be a serial killer—Edward Lester Herzog—although at the time no one knew it. At that point the mousy electronics salesman wasn't even a suspect. He was merely one of dozens of people who had some kind of contact with the victims.

"I often had a person's picture taken so I would have it with their statement. I like to be able to connect a face to the statement. Not all the detectives do that. Maybe I'm being thorough, or maybe it's police instinct, or maybe I'm just overcompensating because I'm a female officer and feel that I always have to do better, be better, not miss anything, prove myself. At any rate, that's how I came to have the photo of Herzog in the stack. At the time it was nothing more than an extra photo."

AJ pulled her lower lip through her teeth as she again stared off at nothing. "When John saw that photo that I just showed you, the one that at the time I didn't think was anyone, he cried out that it was the devil.

"He ran into his bedroom and hid behind the bed. I sat there with him half the night. I couldn't understand what he saw in that photo that I couldn't see, but I sure as hell knew that he saw something evil."

AJ looked up and forced a smile. "I've got a little boy of my own, so I'm pretty good at comforting little boys."

Her smile ghosted away. "I hated seeing John so terrified and knowing that I was the one who brought that terror to him. The compensation for my guilt is that I know that had we not stopped Herzog, who at the time wasn't even a suspect, he would have gone on to murder more young women.

"Killers like that tend to think they're smarter than the police. Killing fulfills an inner need. Oftentimes those types of killers are incredibly difficult to catch. The more murders they commit without getting caught, the more confident they become. They don't stop unless they're stopped. John did that.

"He always made me promise not to tell Kate about him seeing the devil. He grasped that he was helping people, but he didn't want you involved, didn't want you to be anywhere near the danger. As scared as he was, he was a brave man, too.

"You need to know that, Kate. You need to know that despite how afraid he was, he helped stop Eddie Herzog from killing any more young women."

And in turn, Kate thought, he himself was slaughtered.

CHAPTER TEN

Kate poured Detective Janek another cup of coffee while trying to sort out a flood of conflicting emotions. She wouldn't have wanted John involved in any way, but on the other hand her brother had done something good, something truly worthwhile. It bothered her that John had been burdened with such a terrible secret, but what was most distressing was that the kind of men he had feared since he was little had been brought into his life. AJ had brought those men into his life.

"So you never told anyone on the police force about John helping identify Herzog or any others?"

AJ gave her a look. "If I had told anyone in the department I'd likely have been fired and a flock of lawyers would have descended on us, demanding that every one of the convictions I'd worked on be thrown out—and they probably would have been. I'd have been condemned by the press for manipulating a helpless mentally handicapped man who didn't know any better.

"Worse, though, word would have gotten out and John would have been dragged into a public spectacle. I'd have been sent off to traffic duty—if not the unemployment line—and John would have been prey for every kook, sleazy reporter, and religious nut within a thousand miles. His house would have been a circus and John would have been at the center of it, terrified, without me able to protect him any longer. Secrecy was essential to protecting him."

"Then why is he dead?"

AJ let out a heavy sigh as she merely shook her head.

Kate rubbed a thumb up and down the side of her coffee cup. "I guess I can see the spot you were in. But that still doesn't make it right."

AJ stared at Kate for a long moment, then broke the gaze and reached over to her satchel, bringing out a white envelope. She pulled out a smaller stack of photos than she had the first time and again drew the rubber band back over her wrist.

AJ carefully took a photo off the top and slid it across the table so that it was facing Kate. She didn't say anything. The face of the man in the photo looked unremarkable.

Kate knew what the detective wanted. She looked up and reached across the small table to take the stack of photographs out of the woman's hand. She picked up the first photo AJ had shown her, put it on the bottom as she leaned back, and then looked at the top picture. It too, was unremarkable. She moved it to the bottom. She quickly shuffled through the stack, one at a time, briefly looking at each face. She only had to look at each one for a second to know that she felt nothing before moving it to the bottom of the stack.

When she recognized the first photograph and knew she had been through the entire stack, she handed the deck of photos back to the detective.

"Nothing. I didn't feel anything from any of them. I guess I can't really do it. The other one, the one of Herzog, must have been a fluke. Is that what you wanted to know?"

AJ was slow in answering. "What I want is for you to tell me the truth. If you didn't have a reaction to any of the photos, then that's what I want to know."

The detective returned the photos to her satchel, but came up with another envelope, this one manila.

Kate heaved a sigh and snatched the envelope from AJ's hands before she could even take out the photos. Kate drew the rubber band back over her own wrist and started shuffling quickly through the photos, growing irritated that the detective kept pushing this right after John had been murdered.

She hurried through the stack of photos as scattered thoughts raced through her mind. Life was going to seem empty without having to do all the things she had done for John. What was she going to do with John's house? She had grown up there. She could move back, but she couldn't imagine living in the house where he had been murdered. Should she sell the place, maybe do the same with her uncle Everett's place?

She was hardly paying any attention to the procession of men she was seeing, when the eyes of a man rocked her like a lightning bolt. The photo brought her thoughts to a sudden halt.

Her hand with the photo froze. She couldn't look away from the eyes in the photo. Her insides felt as if they twisted into a knot. Her mouth went dry as a sheen of cold sweat broke out across her face.

"What do you see, Kate?"

Kate finally looked up from the terrible eyes in the photo to the detective's dark, steady gaze.

Kate swallowed. "Him. This is the one you want."

She handed the photo to AJ. The detective turned it over to read the name on the back.

"Really," she whispered to herself before taking another look at the face. She finally took the rest of the photos from Kate's trembling fingers.

"Like Herzog?" she asked. "You had the same kind of feeling that you had when you looked at Edward Lester Herzog?"

Kate nodded weakly. She was shaken by the eyes in the photo but managed to find her voice. "Is he someone you have in jail? A test the way you did with John? Someone already convicted?"

AJ shook her head. "No. Not yet, anyway. He

made me a little suspicious, but no more than a lot of other people."

"John's body is hardly even cold, yet. Do you really expect me to step right in and take his place, now? Is that it? You expect me to help you ferret out killers?"

AJ leaned back in the booth and folded her arms, the stack of photos still in one hand. She fixed her dark gaze on Kate. In that moment she looked very much the intimidating police detective, a woman of focused intensity.

"Recently," she said in a soft voice, "the decomposed remains of a child were found by workers in a landfill—just a few random bones. We brought in cadaver dogs to find the rest. Instead we found another boy's body, a more recent kill that was still mostly intact. I'm looking for who killed them.

"The man in the photo has a little boy. I suspected that he beats the boy even though I had no proof of that. But I saw the look in that little guy's eyes. He lives in an area of the city with lots of unattended kids, lots of fatherless kids. The last boy we found had lived with his single mother about a mile and a half from the man in the photo.

"We haven't identified the first boy, yet, but we did the second. I'm the person who showed up and introduced that boy's mother to what would turn out to be the worst day of her life.

"Having a little boy of my own, I could understand her reaction and sat with her for a couple of hours. Not that it did much good. She was hysterical and in shock. She said her son had come home from school and was at home when she got in from work. Once she was home, he was allowed to go out to play with his friends. That was the last time she saw him.

"Her ex-husband is a drunk. She lived with her mother for a time after he left her. She moved several times. He never came to see his son. She hasn't seen him in years. He lives out of state, now. She had one ex-boyfriend who was a womanizer and had simply moved on to other women. She couldn't imagine anyone having a grudge against her, or who hated her. She seemed like a quiet woman, minding her own business, with a job, doing her best to make ends meet."

AJ turned the stack of photos in her hand, showing Kate the one on top, the one that had rattled her. "The only reason I even interviewed this guy is because he called the sanitation department complaining about his trash not being picked up. That put him on our radar. It was simply another of many clues that we routinely follow up.

"He seemed like nothing more than an irritated guy who works nights as a tractor-trailer mechanic and wanted his trash picked up on schedule. I told him that I was questioning him because I wanted to know if he could tell me anything unusual about the sanitation workers who picked up his trash. A few of them made me suspicious. He said he only knew that they missed his trash a lot and he wanted something done about it.

"So, you tell me, Kate. What would you like me to do about the man in that photo? What should I do about you picking him out? Should I just forget about him until someone else's child is murdered? Let another life be cut short? Let another mother have to go through that kind of hell?

"Should I pretend you didn't have a reaction to that photo in the hope that maybe we'll catch the killer after he kills the next boy, or after he kills a few more? Maybe we'll find a good lead, then. Is that okay with you? Should I forget about the guy you just identified because John's body isn't even buried yet and instead wait for some more bodies to show up?

"You tell me, Kate. Is that what you want me to do?"

"No, of course not," Kate said in a quiet voice as she cleared her throat. "I don't want him to hurt anyone else."

"Well neither do I. John was just like you. He didn't want those men to hurt anyone else, either."

CHAPTER ELEVEN

I'm sorry if it seems I'm being insensitive to your loss today. I know it may seem that way, but it's not true. John was your brother, but I thought of him as a friend, and I thought of myself as his protector. I feel that I failed him.

"Sure, there are bad cops, lazy cops, cops who don't care, just like there are bad doctors, crooked lawyers, and lazy bricklayers. But most cops sincerely want to get the bad guys. That's why we become cops in the first place. We fight to put these animals in cages where they can't hurt anyone. We fight to protect innocent people from predators. That's our calling. That's what we're born to do.

"I don't think most people begin to understand how fragile civilization really is. Depravity and mayhem are always there, just below the surface. We fight to suppress it.

"Killers are relentless, so I have to be relentless. I have to press. I have to ask tough questions of people who are hurting, just like that mother was, just like you are right now.

"If I had a photo of the guy I thought might be the one who broke in the face of the woman you work with—Wilma, the one you visited in the hospital, the one likely to die—wouldn't you want me to bring you the photo before he can do it again?"

Kate simply nodded, feeling at a loss for words right then.

"I've seen the things these kinds of monsters do," AJ said. "Every night when I close my eyes to go to sleep I see them again. Tonight when I try to go to sleep I'll see what your brother looked like when I walked into his living room today.

"If I had photos of the man I suspected in John's murder, wouldn't you want to see them? Wouldn't you want someone else to have helped stop John's killer if they could have?

"You just did that for some other unsuspecting family, some other mother and father, some child who is alive right now who might otherwise soon end up in a landfill. Should I not use what I just learned and instead let other people be murdered?"

Kate swallowed before answering. "Of course not."

"The reality is that most criminals get away with their crimes most of the time. Every day serious crimes are committed but never reported and if they are they're rarely solved. The public usually only hears about the ones that are solved. Victims are hurt all the time—beaten, stabbed, choked, shot. They frequently don't want to file charges or testify for fear the attacker will come after them again.

“We find bodies all the time dumped in streets or empty lots and the killer is never caught. No one knows anything. Everyone usually remains silent.

“Don’t get me wrong—we solve a lot of murders. A guy kills his wife or girlfriend, we figure it out. They leave a lot of forensic evidence. We’re pretty good at what we do and we solve a lot of really difficult cases. But you rarely hear about the stacks of cases that go nowhere.

“When we do catch one of those criminals with a long history of arrests, they’re protected by ever-increasing layers of lawyers, regulations, and procedures. Much of the public is in favor of even more restrictions on the police. More and more we’re made out to be the bad guys.”

Kate pressed her lips tight for a moment. “I don’t know if I believe that’s true—that most people think the police are the bad guys.”

AJ sat back, studying Kate’s face for a moment. “About six months back I was working a home-invasion case. Someone broke in, robbed an elderly lady, raped her, and then stabbed her to death. Her family was in shock and couldn’t understand why anyone would do such a thing to the old woman, why they didn’t just steal her money. Why did they have to hurt her or kill her?

“We’d been there all day. A couple of the uniformed officers, Hickman and Rodrigues, were changing shifts and asked me if I wanted to go with them to get a bite to eat. I'd been on my feet all day, was running out of steam, and knew I was going to be there until late that night, so I took them up on their offer. We went to a sandwich shop on a busy street not far away.

"When we walked in, the young woman behind the counter looked the uniformed officers up and down as they were looking up at the menu. Then she said, 'You can't come in here.' "

"They were puzzled and asked what she was talking about. She said, 'Didn't you see the sign on the door? This is a gun-free zone. You can't come in here with guns. Especially cops.' Before Rodrigues could say anything, Hickman tapped him on the arm and said real quiet-like, 'I'd rather get home to my kids than file a complaint. There are plenty of other places along this street.' Rodrigues made a sour face but they both turned to leave.

"I leaned an arm on the glass case covering the area where the young woman made the sandwiches and said to her, 'I'd like you to give your family and coworkers a message.' The young woman made a face and asked what I meant. I said, 'Tell them that if a wide-eyed tweaker, all the muscles in his face twitching from a big hit of meth, ever comes in waving a gun or puts a knife to your throat, I'd like them not to call these officers and instead call me.'

"Real snotty like, she asked, 'Why, what do you

do?' I opened my jacket so she could see the badge on my belt, then leaned in a little and said, 'I'm a homicide detective. I'm the one who will come to draw a chalk outline around your corpse.' "

Kate couldn't help smiling a little. "What did she say?"

AJ flicked a hand dismissively. "Oh, you know, she called me the usual names. Hickman and Rodrigues liked it, though. Cops love good sarcasm."

"Well, you could have gone to the shop owner or the company and I'm sure—"

"That's not the point. Of course I could have complained and I probably could have gotten her fired. But that's like spitting into the ocean. The point is, our culture is changing. People more and more view law and order, and view the police who are representatives of law and order, as oppressors rather than protectors.

"I see countless glares, rolled eyes, and middle fingers directed at us. Go for a ride with me in a cop car sometime and see how many times you hear people yell names or that they hope I get shot or raped.

"Those are the cracks appearing in civilization.

"We call it sympathy for the devil.

"Despite all that, we still do our jobs, because most of us want nothing more than to protect innocent people from harm. That's our calling in life, what we want in our hearts to do.

"This kind of thing with John—with you—is outside the rules. Yet how can I ignore it and still live with myself?"

Kate stared at her hands for a while without really seeing them. "I never thought of it that way."

"You shouldn't have to. I don't like showing you those photos any more than I liked showing them to John. I wish I could put a lot of the things I've seen out of my mind."

"I guess that I can't imagine the things you've had to see," Kate said. "I don't know how you can do it."

"Because if I can stop a killer," AJ said as she leaned in on her forearms, "then it's all worth it. But it seems like more and more we're losing and the bad guys are winning. Cities have broken down into feudal fiefdoms where thugs and gangs control large parts of them. Their numbers grow by the day.

"There are places in Chicago I can't go to investigate a murder without a whole platoon of backup, like the king's sheriff riding into hostile territory with a full complement of armored knights. There are lots of innocent people in there just trying to live their lives amid chaos and ceaseless violence.

"Their lives are hell. I do my best to fight for them and take the devils out of their lives.

"I lie awake at night, going over every detail

of cases I work, trying to think if I've missed anything. I lie awake thinking about those two boys in the landfill, their bodies buried in garbage, and about my own little boy sleeping in the next room. I want to catch killers before they can kill again."

"And John helped you do that," Kate said, as the enormity of it all pressed in on her.

AJ nodded. "I don't like doing this to you any better. But despite my initial skepticism, I came to know that what John could do was not only real, it was absolutely reliable, and because of him I was able to catch killers before they could kill again.

"It's obvious you have that same ability."

As AJ turned to put the manila envelope with the photos back in the satchel, Kate stretched her arm across the table. "Wait. Give them back."

AJ looked up. "Why?"

"I didn't look through them all."

When the detective handed them back, Kate shuffled the photo of the man with the terrible eyes to the bottom of the stack and continued looking through the remainder.

Three photos later, she was jolted by that same, sickening sensation, that same ice-cold flash of fear as she looked into the eyes of a monster. She held it off to the side, turning it over, and quickly went through the remaining photos to see if there were others. None of them looked anything but ordinary.

"This one," she said, leaning in to hand the photos to AJ. "He's like the others, like Herzog and that last man, the one who killed the two boys. I got a similar feeling from him."

AJ's brows drew together as she looked at the photo. "This isn't a man."

"What?"

She turned the stack of photos back so Kate could see the one on top, the one Kate had picked out. "This isn't a man. It's a young woman."

Kate's attention was riveted by the eyes in the photo. She forced herself to look away from the eyes to look instead at the person. It wasn't easy, but when she did, she saw that it was indeed a young woman with long, straight, dishwater-blond hair.

"I didn't notice at first," Kate stammered, realizing that the explanation sounded silly. "Who is she?"

AJ stared at the photo again for a long moment, then put all the photos back in the envelope and returned it to her satchel.

"Her name is Rebecca Wells. The rest of her family were all murdered in their sleep. Mother, father, and a teenage brother. Both parents had been brutally stabbed several times with a butcher knife and died in their bed. It looked to have been a swift kill before they could wake up to defend themselves.

"The boy apparently did wake up. He was stabbed dozens of times as he struggled down the hallway trying to escape. The killer finally cut the boy's throat. That ended it.

"The killer then took a shower in the parents' bathroom, in all likelihood to wash off the blood. Now that I see this photo, I wonder if maybe there was something symbolic about it.

"Rebecca called the police from a house down the street a ways, saying that someone broke in and was murdering her family. She said that she only caught a shadowy glimpse of the killer as she ran out. She begged the police to hurry. The neighbors said she came to their house in nothing but a nightgown.

"When I interviewed her the next day, Rebecca was dressed nicely. Her hair and makeup were in order. She was as calm as could be. She was nonchalant, almost indifferent, as she described what she had been through. She read her statement carefully to make sure I had gotten it correct. She asked that I put a comma in one spot. She even smiled occasionally."

Kate frowned. "That sounds pretty damn suspicious."

AJ spread her hands. "Everyone reacts differently. Certain kinds of killers simply have no empathy for their victims. But profilers say that it's sometimes the way ordinary people react to horrific events. The emotional part of their brain kind of switches off so as not to have to confront the reality of what happened. They try to retain their sense of normality by acting normal."

"I still don't see how she could be so calm."

AJ arched an eyebrow. "How did you? You didn't cry. Since you arrived at John's house you've been cool and collected. You even smiled at me a few times as I asked you questions."

Kate didn't remember smiling. Apparently, AJ remembered such details.

"Maybe on the outside," Kate said, "but not on the inside."

"People often wear a public face. You seemed alert and aware to me. The only emotion you showed was anger at the person who had killed John. You didn't freak out, though. You answered calmly. You asked relevant questions. You took in everything when you went into John's house, pointed out details that were out of place and out of the ordinary. I wouldn't think it out of context for you to ask me to fix a comma in your statement."

"I ask questions for a living." Kate took sip of coffee. "That's my job. I focus on small details in order to find out what's really going on. I guess I fell back on that conditioning. I wanted to be accurate in order to be helpful."

"Well, this young woman is highly intelligent.

She graduated high school a year early and went right into advanced classes in college. She reacted much like you, but with even less emotion."

"What kind of advanced classes?"

"Chemistry and math."

"Subjects that don't have as much human interaction. Dispassionate facts and numbers."

AJ nodded. "Rebecca told me that she ran for her life when she heard her brother's screams. She said it in a way that was coldly logical and made perfect sense. Most people would run from that kind of life-and-death danger.

"Still she was one of a half dozen people on my short list. When I questioned her, she insisted that she had never been abused, and that her father and mother were normal, loving, if slightly annoying. She said that her brother had his own interests, mostly online gaming, and didn't really pay much attention to her, she thought because she was so much more intelligent than he was. The neighbors said they had never heard any fighting and that the parents were nice people. Her brother's friends confirmed her assessment of him.

"From the way the sheets were arranged, it looked like the killer stood at the side of the bed, slammed the knife into the father three times first, then jumped on the mother, straddling her and stabbing her in the chest a dozen times or so.

She drowned in her own blood. The brother was stabbed in the back the first time as he ran into the hallway. Nothing appeared to be stolen from the house. Murdering three people that way—stabbing them to death so violently in their sleep apparently just for the hell of it—is an extreme kind of killing."

"Especially for a woman," Kate said.

"Not necessarily. Women can be the most vicious of killers. They can be as heartless and cold-blooded as any male killer.

"Now, because of you, we just may be able to stop a rare kind of psycho—a female serial killer in the making. A sort of female Edward Lester Herzog. Once they get started, they're hard to find. You've helped me isolate a killer, just like John did."

Kate was unnerved by the description of the murders. With John's murder and the photos of killers, it felt like she had been unexpectedly dropped into the middle of a horrific dream.

"It at least gives me some measure of peace to know that John was doing something to help stop the men he called the devil."

"That's why I used him," AJ said, "and why I hated using him. He was helping me catch evil men, and, in a way, I was taking the devils out of the world for him. I only wish I could have caught that last one, the one who came too close, the one who didn't want to be seen for who he was."

CHAPTER TWELVE

Kate let out a sigh. "But how could the things John was doing be real?"

"You had the same reaction he did to the same photo of Herzog. You had that same kind of reaction to the other two photos. It's not just John, it's you, too."

"I know, but . . ." Kate ran her fingers back through her hair in frustration.

She remembered that her boss had once told her that he didn't understand it, but she seemed to have some kind of radar for the rotten apple in the barrel. She always thought she was simply conscientious at what she did—paying attention to details, looking for patterns and connections, picking out inconsistencies in things people told her. He told her that she might not to be able to see it within herself, but she had a unique, uncanny ability to focus in on the responsible party.

Even so, she wasn't able to do that by the look in their eyes. At least, she had never been aware she was doing anything of that nature. Of course, in her job she dealt only with lowlifes, liars, cheats, and thieves, not killers.

"What's happening to me, AJ? John being able

to do things like that—recognize a killer—is one thing. Even though I never believed him, he's always said he could tell if people were bad. But I've never been able to do that sort of thing before."

Leaning back in the booth again, AJ studied Kate's eyes for a long while before speaking in a quiet tone. "I believe that seeing that photo of Herzog was what's called a trigger event."

Kate squinted her skepticism. "A trigger event."

Detective Janek seemed to have uncovered more than simply what she had learned with John.

"That's what it's called."

Kate stared at the other woman. "I don't understand. I could never do it before. Maybe John could, but I couldn't."

"You don't really know that."

"What do you mean?"

"Your chances of being hit by lightning are better than your chances of actually running across a serial killer in person. They only loom so large in our minds because their crimes are so horrific. They are everyone's bogeyman, and yet the vast majority of people will live their entire lives without ever seeing a serial killer, or even a garden-variety murderer, for that matter. Your chances of seeing a killer are further reduced because you don't do drugs, you don't turn tricks, you don't live in a dangerous neighborhood.

"The photo of Herzog, printed from a negative, is undoubtedly the first killer you've ever seen. It hit you at an emotional level. That triggered your awareness of an ability you didn't even know you had."

"But John was able to do it since he was little."

AJ opened both hands in a gesture of the unknowable. "My guess is that when John was very young, maybe with his mother holding his hand, he crossed paths with a murderer. In that chance moment, he looked up into the eyes of a cold-blooded killer, much the same as you did tonight.

"It was most likely an accidental sighting on John's part, but as random as it was, seeing that level of evil in a killer's eyes"—AJ tapped her temple with a finger—"triggered his conscious awareness of his innate ability.

"Because it started when he was so young, he was always tuned in to it. Going out caused him anxiety, most likely because one time when he was out, he saw a killer.

"As he grew older he likely learned to recognize varying degrees of that cunning quality in lesser criminals and the various degrees of depravity in between. Regular criminals are a lot more common, and while capable of murder, they haven't yet crossed that lethal line. I suspect that as time goes on you will also learn to have a more granular feel for it.

"The point is, like John, you've always had the ability to recognize whatever it is the both of you see in a killer's eyes. You were born with that ability to see evil. You just haven't ever seen a killer before to trigger your awareness of it."

"But what was it, exactly, that John could see when he looked at certain photographs? What is it that I see?"

With her fingertips, AJ slowly turned the cup around and around in its saucer as she considered how to answer. "In the beginning," she finally said, "I asked myself that question a thousand times. I could see what John was clearly capable of doing, the same as you just did, but my head told me that it wasn't possible. I couldn't do it. I've never heard of anyone who could. I couldn't comprehend what John was able to do. To try to make sense out of it I started doing research."

"Research? How do you research something like this? It's not like you can go online and search for 'devil sightings.' "

AJ smiled. "Actually, it turns out you can."

She waved off the distraction, returning to the matter at hand. "I wasn't even sure exactly what it was I was looking for, except that I needed to find some kind of common thread among killers, some key thing that made John able to detect them.

"There were endless dead ends along the way, endless crazy theories about killers, and an endless number of both sincere and deluded people who believe the devil walks among us—that kind of thing. I knew, of course, that it wasn't really the devil that John was seeing."

Kate idly tapped her thumb on the side of her cup. "Ever since he was young, that was what John called people who scared him the most. I always knew that it was simply his word for a truly frightening person."

"After showing him enough photos of killers I figured that much out," AJ said.

She looked back up at Kate, returning to her story. "Whenever I could find the time after I put Ryan to bed, I did research. If I found a promising book, I'd read it. None of them were helpful. After countless dead ends I began to find little bits and pieces of things that weren't crazy, pieces that felt right. That enabled me to refine my search.

"In the end, it was your brother who finally gave me the key."

"John?" Kate frowned. "What key could John give you?"

AJ laced her fingers together and leaned in on her elbows. "I asked myself, what was the primary characteristic John presented when he recognized that these men were killers?"

In that instant, Kate knew.

"Fear."

AJ showed her a small smile. "That was also your reaction to the photos. That's the thing that links it all together."

"Fear? But how?"

AJ pressed her lips tight in thought for a moment. "As man evolved, one of the abilities we developed—like most creatures—was fear. That was the key."

"Fear? Fear is an ability?"

"Of course," AJ said with a one-handed gesture. "It's basic to survival. Fish fear herons, so they hide. A deer hears wolves approaching and it runs for its life.

"If our ancestors weren't afraid of saber-toothed tigers—or whatever predators they had back then—they'd have been eaten. People with too low a level of fear more easily fell prey to predators. People who were afraid ran away or hid to survive another day. Because they survived, they passed that trait on.

"Fear of dying is a basic survival mechanism for most creatures. Over hundreds of thousands of years it has evolved into a finely tuned ability in us all. We don't have to intellectualize it; we're born with it.

"That inborn sense is so highly developed that we don't even realize the countless clues we're using. Our brains simply register the sum total of those clues as an instantaneous fear response—a gut reaction."

“So we were afraid of saber-toothed tigers and snakes and spiders. So what?”

AJ arched an eyebrow. “The predator we learned to fear the most was our own kind. Man is the most dangerous predator walking the face of the earth. He is also the most complex. We need to get along with other people as a matter of survival, and yet our ancestors also had to be wary of others of their own kind who very well might intend them harm.

“While brute force needed no subtlety, predatory individuals learned to offer strangers a smile, or friendly small talk until they could get close enough to strike. Even today, serial killers are frequently exceedingly charming individuals.

“That meant that potential victims had to learn to key in to little clues if they were to survive. Predators in turn had to learn to fine-tune their skill if they were to survive. It was an ever-escalating war of natural selection between predator and prey.

“Man is both.

“As a result, over many millennia we developed a keen sense for telling when others mean to do us harm. That sense of fear is one of our most valuable skills.”

Kate made a face. “I don’t know . . .”

“When you see a guy out of the corner of your eye as he walks up behind you and you suddenly get goose bumps, that's the product of evolution meant to protect you. Your inherent sense of fear picked up on clues that his approach was not random or innocent, but predatory. You probably couldn't identify the individual reasons, but your goose bumps show that your highly developed human brain has already identified them.

"When you walk to your car and notice someone standing nearby watching you and for some indefinable reason he gives you the creeps, that's your inner fear analyzing a vast collection of tiny clues and urging you to get in your car, lock the doors, and get the hell out of there. You don't have to consciously evaluate the situation.

"These days we're supposed to ignore our inherent fear of threat. We're told that it's wrong, that it's immoral, it's prejudiced for us to be afraid of others. We're made to feel shame for our fear. Yet this birthright of fear is what has enabled mankind to survive. When it comes to matters of life and death, fear helps to keep us safe."

"And so you think that because of John's limited mental capacity he didn't comprehend such complex social pressures and instead relied on his baser instincts more than most people?"

AJ nodded. "I think so. He didn't have the social filter that says fearing other people is prejudging them."

Kate felt a bit guilty for telling John that very

thing, that he shouldn't judge people without knowing them.

"I've seen the grainy surveillance video of the attack on your friend Wilma," AJ said. "Passersby ran to help her once she was down, but they avoided looking at the men who attacked her, avoided looking at evil. That woman where John worked, the one who was robbed in the alley, wouldn't turn around to look at the man who was threatening her. She couldn't bring herself to look at evil. Most people refuse to see evil.

"Criminals look for that kind of person, the ones preoccupied on their phones, or looking in windows, or simply spaced out. Most criminals want to avoid risk and keep the odds in their favor, so they look for the easiest prey. There is always plenty of it, so why take a risk?"

"That would mean that the predators have also evolved and learned a counter-skill."

AJ smiled. "Exactly."

Kate had never thought about it in quite that way.

"As a police officer I watch a person's body language for any possible threat the person may represent. We're trained in self-protection, but that threat profile originates in our primitive fear. I use that fear to help keep me from being hurt. That is, after all, the purpose of our fear."

Kate had a hard time imagining AJ being afraid

of anyone. “I’ve seen plenty of people who don’t fit your description. They don’t try to hide who they are.”

“You’re right,” AJ conceded. “Predators come in all varieties. There is certainly no shortage of predators who are loud, arrogant, and aggressive. There are thugs and gangs of every sort. They deliberately try to intimidate people. They pick fights, bully, rob, brutalize. They’re the animals who beat their wives and girlfriends. They’re the ever-growing packs of jackals snapping at the edges of society.

“Even though they’re a different kind of predator, that doesn’t make them any less dangerous. They have no empathy for others. If they corner you, you give them what they want and run—if you can.

“They are the ordinary rabble in the world of the wicked—the kind those with a brain and a halfway healthy dose of paranoia avoid. But there’s another kind of predator who is altogether different. They are not the scavengers. They are the wolf in sheep’s clothing blending in, giving us no warning signs. They kill for the sake of killing. They are the unseen terror in the night. *Everyone* fears them.”

Kate rubbed her arms as she listened.

These were John’s devils, these were the bogeymen.

AJ’s gaze focused into the darkness outside

the window. "In my search for a way to explain what John could do, I found a book by an author named Jack Raines. By the way his book reads, I suspect that at one time he may have helped build psychological profiles for law enforcement. His book is largely about this last kind of super-predator."

"What's this book called?"

The detective's dark eyes turned back to Kate. "*A Brief History of Evil.*"

CHAPTER THIRTEEN

That sounds like an unpleasant read," Kate said.

AJ shrugged. "Yes and no. It wasn't what I expected. For the most part the book doesn't deal with the lower-level Edward Lester Herzog type—"

Kate leaned forward. "He considers someone like Herzog 'lower-level'?"

"On the predatory food chain, yes. Raines believes that there exists among us a whole different kind of rare individual who is entirely more dangerous."

"So this book is about these, what . . . super-predators?"

AJ gazed into Kate's eyes. "And in part about those rare individuals who can recognize these top-level killers among us."

"You mean recognize killers the way John could?"

AJ leaned back in the booth. "That's what I wanted to know. The book deals with how both killers and their opposite are connected in a broad historical context."

"What do you mean, connected?" Kate asked. "Connected how?"

"That's what I needed to figure out in order to understand John. The problem was, Raines wasn't specific enough. By reading between the lines I could tell that he understood those connections quite well, but they weren't the focus of the book.

"I needed to talk to him to find out more. I tried to find his phone number. It wasn't in any of the police reference resources. It was like he didn't exist.

"So I called up his publisher, thinking it would be simple for them to put me in touch with him. People there weren't in, they were on vacation, they were sick, no one would return calls. I believe his book was relatively successful, but his publisher seemed disorganized and uninterested."

"Maybe they thought you were an aspiring author who wanted to submit a manuscript or something."

"Could be. I repeatedly left my name and number asking for Jack Raines or someone familiar with him to call me. I didn't want to leave messages with just anyone saying that I was a police officer for fear that someone there might call my department, instead of me, asking what I was calling about. That would have opened a whole can of worms."

"And possibly expose John," Kate said.

"Exactly," AJ said with a single nod. "So one day a woman named Shannon Blare finally returned my calls to see what I wanted. She sounded rather put out by my repeated calls. I told her I was calling about Jack Raines. She said that she was the editor for a number of writers and wanted to know what my interest was in that particular author.

"I told her that I was a homicide detective and I wanted to talk to Mr. Raines about some of the theories in his book.

"She got all quiet."

"Why?"

"I don't know. I asked her for Jack Raines's number. She told me that he was busy working on a new book, but the next time she spoke with him she would pass my number along.

"I didn't understand her reluctance, but I especially didn't want her calling my department, so before she could hang up I told her I had a test for lieutenant coming up, and as part of my work on the most intelligent kinds of killers, I had read *A Brief History of Evil*. I told her it would really help me out if I could ask him a few questions. That seemed to calm her down. I said I understood that she was only protecting his privacy and asked her to at least email my phone number to him."

"I take it he called?"

AJ nodded. "Just a little over a month ago. He was aloof. I suspected he'd had enough calls from wannabe private detectives, or cranks, and they never really understood the premise of the book. I answered as 'Detective Janek' so he would know I was a police officer. I asked him a few questions about specifics in his book in order to dispel the notion that I wanted to become an author myself or have him write the story of my life or some-thing. He gave simple answers and asked a few questions of his own. As a detective I know when someone is doing the dance with mc. He was dancing."

Kate understood what Detective Janek was talking about. She often had to do the same kind of thing when she questioned reticent people about serious issues.

AJ gestured with a sweep of her hand. "I finally steered the conversation to the heart of the matter and told him that I had someone who matched the abilities he theorized in his book.

"There was a very long pause, and then he said, 'It isn't a theory.' I asked him if he was sure. He asked me instead what made me think that I might know such an individual. It was obvious to me that we were still dancing. I wanted to bring it to an end."

Concerned, Kate said, "So you told him about John?"

"Yes, but I didn't name him. I simply told him that I had a man capable of the things I thought he was touching on in his book, the things connected to his larger theme. He asked me if all the people in my department were big believers in his work.

"I told him that no one in the department knew what I was doing and wouldn't believe me even if I told them. I said I didn't dare tell anyone or I would not only lose my job but endanger this individual. I told him that I knew the stakes, that my phone call to him was outside the scope of police procedures and could cause me a lot of problems. I told him that while I'd very much like to talk to him about the matter because I thought he could help me understand it better, I couldn't discuss it any further unless I had his word that he would keep it strictly between the two of us.

"He said that he was glad to hear that I was being cautious and he would keep the call confidential. His tone changed a little, then. He became more focused. He asked me what I was dealing with—what I believed I had found and why I believed it.

"I told him that I had a mentally handicapped individual who wasn't the kind to try to impress me or flatter me or con me. In fact, this individual was reluctant. Jack said the mental handicap would help explain his ability, if that ability was in fact actually true.

"I told him straight up that this man could identify killers from photos on film printed from negatives—something mentioned in his book. He asked how sure I was. I told him that in all the tests I'd done, and I'd done a lot, he had never once been wrong. Not once.

“In the silence, I could almost hear the guy thinking. He dropped the formality and told me that he suspected I was a professional or I wouldn’t be a detective and I wouldn’t have gone to the lengths I had, but detective or not, I needed to be painstakingly careful not to tell anyone what I had stumbled upon. He said that he didn’t think I fully comprehended what I was dealing with.

“I told him that I knew quite well what the individual I was dealing with was capable of. He said that wasn’t what he meant. That in turn gave me pause.

“He told me that the new book he was working on dealt with the connections he had only hinted at in his first book, and asked if he could interview this person.

“I told him no, that an expert had advised me to be painstakingly careful to protect him. He laughed.

“He had a nice laugh. You know how sometimes an easy laugh tells you a lot about a person? It was that kind of laugh.

“I laughed, too, and in that moment I think we had established something of a real and trusting relationship. We both understood that we were well outside the orthodoxy of regular police work or even accepted principles of criminal behavior, much less criminal law. We were both outsiders in something that others wouldn’t want to hear or believe, but we both knew to be true.”

AJ pointed back and forth between herself and Kate. "Kind of like you and me. We both know we're touching on something out of the ordinary, something others wouldn't believe, but we've seen it with our own eyes. You know what I mean?"

Kate nodded with a sigh. "I know exactly what you mean."

"Anyway, Jack said that not only were there exceedingly rare individuals like the one I had encountered who possessed a refined ability to recognize threat, there were also predators who, as a consequence of their own natural selection and evolution over tens of thousands of years, had developed the corollary ability to recognize those individuals."

Kate's brow drew down. "Predators who know which prey recognizes them?"

"Exactly." AJ leaned in again, lowering her voice as if the walls might have ears. "That means that not only can people like John—like you—see evil, but evil can see you."

AJ straightened back up, letting that sink in for a moment.

"Jack says those rare killers can recognize people with that special kind of vision—and they don't like it. Not one bit. He said that a regular criminal will typically avoid a person who looks them in the eye, a person who is watching them, who suspects them, and instead look for weaker prey.

"This kind, he said, will do the opposite. They will go after a person who can see them for who they are."

Kate was frowning. "You're saying that despite your secrecy, one of these sorts of super-predators may have somehow recognized John for his ability and killed him?"

AJ shook her head in frustration. "I don't see how."

"Maybe it's simpler than that. Maybe John was on his way home one day and happened to cross paths with a killer," Kate offered, "the kind he thought of as the devil—you know, a regular killer, not one who recognizes John for his ability. Maybe without thinking John hit him over the head and then chained him up. John wouldn't always think things through. He would sometimes act on impulse and later on not know how to untangle himself from the situation."

"That makes sense," the detective admitted. "Even an ordinary killer would have been more than John could handle."

After a moment Kate asked, "What about me? Did Jack Raines have anything to say about someone like me?"

"In a way, yes." AJ's finger traced the contour of the handle on her cup as she thought about how to explain it. "Jack says that an ability like John's is incredibly rare. He says it's a mutation wired to the person's perception."

"I don't follow."

"Neither did I," AJ admitted. "Jack said to think of it as the way owls evolved, taking advantage of genetic mutations that enabled them to see better in the dark. He says that a genetic mutation resulting in John's ability is relatively new on the scale of human evolution and it runs in families the same as any other genetic trait.

"Life is always in the process of evolving. Some mutations help, some hurt. The ones that help us survive are passed on; the ones that hurt die out.

"Like I told you before, for most people the chances of actually seeing a murderer are pretty slim, but it obviously does happen. Since seeing that kind of individual is a rare occurrence, the genetic mutation to identify them is rare. Yet being able to see a truly evil individual for who they really are is a lifesaving ability, and as such, as rare as it is, it would tend to pass on genetically. Thus it runs in families.

"Jack says that this ability can lie dormant until a trigger event—a sighting. If he's right, you've always been able to see what John could see. You just never knew it before because you never saw a killer before."

One time when she had doubted John about a man he had seen in the neighborhood, she told him that he couldn't tell if a person was bad just by looking at them. John had fixed Kate with a look that gave her pause and he said that if she ever looked into the eyes of the devil she would know it, too, just like he did.

"Jack said he has been studying the history of these rare predators. I told him that it wasn't the history of killers I was interested in so much as the connections he'd hinted at in his book. I told him that I thought those connections were somehow at the heart of all of this.

"He said I was right about that in more ways than I even realized. He said that all those connections created nesting events."

"Nesting events?"

AJ shook her head in frustration. "He said that was the heart of the matter, but he didn't have the time to get into that part of it with me right then."

AJ saw the worry on Kate's face and softened her tone. "Look, Kate, maybe after things settle down you could talk to Jack Raines. I'm sure he could help you understand all of this better. I'm probably doing a pretty poor job of explaining it. Maybe I'm making more of it than is warranted."

Kate wasn't about to be put off. "I can recognize the worst kind of killers, they can recognize that I know them for what they truly are, so that makes me a target. Isn't that about the sum of it?"

AJ sat back. "I guess it is."

"It sounds," Kate said, "like Mr. Raines had pretty good reason to tell you to keep John's identity a secret."

"Yes, and now yours as well."

"What now?"

AJ yawned. "I asked Jack if he had any suggestion as to what I should do about all of this. Of course, at the time I didn't know that you could do the same thing John could. Jack said to give him a little time to look into it and he would see what he could find out."

"But you said you didn't give him John's name."

"I didn't."

"Then how is he going to be able to look into it?"

"He simply said to give him some time to look into it." AJ opened her hands. "I'm not sure what he meant. I haven't heard back from him since then."

Kate felt a shadow of worry for Jack Raines. Even though she didn't know him, she worried that in the kind of research he was doing he could very well encounter one of those killers, and she didn't think that, like her, he would be able to see them for who they were.

CHAPTER FOURTEEN

AJ yawned again, making Kate yawn with her. "It's been a long day. I appreciate the coffee and the confidential conversation—and getting to know you better—but I guess it's time I get home and kiss my kid. The big one and the little one. On days like this it helps me to remember that there really is good left in the world."

Right then, Kate couldn't find much of the good. John's murder was a crushing blow, but finding out what he had been doing, as well as what she was able to do, made the world that Kate thought she knew feel foreign and hostile. She was exhausted and knew that she needed to get some sleep, but she doubted she would get much.

"I've got to be at John's house early," AJ said. "We have a lot of investigation still to do and evidence that needs to be processed. We also need to interview all the neighbors. Between combing through the crime scene and trying to find someone who might have seen or heard something, I'm hoping that I can find pieces of this puzzle that will lead me to John's killer. It's going to be several days yet before we're finished up at his house and we can turn the place over to you."

Kate couldn't help remembering the blood all over the living room. She imagined that even after it was cleaned up, she would still see it, if only in her mind's eye. The place, for her, would always be haunted by ghosts.

"You said that a lot of murders go unsolved."

"This isn't one of those kind," AJ insisted. "We're going to catch this guy. In the meantime, I suggest that you wait until after the place has been thoroughly cleaned before going back there. I'll get you those names of some reputable companies that can handle it for you."

Kate couldn't bear to worry about such details right then, so she simply said, "All right."

AJ slid out from behind the table and stood. "Here, give me your phone."

Kate pulled it out of a pocket, unlocked it, and handed it over. The woman started tapping away with her thumbs, then took her own phone out of her jacket pocket and made entries into it.

"I put my name and cell in your contacts list, and yours in mine, so if you want to know anything at all, just call me. If I can't take it, I'll get back to you as soon as possible."

Kate set her phone down on the counter beside her laptop. "Okay. Thanks." She could only imagine how busy the detective must be.

"I wish I had more answers, Kate. But for now I wanted you to know about your brother—that he was a good man. It was important to me that you know he helped put a couple of killers away for life and in all likelihood saved other people from being murdered. You've done the same thing tonight. You don't know how much I appreciate it.

"No one other than you and I will know about this, but it will help stop two killers. I'm going to make sure that guy is never able to harm another child. I want you to hold on to that. In all the terrible things you've learned today, that's something good. You helped keep some good people alive."

Kate nodded and thanked the detective as she walked her to the door. She supposed that sooner or later the woman was going to want to show Kate more photos. In a way, it gave her an inner rush to know that she was able to help stop such animals.

"Please, when you have time, or if you learn anything, keep me informed?"

AJ flashed a sympathetic smile. "I'll be in touch—I promise. I'm hoping that as soon as I start questioning people and develop some leads you might be able to help me identify the guy who did this to John."

"Gladly," Kate said, and meant it. She wanted John's killer found and punished.

She wanted him dead.

AJ turned back from the doorway. "Look, Kate, I want you to know that I'll keep digging, but I don't think this is going to turn out to be an ordinary case. There are too many strange things about it."

"Like John chaining a killer up in his basement?"

"That would be at the top of my list, especially since I knew John and I would never have thought him capable of doing such a thing. Knowing John, he had to have had a powerful reason."

Kate frowned, staring down at the floor as she ran the conversation back through her mind. She looked up. "I just thought of something. When John was on the phone with me when I got back in town, before he told me to run, he told me that he'd gone to put flowers on our parents' grave."

"What of it?"

"He said that someone was watching him."

AJ's brows drew together over her dark eyes. "Really."

"I told him that it was probably just someone putting flowers on another grave—and it probably was. John was pretty fearful when he was out by himself, so he might have imagined it."

"I don't really believe in coincidence," AJ said.

"I have to tell you, I never have, either. That's why I'm mentioning it."

"I wish I understood what the hell was going on and what it all means."

"You think you're confused?" Kate asked. "I'm upside down and inside out."

AJ smiled reassurance. “I’ll be there to help you figure it out. You won’t be alone in this, I promise.”

“Thanks. That means a lot to me, it really does.”

AJ handed Kate a card. “I put my number in your phone, but keep this handy as well, just in case. It’s my personal card. It has my cell and my home phone number, so you should be able to get me anytime, day or night.”

The card had a City of Chicago badge printed beside her last name. “Just like the one you gave John?”

She nodded with a deadly serious demeanor. “Listen, Kate, don’t be afraid to call me. Anytime. I mean it. I don’t live that far from here.” She leaned in and pointed. “See? There’s my address. I can be here in no time. Lights flashing, guns blazing.”

Kate smiled as she used her first finger to mimic the detective’s earlier imitation of a gun. “Guns blazing.”

“I mean it, Kate.”

“I know.” Kate knew that AJ wished John had listened and that he had called her. She very well might have been able to help him. AJ didn’t want Kate to make the same mistake of not calling for help.

“Will you call me if you hear any more from Jack Raines?”

“Absolutely.”

AJ paused in the doorway, as if trying to decide something. She tapped the palm of her hand against the doorjamb, considering. She finally turned from staring off into the darkness to look back at Kate.

"Angel."

Kate's nose wrinkled. "What?"

"My first name. It's Angel. Angel Janek. You asked me before what the 'A' in 'AJ' stood for. It stands for Angel."

Kate folded her arms and shrugged. "That's a great name. A wonderful name. Why wouldn't you want to tell people?"

AJ made a sour expression. "I'm a female homicide detective. I have to be tough if I want to be respected. Angel just sounds . . . I don't know, froufrou. I've always been afraid that if people knew my name was Angel they wouldn't take me seriously."

Kate studied the other woman's eyes for a moment. "I think the perception of a person's name is shaped by their character. Genghis Khan sounds like he could be a monk in a monastery if you didn't know anything about him. The name only sounds intimidating because the man was.

"As strong as you are, I don't think people would take your name lightly. You said yourself that day by day there is more sympathy for the devil. I bet that the people on our side of civilization would think of you as an avenging Angel."

"Avenging Angel." AJ smiled. "I like that. I should have met you sooner. But I think I'm stuck with AJ, now."

As she walked to her police cruiser, she turned, walking backward for a moment, pointing her finger gun at Kate like she had in the police car.

"You're everything John said you were, Kate Bishop."

As she watched the woman climb into her police cruiser, Kate smiled at the thought of the way she was always an invincible hero in her brother's eyes, but then the smile faded.

Kate leaned a shoulder against the doorjamb and folded her arms as she watched the tail-lights of the unmarked police car vanish down the empty street.

CHAPTER FIFTEEN

Bare branches clattered together as they swayed to and fro in fitful gusts of wind. The night felt hostile. Somewhere out there in the darkness was a man who had murdered her brother. Watching the taillights of the police car vanish into the darkness, Kate felt an unaccustomed, crushing weight of loneliness.

Something else she had never really thought about before also occurred to her. Besides the man who had killed her brother, there were other killers out there as well. There always had been murderers and always would be. Some of them got caught. Some didn't.

At that very moment some of those killers were on the hunt. Some would find their prey. This night, every night, someone would die at the hands of one of these human monsters. This night, every night, there were people going about their lives who didn't know that they were about to meet a violent end.

Kate closed the door and locked it.

On her way to the kitchen she saw the flashing light on the message machine. Exhausted, she ignored the message light and instead went into the kitchen, unplugged the coffeemaker, rinsed the pot, and put the cups and spoons in the dishwasher.

When she flicked off the lights, she paused to look out the window into the backyard. With the lights in the kitchen off she could finally see into the darkness outside. The private backyard was dark, silent, empty.

Her laptop was still on the counter, where she had left it plugged in to charge when she stopped off at home before going to the hospital to see Wilma. Despite how tired she was, she gave in to a nagging thought. She put her phone in the pocket of her jeans, unplugged the laptop, and took it to the table.

Kate sat in the dark kitchen for a time, staring at the bright screen, feeling an odd sense of anxiety about what answers it might hold. She knew she should go to bed. It was already late. She had gotten up at four that morning to catch the earlier flight. She was beyond tired—both emotionally and physically—and already well into her second wind.

The thought of genetic mutations and the evolution between hunter and prey and all the rest of it was starting to feel distant to her. Kate had trouble fitting it into her sense of life, her sense of reality. She had always thought of the world in terms of lots of good people and some bad people. Simple as that. What had seemed compelling as AJ had described it was beginning to lose its hold on her.

Most of the people at KDEX Systems were good

people. Her job was to find those few who weren't and get them out of the company. Some of those were really bad people. But there were much worse people in the world, people she had never encountered before. People like Edward Lester Herzog.

John had encountered one of that kind.

She needed to call the funeral home, but it would have to wait until morning. There were a number of other demands swirling through her mind. She needed to get back to work and give her boss a report about Dallas. The office, she knew, would be a bit frantic that she address other pending cases. Dallas had diverted a great deal of her time—more time than usual—but it had proven necessary.

Despite her apprehension, she finally opened a page for Amazon and typed in "A Brief History of Evil."

She clicked on the link to the book by Jack Raines. The cover was a decidedly dark illustration of a wet, narrow cobblestone alley between the irregular shapes of old buildings constructed of beams and stucco. She thought it looked like a scene out of the Dark Ages in Europe. In gloomy corners here and there she could see what looked like bundles. It could have been accumulated debris, or even the artist simply being vague with the treatment of shadows.

Or they could have been bodies.

It certainly didn't look like the kind of place one would want to walk alone at night.

It looked like the kind of place where one would not be at all surprised to find bodies.

A Brief History of Evil had a two-star rating out of five. Kate was surprised that people didn't think much of it.

There was a list of one-star reviews in a line down the right side, punctuated by a single two-star review. Kate had to scroll a long way down to find any of the better ratings.

The top "Most Helpful Review" from a confirmed purchaser had given the book one star. The review had been voted most helpful by seventy-eight people. Kate scanned down the length of the long review to get a general sense of what it had to say. The reader was indignant that the book had even been published. Apparently seventy-eight others agreed with him.

While seventy-eight wasn't anywhere near a significant number for books that sold in the tens of thousands, the review was pretty damning, because the reviewer said that he had worked in law enforcement his whole professional life, specializing in criminal profiling, and he hated to see this kind of sham profiling by amateurs who didn't know what they were talking about. He said that the book was mostly pop psychology and wordy filler and Raines was a phony giving the real professionals a bad name.

Kate's heart sank a little. She had thought that maybe this book by Jack Raines would have some answers and be able to help her understand what John had been able to do—as well as her own reactions to the photos AJ showed her.

Another reviewer felt she had been duped into buying what she expected to be a book about the history of serial killers, but it was more like the stuff an amateur would self-publish and any good reviews were probably written by the guy's mother.

The next review said that the book was written at a fourth-grade reading level and repeated itself ad nauseam. Another reviewer agreed, saying that the awkward writing was an embarrassment to the English language and Raines really needed to go back to school and learn the basics. Many recommended other books.

Kate's awareness from analyzing a lot of data at her job told her that such a tiny number of reviews compared to how many people had read the book were meaningless. Still, almost all of the people who reviewed it gave it one or two stars.

While Kate knew that the relatively small number of people who had written bad reviews were unreliable guidance, what was troubling was that a lot of reviews were by police officers who said that the author didn't know what he was talking about. They pointed out that Jack Raines didn't understand police procedure or know how investigations were actually conducted. Few as there were, they left a wedge of doubt in her mind.

Kate was a little surprised by how vicious the reviews were, since it wasn't a book promoting a political view. It was supposedly a book about the horrors of the murderers among us. She reminded herself that the people who haunted the internet loved to hate. There were, after all, lots of people who gave a thumbs-down to videos of kittens.

Something bothered her, though, something that seemed a little off about the reviews. Kate couldn't quite put her finger on it. It felt to her like what she was seeing might be an inkling of a contrived agenda that the retailer's algorithms—designed to detect false promotion, not malice—would overlook.

She wondered if she thought that only because she was so tired. Or because in her job she was so used to looking for ulterior motives that she always tended to suspect everything and everyone. Or maybe it was because AJ had made so much of Jack Raines, and the reviews didn't seem to match what the detective said.

While most of the reviews agreed in their blistering criticism, buried down near the bottom there were a few good reviews that were passionate in their defense of the book, but those were lost beneath all of the negative reviews.

Kate's heart sank a little. She wondered why AJ

had thought so much of the book that she would call Jack Raines.

Kate had been planning on ordering the book that night. Disappointed, she instead closed the cover of her laptop.

When AJ had talked about the book and Jack Raines, it had given Kate the spark of some indefinable hope, but now, like her brother's life, that spark had been extinguished. She felt hollow.

As she headed down the hallway to her bedroom, turning off lights along the way, she felt like something potentially valuable, something that would help her understand what John could do, what she could do, had just been lost to her. In the dark hallway, she felt silly for having harbored hope of some kind of larger explanation to it all, some understanding of the connections. AJ had said that it was the connections of everything that had intrigued her.

Kate knew, though, that not everything in life could be explained or connected. She guessed that what had happened to John and her with those photos was one of those mysteries that would simply never be explained.

People often believed things because they wanted them to be true. AJ must have wanted what Jack Raines told her to be true.

Kate began to wonder if she had been fooling herself about the photos, fooling herself into thinking that she had some kind of latent ability.

Perhaps it had been dumb luck or a simple hunch. After all, she was pretty good at hunches in her work, pretty good at picking out the guilty party. But having hunches was different from being able to tell that someone was a killer.

As frightening as it had been to look at the photos of killers, there had also been something oddly electrifying and exciting about it—like as a child finally finding someone when playing hide-and-seek. A discovery. It was a sense of a small triumph, or an insight.

At least it had been. Now that sense was fading.

As she kicked off her shoes and unbuttoned her blouse, she dismissed *A Brief History of Evil* as a dead end. Somehow, it was depressing to do so. She felt as if she had just lost a bit of hope for finding out what had really happened to John, a bit of hope for shining a light into a dark corner of her own mind.

Looking into the bathroom mirror as she washed off her makeup, she wished she could talk to John about it all. He wouldn't have been able to help her understand any of it, of course, but he would have listened patiently, smiling at her the whole time.

When she curled into the fetal position on her side and pulled up the covers, she finally began to cry.

CHAPTER SIXTEEN

Kate slung her purse up onto the table before walking through the metal detector.

"Good morning, Miss Bishop," came a familiar, husky voice from behind the security podium on the far side of the check-in station.

Kate smiled briefly at the bear of a security guard dressed in a dark blue shirt and black tie. "How have you been, Carlos?"

"My wife still cooks me dinner, so I guess I can't complain."

A small group of well-dressed people waited as the two security women, in the same security uniforms, inspected purses, bags, and briefcases. After Theresa, one of the two, had performed a cursory inspection of the contents of her purse and handed it back, Kate thanked her and then hooked the strap over her shoulder.

Carlos lifted a page on his clipboard. "My printout says you aren't scheduled back until tomorrow."

"Caught the culprit, caught an earlier plane," she said in simple explanation.

"Ah," he said with a knowing nod. "Good for you."

Carlos called her name as she started for the elevator. She turned back to see what he wanted.

He stepped away from his station to come over to her. “Listen, Miss Bishop. I think you should know that one morning, a couple days back, this young man came in wanting to know where your office was. He said he had an appointment with you.”

Kate frowned. “An appointment with me? For what?”

“He said he was here to apply for a job.”

Kate’s frown deepened. “Not only do I not have any appointments with anyone, I don’t handle that kind of thing.”

“I know. He told me that a friend of his, a Mr. Baker, had told him that he was to go see you about a job. He said that this Mr. Baker was supposed to have set it up.”

“I don’t know a Mr. Baker.”

Carlos didn’t look at all surprised. “I was pretty sure you didn’t. People sometimes try talking their way past us. They think that if they can see someone in person they have a better chance of making a pitch to get a job.

“I didn’t like this guy’s attitude. He was acting like I was a petty annoyance preventing him from getting in to see you. Rather than tell him that he wasn’t on my list of scheduled visitors, or that you didn’t do any of the hiring, I told him you weren’t in. He asked when you would be back. I didn’t want him getting in your hair, so I told him that you had gone to Atlanta to open a new office and you would be gone for the rest of the year."

Kate smiled. They didn't have an office in Atlanta. "What was his name?"

"He said his name was Bob."

"Bob."

"Yeah, but he didn't look like a Bob to me."

"Did he say anything else?"

Carlos shook his head. "No. When I asked his last name he flipped me off and left."

"What did he look like?"

Carlos scratched his jaw as he thought. "Curly bleached-blond hair cut close to his scalp. Brown eyes. About your height—five-nine, five-ten or so. He was wearing baggy blue shorts and a D.A.R.E. T-shirt. Black with red lettering. Hardly what one would wear to a job interview at KDEX."

Kate nodded as she tried to think of who the guy could be or if she had ever heard of anyone by the last name of Baker. Neither sounded familiar.

"All right, thanks, Carlos. If you see him again let me know."

He gave her a friendly wink. "I got your back."

Kate smiled. "You always do."

She glanced past him, out the tall glass doors, to the confection shop at street level in the office building across the street. Painted in arched gold lettering on the window it said "Baker and Chocolatier."

At the elevators she pushed the button for the eleventh floor. As she waited in silence with a few other people, she looked at herself in the smoked mirror between the elevators. She looked crisp and professional in a black skirt and jacket paired with a pale yellow top, but she groaned inwardly at the way her jet-black hair looked. She hadn't had time to wash it for several days and it hung limp to her shoulders. She used her fingers to comb the long bangs to the side a little, trying to make them look naturally disordered, rather than simply dull and disordered.

About a year before, she had dated a man who one day asked her if she would consider coloring her hair to a lighter shade. She had been more than a little surprised and had asked him why, and if he didn't like the way she looked. He had hemmed and hawed and said that he only meant that maybe she wouldn't look quite so intimidating if her hair were a lighter color. Kate didn't know what he was talking about. He said that her black hair made her look like the Angel of Death. If nothing else, it had been the death of their brief relationship.

The gold-toned eye shadow she liked because it went well with her green eyes helped hide how tired she was. It was good enough. Her hair and fatigue were only passing concerns in a roiling sea of grief, confusion, and questions. In between those cascading thoughts, she tried her best to go over in her mind the report her boss, Theodore Harper, would need.

Standing in the back of the elevator, she looked at each person's eyes as they walked in after her. If anyone met her gaze she flashed a brief, polite smile.

Walking down the main aisle on the eleventh floor, past the walls of shoulder-high work-stations, each with a computer terminal, she slowed to a stop beside Wilma's empty station.

Karen, the woman working at the next station over, turned her chair around to lean out and look up at Kate. "Wilma died early this morning."

Kate swallowed. "That's terrible. I feel so sorry for her family."

Karen nodded. "We're passing around a card for her kids."

"Let me know when you get it back, will you? I'd like to sign it."

Kate could tell by the woman's stricken expression what she already knew. "I'm sorry about your brother, Miss Bishop."

Kate forced a perfunctory smile. "Thanks, Karen. John was a gentle person and I'll miss him."

Not wanting to invite conversation, Kate glanced back at Wilma's desk. Karen seemed to understand and nodded before swiveling her chair back around to her computer.

In Wilma's work area, partially deflated foil balloons saying "Get Well Soon" still floated at the ends of drooping strings tied to the handle of a mug with the words "World's Best Mom" on it. The computer screen was dark. Flowers in simple paper cones had been laid over the keyboard and desk while vases with cut flowers stood to the back. Unlit candles with ribbons and bows sat among the multicolored flowers and stands of cards. Three teddy bears rested among the items left on the desk.

Kate wondered what the hell a dead woman was supposed to do with teddy bears.

Everyone likely knew that Wilma had not been expected to live. All of the flowers and candles and cards were the modern equivalent of grave goods.

The thought came with the memory of a TV program on early humans and how it was believed they had lived. The program had shown a grave from the early Bronze Age.

The archaeological and forensic investigation had revealed evidence that the remains had been covered with flowers and beads. One of the curiosities found in the grave along with some stone tools had been the remains of a small figure made of bones, possibly fleshed out with straw, and dressed in a bit of sewn leather. It struck Kate how much Wilma's desk was not so very different, in spirit, from those early human graves.

Like John, Wilma was gone. Her life snuffed out by a monster who killed people. In Wilma's case, a monster who killed for the fun of it. And teddy bears were somehow supposed to soothe her family's sense of anguish and loss?

It unexpectedly angered Kate that teddy bears seemed to have come to take the place of a burning rage for retribution. They had become civilization's impotent response to senseless murder.

She supposed that there was really no way people could fight back, and this was the only way in which they could express their sorrow and sense of loss. They were trying to cover over something that was nakedly savage with something that would seem kind and gentle. Kate would rather the guy who did it have his skull crushed in.

Along with the guy who had killed her brother.

With a deep breath, she tried to let go of the sudden flash of raw anger.

Down the broad hallway at the far end of the room, Kate went into her office and set her purse in a bottom drawer. She stood over her desk, surveying the collection of yellow sticky notes. They were a map of sorts, a visualization of problems, intended to help reveal any connections. She was the only one in the company who did it that way. Other people kept lists on their computers. Kate liked something more tangible, something she could look at, touch, and move.

She often tried rearranging pieces of the sticky-note puzzle to give herself a fresh view of the problems, to see them in a different way, in order to help pick up on any connections. Sometimes security issues had connections. Multiple components made problems exponentially more difficult to solve.

With a variety of things vying for her thoughts, Kate had trouble focusing on what the notes said. She knew, though, that none of the issues on them were urgent. Unlike the problems she had encountered in Dallas, they were relatively petty. They needed to be dealt with, but none were security emergencies.

Before she got involved with her report to her boss, she sat and picked up the desk phone. After she dialed the funeral home she leaned back in her tall leather chair. Eyes closed, she swallowed, steeling herself as the phone rang.

When a man answered, she sat up. He remembered her from when they had buried her parents. He expressed his sympathy for her recent loss. It sounded sincere, and probably was. She couldn't imagine a job where every customer was grieving.

She explained the life insurance policy she had taken out on John after her parents had both died, naming the funeral home as the beneficiary. Kate couldn't bear the thought of benefiting from the death of a loved one, so it had deliberately been set at enough to cover the expenses and no more. They told her not to worry and promised that they would handle everything. He said the funeral could be the following week. She requested that he let the people at the Clarkson Center know about it.

After replacing the receiver, she sat for a time with her hand still resting on it. It was a relief to have such a painful task out of the way. It had been a call she had been dreading making, but now it was done. With her parents gone, and now her brother, Kate realized that she no longer had any living relatives. Even her Uncle Everett was dead.

While John's death was a painfully fresh wound, at the same time, like the deaths of her parents, it was already beginning to seem like ancient history. John's life was done. It made her feel a little guilty to be still among the living, moving on with the mundane matters of life while leaving the dead behind.

But as much as it hurt, there was nothing else the living could do.

She turned her mind back to work.

CHAPTER SEVENTEEN

Several offices down the hall, Kate walked through an open door with the words THEODORE HARPER, PRESIDENT engraved in white letters on a black plaque. Inside, his secretary looked up from behind her tidy desk.

"Kate!" the woman said with a sudden, broad smile. "He already heard that you're here." She pointed a thumb back over her shoulder. "He's waiting for you."

When she heard him call her name from the next room, she went into the inner office and closed the door behind herself. The rich wood panels around the office were raised away from the wall with a gap between each panel, creating a black grid in the background. It always reminded her of the clean designs of the Art Deco era. She had always suspected that it was a deliberate juxtaposition to the nature of their business.

He rose up on the other side of his broad mahogany desk as she crossed the carpet. "Kate, what are you doing here?"

She showed him a frown. "I work here, Theo. At least, last I knew I worked here."

"Of course you work here, don't be silly," he

said with a whisk of his hand. His expression took on a pained look. "What I mean is . . . well, we all heard about John. I'm so sorry, Kate. You don't need to be coming into work right now. You should take some time to—"

"Thanks," she said, cutting him off as her gaze fell away from his. "But I think the best thing for me right now is to keep busy."

He rested a hand on a hip for a moment. "I understand." He lifted the hand to gesture. "I heard you weren't supposed to be back in town until late today."

Kate knew him well enough to know that despite his sincere sorrow for her personal tragedy, he would be eager to find out what had happened in Dallas. While he wasn't yet aware of the details, he would already know it had been serious.

"I wrapped things up ahead of schedule and was able to switch to an earlier flight. Besides, the head of their operations, Tony Sexton, wasn't too pleased having me around."

Theo Harper arched an eyebrow. "So he told me."

"Really," Kate said. "He never mentioned that he had called you. What did he have to say?"

The corners of Theodore Harper's eyes pinched into branches of small wrinkles as he squinted at her. "He started out telling me that I needed to fire that stupid bitch I'd sent down to his office because—and I quote—she didn't know her pretty little ass from a hole in the ground."

Ordinarily she would have had a flippant remark, but she wasn't in the mood and instead said, "I'm sorry he dragged you into it, Theo."

He didn't show what he thought of it one way or the other. "That's what I'm here for."

"When was this that he called?" Kate asked.

"It was about a week after you first got down there. I told him to let you do your job. He said that he couldn't go along with that kind of interference. I told him that in that case, if he didn't feel that he could cooperate with your security audit, I would reluctantly accept his resignation.

"That surprised the hell out of him. He started backpedaling, making excuses. He said he'd only meant that he didn't think I was aware of what you were up to. He said he was only trying to spare the company any embarrassment. He tried to tell me that if I really knew what was going on he didn't think I would have so much confidence in you.

"When he finished babbling, I told him I had complete confidence. He stammered that what he meant was that he knew his operation and his people and he wanted to make sure I was aware of everything." Theo waved a hand. "All that kind of crap."

That explained a few things. Kate couldn't help smiling. "Thanks, Theo. I appreciate the support."

He shrugged, dismissing it as a small thing. “So what happened down there, anyway? I thought it was a simple security audit. It shouldn’t have taken more than a few days, a week at most. What’s been going on all this time?”

Kate took a deep breath, ordering her thoughts, trying to keep them off the memory of pools of blood in her brother’s house. “Well, when I started looking over things, I thought that something with the orders versus production didn’t look right.”

Theo’s frown deepened. “There are meticulous production records and our shipping procedures require delivery confirmation of those parts. That means they have to tally.”

Kate spread her hands. “Well, they did tally—as long as you took into account lost shipments that had been replaced.”

“Replacing lost or damaged shipments is a contractual requirement. We always take care of such issues in the course of business. The production figures would include replacements, so everything should tally.”

“I know, and they did, but with the exception of one mounting rig the lost shipments were all sensitive equipment. To double-check, I called Corrine Industries, one of the companies that had gotten replacements for several lost shipments. We had production records for the guidance components and confirmed delivery receipts for those components. It looked for all the world like Corrine Industries had received the guidance systems and dropped the ball, like something was very wrong in their operation. The problem was, the guy I talked to, Gerard Laza, is the guy who checks in, looks over, and signs for the shipments."

"So?"

"So, he said he never received the original shipments, so, assuming they had been lost, he had requested replacements."

"Maybe he has a faulty memory. Maybe they actually lost track of them after they received them. Maybe they never went to the proper production department. Maybe they have security issues. More likely he screwed up and was covering his ass."

"I thought the same thing at first, but I went back through the shipments going to Corrine Industries and this guy—Gerard Laza—was indeed the one who had signed for all of the shipments, including the ones he said he never received."

"So he really did receive them." Theo was giving her a questioning look. "So he's dirty?"

"The signatures on the deliveries in question looked off to me," she told him.

He squinted with one eye. "Off?"

"Yes, like someone had forged his signature."

Theo, a big, thick-boned man, straightened and

peered down at her. "So now you're a handwriting expert?"

Kate shook her head. "No, but there was something about it that didn't feel right."

"What do you mean?

"Laza was emphatic that he had a good memory and he insisted that he had never received those original shipments. So I flew in to Corrine Industries with the signed bills of lading and confronted him with them in person. I didn't want him to get them in an email or a scan. I wanted to see the look on his face when I showed him his signature.

"He stammered and admitted that it was his signature. The guy was completely confused. He didn't try to lie his way out of it. He seemed crushed that he didn't remember signing those bills of lading."

"So he didn't remember them, screwed up, and lost track of them in their system. It could even be that he's simply undependable. The guy even admitted recognizing his own signature, so what made you still think it was a forgery?"

Kate made a face. "I don't know how to explain it, Theo, but something about the whole thing didn't feel right. Since all but one of the replacement shipments were sensitive guidance components—not some of the more innocuous stuff—that alone made me suspicious. It was too much of a coincidence that with only one exception it was guidance components that were lost, not gyro frames or simple machined mounting blocks.

"Besides, the guy in charge of scheduling in our Dallas office, Matt Fenton, just gave me the creeps."

Theo shot her a suspicious look. "What do you mean, he gave you the creeps?"

"I don't know." Kate's mouth twisted as she tried to think of how to explain it. "When I first arrived, I asked Tony Sexton to introduce me to the heads of all of his departments. I always do that when I go to a place I haven't been before. It sets up an expectation of cooperation.

"So Sexton called them all in and said that I was there from the head office to confirm that they were all doing a superb job for KDEX Systems. Sexton told me—in front of the dozen or so people he had called into the conference room—that they were all proud of their operation and were looking forward to showing me how well everything was run. He almost made it sound like I was there to give them all awards, rather than to do a security audit.

"As each person was introduced to me I shook their hand. When Matt Fenton shook my hand, he looked me in the eye and smiled. It made the hairs on the back of my neck stand up."

Theo's brow twitched. "Why would you have that reaction?"

Kate shrugged. “Doesn’t that ever happen to you?”

Theo snorted a laugh. “No, can’t say that it does.”

“Maybe it’s just me,” Kate said, dismissing it with a flick of her hand. “Anyway, after I started reviewing everything and then talked to Gerard Laza at Corrine Industries, I wanted to dig deeper into the shipping department.

“I wanted to go over things with this Matt Fenton character and ask him some questions about the details of his procedures, but if he wasn’t out sick, he was always too busy. Every time I wanted to meet with him he just so happened to be unable to make the meeting because coincidentally a problem had cropped up that he needed to resolve. Every time. I don’t like coincidences.

“Of course, there are other ways of looking into the things I wanted to know. As I looked deeper into the details of the plant and their operation, I was able to eliminate a whole series of possibilities. From the pattern of the problems I strongly suspected that it wasn’t accidental.

“It began to look to me like a scheme to sell guidance systems on the black market.”

Theo wiped a hand across his mouth. His tone turned grave. “That would be bad.”

Kate agreed with a nod. “So, I went to Tony Sexton and told him that I had come across some matters of significant concern. I told him that whatever was going on, it was serious and it was deliberate.

"I told him that there were a number of sensitive guidance systems that I believed were unaccounted for, and I suspected Matt Fenton."

"What did Tony have to say to that?"

"He didn't believe me, or I should say he refused to believe me. He told me that my accusations were baseless and insulting. He said that I had it all wrong, that Matt Fenton was an active flight officer in the National Guard and he was a great asset to the company. Sexton had personally recruited Fenton and was positive that he was golden.

"I told him that I respected his opinion but I was going to get to the bottom of it and I wasn't leaving until I did. I said that if Fenton was innocent, as Sexton claimed, then my investigation would exonerate him. I instructed him not to say anything to anyone.

"He asked me what the hell made me think I could stop him from saying something to Matt Fenton. I told him that if I ever found out that he had breathed a word to anyone of what I had just told him in confidence, I would first fire him on the spot and then make a call to my liaison at army intelligence—"

"Jeff Steele?

"Yes, that's the guy, but I didn't use his name. I only told Sexton that I would hate to have to report to army intelligence that my security audit had turned up irregularities and the former head of operations had compromised my investigation which made me suspect he might be involved. Sexton didn't say a word, but his face turned beet-red, so I left."

Theo was smiling out of one side of his mouth. "That must have been when he called me. So then what?"

"The further I dug into the matter, the more obvious it became that the problems could only be deliberate. Whoever was at the center of it was doing their damnedest to make it look like incompetence on the part of our customers, like Corrine Industries, rather than a problem with KDEX."

"But what you're describing seems . . . I don't know, too simple to be the real answer."

"It's precisely because the whole thing was so stupidly simple that it seemed impossible it could be deliberate.

"I gave Matt Fenton plenty of freedom to avoid me and let him think I hadn't found anything and was looking into other areas of the operation. It took me a while, but I laid a trap by going behind his back and scheduled a shipment that was locked down in a way that only he could intercept it—but he didn't know that.

"The shipment supposedly contained the first batch of our latest generation of guidance systems. It went out in regular fashion with the proper tracking documents. The thing was, I had our security intercept the consignment at the shipper and take possession of it. So I knew for a fact that the guidance systems never arrived at Corrine Industries—security still had them under lock and key. Yet Fenton turned in signed delivery confirmations for the phantom shipments along with all his other paperwork. It was 'signed' by Gerard Laza at Corrine Industries, just like he did with all the other shipments, making it look like it had been delivered."

"This shipment that was never shipped? And yet he turned in signed receipts confirming that it had been delivered?"

"That's right. The only one who could have forged the signature confirming delivery on the bill of lading was Matt Fenton."

"So we're paying this asshole six figures a year to steal guidance systems from us?"

"Not anymore. I gave him enough nuggets of my evidence for him to know that I had him dead to rights. He knew it could get very ugly for him, very fast, so when I put a resignation letter in front of him, one I had personally written for him, one that included an agreement to immediately surrender his pension and health benefits, he signed it.

"I had the heads of our Dallas corporate security standing in his open doorway, watching while I had this conversation with him, ready to escort golden boy off company property. I think he just wanted to get the hell out of the building. As soon as he signed everything, security escorted him to the front doors."

Theo rested his fingertips on his desk as he leaned toward her. "So you just let him resign and leave? He stole sensitive and very expensive equipment and got away with it? That doesn't sound like the Kate Bishop I know so well."

Kate leaned in herself. "Are you kidding? These were missile guidance systems. I knew that if I called the district attorney they would have to investigate, Fenton would lawyer up, and the whole thing would take years and then likely get plea-bargained down—at best—and that's only if Fenton didn't flee while he was out on bail. So I told him he was free to go."

Theo was speechless as he wiped a hand down his face, wanting her to go on.

"Instead of letting Fenton get lost in the legal system, I had already called Jeff Steele, our liaison with the army, and filled him in.

"Matt Fenton knew he was out of a high-paying job, but he thought he had at least gotten away with stealing what were some very expensive items. He'd probably sold those items on the black market or to foreign governments. He was happy as hell to be escorted out of the building.

He probably had his car keys in his hand on the elevator ride down to the first floor. When our security guys took him out the front doors, Jeff Steele and his team were waiting. They took him into custody. I think our reservist has been checked into the Army's Grey Bar Hotel."

Theo took a deep breath as he considered it all. He finally smiled conspiratorially. "Now, that sounds like the Kate I know. So that's what took you so long in Dallas."

She nodded. "That's what took me so long in Dallas."

"What did Sexton have to say once this was all uncovered?"

Kate shrugged. "He shook my hand, thanking me for resolving the 'glitch' in their operation, then he said he had a meeting and had to go. I'm sure he was glad to have me out of his hair. My investigation showed that he didn't have anything to do with it, other than the fact that the scheme worked because he was too arrogant to see what was going on right under his nose."

"You would think he would be thankful that you had absolved him of any wrongdoing."

"You would think. Since Fenton and my file with all the evidence are now in the hands of the army, there was no need to follow anything up with Sexton, so I caught an earlier flight."

"Well," Theo said, "I'm certainly glad that those hairs at the back of your neck still seem in good working order." One eyebrow lowered. "I'll deal with Tony Sexton myself."

Kate smiled. "I thought that maybe you would," she said as she pulled her vibrating phone out of her jacket pocket.

It was a text from Brian, in the IT department, asking if she could come down to see him right away.

Kate waggled her phone. "I need to go see Brian."

Theo finally sat down and leaned back, locking his fingers behind his head. "It's always something, isn't it?"

He'd said more than he could know.

Kate slipped her phone back in her pocket. "I guess I'd better go see what Brian's problem is."

"Good luck down in the hive."

"The hive" was what he called the tenth floor, where all the computer operations were located.

"And Kate, if you feel the need, please, for god's sake, take a few weeks off. I'm not just saying that—I mean it. With what just happened with John, you may find that you need some time. If you do, take all the time you need."

"I appreciate that, Theo." Kate smiled briefly. "I'll think about it, I promise," she said before heading for the door.

CHAPTER EIGHTEEN

Kate marched past the long stretch of glass panes down on the tenth floor. She was already tired from the long meeting with Theo, and now she knew it would be another long meeting with Brian.

Beyond the glass, in a freezing-cold room of their own, were row upon row of servers, each row with a lettered blue endplate. It always reminded her a little of visiting the library when she had been a girl and seeing the rows of shelves filled with adventures and mysteries. What all the servers contained were, to her, mostly mysteries. Even from outside the room she could hear in the background the constant drone of white noise from all those machines going about their inscrutable tasks. Beneath her feet, miles of cables and wires ran under removable floor plates.

Opposite the server room were offices filled with people in charge of overseeing the computer department. A few of the people inside waved at her from their desks as she passed their open doors. She returned the gesture without slowing.

At the far end of the tenth floor, she finally reached Brian's room, set by itself at an angle across the corner. Everyone called it "Brian's cave." Theodore Harper's management genius was in leaving people like Brian alone to do what they did best. Kate supposed that applied to her as well. Theo didn't always understand how certain people got results, but he recognized what they were able to accomplish and so he gave them the latitude they needed. Thus, Brian was left alone to work in his triangular cave.

The wastebasket just to the left inside the door was overflowing with empty diet cola cans. As usual, the room was semi-dark, with three big monitors providing most of the light. Brian had on a green plaid shirt with the sleeves rolled up and the front open over a gray T-shirt. Since he would sometimes stay in his cave for days on end, he frequently had a good growth of stubble, but today he was clean-shaven. Surprisingly, for someone who seemed to care little about his appearance, his brown hair was neatly trimmed and always kept in order, even if most of it was too thick and too short to lie down.

The monitors lit the side of his smooth, pudgy face when he looked up. "Kate!" he said, sounding oddly relieved to see her.

He reached out, grabbed the back of an empty chair at the other side of the long counter holding the monitors, and spun it around for her.

"Here, why don't you sit down?"

Kate sighed inwardly. Whenever Brian wanted her to sit down, it was more likely than not to be a long time before he was finished. He liked to show her things, pointing out relevant issues across the expanse of monitors. New topics he wanted to tell her about continually popped into his head. Brian found his electronic cosmos intoxicatingly interesting.

As he explained various issues to her he often became more and more excited, while Kate usually got more and more lost. He had virtually no comprehension of how little others actually understood of the things he was talking about. Knowledge of all things computer-related seemed to ooze from his every pore, as if computer code were part of his DNA.

Kate had long ago learned not to ask Brian to explain too many things if she didn't think she needed to know exactly what he was talking about, because in his excitement to explain them he would only end up veering down a variety of side trails, often for hours, wandering around in the intricacies of ancillary information before she was able to shoo him back to the main path. He saw all the information in his head as an ever-expanding universe of data points that were all linked in one way or another and all profoundly intriguing.

She often had trouble getting him to stay on subject because to Brian there was no such thing as a discrete subject. It was all part of a whole, and separating out a slice was impossible.

The things he told her about were usually wrapped in a word salad of technical details that he thought she would surely want to know. She rarely cut off his explanations because, to Brian, they were his evidence, and they mattered to him the same way her evidence mattered to her. While all those bits of information were often frustratingly scattered, she respected his unique view of how they were interdependent, and even if the details weren't all important to her, they were to him, so she let him go on until he got to the parts that she needed to know about.

Because she listened patiently, Brian loved explaining anomalies to her. She had learned such patience from listening to her brother's tedious explanations of the most ordinary things. One time it had taken her brother fifteen minutes to explain how the bus door worked and how the driver operated it. It had been no less important to him than the things in Brian's world were to him.

In Brian's case, though, those anomalies were not only profoundly complex, but sometimes profoundly important to the security of the company.

Kate pulled the chair around and sat down. "So what's up?"

He looked over at her, concern tightening the soft contours of his face. "I heard about your brother. I'm sorry."

Kate's focus was drawn past him to the news stories about it hovering in the upper corner of the far monitor. Brian usually knew about things before anyone else. He seemed to have spider-webs everywhere, vibrating with information for him to snatch up. He was protective of the people at KDEX and watched for anything that might affect them.

Kate deliberately didn't read any of the news on his monitor. Some was video from TV stations, with static news anchors sitting at their desks, eyes caught half closed in stop-frame, red triangles over their chests, waiting to be clicked on so they could come to life and report on the murder. Kate was trying her best to remember her brother as he had been when alive.

"Thanks, Brian. John was a gentle being. I'm going to miss him."

Brian nodded with sincere understanding. "I wish I could have known him."

It occurred to Kate that they probably would have gotten along quite well. "So what's up? Why did you want to see me?"

Brian leaned toward her, his eyes intense with concern, and an odd glint of glee. "We've been hacked."

Suddenly alert, Kate sat up straighter. "Who's on it?"

"No one but me knows about it, yet," he said in a low voice, almost as if he didn't want anyone to hear, even though there was no one else within earshot.

Kate got up and closed the door, then sat back down.

She crossed her legs and locked her fingers together over her knee. "What do you mean, no one but you knows about it?"

"I didn't want to say anything to anyone else until I talked to you about it."

"Why? You know I'm no computer expert."

He tilted his head toward her. "Because this is a very weird kind of hack."

To Kate, most of the things in Brian's electronic world were weird. "What was so weird about it?"

"It was a probe of specific files. It started several weeks ago. I've been watching, waiting to see what they were after."

"Isn't that rather dangerous, letting it go on like that?"

He shook his head. "It wasn't an APT."

"An APT?"

"An Advanced Persistent Threat. Those frequently come from foreign nations—China, Russia, Iran. There are teams in China dedicated to writing malware just to try to break into our systems. I think the Chinese alone probably have more people trying to break into our systems than we have working here.

"Then there are syndicates dedicated to stealing intellectual property or information and selling it. They can have hundreds of thousands of botnets at their command. They use them for everything from saturating online ticket sales for popular concerts so they can scoop them up to be sold for an outrageous profit, to using malware to try to break into allied systems, much like impersonating a janitor and using their key ring to open doors.

"These syndicates are big organizations, frequently offshore. They're run like any big business, with huge departments dedicated to nothing but writing malware to bypass specific types of security defenses or even just to get into a particular company or government agency. A lot of that kind of code is sold on private channels to the highest bidder—like people wanting to get into KDEX.

"They're always finding new ways to hijack employee machines and plant subroutines in our system, continually trying to connect our data with their mother ship. If that succeeds, they have a conduit right into everything—emails, passwords, designs, that kind of stuff. They mine the data and analyze communications, looking for passwords or anything of value. Those kinds of attacks by crime syndicates and foreign governments are happening twenty-four hours a day. Thousands a day.

"Since we manufacture weapons components, we're also a big fat target for hacktivists—people intent on destroying the nation's defense structure. Political hacktivism is the subversive use of computers to create anarchy by destabilizing and destroying our world."

Kate's mind was spinning with the hopeless nature of internet security. "Seems like the bad guys outnumber us."

"If people only knew how lawless and out of control the internet criminal activity really is . . .

"Here, let me show you." He laid a keyboard in his lap and started typing. "This is an attack map developed by the Norse Corporation, a company we use."

He typed in "map.norsecorp.com," and a map of the world opened. He pointed at the screen.

"Hack attacks show up as streaks of light shooting across the globe from their source to their target. Here below the map the attacks are logged. The number of attacks is so massive they're logged to the thousandth of a second."

Kate was stunned by what she was seeing. "It looks like World War Three."

"These are hack attacks happening in real time," Brian said. "There are times when it looks even worse than what you're seeing at the moment. Norse created a galaxy of honeypots, millions of them, in hundreds of data centers all around the world. They mimic computers, servers, mobile devices, office equipment, just about everything. We use them because one of the things they track is attacks on industrial equipment. With these attack logs we can see where the attacks are coming from and what the threat environment is at any given moment."

The map was in continual turmoil as the targets lit up in rings of varying sizes and colors, depending on the density of the attacks. At times it looked like the surface of the sun.

"It's like the fourth century all over again with the Huns invading, pillaging, and destroying lives and everything people have built," Brian said. "The sheer amount of damage is staggering. Crime on a massive scale grows all the time and is rarely punished. A lot of it is other countries hacking into everything we have. It's like there is no longer any law and order. No one and nothing is safe anymore. It's like civilization itself is beginning to crack apart."

It revealed a world of criminal activity and cyberattacks that Kate had never fully appreciated.

"It's certainly frightening," she said. "But what about this hack you wanted to tell me about?"

He took a drink out of a diet cola can before going on. "So, besides the sophisticated software tools we use, I also have honeypots set up."

"You said that word before." Kate cocked her head. "Honeypots?"

Brian gestured with the cola can toward the server room. "In our case we have servers that are there solely to be attacked. Whereas Norse has a galaxy of sensors set up around the world, I have a honeynet set up in-house. By mimicking vulnerable systems, they draw in zero-day exploits and newly created malware. I get alerts when they're attacked. They have a lot fewer false positives than the regular intrusion-detection systems and are a lot simpler than the complex firewalls we use. They're a great early-warning system."

"Okay, so you're using sticky traps to catch the cockroaches."

Brian smiled at the way she'd put it. "In one of them—the server in row B, rack twelve—I use decoy password vaults. It's a tar pit. That's how I picked up on this intrusion. A honeypot is great for capturing this kind of activity. Since there are no legitimate connections on that server, once activity popped up I knew about it immediately. It was a very small intrusion. Lone criminals like this are extremely rare anymore. Like I explained, it's almost always a criminal syndicate or foreign government."

He clicked a few keys, bringing up a window.

"This was the only thing they got into. They weren't interested in anything else. That's what is so weird about it. It was a relatively unsophisticated discrete intrusion, not an APT. This was the sole target. One of the files in here was the only information they stole."

"I'm listening," Kate said as she frowned more closely at the screen and saw a list of a few dozen names she recognized.

"This is a specific folder with our top executives. It has their personal information—Social Security numbers, cell phone numbers, home addresses, all that kind of sensitive information. It also has their work and travel schedules."

Kate met his gaze. "If they were identity thieves they would have gone after the entire employee list and all their data, not a small list of executives. Executives would be a different kind of target."

Brian nodded as he tapped a specific spot on the screen. "Your name is on this list."

She looked where he was pointing. "So they got into the files of all of our top executives?"

"Yes."

"Damn," she whispered.

Brian smiled. "Not exactly."

Kate frowned. "What do you mean, not exactly? You just said they did and all that information is in there."

When he merely smiled, Kate leaned back as she used a thumb to glide her hair back over her shoulder. "Okay, Brian, what's going on?"

"These are internal corporate files, not something used for paychecks or tax reports or anything else. It's a list that I use to keep track of executives. You know, so I know where they are if

I need them, or if someone comes and asks where so-and-so is if they're out of town, or needs a phone number. This is just a file sitting in the honeypot—a worm on a hook."

Kate was bewildered and more than a little irritated. "So you're offering up our personal information as bait to see if someone will steal it?"

"Not exactly."

She leaned in, then, and looked more closely at her own information. "Hawthorn Street? Brian, I don't live on Hawthorn, and my Social Security number and phone number are wrong."

"Of course they're wrong," he said with a sense of pride.

"What the hell good could it do you if it's all wrong?"

"It's not really wrong," he said. "It's encrypted. Well, obfuscated to be precise. It's a substitution cipher."

Kate blinked. That made sense.

"But encryption doesn't look like that. Encrypted files aren't in a simple English form like this."

"That's because this is my own encryption. Security by obscurity. I created my own obfuscated code."

"What are you talking about?"

Brian pulled open a drawer and took out a cheap, yellow tablet. He folded back most of the pages, then set it on the desk. A graph, written out by hand, took up most of the page.

"It's this kind of encryption. One character is substituted for another, but without this key, the data in the file is meaningless."

Kate pressed her fingertips to her forehead as she took a breath, trying to control her sense of confused frustration.

"Brian, we have the most sophisticated encryption available, provided by the government."

"Yes, but encrypted information isn't targeted in this way. Remember, this is a honeypot, designed to draw attacks. This folder contains the most important people in the company, people who could be kidnapped and held hostage or bribed or whatever. That's why the home addresses, travel schedules, and phone numbers are wrong. This is a decoy. This is sensitive information hiding in plain sight."

"I don't understand how it works."

He started pointing to horizontal and vertical lines on his table. "This is how the information is decoded. I invented the code myself. You would need this graph to decode the information in the file—"

"And because the information in the file looks real, no one would have any reason to suspect that it's not correct, so they wouldn't realize it needed to be decoded."

He grinned that she was finally starting to understand. "It's my way of protecting all of you."

Kate felt a chill of icy realization. "So this

means that someone was trying to get information about these top executives, but what they got wasn't correct."

Brian nodded. "They lifted your file, specifically. The others were untouched. That's what set off the alarm on my honeypot. Someone is looking for you, or possibly looking for your schedule to know where you are at any given time."

"Or maybe they simply lifted one random file to see if they could and then they intend to come back for the others."

"Could be."

Kate took a deep breath. "I'll call security and let them know that there has been an attempt to get personal and travel information about upper-level executives. You may only have gotten a hit on my file, but that doesn't mean they aren't after information on other people."

He nodded. "They could be intending to come back after the other names on the list. I wanted you to come down here so I could let you know that it was your file they lifted. Even if, coded, it's full of mumbo jumbo, it had your name on it, and that's the one they took. I thought you should know."

Kate let out another settling breath. "Yes, of course. Thanks, Brian. You notify the rest of the department about what's going on. I need to get security involved. It could be anything—kidnapping, ransom, terrorists."

"Or just someone fishing for information to sell."

When her phone vibrated, she lifted it partway out of her pocket, tilting it, so that she could look at the screen.

It was AJ.

"I need to take this."

Brian nodded as she stood. She went out into the hall, where she leaned back against a wall as she answered the phone.

"AJ, did you find out something?"

"Nothing yet, I'm afraid."

There was a brief pause. Kate's heart sank a little. She had thought AJ would have news that they had found the killer.

"Kate, I need your help."

"My help? What do you mean?"

There was another pause. "I need you to look at some photographs."

Kate let out a sigh. "Is that really—"

"A twelve-year-old girl disappeared. I have over a dozen people I'm looking at. One of them may very well be the person who took her. Girls abducted like this are usually dead within short order, but it's possible that she's still alive. If we can find her in time . . ."

Kate could read the tension in AJ's voice.

She glanced up at the clock at the end of the hall. It was already getting late in the afternoon. She needed to order security details for Theo and the other executives, but that wouldn't take long. Brian would get other people in on the breach to see what they could find, but knowing a little about how those things worked, she figured that the chance of them learning anything helpful was about zero.

"On one condition," Kate said.

"Condition? What condition?"

Kate paced a ways down the hall and back. "AJ, I don't know if what I did last night was real. I don't know how it could be. Maybe it was some kind of fluke. It doesn't make any sense to me. Last night it kind of did, but today . . ."

"So what is it you want?"

"I want you to test me—like you did with John. You know, with photos of convicted killers mixed in with normal people. I need to know if what I did last night was real or if I'm imagining things.

"I don't want to point someone out for you unless I'm sure in my own mind that I'm not imagining that someone looks guilty. I want to know for certain that what happened last night wasn't only real, but that it's reliable. I'm willing to help, but first I have to be convinced myself."

"Of course," AJ said immediately.

"When and where?"

AJ was silent for a moment as she considered. "I have a small office at home. I didn't keep any of this kind of stuff at the station for fear that someone might come across it and start asking questions. That could have exposed John. Come over to my place. I gave you my card. My address is on it."

Kate had already pulled out the detective's card and was looking at the address beside the printed badge.

"I have to do a few quick things here at work, then I'll be on my way," she said. "But rush-hour traffic has already started, so it will take me a while to get there."

"I'm still at work, too. My husband is home making a big pan of lasagna. Have dinner with us. After we have a quick bite to eat, you and I can go in my office, lock the door, and look into the eyes of the devil. All right?"

"All right," Kate said, smiling a little at the way AJ tried to lighten what was a dark and serious subject. "As long as I know for sure that I'm not just guessing."

"I need you to be sure, too—the same way as I needed to be sure about John. If you aren't sure then it just sends a lot of officers and resources off on a wild-goose chase that lets the real killer get farther away."

"That's my fear. I'll be there as soon as I can."

CHAPTER NINETEEN

Perfect timing," AJ said as she opened the door. "I just got home myself and my husband says his specialty is done to perfection." She rolled a hand in invitation. "Come on in."

The aroma of the lasagna filled the air and reminded Kate that she'd only taken the time to eat a protein bar for lunch. With it being a chilly night, the warmth that enveloped her when she stepped inside felt welcoming, too.

It was a bit jarring to see the detective in jeans and a sweater. They showed off her shape better than the suit she wore for work. Kate hadn't taken the time to go home and change, so she felt overdressed.

"Sorry to be asking you to do this before I help you," Kate said.

"Don't be." AJ glanced back over her shoulder. "To tell you the truth, I could use the reassurance myself."

Kate nodded in relief as she followed the detective through the entry hall. A stairway immediately to the right had a varnished handrail that looked to have been restored with care.

The living room opening up from the entry had a couple of comfortable leather couches and chairs on a beautiful area rug that was mostly black with gold patterns flecked with green. The heavy glass coffee table had an arrangement of white silk flowers along with several colorful plastic toy trucks. A big TV, now dark, sat at the far end of the room. To the right, a broad archway in the living room opened to the dining room beyond. The small dining table was set and there was already a salad bowl in the center.

"You have a lovely home," Kate said.

"Thanks. It's a good castle to come home to."

A big man, holding a pan with oven mitts, came in through a swinging door from the kitchen.

"Kate, this is my husband, Mike. And that shadow behind him is Ryan."

He smiled over at them as he set down the pan of lasagna, then pulled off the mitts as he came over to shake Kate's hand. She didn't know what she had been expecting, but he fit the bill of a husband for a woman like AJ. Mike Janek was a wall of a man, a formidable force moving through the house that almost seemed too small for him. His dark blue T-shirt had trouble containing the bulk of his muscles, especially his neck, shoulders, and arms. His powerful upper body narrowed down to a trim waist. He was a big, broad force looming over her.

"I'm sorry about your brother," Mike said with sincere concern on his well-defined features.

He wasn't handsome the way a male model was handsome, or the way TV stars were handsome.

He was handsome in the way that a big, intimidating, powerful-looking soldier was handsome.

But it was his brown eyes that held her breath in. She had never seen eyes like his.

They were the eyes of a killer. . . .

And yet they weren't.

She wondered if maybe she thought his eyes looked like those of a killer because he was so physically intimidating. It was a bewildering mixed signal. It made Kate feel unsure of her ability to actually know the truth about the guilt of a person from their photograph. The night before, with a relatively small sampling, it had seemed to work. Kate was rattled, seeing in his eyes that he had killed people. She couldn't understand it.

"Thank you," Kate said.

Her hand felt impossibly small in his big fist. She was thankful he didn't squeeze too hard.

He tilted his head. "Come on and have a seat. Dinner is served." He put a hand on his boy's head of sandy-colored hair, the way one might grasp a basketball. "Ryan, say hi to Kate."

Ryan smiled and said, "Hi," from the safety of his father's shadow.

"You left your trucks on the coffee table," AJ told her son. "Is that where they belong when you're done playing with them?"

"Yes," Ryan said with open mischief in his grin as he twisted his fingers together, but it was only a brief moment before a look from his mother had him running off to collect the trucks.

On the way to the table, Kate said, "So, Mike, do you cook professionally?"

He let out an easy laugh. "No, I'm afraid my family would have to live in the car if they had to depend on my cooking ability to earn us a living. I have a few specialties I like to make from time to time when Kate is going to be home late, but they're the limit of my cooking talent. I'm a personal trainer."

AJ gave him a friendly slap on the back on their way toward the table. "A personal trainer to the stars. He earns enough at it for me to be able to afford to be a cop. He used to be an Army Ranger, so he gets retirement from that as well."

"Ancient history," he said with a sigh. "Now I get to tell other people what to do—not that they listen. I have to admit that I miss the days when I could shoot my customers."

Kate wondered how much truth there was to that, and if maybe that was what she saw in his eyes. A lot of soldiers had killed people in the wars in the Middle East. It was a different look than in the photos she had seen—not as frightening.

As Mike dished out lasagna and salad while Ryan commented on a stream of subjects from TV programs to the tooth that recently had come out, Kate couldn't help but think how much she missed a family around the dinner table.

She asked Ryan what he wanted to be when he grew up. He said he wanted to be a police officer and arrest bad guys. And that he wanted to have teeth. He pointed out two missing front teeth. His mother told him to put his remaining teeth to good use and eat.

Dinner was filled with small talk and easy conversation about the incidental things in life. It felt good. Kate could tell, though, that AJ wanted to get on with the important business at hand. Ryan, busy chewing, quietly looked back and forth between the adults as they talked about work and traffic and the price jump in coffee.

Kate had trouble thinking about anything but the task ahead, of looking into the eyes of murderers. She didn't know if she was more afraid of seeing murderers in the photos, or not seeing them. In her job any edge over bad people was an asset. Any kind of information was a weapon to get to the guilty party. She liked having an edge over people who didn't see her coming, didn't know what she knew. So, from that standpoint, she was hoping it worked.

When dinner had finally ended, Mike offered to make some coffee.

AJ stood and laid her napkin on the table. "How about you bring us some in a little while? We have some work to do."

Kate stood as well. "Thanks, maybe later, like AJ says."

Mike shrugged. "Okay, Ryan and me will clean up. Right, partner?"

"Right," Ryan said with a firm nod and a grin. Kate had to smile at the way he looked like a perpetually happy kid.

Kate couldn't help thinking of the contrasts of a happy kid, good parents, a loving family, a soldier who'd had to kill people, and a police officer who dealt with dead bodies and murderers all day long.

It was a struggle between good and evil in uneasy balance.

She also couldn't help thinking that AJ had asked her to come to see if she could recognize killers, and she had already seen one.

CHAPTER TWENTY

Down the hallway, AJ used a key to unlock a room on the right, opposite the bathroom. When she pulled the key out of the deadbolt lock, she gestured farther down the hall.

"The master bedroom is down at the end. Ryan's room along with a guest room are upstairs. I have to keep this locked to keep a certain curious little boy from messing things up in here."

The detective flicked on the light switch. It looked like a spare bedroom that had been made into an office. The walls had been painted a deep, dark brown, giving the room a serious, profes0sional cast. There was a tall gun safe in the corner—tall enough for long guns. Boxes of ammo were lined up across the top of the safe. This was not a cheerful place. It was a place that meant business.

Against the wall with the door stood black metal shelves holding semi-clear plastic tubs, all the same size. They appeared mostly to contain stacks of papers. Some were labeled, some not. Opposite the shelves was an older oak desk, its side up against a window. There was space underneath so a person could sit on either side with their legs under the middle.

AJ gestured to one of the chairs. "Why don't you have a seat?"

While she sat in an old wooden chair with arms, AJ pulled down several translucent tubs from a top shelf.

"How do you want to do this?"

"What do you mean?" Kate asked.

AJ set two plastic tubs on the end of the desk. "Do you want to see batches at a time, like we did at your house last night? Or should I just get them all out at the same time? You tell me how you want to look at them."

Kate flicked her hair back over her shoulder. "I think the best way would be if you test me with all the photos you have. All the ones you showed John. If you have more than that, show those to me, too. I want to see everything.

"There's no real purpose in separating them into batches. Unless there's some reason you want them in separate batches? Some kind of order you want to keep them in?"

AJ shook her head as she set another tub on top of the two already there and pried off the lid. She took out all the blocks of photos and removed their rubber bands. She started stacking the photos on the desk in loose piles.

"I have a ton of photos of witnesses—a lot more than photos of convicted criminals. No need to worry about keeping any of them together or keeping them in any order. Their only real value is with you. I guess that without really knowing it, this is the reason I've been collecting them all."

"How many murderers are in all of these photos?"

"Enough" was all AJ said.

She clicked on a desk lamp and extended it up out of the way to give them room, then pulled up a rolling office chair and sat down on the opposite side of the desk. Kate pulled several of the piles close.

"Does it matter if I pull some out and don't put them back in where they were with the others?"

"No," AJ said as she leaned in on her elbows. "Do whatever you want, however you want. There's no reason any of them have to stay in any particular place. They're random photos."

She set the empty tub to Kate's right. "The ones you've looked at we can put in here. When it's full, I'll put it away and give you another empty tub."

As she picked up a batch of photos off one of the piles, Kate felt like she was once again descending down into some kind of psychic black hole, afraid of what she might find, afraid of what she might not find. Some part of her was afraid that it was going to work again. But some bigger part of her was afraid that it might not.

As shocking as the experience the night before

had been, she'd had time to think about it, so she was more prepared this time. This time, she knew what to expect. This time, she planned to use her knack to compartmentalize information, to prioritize, in order to focus her attention on what was most material.

Kate looked at the first photo, saw nothing out of the ordinary, and laid the photo down like she was placing a card on the table.

"Here we go," she said, "down the rabbit hole."

Elbows on the table, AJ locked her fingers together as she leaned in a little to be able to see the faces on the photos Kate laid down.

Kate started a bit slow, taking a few seconds to look at each of the first photos. It wasn't long, though, before she was moving through the photos quickly, dismissing each face she saw in less than a second. Because she wasn't seeing anything that brought her to an abrupt halt, she began to worry that she might not be giving each face adequate time to register, but that notion was swiftly dispelled when the first killer met her gaze.

Not allowing herself to be overwhelmed by an emotional reaction, like the first time, she made sure to not merely look at their eyes, but to take in their whole face. Kate only paused briefly before putting that first photo of a killer face-down beside the face-up stack she had already looked through.

AJ made no comment and showed no reaction. In fact, Kate didn't really know if AJ saw the face of the hollow-cheeked man before she placed it facedown on the table. There were some notes on the back, but Kate didn't try to read them.

She made her way through photo after photo, not letting the memory of the one she had put facedown slow her. This time she was determined not to let the eyes of any killer disrupt her task or prevent her from seeing everything about them.

At the next photo that momentarily hit her with that same jolt of recognition, she put it facedown atop the first she had already set to the side and continued on almost without pause. She was able to disregard that momentary recognition of evil and go back to looking at faces, mostly of men.

Kate moved methodically, looking at all of the photos in her hand one at a time, as if looking at cards, and setting them down on the pile, faceup, when the card wasn't useful. She moved through the stacks quickly, taking a fresh handful without pause. When the stack of photos she had been through had grown big enough, AJ pulled it away and put it in the tub to the side.

Every once in a great while Kate would meet the eyes she knew to be those of a killer. One of them was a stocky woman with dark hair pulled back into a ponytail, the different lengths and stray strands sticking out in disarray. That photo she placed in a second pile. She noticed that she had already placed another one in that second pile.

Before long, she put a photo she encountered facedown in a third pile. She was beginning to understand why. That third pile helped her move more quickly. AJ sat stone-faced as she watched.

Kate was so absorbed in the photos that at one point she glanced up and noticed that AJ had a cup of coffee. There was another with a carton of cream beside it. Kate didn't really want any coffee. She felt driven to look into all the faces.

As she put the last photo in her hands down faceup on the stack before her, she looked up at AJ.

"I need some more."

"That's all of them. You've looked at them all."

Kate blinked. "How long has it been?"

AJ reached out and took away the last face-up stack. "An hour and forty-five minutes."

She put the stack in the plastic tub. After replacing the tub on the top shelf, she sat down, looking into Kate's eyes.

"Not one of the ones you put in the face-up stacks was a killer. Not one. You didn't miss a single one."

Kate glanced at the three piles lying facedown to the side. The one in the middle was bigger than the one on the left, and the pile on the far right was bigger yet.

"The real question is, are there any innocent people in those piles?" Kate asked. "Did I get any wrong?"

"Well, let's see."

AJ picked up the first pile and looked at each one, turning each over after looking at the face to read what was written on the back.

"These are all killers," she announced after a time. "Serious, nasty killers. They've all been convicted and are in prison. One has already been executed. I hope to god that none of these monsters ever get out to kill again."

Kate pushed the second pile across the desk. "What about these?"

AJ was watching her again. "Why did you put these in a different pile?"

"Because they are a different kind of killer."

AJ's brow drew down over her dark eyes. "Different?"

"That's right, different."

AJ finally looked at each face and then read the back.

"They are different," she finally said. She turned around the last photo, of the woman with the wild hair. "This woman, for example, killed her husband. It wasn't the killing of a stranger or anything like that. They fought all the time. One day when he was drunk on his ass and she was a bit drunk herself, she shot him. It was spur-of-the-moment, but had been building."

"That's how they are different," Kate said. "They aren't premeditated murders of a stranger or a particular type of victim. They were a different kind of killing. Someone they knew, probably knew quite well, like a wife or girlfriend. The first stack were predators. These people aren't predators. Still, they are killers."

"And what about the third pile?" AJ asked as she picked it up.

"Bad people," Kate said. "In some cases, very bad people. Some of them very well might one day kill, but they haven't killed anyone yet. They haven't crossed that line."

AJ went through the stack, announcing some of the crimes associated with the person in each photo.

"This guy is an armed robber. This one does home invasions, leaving the victims terrorized. This one pistol-whipped a store clerk in the course of an armed robbery. This one, and this one, both violent rapists, but they never killed their victims. This guy stabbed his wife in the legs several times with the intent of crippling her to keep her from going out and seeing other men, but he didn't intend on killing her. A bunch of these are men who beat their wives or girlfriends to a bloody pulp. Robbery, burglary, arson," she ticked off as she shuffled through the photos.

Her gaze finally turned up after she'd looked at

the last one. "How were you able to tell the difference?"

Kate shook her head. "I wish I knew. I can just see that they're cruel. In the others, I can see in their eyes that they've crossed that line and murdered someone."

"What made you put these here in the first pile?"

Kate felt somewhat shaken and uneasy. "They are altogether different. They're the ones that John would have said were the devil."

AJ let out a deep breath as she drummed her fingers on the desk, looking down at the three piles.

"Well?" Kate finally asked. "How did I do?"

AJ looked up, staring at her again in that way that was so unsettling. "You passed the test," she said in a low voice.

Kate wanted more detail than that. "What grade do I get?"

"You get a one hundred. You didn't get a single one wrong. Not once. Not a single innocent person, not a single killer, not a single violent criminal. Not one."

"Has your husband killed people?"

AJ showed no reaction to the question. "He was a sniper in Afghanistan."

"And you've never had to shoot anyone to defend yourself." It was a statement, not a question.

"No. I'm just a detective. I've only had to draw my gun a few times over the years. I've never had to kill anyone."

That had answered Kate's last two questions. "Okay, now I have one hundred percent."

AJ wiped a weary hand across her face. "I guess I hadn't thought about the two of us."

Kate sat back, taking a deep breath as if coming out of a daze.

"What about the missing girl?"

AJ got up and pulled a manila envelope out from under her jacket on a lounge chair. She tossed the envelope on the table.

Kate opened the envelope and took out the small stack of photos. Without asking any questions or waiting for instructions, she started shuffling through the photos, tossing the ones that didn't mean anything to her across the table toward AJ, as if she were dealing cards.

Near the end of the stack she pulled out two photographs and then finished looking at the rest.

"These two," she said, with one finger on each as she slid the photos across the desk so that AJ could see them.

"Shit," AJ said under her breath. She pulled her phone out of a pocket, unlocked it, and then hit a number in speed dial.

"It's AJ," she said when someone answered. "Pick up the Dominguez couple. Yes, both of them. Yes, I'm serious. Get them down to the station." There was a pause. "Never mind that, just get them each into an interrogation room. I'm on my way."

When she hung her phone up, Kate asked, "Who are they?"

AJ looked at her a long moment. "A man and his wife who are doing a remodeling job on the front porch of a house a few doors down the street from the missing girl. The husband does most of the work, the wife is his gofer."

AJ threw her straw-colored, faux-alligator leather jacket around her shoulders and stuffed an arm through a sleeve.

"I have to go. Thanks, Kate. You don't know how much this means to me—everything you did. But I gotta go."

"The girl is already dead," Kate said.

AJ froze, her other arm partway into the sleeve of her jacket. "How could you know that?"

"I can see it in their eyes. They have no empathy. They're bad people and have been for a long, long time, but this was their first kill. They just jumped from the third pile to the first. They skipped right over the middle pile.

"I think their intent was to ask for ransom. The man is somewhat mentally retarded. He raped the girl—"

"Raped her? How do you know that?"

Kate blinked at a question about something that

was so obvious to her. “Haven’t you ever looked into a man’s eyes and known that if given the chance and if he could be reasonably sure he could get away with it, he would rape you?”

AJ frowned as she stared. “No.”

“Oh. I thought everyone could tell that.”

“No, they can’t. What about the rest of it?”

“Like I said, the husband has limited mental ability. He acts on impulse. He’s raped before. The wife got some kind of perverted pleasure out of hurting the daughter of a ‘rich’ family. The husband had sex on his mind; the wife thought the girl was getting what she deserved. The husband’s urges overran his sense of self-preservation. The wife is the one who decided they needed to kill the girl, but the husband took part. They used knives.”

“Knives.”

Kate nodded. “These two are monsters. Now they’ve killed for the first time. The barrier is gone. It will come easier for them the next time.”

“You could read all of that in their eyes?” AJ asked as she finished shoving her arm through her sleeve. “Just from their photo?”

Feeling a bit self-conscious, and not wanting to oversell what she could see, Kate shrugged one shoulder. “I could see that he’s a rapist. I’m pretty sure that’s how it went.”

But she knew that was exactly how it went. She could see it in her mind’s eye. She could see the girl, naked from the waist down after being raped, screaming in terror as the two started cutting her.

AJ leaned down. "How can you know all this? John couldn't do that."

"He couldn't do it because he didn't have the intellect to evaluate what he was looking at. He could only react emotionally to what he saw. He was so overwhelmed with fear that he couldn't really get beyond it. I can."

AJ pulled her car keys from a jacket pocket. "Kate, you give me goose bumps.

"Thanks for this, but I've got to get down to the station. If you're right, I have to get a confession out of them so we can recover the body. If you're right, the girl they butchered and her family deserve at least that much."

CHAPTER TWENTY-ONE

Kate let out a weary sigh as she latched the deadbolt on her front door. All she wanted to do was fall into bed and go to sleep.

The day before, she'd gotten up early to catch the flight back from Dallas, only to come home to see Wilma in a coma in the hospital and then to be dropped into the middle of her brother's murder scene. Later that evening she had been shaken by AJ's revelations of what John could do, and further, by the revelation of what she could also do.

After such a terrible day she had gotten little sleep. She couldn't help imagining how terrified John must have been, all alone and helpless. She couldn't help feeling guilty.

Her first day back at the office, as always, had been busy, long, and tiring—and upsetting, when she learned that Wilma had died. Two people she knew, murdered. She changed that to three people—her Uncle Everett made it three.

She was also concerned about a hacker going after executive information—after her information. She wondered who had the file with her name, and why. Kate didn't like unexplained connections.

It felt like events were rushing headlong at her. Besides the things she needed to catch up on at work, her brother's funeral was going to be in a few days. The people at the Clarkson Center had liked John. Kate was sure that some of them would want to go to his funeral.

On top of all that, she hadn't realized how draining it would be to look through all the photos at AJ's house.

Or to look into the face of so much evil.

In the back of her mind she was also upset over learning that John had been working with AJ to identify murderers. She could certainly understand AJ's reasoning, yet despite the precautions AJ had taken, Kate knew that it had somehow put John into the clutches of a killer.

She remembered that AJ said she had learned from the book by Jack Raines that not only were there rare people like John and Kate who could look at a killer and know them for what they were, there were equally rare predators who were able to recognize people with that ability, and they wanted very much to eliminate them.

The fact that the killer had removed John's eyes was no coincidence. She didn't know how he had found John, but Kate knew that it had to be that kind of killer who had murdered her brother—one who was able to see John's ability. But how had he found out about John?

A sensation of icy dread suddenly washed through her as she realized what had been nagging at her.

The photos of Kate that had been on the refrigerator at John's house were older photos that John had taken himself with his old, simple film camera. He'd had the negatives developed at the nearby drugstore. When Kate had gone through the house with AJ the night of the murder, those photos had been missing.

There were predators who could recognize her ability to see them for what they were.

Kate felt as if her heart had come up into her throat.

If she could see evil, then evil could see her.

And the photos of her that had been on the refrigerator at her brother's house were now missing. It had to be that the predator who had recognized and killed John for his special kind of vision had taken those photos because of what he also saw in Kate's eyes.

The devil had her picture.

The lamp on the side table beside the couch suddenly clicked on. Kate jumped.

She put a hand over her hammering heart as she realized that the lamp was on a timer. With the shades drawn it was meant to look from the outside like someone was home. In the gloom, she saw the red light still blinking on the answering machine. She hadn't bothered to stop long enough to check that message and erase it. She saw that there were now three messages.

Kate just wanted to brush her teeth, take off her

makeup, maybe take a quick shower if she could muster the energy to stand that long, and go to bed. She knew that she needed sleep in order to be able to think clearly. She headed for the kitchen to set down her laptop and plug it in to charge for the night.

As she walked into the kitchen, out of the corner of her eye she caught a glimpse of something moving outside the window over the nook. She set down her computer case and peered out the window, but with the under-counter lights on she couldn't really see much out the window. She wondered if the door on the shed had come unfastened. The wind sometimes worked the latch loose.

She flipped open the deadbolt, thinking she ought to run out back and secure the shed door. She opened the kitchen door enough to stick her head out, trying to see better. She couldn't really tell if the door on the shed, at the far end of the backyard, was closed or not.

Fitful gusts of wind clattered branches together, sounding like bones rattling. She hated windy nights. She debated whether the shed door was important enough for her to go stumbling out in the dark and risk breaking her neck tripping over a tree root. The light over the back door had burned out and she hadn't gotten around to changing the bulb. She tried to remember where she'd left the flashlight last, but she was too tired to think.

The shed door might bang around a little if the wind picked up, but it wasn't going to blow off. She decided to go to bed instead. She shut the kitchen door and turned the deadbolt.

Curiosity, or maybe it was merely an ingrained sense of obligation, finally got the better of her on the way out of the kitchen. She pressed the play button on the answering machine.

A mechanical voice reported the time and date. The first message had been from several days before Kate had returned from Dallas.

"Miss Bishop," a voice said, "my name is Jack Raines."

Kate was instantly wide awake.

"I'm . . . an acquaintance of your Uncle Everett. As I'm sure you must know by now, he was murdered a few weeks ago. I only just found out that Everett had relatives. If no one has informed you yet, then I apologize for being the one to bring you the news this way."

It was a bad cell connection and it was hard to hear. Kate leaned closer to the phone. "Miss Bishop, I'd really like to talk to you as soon as possible." There was a pause, as if he wanted to add something, then changed what he had intended to say. "Please call me as soon as possible."

Kate stood stiff and wide-eyed as he gave his name again and his phone number.

Why would Jack Raines be calling her? AJ said

that it had been difficult for her to contact him.

"Please," he added, "call me as soon as you can."

She wondered if he wanted to tell her something about her Uncle Everett. Or possibly about his murder.

Kate had intended to talk to AJ about Jack Raines after dinner and after looking at the photos. Kate had wanted to ask about the reviews from law enforcement personnel that said Jack Raines was a phony, or a detective wannabe, and that he didn't know what he was talking about. AJ had seemed to think a lot of him. Kate wanted to know why there was such a discrepancy. But the photos had been the priority and then AJ had left in such a rush there hadn't been time to bring it up.

She thought from what AJ had told her that Jack Raines might be able to provide better explanations, or at least context, for what she and John were able to do, but the reviews had caused her to dismiss Jack Raines as a legitimate authority.

Kate pressed the play button for the next message. It had been left the day before. It was also from Jack Raines and nearly identical. The connection was much better this time. His voice struck her as intelligent and sincere.

Kate had dealt with people who sounded intelligent and sincere, but turned out to be con artists of one sort or another. People who were stealing from KDEX, or up to no good of some kind, could almost always make their excuses sound perfectly reasonable. That type of person was good at sounding convincing, much the way serial killers were often charming.

Maybe that had been what fooled AJ. Maybe the reviewers, who were real criminal profilers, were right about the book. Or, maybe they were the ones deceiving readers.

With trembling fingers, Kate pressed the play button for the final message. It had been left earlier that day but it started a little differently. "Miss Bishop, I realize that I must sound like a crackpot or something, and that's probably why you're not returning my calls, but it's very important that I speak with you. I don't want to explain why on an answering machine. Please call me as soon as possible."

She could read the stress in his voice.

He again left his phone number. Kate played the last message over so she could write the number on the back of AJ's business card. After thinking about it a moment, she pulled out her phone and also added it to her contacts list. Her name and number were blocked, so if she did decide to call him on her cell, he wouldn't be able to see her number.

Because of the nature of her security position, her number and home address were unlisted. The people she dealt with knew to give out her office phone number, and not her cell number. If someone called KDEX wanting to speak with her and she was away from the office, they connected the call to her cell rather than give out her number, or they took a message. She usually returned calls on the landline in her office.

KDEX computer-security people had seen to it that the cell number had never appeared on the internet search sites where such information was typically available. Brian, ever watchful over her, had gone to even greater lengths to insure that she was invisible and to a certain extent off the grid.

That was probably why Jack Raines had called her home phone—it was an old number that he might have gotten at her Uncle Everett's place. She hadn't spoken to her uncle in years and he wouldn't have known her cell number, but he might have had her home phone number.

It also occurred to her that the hacker who had lifted her personnel file had gotten garbage information. Her cell phone in that file was wrong, so whoever stole that file wouldn't have been able to call her cell. But they might have been able to find the old number of her landline.

Kate reminded herself that Everett had been murdered.

John had been murdered.

She unlocked her phone and with her thumb

scrolled through her contacts list. She stopped at a listing under S and pressed the cell number.

After it rang half a dozen times, he answered.

"Jeff Steele."

"Jeff, it's Kate Bishop."

"Kate—good to hear your voice. Kind of late for you to be calling. Are you checking up on your friend from Dallas?"

"No. This is about something else."

Because Jeff Steele had occasionally pulled off the seemingly impossible for her, Kate sometimes called him her "man of steel." He was the one she called with difficult security situations. She had one of those now.

His tone immediately changed. "What is it? You sound upset."

"I need a favor."

"Anything. I owe you more than one. What can I do for you?"

"Can you please find out what you can about a man named Jack Raines. R-a-i-n-e-s."

"Jack Raines. Got it. What's this about? What kind of trouble is he causing for KDEX?"

Kate hesitated. "It's nothing like that," she said. "Could you please just find out what you can for me?"

"Not a problem."

"The sooner the better."

"Are you in some kind of trouble? Is this guy causing you—"

"No, it's not that," Kate said as she paced across the living room, holding the back of her neck with her free hand. She cleared her throat. "My brother was murdered."

"John? John was murdered?"

"Yes, just yesterday. I found out about it when I got back into town yesterday."

"Good lord, Kate, I'm really sorry to hear that. Is there anything I can do? Anything at all, just name it."

"Yes, find out what you can about Jack Raines for me."

"Do you think he's involved in the murder somehow?"

"No, it's nothing like that. This is about something else. I've become friends with the detective working on my brother's murder. She told me about a book called *A Brief History of Evil* written by Jack Raines, but I don't know if the guy is legit. She only mentioned it because she thought it might explain some things about my brother."

"What kind of things?"

Kate pressed trembling fingers to her forehead, doing her best to hold back tears. "Jeff, I'm exhausted. Can we talk about it once you see if you can find anything on Mr. Raines?"

"Sure. Sorry, Kate. You get some rest. I'm on it. I'll call you."

"Thanks Jeff," Kate said before pressing the END CALL tile.

With the back of the hand that held her phone, she wiped a tear from her cheek on her way down the hallway.

She turned off the hall lights, then sat on the edge of her bed and opened the bottom drawer of the nightstand. She slid her fingers into the recesses of the safe and let her muscle memory quickly press each finger in the correct sequence. The safe door popped open.

She reached in for her semiautomatic handgun. As she lifted it, she slid her trigger finger over the raised indicator behind the ejection port, confirming that it had a round chambered. She always kept it loaded and ready to fire, but she still always checked.

It had been Jeff Steele who suggested she get a gun, a Glock 19 in particular. It was difficult to legally possess a gun in Chicago, but Jeff had helped her get through the tangle of legal requirements so that she had all the proper permits. He had also used his contacts to get her proper instruction on using the weapon.

She set the gun on her nightstand before going into the bathroom to get ready for bed.

She knew. The devil was on the hunt.

CHAPTER TWENTY-TWO

Late in the afternoon the next day, Kate finally had time to head down to the tenth floor. As she walked past the long stretch of glass panes, past the rows of servers continuously humming away at their work, she thought about how all the while, every moment of every day, they were ceaselessly being attacked from all around the planet.

Most people didn't realize that computer security was a losing war. There was no longer anything in the digital realm that hadn't been successfully attacked. Nothing was secure anymore. Now, it was a matter of damage control.

It really was the modern equivalent of the Huns rupturing every crack in the defensive walls, swarming over the civilized world, and leaving ruin and destruction in their wake.

It at least felt good to walk after sitting all day in long meetings with various departments, going over laundry lists of issues. At the top of the list of general security concerns had been executive security in particular. The nature of the breach Brian had discovered was certainly sobering.

Even though the intruder had gotten into only one of Brian's honeypots and had stolen only useless, fictitious information, it was worrisome that it had been executives the hacker had gone after. Executives on that list had been made aware of what had happened and that security in general had been heightened.

Walking into Brian's cave, she hoped to hear that he had learned something useful. If it was an intrusion from overseas it was somewhat less of an immediate threat, but since Brian thought that it was an individual or small group, if the hack originated somewhere in the Midwest, and especially in the Chicago area, it was cause for immediate concern.

The monitors were off in Brian's cave. There was no telling how long he had been gone.

She glanced up at the clock and saw that it was half past five. The day had flown by before she had realized it. Since Brian kept odd hours, she knew he could easily be at home asleep and not show up until the dead of night. Even if he was awake, working from a laptop at home, he usually left his phone turned off. For someone so fused into the world of technology, he remained oddly divorced from its most useful purposes.

When her own phone rang, Kate pulled it out and saw that it was AJ. She leaned a hip against the counter in Brian's empty cave and clasped her elbow with her free hand as she held the phone up to her ear with the other.

Kate resisted the temptation to start out by

asking if the detective had found John's killer. "Hi AJ."

"Hi Kate. I just wanted to check in and see how you're doing."

Kate knew by the sound of the woman's voice that she had something more on her mind than checking up to see how Kate was feeling. As sympathetic as AJ was about John's murder, she was also determined and focused in her job. Kate wondered if AJ had an urgent case and wanted her to look at more photos.

"I'm good. What's up?"

"Hey, listen, Kate, Ryan had such a good time with you last night we'd like you to come spend the night with us. We have a nice guest room."

Kate was momentarily mute with surprise.

"You want me to come over and have a play-date with your son?"

"Sure, he'd enjoy that. But more than that, so would Mike and I."

"You know, AJ, I like you and all, but you're a really bad liar."

AJ let out a sigh that she wasn't fooling anyone. "Kate, you're all alone. It's a difficult time for you to be alone. Come have pizza with us and spend the night. It will do you good to be around some friendly faces."

Kate's suspicious nature had already kicked in. "On one condition."

"What do you mean? What condition?"

"Only if you tell me the truth of why you want me to spend the night at your house."

In the silence, Kate wondered if the call had been dropped.

"AJ, all I'm hearing are crickets."

AJ finally answered. "We caught the guy who killed Wilma."

Kate's weight came off the table as she stood up straight. "You got him? That's great. But what does that have to do with me spending the night at your place?"

Again there was a pause before the detective finally answered. "Other than a small amount of money, the guy didn't have anything on him. No wallet, no ID. Nothing else . . . except a piece of paper with your name and the address of KDEX."

"My name?"

"That's right."

"Let me guess. Curly, bleached-blond hair, brown eyes, five-ten or so, wearing baggy blue shorts and a D.A.R.E. T-shirt. Black with red lettering."

"How the hell do you know that?"

"SWAG."

"Swag?"

"Scientific Wild-Ass Guess. I bet he says his name is Bob."

"Yeah, as a matter of fact he did, but I'm pretty sure that's not his real name. We're running his prints to see if we can identify him."

"You said it was nearly impossible to catch the guys in these kinds of random attacks. How did you get him?"

"We found a surveillance camera in the lobby of the building next door and we got lucky. There was a mirror on the wall beside the entrance where the camera was aimed. We caught the whole thing from the reflection in that mirror. From that, we knew what he looked like. An alert officer spotted the guy hanging around the area, just around the corner from the KDEX entrance. Since he had your name in his pocket, and was lurking around where you work, I suspect he got frustrated waiting to catch you the other day and took his frustration out on Wilma. I think that he came back looking for you."

Kate felt a pang of anguish for Wilma being in the wrong place at the wrong time, along with a dose of fear for herself.

"Why was he looking for me?"

"That's the question that really worries me. The guy isn't talking. Won't say a word, except that he wants a lawyer. And medical attention."

"Medical attention? For what?"

"He has a broken bone in his hand. It's pretty swollen. Small wonder, considering how hard he hit Wilma."

"Do you have enough to convict him?"

"It was a swarm attack, as it often is in these cases. There were seven guys in all. But when the guy who attacked Wilma swung around with the force of hitting her, there are several frames with some pretty clear shots of his face."

"I hope he gets locked up for life."

"Me too, but that's not what concerns me at the moment. What worries me is why he had your name on him when he killed a woman where you work, and why he was hanging around there again."

"Do you think he could be the guy who killed John?"

"No. He has a pretty good alibi for that."

"What's his alibi?"

"John's killer was chained up, so it couldn't be the same guy we arrested. Unless this guy unchained himself, went downtown, attacked Wilma, then went back and locked himself up again in John's basement, then escaped a second time and killed John, and then came back to your offices again.

"I'm not ruling anything out, but with all the DNA evidence at John's house from the paper plates the guy was eating off of, it will be easy enough to eliminate this 'Bob' as the one chained up in the basement.

"Are there any security cases you're working on that would make someone want you dead? Maybe the case you had in Dallas?"

Kate shook her head. "I don't think so. The cases I deal with are generally petty theft and white-collar crime. There are sometimes bigger criminals involved, like in Dallas, but that guy is in the custody of the army."

"You sure they still have him?"

"I would have heard had he been released."

AJ sighed into the phone. "Well, right now what has me the most concerned is that I don't know what's going on or why. Someone killed John, and now this guy who murdered Wilma has your name in his pocket. Until we can start connecting the dots, I'd feel a lot better if you were sleeping at my house where I know you will be safe."

"Isn't it outside of police policy for an officer to be unofficially protecting someone in their home?"

AJ huffed a laugh. "Get real. We're already well outside department procedure and official policy here. I'm certainly not going to report that I have you staying at my house.

"Don't be stubborn about this, Kate. I don't like thinking about you asleep all alone in your house right now. I think the real guy who killed your brother is still out there and now this second killer had your name in his pocket. I don't know why. Until we can catch the guy who killed John, come stay at my house where Mike and I will know you're safe, all right?"

Kate couldn't help thinking about John's killer having photos of her, or the way she had thought she saw something out the kitchen window and the way she felt when she had tried to go to sleep after putting her gun on the nightstand. It had probably been some trash blowing around in the wind. But still . . .

"What kind of pizza are you having?"

AJ chuckled. "Whatever kind you want. Name it. As long as it's Mike's special vegetarian pizza that he says builds strong bodies. There's plenty. He always makes several. It's enough to have leftovers for a few days."

"AJ . . . I had several messages left for me on my home phone."

"From who?"

"Jack Raines. He wants me to call him. I haven't yet."

Kate leaned her shoulder against the door-frame. She saw one of the KDEX security personnel down at the far end of the hall. He was standing at ease, hands clasped in front, watching her. Plainclothes security was watching all the executives.

"AJ, I'm hearing crickets again."

"Why does he want you to call him?"

"He only said that it was important."

"How did he jump from me telling him about John—without me giving him John's name—to calling you?"

"That's what had me concerned. He mentioned that he was an acquaintance of my Uncle Everett, though. So maybe that has something to do with it."

"The same Uncle Everett who was murdered a few weeks ago?"

"That would be the one. But we have different last names."

"If you have different last names, how did Jack Raines connect your uncle to you?"

"I don't know. Everett's lawyer contacted me about the will, so maybe the lawyer told him about me. Maybe he only wants to talk to me about my uncle for some reason. Maybe that's all it is.

"Or maybe my uncle could do what John and I can do. You said that Jack Raines's book claimed this ability is hereditary, that it runs in families."

"That could be it," AJ said, deep in thought. "He said he's working on a second book that was going to go into more detail about it. Maybe he wants to interview you for research into that book. Did he say anything else?"

"He left three messages. In the third one he said that it was very important that he speak with me. He said he didn't want to explain why on an answering machine. He asked me to call him as soon as possible."

"So why haven't you called him?"

Kate hesitated. "I don't know. I guess with all the things that have been happening I'm suspicious of everything. I wanted to talk to you about it first."

"Call him. I think he's one of us. I think he's

someone we can trust. I really do. He understands about people like John—like you. He could end up being a great help to us in understanding what you did last night with those photos."

"You really think so?"

"Yes. You were right about the couple. We got their confession. It went down just about like you said it did—the rape, the knives, all of it."

Kate wanted to bring up what the reviews from law enforcement people and criminal profilers had said about *A Brief History of Evil*, but if she was going to have dinner with the Janek family and spend the night, it would be better to talk to AJ about it then. They could even go over the reviews online together. Maybe AJ had an explanation for them. Maybe these reviewers were people in the law enforcement bureaucracy, and, as AJ had explained before, such people resented the kinds of things Jack Raines had brought up in his book. Or maybe she would be shocked by them.

"How about I come over and have dinner with you, we talk about it, and then afterward we can go in your office and call Mr. Raines together?"

"Perfect. I'd really like to talk to him again. And thanks, Kate."

"For what?"

"For not giving me all that 'I don't need protection' crap."

Kate smiled. "I don't know that I need

protection as much as I'd like more of Mike's cooking and Ryan's conversation."

AJ laughed. "See you when you can get here. —Oh, and the neighbors across the street are having a fiftieth-wedding-anniversary party. It's going to be a big shindig. They have a large family with lots of children and grandchildren. Besides the ones who live here, they have friends and relatives coming in from around the country. So, sorry, but you'll probably need to park a block or two away."

"All right." Kate glanced up at the clock again. "I'll be leaving work soon."

As she slipped her phone into her pocket, the security officer started toward her. The security personnel were supposed to blend in and be rather invisible. In his dark gray suit and striped blue tie, Bert looked like he could be any of the businesspeople who worked at KDEX or regularly visited, which was the point, except that perhaps he looked a little too bulky to fit comfortably into the suit. As he came toward her, he looked like he wanted to talk to her about something.

Kate met him halfway down the hall. "What's up, Bert?"

"There's a guy waiting for you in your office."

Kate tilted her head toward the man. "A guy. In my office."

"Says his name is Jack Raines."

CHAPTER TWENTY-THREE

How did he get in the building?" Kate asked after a moment of silent brooding as she rode up in the elevator with Bert.

Security was supposed to be heightened. Granted, an author hardly seemed like a security threat, but still . . .

Bert glanced over at her. "I assumed you knew him or maybe that he was coming."

"Why would you think that?"

For the first time, concern darkened his coarse features. "He told Carlos down at the security desk that he flew into Chicago as soon as he heard about your brother's death. He said it was shocking and awful. He said he was upset, and he could only imagine how upset you were. He asked if you were okay. He said that under the circumstances he couldn't understand why in the world you were at work. To tell you the truth, that's kind of what all of us have been thinking."

Kate looked at the man's face reflected in the polished brass panel studded with two vertical rows of buttons. "Better to sit home all alone and cry?"

Bert arched an eyebrow. "I guess you have a point. Anyway, he asked Carlos where and when the funeral was taking place. He has a bouquet of flowers. He asked if they had a vase to put them in and asked if they could hold his carry-on bag at the security station. Carlos said yes about holding the bag but said he would have to ask you about a vase. Then he sent the guy up."

"I see," Kate said, her gaze returning to the doors.

"Is this some kind of problem?"

"No, it isn't that," she said. "It's just that I wasn't expecting him and since I didn't put him on the schedule I'm surprised that security let him come up."

"Carlos would have stopped him if he seemed at all like he was any kind of trouble," Bert said, his tone echoing her own tension. "To the contrary, Carlos talked to him for a bit and thought he was a nice guy. Do you want me to escort him from the building?"

Kate waved a hand in a dismissive gesture as the elevator came to a stop and the doors glided apart. Jack Raines had a lot of bad reviews of his book. Maybe he was an awful writer, but that was no reason to treat him like an intruder and throw him out. She and AJ did want to talk to him, after all.

Still, the whole thing didn't make any sense. Why was he there and what did he know about her? How did he know about her? There were too many missing pieces and unexplained connections to suit her. She guessed that there was only one way to get to the bottom of it.

After taking a few steps toward her office, Kate turned back. "Do me a favor, Bert?"

"Do you want me to go in with you?" he guessed, obviously concerned. "Or maybe go wring Carlos's neck?"

"No, no, it's okay. I've heard of Mr. Raines before—he's an author and he wrote a book I'm interested in, that's all—but I've never met him and it's getting late and it's been a long day. Maybe you could hang around out here for a bit in case I want a way to cut the conversation short so I can go home?"

"Miss Bishop, besides our regular duties of watching for anything suspicious in the building, everyone in security has orders to keep an eye on all the executives. You're my gal today. Consider us engaged until you want to leave. After I escort you to your car, then, if you want, you can give me back the engagement ring. If not, and you want, I'll go home with you and sit in your living room all night while you sleep."

Kate smiled as she nodded. "Okay, thanks, Bert. And I'll be staying with a friend tonight."

First Bert, then AJ. It was reassuring to know that both at work and away from work she was going to be well protected until they got to the bottom of things.

Bert looked like a sentry at a guard post as he

stood with his back to the opposite wall not far away—far enough not to look intrusive, but close enough to watch over her office. He clasped his hands in a relaxed manner.

When Kate walked into her office, the man waiting inside stood and she was abruptly face-to-face with Jack Raines.

She knew the instant that she looked up into his eyes that this man was a stone cold killer.

And yet, at the same time, he wasn't.

His eyes revealed traits both terrible and tender. He looked crazy dangerous. He looked calm and compassionate. In his eyes she saw barely restrained violence. In his eyes she saw a reasoned, resolute, intelligent man. It was all somehow mixed together in a way that was at once terrifying and captivating. He frightened her and at the same time made her feel safe.

Looking into his eyes took her breath away.

It was such a bewildering emotional reaction, unlike any she had ever had before, that she could only stare.

She had been expecting to see a dreary, drab author.

Jack Raines was anything but dreary and drab.

He gazed back, seeming equally transfixed. The way he looked at her made her feel as if he was gazing into her soul, taking the measure of her character.

"I can't help being overwhelmed whenever I

see eyes like yours," he finally said under his breath, almost as if he didn't realize he was saying it aloud.

"Eyes like mine?"

He nodded. "Even though I've seen eyes like yours before, I'm never fully prepared whenever I see them again.

"But I was especially not prepared for yours."

Kate didn't know quite what to do. It wasn't like her to be at such a loss for words.

More than anything, she wanted to reach out and put her hand on his arm, to test if he was real. Given what she saw in his eyes, she had trouble believing he could be real, much in the same way that it was disorienting to see a statue in marble that was so lifelike, so filled with force of personality, that you simply had to touch the cold stone to convince your brain that it wasn't flesh and blood.

She resisted the unexpected impulse to touch him.

He seemed to grasp her unease and smiled. It was an easy smile, genuine and warm.

"I'm sorry." He held out his hand. "I'm Jack Raines."

"Kate Bishop," she said half under her breath as she looked down at his big hand. Finally she took his hand and shook it.

His grip was reassuringly firm but not too tight. It somehow conveyed more than any other handshake she'd ever had. His touch seemed to reveal the same mesmerizing contradictions she saw in his eyes.

She remembered shaking hands with Matt Fenton, the crooked head of shipping in Dallas she had eventually turned over to army intelligence. She had told Theo that shaking hands with him had made the hairs on the back of her neck stand on end.

Jack Raines's handshake and smile were the polar opposite of that experience. Even so, neither his eyes nor the warmth of his handshake entirely disarmed her. She was already suspicious of too many things to be so simply put at ease.

"What do you mean about eyes like mine, Mr. Raines?"

"I think you know what I mean," he said with a ghost of a smile.

"I do?"

His smile grew a little broader, softening the incisive glint in his eyes, giving her his answer in no uncertain terms.

Kate felt the first genuine wave of fear under the gaze of this man. He put her off balance unlike any man she had ever met before. AJ had read in Jack Raines's book that there was a rare kind of predator who would be able to look into her eyes and recognize her ability.

She wondered if this was one of those rare

predators. She wondered if he was looking at her as prey. Was she a mere mouse in a meadow, gazing up at a raptor plummeting down toward her?

And yet his eyes were markedly different from those of the cold-blooded killers she had seen in photos, even if he did share traits with them.

But then again, she was no expert in such matters, so how was she to know that such a rare predator wouldn't strike her in this very way? She was suddenly acutely aware of the distance to the door of her office, and Bert out in the hall.

What was perhaps most surprising was that Jack Raines seemed to be a man not the least bit interested in the affectation of a conversational dance, and by the way he started without any pretense, he wanted her to know as much. She didn't know if that represented benevolent purpose, or a window into lethal intent.

Whatever he was, she knew that she had never met a man like him before. Most men had always struck her as rather dull and hollow or, at most, one-dimensional. None had ever sparked anything in her, any kind of emotional response. She often wondered if it was just her. She often feared that there was something missing in her and she was simply incapable of caring.

In the back of her mind, though, she had always thought that a man like this, with eyes possessing such mystique, a man who could have such an effect on her, must exist, but until that moment she had never met one.

Kate finally forced herself to break his gaze to take her hand back in order to close the door. She retreated into her analytical mode and deliberately made herself ignore his eyes in order to take in the rest of him, much the way she had done with the photos at AJ's house the night before.

By habit, she noted where his hands were as she mentally measured his distance from her.

He wore blue jeans and a white shirt with the sleeves rolled up. It fit him well. In fact, it fit him perfectly.

He was a little taller than her, with a pleasing build—muscular, but not overly so like Mike, AJ's husband. His neat, light brown hair went astonishingly well with his spellbinding brown eyes. He wasn't sporting the shaggy stubble or beard that seemed to be in fashion, allowing her to see the clean lines of his features.

He looked to be the sort of man who made his own decisions rather than rely on trends to dictate his style. Everything about him seemed deliberate, from the way his hair fit his features to the way his jeans fit his form. That lack of style conformity made him stand out, not because he was odd-looking—quite the contrary—but because he was so uniquely his own man.

He was probably the most exquisite, arresting,

bewitching man she had ever met. It felt like a knot tightened in her core.

"Why are you here?" she asked, trying not to sound rude.

"Because you didn't return my messages."

She didn't want to get into the reasons as to why not, so she didn't explain. He had a leather jacket draped over one arm, and in the other, like he might have cradled a precious newborn, he held a bouquet of flowers wrapped in a paper cone.

He seemed to realize that he hadn't been very considerate in the way he had started the conversation, so as he offered her the flowers he started over.

"I'm sincerely sorry about your brother's death. Please forgive me for showing up unannounced and unexpected like this."

"Then why did you? Did you come just to offer your sympathy? Or because I haven't returned your call yet?"

He straightened a bit. "No, no, it's not like that at all. I came because I'm worried for your safety."

It wasn't the kind of answer she had been expecting. Kate took the flowers he was holding out and set them on the desk.

"How would you know about my brother's death, if you don't mind me asking? For that matter, how do you know me?"

He drew in a deep breath as he glanced around her office and slowly let out a sigh as if trying to think how to condense a thousand things down into what was most important. “I came here to help you if I can.”

That didn’t answer her question. She wondered if he was being evasive or simply didn’t know how to find a way to put into words what appeared to be not only complicated, but meaningful to him.

“Help me?”

“Yes. I’m hoping for your sake that you will give me the chance to give you that help.”

“Help me in what way?”

“Well, first of all it was important for me to show you that what you think of as security is an illusion. You can’t be safe if you depend on those things you be believe keep you safe, but in reality don’t.”

“I don’t understand.”

He held out his arms. “Well, look at me. I have no legitimate business with KDEX, no one here knows me from Adam, you don’t know me. We’ve never spoken. I didn’t have an appointment, and yet I managed to walk right in with the blessing of security and now I have you alone in your office.”

“Carlos is pretty good at reading people.” Even as she said it, she knew it was a pretty lame excuse. It was not an excuse she would have accepted in a security audit.

"Are you so sure of that?" he asked. "Are you willing to bet your life on his ability to read people? Your uncle was murdered a short time ago. You brother was only just murdered. I suspect that you're smart enough to realize that something is going on and you may be in danger. Are you willing to put your life in the hands of someone down in security who can't see in people's eyes what you can see?"

Him pointing it out didn't make her feel any safer in his presence. Her anxiety clicked up a notch.

"Are you saying that you mean me harm?"

"Quite the opposite," he said with a flustered smile as he shook his head. "Miss Bishop, I'm here to try to help you stay alive."

There certainly seemed to be some kind of shapeless threat. The computer hack had targeted her file. The man who had murdered Wilma had her name in his pocket. Her uncle had been murdered. Her brother had been murdered.

More importantly, Kate couldn't begin to imagine how Jack Raines seemed to already know what she had learned about John's ability and about her own ability. AJ certainly hadn't mentioned anything to him or she would have said so. Besides, AJ had spoken to Jack Raines long before ever meeting Kate.

She recalled AJ telling her about the theories in his book, about people who could recognize killers by looking into their eyes. She remembered with a sickening sensation what she had been told about the killer removing John's eyes. Since Jack Raines had dispensed with pretense, she did as well.

"Are there many others like me?"

"Fewer all the time."

"Why?"

"I believe they are being systematically murdered."

Kate stood staring at him, feeling genuinely frightened at the stark clarity of the answer, not the man delivering it, not knowing exactly what to say, when her cell phone rang.

Kate pulled her phone from the side pocket of her jacket and saw that there was no information about the call. She frowned down at the phone. The screen was blank. She couldn't imagine why and ordinarily would have ignored it, but right then she was glad to have an excuse to escape the gaze of a man who so unnerved her, who so captivated her.

"Could you excuse me a moment, please? I need to take this call."

He pressed his lips tighter into an understanding smile. "Sure. I'll go out and talk to your bodyguard."

CHAPTER TWENTY-FOUR

With her fingertips, Kate pushed the door shut behind him as she answered the call.

"Kate Bishop."

"Kate, it's Jeff."

Kate's brow twitched. "Jeff? That's weird—your name didn't show up on my phone."

"It didn't show up because I'm calling on a secure line."

"A secure line? Why?"

"So I can give you the report you asked for on Jack Raines."

"And you need a secure line for that?"

"Yes."

Kate was taken aback. Jeff had never called her on a secure line before. She couldn't imagine why he needed to this time.

"So then you were able to find out something about him?"

"Yes and no. This was a tough one, Kate. You have no idea what you were asking for. This comes close to making us even."

Kate felt a worried chill at the seriousness of his admonition. Jeff Steele was more than an invaluable contact to her and someone she worked with occasionally; he was a good guy. As often as they had talked in the last couple of years, she considered him a friend.

"I'm sorry, Jeff. I didn't mean to cause you a problem or get you into any kind of trouble."

"No," he said with what sounded like a frustrated sigh. "It's not that."

She wondered if Bert was capable of handling the man out in the hall if he had to.

"So what were you able to find out about him, if anything?"

"Well, you asked me to find out if he's legit."

"So is he?"

"Yes. But you aren't going to be able to talk to him about his book."

"Why not?"

"Because the guy's a ghost."

Kate glanced out the open slits between the slats of the blinds on her office window to see Jack Raines approaching Bert.

"A ghost?"

"That's right. For all practical purposes Jack Raines doesn't exist. At least, not officially. He wrote that book you mentioned, but that's about the only time his existence shows up publicly. Other than that, like I say, the guy is mostly a ghost. He vanishes for years at a time before popping up on the grid again, like he did with that book. Even then, any evidence of his existence is pretty thin."

"Jeff, you're kind of freaking me out. What are

you talking about? Is this guy dangerous or something?"

"No, it's not that. The thing is, Jack Raines is known in the upper levels of some of our security agencies."

"You mean he's a threat?"

"No, he's on our side. At least, I'm ninety-nine percent sure he is."

"In other words, you're not positive?"

"How much in life—or in our business—is one hundred percent positive? There's very little about the guy to go on, but what I do know makes me feel confident that he's on our side, if that helps."

"Coming from you it does. What do you have to go on that makes you feel confident?"

"The biggest thing is that he's known at the deepest levels inside some of our agencies—agencies that, as far as the public knows, don't exist, if you follow my drift."

Jeff Steele was a man who knew about those deep levels of security agencies. KDEX produced systems used by some of those agencies. That was why he worked with her. The security audits she conducted had the potential to expose threats to national security.

"I think I do."

"In the past Jack Raines was the go-to guy when there were problems I'm not privy to—problems within the most clandestine circles."

"So then he works for some of our national security agencies? He's a spook?"

"Not exactly," Jeff said. "He has helped them in the past, but as far as I could find out, only on occasion, and then as a consultant or advisor of some sort, not as an employee, but I don't know what his consulting involved. With some of these shadow agencies it's possible that he was more involved than I could find out about.

"The fact that they relied on an outside consultant in that way, rather than on one of their own, speaks volumes. Usually they try to pull that type of person into the fold. In his case, they didn't and then he ghosted away again.

"Then about six years ago he resurfaced when they pulled him back out of the shadows for something. I gather from hints that it was some kind of profiling. Maybe like the FBI does for serial killers—I just don't know. But whatever it is he does is apparently pretty invaluable and they wanted his services. He agreed to do the work, but as seriously interested as those agencies were, the program—whatever it was—was shut down and his services were canceled."

"They went to him for help, he agreed to help, and then they turned down his help? Why?"

"Politics. The whispers I was able to pick up on say that the civilian oversight authorities, meaning political appointees, didn't approve of the kind of services he was offering. The operatives did, but the oversight boards didn't. Bureaucrats being bureaucrats, they didn't want to get their agencies involved with anything they thought could threaten their big paychecks or their pensions, so they saw to it that his services were canceled."

"You mean to say they would rather put the country at risk than work with him? And so they fired him?"

"In a word, yes. What I do know is that it was a choice made for purely political reasons. Some people I know very well were pretty damn upset that the door was closed on him."

"So he decided to become an author?"

"No, that was later. After we turned down his services, he next showed up as an advisor to the Mossad."

Kate blinked, taking it in for a moment. "He went to work for Israeli intelligence?"

"That's right. As soon as he did, he went dark for five years. We think that during that entire period he was working for them, but it's impossible to know for sure. The Mossad aren't exactly chatty, so we can't be positive.

"All I know is that for that five-year period he was off the grid. And when I say off the grid, I do mean off the grid. As far as any of our people know—people whose job it is to know such things—he wasn't just off the grid, he might as well have been off the planet. He ceased to exist."

"That would be consistent with him working under the umbrella of the Mossad," Kate said.

"That's right."

"So you don't know anything about what he offered to do for our intelligence agencies, or what he did for the Mossad?"

"Well, I was able to find out one thing."

"What's that?"

"The Israelis paid him twelve point five million dollars for his services."

Kate put her fingertips to her forehead as she paced across her office and back, not sure she had heard correctly. She glanced through the slats in the blinds again and saw Jack Raines talking to Bert. They were both chuckling and seemed to be getting along famously.

"Twelve point five *million?*"

"Yeah, that was pretty much my reaction, too."

"Do you have any idea what he did in return for that much money?"

"No. I wasn't able to get any information about that part of it. All I can tell you is that the Mideast is a seriously dangerous place."

"Everyone knows that. What's your point?"

"Israel is still on the map, isn't it?"

Kate paced for a moment. "I guess that in that context maybe it doesn't seem like so much money after all."

"That's the point. Like I said, I suspect that he was providing some kind of profiling expertise similar to what our bureaucrats had been fearful of and turned down.

"Apparently the Israelis were only too happy to have his services. When your very existence is at stake, you tend not to be quite so chickenshit about political heat. Israel doesn't have the luxury to wring their hands over things the way we do here."

"Why did he leave his work for the Mossad?"

"I don't have that information. With the way he was turned down here, I think that maybe he thought it was important to get a wider audience than just one intelligence agency overseas, so he wrote that book you mentioned. From what I'm told, that book says more about the nature of his knowledge than anything else known about him."

Kate paced for a moment, trying to let it all settle in.

"Anything else?"

"I wish I could tell you more, Kate, but like I say, the guy's a ghost."

Kate glanced through the blinds again. Jack Raines was standing beside Bert, leaning back against the wall, watching her with those strange, otherworldly eyes.

She thought that he might be the most beautiful creature she had ever seen. At the same time, he set off all kinds of alarm bells in her head.

"I sure wish I had the opportunity to talk to the guy sometime," Jeff added.

“Maybe I can arrange it,” Kate said.

Jeff Steele was silent for a moment. “What do you mean?”

“I’m standing here looking at him. I’ll give him your number.”

CHAPTER TWENTY-FIVE

Kate opened the door and with a tilt of her head invited Jack Raines back into her office.

He spoke as she closed the door behind him.

"Miss Bishop, I'm wondering if—"

"It's Kate."

That seemed to put him at ease. "And I'd really appreciate it if you called me Jack. 'Mr. Raines' sounds like my father.

"I was about to ask if I could I take you to dinner? We could talk over my reasons for contacting you."

Kate opened the bottom desk drawer and lifted out her purse.

"I'll tell you what," she said as she hooked the strap over her shoulder. "How about I take you to dinner, instead?"

He shrugged. "Sure. Do you have anything in particular in mind?"

"Do you like pizza?"

"All except for the kind with doughnut topping."

Kate couldn't help laughing. "Homemade. No doughnuts."

"Homemade? That's the best kind."

"Detective Janek invited me to come over to her place for dinner. I believe you know her. Her husband likes to cook. He's making vegetarian pizza. Are you up for that? For a visit and talking to both of us?"

Surprised at hearing the name, he turned more serious. "I would dearly love to talk to AJ again."

"I know she'll feel the same. Do you have a car?"

"No, I took a cab from the airport. I left my carry-on down at security."

"Hold on," Kate said as she pulled out her phone. "I'd better let AJ know."

When AJ answered, Kate said, "Question for you."

"What's that?"

"Do you mind if I bring someone with me to dinner? I have a date with a man I just met."

"A date?" AJ sounded surprised. "Uh . . . no, not at all. That would be great. Who is the lucky guy?"

"Jack Raines."

AJ let out a low whistle. "I guess you're going to have a story for me. I'd like nothing more than for you to bring him along so we can handcuff him to a chair in my office and interrogate him."

"We're thinking along the same lines."

"Is he as good-looking as the photo on his book?"

"I'll let you judge for yourself."

AJ laughed. "All right. Can't wait to meet him. —I gotta go. There's some kind of commotion at the front door. I think some of the people for the party across the street have the wrong house—again. Third time tonight."

"Okay, we're on our way," Kate told the detective before ending the call.

"What was that about—the business with letting her judge for herself?"

Kate shrugged. "She wanted to know if you looked like as big of a nerd in real life as you do in the photo on your book."

Kate was pleased to see his face turn red. The guy was human after all.

"Just kidding," she said with a smile.

"Well?" Bert asked as they stepped out of her office and she turned back to lock her door.

"She invited me, instead," Jack told him.

Kate looked up as she pulled the key from the deadbolt. "What are you talking about?"

Bert grinned, ignoring Kate as he gave Jack a wink. "Good for you. This lady works too hard. She needs to go out on a date for a change."

"Date? What have you two been talking about?" Kate asked.

"Mr. Raines told me he was going to ask you to dinner," Bert said with a dip of his head toward Jack. "He wanted to know if I thought you would say yes."

Kate frowned first at Jack and then at Bert. "And what did you tell him?"

Bert shrugged. "I told him that he had as good a chance as anyone, but most who have tried have struck out, so that kind of tipped the odds against him." Bert flashed a lopsided smile. "I guess he beat the odds."

Kate looked between the two faces before settling her gaze on Bert. "Are we still engaged until you get me to my car? I guess I'm going to be the chauffeur."

"You bet," he said as he turned and pressed the down button on the elevator.

True to his word, Bert escorted them all the way to her car in the underground garage and put Jack's carry-on bag in the trunk for them before going back to the elevator and his job of watching over the office.

"I need to stop at my house and get some things first," Kate said as she closed the car door. "AJ invited me to spend the night."

"Pajama party?"

"Not exactly. She's worried about my safety. I have to admit, with some of the things that have happened, so am I."

"I hope you're not worried about being alone with me."

Her red flags were still flying because of what she saw in his eyes, but she didn't say so.

"If the Mossad trusts you, I guess I can," Kate said as she backed out of the parking space and put the car in drive.

Jack smiled to himself, but didn't comment as he watched the round, scarred, and scraped concrete pillars of the underground parking structure pass in a blur.

"I thought a woman in your position would have a more prestigious car," he said as they made their way up a ramp to the next level.

She wondered if he was avoiding the topic. "This gets me around just fine."

"Beige? Really? A woman like you?" He shook his head without looking over at her. "What's the real reason?"

"I can afford a Mercedes or something like that," she said with a shrug, "but in a city like Chicago it's safer for a single woman not to attract unwanted attention to herself. And it isn't beige. It's urban camouflage."

He smiled, apparently appreciating the truth.

As they drove up the exit ramp and passed through the security station, emerging out into fading daylight and traffic, he still hadn't said anything about her Mossad comment, so she asked.

"What did you do for the Mossad?" She didn't explain how she knew about it. She glanced over to see him still looking out the side window. "You said that you wanted me to know that I wasn't as safe as I thought I was, and that people who can do what I can are being systematically murdered. I think we're past the 'what's your favorite movie' stage of our date."

"Indeed we are," he said, half to himself.

Cabs honked as Kate worked her way across three lanes of traffic.

"So answer the question. What did you do for the Mossad?"

"I helped them find people like you."

Kate didn't know what she had expected to hear, but that wasn't it. "Why?"

Jack seemed unconcerned with the aggressive way she accelerated past several cars and then slid into an opening in the next lane. She didn't want to miss being in line for the entrance ramp to I-90. In the heavy traffic it would take half an hour to get back around if she missed it.

"As innocent as they may look, there are killers who have high explosives packed inside ten or fifteen pounds of ball bearings and strapped around their waist, or an IED in their backpack. Wouldn't you want that kind of person identified before he got on a crowded bus, pulled out a knife, and stabbed you along with other innocent passengers?"

Kate glanced over. "The Israelis really use people like me for that purpose? Kind of like bomb-sniffing dogs?"

He was still looking out the side window, watching the throngs of people moving along the sidewalk. "Don't ever discount the value of a good bomb-sniffing dog. They're man's best friend."

Kate thought about it as she maneuvered her

way through the stop-and-go traffic, letting in an aggressive cab rather than getting into a honking match. She slammed on the brakes briefly as a guy dashed out between parked cars. She couldn't help looking at his wide eyes as he froze. When their gazes met, she saw that he was just a guy in a hurry, trying to cross the canyon between towering buildings. He waved his appreciation that she hadn't run him over.

"And they really paid you twelve point five million dollars?" she finally asked.

He laughed. "No. I'm afraid your source was wrong."

"He's a pretty good source."

"Well, he's wrong. The fact is that twelve point five million was their opening offer."

"Jeez," Kate said. "What did you counter?"

"I told them that if it was that important to them, then they needed to know that it was that important to me as well, so I would do it but for a fraction of what they were offering."

Kate shook her head. "It would be hard to turn down that kind of money."

Jack shrugged. "They paid me enough so I can continue to try to help people like you. That's what matters."

Kate had more important things on her mind than Jack's past work experience or his salary, but the investigator in her couldn't resist asking another question.

"If the work was that important, why did you quit?"

He finally looked over at her. "Terrorists are determined to kill people everywhere, not just Israel. As killing spreads, it threatens to overwhelm every civilized country. The Israelis were the only ones more interested in finding the killers than finding excuses for them. But I think that it's vital for me to help individuals—good people, innocent people, people who care—wherever they are, even if it's at a private level."

Kate realized that identifying terrorists before they could act must have been what Jeff Steele had meant about bureaucrats not wanting Jack's consulting services. They would be accused of profiling. How would they justify arresting someone because of their eyes? Politicians would rant and rave. Lawyers would have a field day.

She could see that his help would be invaluable to people like her, but only if it was unofficial and kept secretive.

"So you wrote that book."

"So I wrote that book," he confirmed with a nod.

"Did it really help with . . ." She took a hand from the steering wheel and rolled it as she tried to think how to put it into words. "Did it really accomplish what you wanted? Did it really make a difference the way your work in Israel did?"

He glanced sideways at her. "Yes and no. It's a process."

As Kate turned onto the on-ramp, following a line of cars up onto I-90, she said, “Can we not talk in riddles, please?”

“It’s not that I’m trying to talk in riddles. It’s just not easy to explain. While some of it sounds simple on the surface, it’s really a three-dimensional maze of different moving components over time. It’s pretty complex.”

“Well, how about you start with the simple part, then. What is it you do, and why did you come looking for me?”

“Okay,” he said, gesturing with both hands. “Here’s the thing. Your brother and your Uncle Everett had the ability to recognize a killer by their eyes. That’s incredibly rare.”

“How would you know about them?”

“Everett read my book. Shannon Blare, my editor, lets a few messages get through to me if she thinks they’re legitimate. She understands and believes in what I’m doing. She has been my champion at her publisher.

“Everett had a lot of questions, much like AJ did. From speaking with him, I knew he had this ability, but it wasn’t very robust. Although I never talked with your brother, I would bet that your ability, now that it’s been triggered, far outstrips his.”

“Because he didn’t have the mental capacity to process information the way I do?” Kate suggested.

"That's part of it. The total genetic makeup of the individual's mind, all the elements, such as intelligence and analytical acumen, contribute to and shape that ability."

"How do you know that my ability has only just been triggered?"

"By the way you act," he said, as if it were obvious.

Since he sounded sure of it, she didn't argue.

"I believe that it's one of the many connections involved in the larger picture," Jack said. "Mankind's fate has always been in flux—like the way the weather goes through periods of drought and times of flooding."

"It still sounds to me like you're talking in riddles."

"We see a single murder, we don't how they are connected. The purpose of the book was to begin to bring out information on those underlying connections behind historic trends in order to find and help people like you, or people like AJ who know about you, to survive. That's the purpose of the book.

"In Israel I had a limited audience. They believed in me, which was great, but that was only one place. I didn't feel I could turn away from the larger problem.

"In order to begin to tackle it, I first needed to introduce the basic information, hoping that in the relative obscurity of a mostly unnoticed book

I could begin to find a number of these people, like I ultimately found you. The book is also helping to smoke out some of these super-predators, find out how they are going about what they do.

"In the second book I want to bring understanding to those capable of understanding. I know what kind of super-predator is after you and others. What I'm doing won't save the world, but I'm hoping I can save some good people of rare ability. If I can do that, then my life will have been worthwhile. So for now I have to try to find those like you before it's too late."

Kate checked her mirrors as she merged onto the center lane of the interstate and into the stream of red brake lights that stood out in the dreary early-evening light.

"All right, so let me get this straight. There are these two rare types of predator and prey who can recognize one another," she said.

Jack nodded. "That's right."

"That means I can recognize killers, and this certain rare type of top-level killer can recognize me."

"Right."

Kate dared to ask the question. "So, since you recognize me for my ability, you would have to be one of those top-level predators."

Jack smiled. "Very good, Kate. Very good indeed."

Kate swallowed, seeing that traffic was moving

slow enough that if she had to she could jump out of the car.

"Is that what you are, Jack? One of those rare predators on the hunt?"

He smiled in a boyish way as he shook his head.

"No. From what you know it would seem that I would have to be. But you don't know it all."

"What is it that I don't know?" she asked in a tone that told him she expected an answer.

"Your ability is rare. The ability of those elite predators is rare. You are in a way two sides of the same coin. But I'm the rarest kind of all. As far as I know I'm the only one of my kind alive in the world right now."

Kate stole a quick look over at him. "You're the only kind of . . . what? What is it you can do? Recognize killers like I can?"

"No. Unfortunately, I can't tell a killer by looking at their eyes. I wish I could, but I can't. What I can do is look into eyes of those like you and recognize your ability. I can recognize you for what you can do the same as one of those rare predators can. I guess you could say that I can only see your side of the coin."

"Wow," Kate said under her breath as she stared ahead at the road and the traffic.

CHAPTER TWENTY-SIX

"So you mean to say that your ability is to find people like me? You can only identify people who can recognize killers? But you can't spot killers yourself?"

"That's right."

Kate drove in silence for a time, letting her mind run through all the permutations. The good news was that, while she knew by looking into his eyes that he had killed people, his eyes were like Mike's—those of a killer in defense of innocent people, not one who preyed on them.

If, of course, he was telling the truth. For all she knew, she could be sitting in her car with a seriously dangerous man who had found her and now intended to kill her.

"What's it like when you look into the eyes of someone like me?" she asked. "What is it you see in my eyes?"

"What do you see in a killer's eyes?"

"Don't dodge the question by asking one. What do you see, Jack?" With her first two fingers she pointed at her own eyes. "What is it you see when you look into my eyes?"

"A killer. A savior."

"That's not good enough. I want a better answer. I think you owe me a better answer."

Jack stared ahead for a long moment before he gave her that answer. When he did, it came without him looking over at her.

"I guess that the best way to explain it is that it's an emotional experience."

Kate frowned. "Emotional?"

"Yes. It's like looking into the eyes of a real-life avenging angel. Into the eyes of someone elementally human—someone carrying an ancient spark from the dawn of mankind. It's almost an animalistic glint in their eyes. For me, that's emotional.

"At the same time it's terrifying because I know that there are predators who hunt your kind, and I know how very fragile are the wings of such rare, avenging angels."

That was not the kind of answer Kate had expected.

She drove in silence for a time, maintaining distance from the car ahead so as not to run into it while her mind raced.

A raised-up black pickup with tinted windows took advantage of the space to dive in front of her. She backed off and let him have the space rather than antagonize him.

"So . . . what? You expect me to save the world or something?"

Jack snorted a laugh before frowning over at her. "Save the world? You can't save the world. The world is going to do what the world is going to do. It's always been that way. It always will be. This is a struggle as old as mankind. It is the struggle of mankind. All you can hope to do is save yourself.

"When I look into eyes like yours, I see something worth risking my own life to save because I know that it's something bigger than just you or me. That's why I do this. It's my calling and my curse—to be able to see that kind of righteous soul, and yet not have that ability myself.

"But at least I can try to help those like you to protect yourselves. That's what I *can* do.

"I can see the strength in your eyes, but I can also see how easily you can be broken by those you can recognize. That's why I came looking for you—to see if I could help you be safe before they find you and slaughter you."

Kate was taken by the raw emotion of his words. It was the quality she had seen in him, but until that moment had not been able to define. It was genuine goodness without guile. Strength without hate. Intellect without arrogance.

Kate cleared her throat, finally finding her voice. "Thanks, Jack, but I don't think what I can do makes me noble. I was born this way, that's all, the same as having black hair. It's the same as you being born male and me being born female. I didn't work to achieve it."

"In a fundamental way, you're right."

"And when I look into the eyes of killers it's

terrifying," she said. "I don't feel righteous about it. I think maybe you're reading too much into what I'm like."

"Trust me, Kate. I've been with enough of your kind to know exactly what you're like."

She twitched a frown at him. "What we're like? What makes you think you know what I'm like?"

Jack gestured at the radio. "When we got in your car, the radio wasn't on. It wasn't on because you generally don't listen to music."

"So what? I like it quiet."

"You don't like distractions from your ability to think. You're motivated internally, not externally. You don't really understand the way the rest of the world seeks ways to be distracted from life, from what's going on around them, from their own thoughts. You don't quite fathom how they can spend so much time watching TV or listening to music. You don't get why they prefer an imitation of life over life itself.

"You don't have a Facebook page. You don't really get those who do. You view social media as a monumental waste of time, as an opiate of the masses, something for those not like you. You bristle at the thought of being one of the masses."

"So I'm private and I like it quiet. That's not so unique."

He considered a moment before going on. "You can't identify with other people. They make you feel like you don't belong.

"Most of you are loners. It isn't that you don't like people—you do—but people in general let you down. They just don't seem worth your time, and, like I said, you can't comprehend how they put such little value on their own time.

"You know the value of your own life, of your own spark of time in this world. You date little, and when you do you see all the things that make that person unworthy of a piece of your life."

"Maybe I just haven't found the right person. Did you ever think of that?"

"It's not just dating, it's everything. Those like you are almost always loners. Your uncle was a loner, living by himself in a trailer out in the desert. Your brother liked living alone. It's not an overt trait; it's more of an inner compass.

"Most like to find the answers to things, whether it's treasure hunting, research, or some kind of investigative work. You don't accept what shows on the surface. You dig deeper than others would ever think to. I would bet that even your brother, as disabled as he was, liked working puzzles."

Kate had to swallow back the lump in her throat. "Picture puzzles."

"Your puzzles are a lot more complex. You need them to be challenging. You only feel your own strength when you have something hard to push against. Without a challenge there is no reward for you, no sense of self-worth, so you seek out things that are not easily accomplished. You don't like unearned accolades. For that reason you also don't like to gamble.

"You feel that there is so much more that you don't understand and you hunger to know it all. You want to find answers. That's why you gravitated toward the kind of work you do."

"Okay, so I'm a self-starter and I work hard. That's not all that unusual."

"You have an attractive smile, especially with your eyeteeth."

This time, Kate gave him a serious frown. "My eyeteeth? What are you talking about?"

"They're on the long side of normal eyeteeth. They are a minor characteristic of your kind—part of your genetic makeup. They evoke the look of fangs and for good reason. Fangs are suggestive of the nature of your entire makeup. It gives you an edgy look."

She glanced over at him again. "Edgy."

"Yes, especially when you smile." He looked at her for a long moment. "You know the way looking into the eyes of a killer gives you a chill of fear?"

"What of it?"

"When a killer looks at you, he doesn't see what I see. He gets that same chill of fear. Your eyes are intimidating. Everything about your nature, including your vestigial fangs, is intimidating to them. You are the thing they fear most. You are a direct threat to their survival. That's why they want to kill your kind."

"I'm no avenging angel, and now you're making me sound like a vampire hunter or something."

He was still watching her. "In a way you are. Those you can recognize are extremely dangerous. But so are you. For example, you watch my hands because you know that is where the threat will come from, if I am a threat. Most of your kind instinctively take up some kind of defensive training—from martial arts to combat weaponry."

"Martial arts," she admitted. "I do it for the exercise."

"Uh-huh."

"No, really. It keeps me in shape. I think it's good training to have in my line of work, but it's interested me since I was a girl." She tried to think back to when that interest had started, but couldn't remember a time when it hadn't interested her. "I'm not exactly sure why."

"It's an inherent interest born of an elevated recognition of the very real dangers in the real world and a desire to defend yourself. Your instinct, your temperament, guided you to that interest.

"Right now, because of the way you look at the world, the way you analyze and question everything, the way you work out all the possibilities, you're sitting there thinking that you still don't know for sure if you might not be sitting in a car with a rare predator who has hunted you down and now that he has looked into your eyes and seen you for who you are, is lulling you into complacency and intends to kill you."

Kate felt a chill, as if he had looked into her soul, as if he could read her mind. No one before had ever been able to read her so well or so accurately. It bordered on being creepy.

She felt the sudden, urgent need to shift the subject off of her. "So you weren't trying to save the world, then, working for the Mossad?"

He rubbed his eyes. She thought he looked tired.

"I try to find people with your ability. It not only saves your lives, but those lives you save through your ability. The Mossad listened. They wanted my help. They wanted to save those innocent lives."

Kate thought of the way she had helped AJ, and because of that, lives might be saved. It was difficult to turn away when you knew that you could make a difference. It sounded like Jack felt that same way.

"But you're right. As much as I would like to, I can't save the world," he said. "As much as you would like to, you can't save the world. Each of us does what we are driven to do.

"I guess my kind, if I have a 'kind,' doesn't like seeing your kind slaughtered. While you can't save the world, the world still needs those like you who have the courage to see evil. Most people don't want to see evil. You can't help seeing it, but you have the courage to recognize it."

"Are there many of my kind left?"

"Not many. Too few."

"Have you been successful at helping them?" She glanced over at him, his face lit by the dash lights as day was turning to night. "Have you helped those you can find stay alive?"

He stared off into the distance. "Not as often as I would wish. I found one a few months back. A young man. Sharp, brilliant even. He grasped the things I was starting to explain to him. He was beginning to comprehend the connections of it all and his link in those connections. The world was new and bright and fascinating to him."

"Were you able to help him?"

Jack was still staring off at nothing. "I'm the one who found his body. It was a horrific scene. It always is. I don't know how they found him, but they did. The new, bright, fascinating world was over for him. A predator had ended it.

"I didn't learn about your brother in enough time to get out ahead of whatever is happening. I tried to warn AJ to be extremely careful to protect him."

Kate nodded. "She told me."

He looked down at his hands. "But I didn't learn about him soon enough. I hope that, with you, I have."

At hearing the anguish in his voice, Kate

swallowed back her own sense of helpless terror. He saw the look on her face.

"Sorry, I'm not trying to frighten you."

She accepted his apology with a nod. "What is it that you think could be changing? You said something was changing."

He gestured out the side window after a few moments of silence. "What do you see out there?"

Kate glanced out the window. "I don't know. The city. Lots of streets and houses. Why? What do you see?"

"Ceaseless brutality and depravity—every sort of evil growing stronger," he said, almost to himself. "Anarchy."

"You think evil is growing stronger?"

"Those streets are controlled by gangs. Hundreds of gangs. Thousands of gang members. Tens of thousands. All of those neighborhoods are controlled by gangs. They didn't used to be that way. We let that evil grow. The people who live there are virtual prisoners. Right here in the middle of civilization."

"Criminals are nothing new," Kate said. "Some streets have always been dangerous."

"To some degree, yes, but more and more cities are now controlled by violent gangs. They spread drugs like an infection. They rule through fear and intimidation the way feudal barons ruled. They rape, torture, and murder indiscriminately. They have no remorse. They have no empathy for others. To them, other people are just slabs of meat.

"They are, quite simply, ruthless killers and they will kill anyone for any reason or for no reason. Or just for the fun of killing another living human being so they can watch them die. It is not yet anywhere near as bad here as it is in other places, like Mexico. But one day it will be.

"Consequences are gradually fading. A corroding civilization increasingly turns a blind eye to it, or explains it away, or even justifies it. We simply learn to live with it.

"For every killer who is put away for life, ten more killers spring up. For every impotent new law, they become more lawless. For every difficult battle won, a dozen more are lost.

"Despite everything, evil grows more vicious."

"Like I said, that's nothing new," Kate said.

He shook his head. "It's hard to see a trend when you're in the middle of it, especially trends that span hundreds of years. Yes, there have always been killers and there always will be. There has always been a back-and-forth balance between those who kill and those struggling to be above killing.

"In the middle of a trend, everyone's focus is too narrow. You have to be able to see those connections in all of mankind," he said. "Not just what's out there."

"The police work hard to stop gangs," Kate said. "They know the problem and are working to get it cleaned up."

Jack shook his head. "If you believed that in your heart, you would buy the kind of car you would like to have, not the kind of car that helps hide you from predators."

"You're saying that you think some of the people out there are born to be killers and given an opportunity they will kill?"

He smiled to himself, as if she had said something ironic. "Not even close," he said, cryptically.

"What do you mean?"

He gave her a look like she'd asked for it. "Dozens or even hundreds of young girls on the internet will pick out a victim and torment them relentlessly, constantly urging them to kill themselves, goad them into suicide.

"Dead is dead. Killing is killing. People can make excuses all day long, but those twelve-year-old girls are killers just the same as the thugs out there on those streets. Each ended another person's life. Were each of them born to be killers? Why do you think supposedly innocent girls would do such a thing?"

Kate was at a loss for an answer. "I can't imagine."

"What is it they share with the gang members out there on those dark streets?"

Kate lifted her hands from the wheel in a helpless gesture. She had no answer.

"You think about it," he said, "and let me know when you have an answer."

Kate knew he was getting at something, but she didn't know what. As for the twelve-year-old girls, she had never been able to understand that sort of thing.

She had survived being twelve, but she tried not to think about what was out there, off the interstate, in that dark warren of streets and neighborhoods, those no-man's-lands where even the police feared going. AJ had told her how dangerous it was, even for police, to go into those neighborhoods. In a civilized city, there were places even the police dared not go.

And Jack was saying that there was some connection to twelve-year-old girls on social media?

If there was, she didn't see it.

Yet Jack was right; it was part of why she drove a nondescript car. She didn't want trouble to see her. She didn't want to catch the attention of evil. She knew it was dangerous out there, but there was nothing she could do about it, except, like everyone else, try not to be noticed. It was just the way the world was.

She realized that he was right. There was no saving the world. The world was going to do what the world was doing to do.

All she could hope to do was save herself and as a result the lives that her ability might save in the future.

"So, how does all of this tie together? What are the connections that link everything? What is it you intend to write about in your new book?"

"Tell you what, why don't I explain it when we talk to AJ?"

Kate nodded. AJ, too, would want to know what he had to say.

Kate glanced up at the exit sign for O'Hare Airport spanning the interstate as they drove under it. "We'll be to my house soon, and then AJ's place isn't far."

CHAPTER TWENTY-SEVEN

So how did you find out about John?" Kate finally asked as they drove on through the darkness. The traffic had thinned out a bit and was finally moving at a good pace, but it was still a snaking river of lights.

Jack Raines smiled. "Trying to find the answers to those things you don't understand, those things that trouble you. Like I said, it's part and parcel of your nature."

Kate had hoped that asking the question out of the blue would trip him into answering before he'd had a chance to think about it. It was a technique she sometimes used in her security investigations. It worked pretty well for most people. It hadn't worked with Jack, so she asked him directly.

"Jack, I'd like to know how you found out that AJ was working with my brother. She didn't tell you who she had found with that ability because she was protecting him, and she certainly couldn't have told you about me since we hadn't even met when you talked to her. How did you find out about John and me?"

"It wasn't all that hard," he said.

"I didn't ask how hard it was, I asked how you found out."

"I hacked Detective Janek's phone."

Kate was taken aback. "Hacked her phone?" She glanced over at him. "What are you talking about?"

"When AJ called me, she told me that she was working with a person who could do the things I described in my book. That was part of the purpose of the book—to help me discreetly locate people like her so that I could try to help. She said that she had tested this man with photos printed from film negatives and he never missed a killer among the photos, so I knew this was an important contact."

"But AJ told me that she never told you anything about my brother, not even his name. I believe her."

"She was telling you the truth. Once she had convinced me that she really was in contact with one of these people, and that she was using him to help her find killers, I had what I needed."

"You used your contacts in the Mossad to help, didn't you?"

"No. I could have, but I didn't need to for something that easy. AJ had already given me what I needed."

"That easy? What do you mean? What did she give you?"

"She gave my editor her cell number and email address. Once I had those, I simply hacked into her iPhone account—"

"What do you mean 'simply'? I have it on good authority that iPhones have bulletproof encryption and not even the FBI or NSA can hack into them."

"There are hard ways to do things, and then there are easy ways," he said. "Trying to crack the encryption is the hard way."

Kate turned on the blinker to change lanes past slower traffic. "So what's the easy way?"

"I cracked her iCloud account—"

"How could you do that?"

"Easy. Go to iCloud. To get into your account, it asks for your password. I said I forgot my password. I needed AJ's birthdate which was easily findable on a social network. Then it asks a few personal questions. In AJ's case, the first 'security' question asked for her 'ideal job.' That one only took me one try. Detective. Next it asked what city she was born in. Chicago. With that, I was in. How hard is that? I didn't even need to use any brute-force software to break her password."

"And that got you into her iCloud account?"

"Sure. How do you think celebrities get their private photos stolen and posted all the time? Even difficult passwords can be bypassed by answering personal questions and it's usually pretty easy to find what you need simply by going through their social media. I advise you not to keep any naked photos of yourself on your phone."

Kate shot him a look. "Why would I have naked photos of myself on my phone?"

"Not saying you would—your kind wouldn't. I'm only saying that other people do that, and more often than you would think."

"Okay, so you got into her iCloud account. Knowing AJ, I'd bet there were no naked photos of her there, so how could you possibly find something in there that could lead you to my brother?"

"Once I was into her account, I was able to track the location of her phone through its GPS, so I knew where she was at all times."

"But how?"

"I hate to say it again, but it was easy. Apple calls it 'Find My Phone.' It shows you exactly where the phone is at all times. You can even zoom in and tell what room of their house someone is in. Since I knew she was working with someone with the ability to recognize killers, and she told me that it was outside police procedures and that she hadn't told anyone at the department, I knew that she would have to do it after work.

"I kept track of her locations through her phone day and night, and from that I established patterns."

"What good would that do you?"

"Well, I could see where she spent the night, so that told me where she lived. I could even see her move around in her house. I could see where she slept all night so I even knew where her bedroom is in her house.

"I could see her going to a number of different locations throughout the day. Those locations changed throughout her work week, so I knew those were most likely different cases she was working. She would sometimes spend several days at one location, or repeatedly returned there, no doubt investigating a murder.

"Then, I could see her go back to one spot on a regular basis during the day. The map showed that to be her precinct where she has an office—northeast corner of the building, by the way.

"I now knew where she lived. I knew where she stopped for coffee in the morning. I knew where she worked. I knew how she moved about. I could see her going about her life and work. I now knew how her locations fit patterns.

"Then there was this one place where she went quite often, always in the evening. She frequently spent several hours there. It didn't fit the pattern of her work and home life."

Jack held up a finger to make the important point. "I knew, therefore, that it had to be the home of the person she was working with, outside her official work, the person she had called me about, the person who could identify killers. It was then a simple matter of finding out who lived there: John Allen Bishop."

"Jesus Christ," Kate muttered, shaken by how easy it had been to track down her brother.

"I had already spoken with Everett on the phone and knew that his ability was sketchy. I had hopes that even though it was weak, he might have family members and it might be stronger with them. The ability runs in families."

Kate nodded. "AJ told me."

"I needed to see him to try to find out how much he was actually able to do, and see if I could find out the names of his relatives, so I flew out to Nevada. I needed to look into his eyes.

"By the time I got there he was already dead. The sheriff referred me to Everett's lawyer. He was able to give me the names of the only next of kin: John Allen Bishop and Kate Bishop. In between working on my book and searching for some others like you, I called John's house, but could never get hold of him."

"John was afraid to talk on the phone. He often wouldn't answer it when it rang," Kate said. "So then you heard from AJ?"

Jack nodded. "When AJ called me about this person she was working with, she didn't tell me his name, so I didn't know at the time that he was a relative of Everett. Once I eventually traced her activity I discovered it was Everett's nephew, John. I was looking for another person at the time and was traveling, so by the time I connected all the dots, it was too late.

"That leaves you as Everett's only other living relative. I had your number from Everett's lawyer."

"Why use my home phone and not my cell?"

Jack arched an eyebrow at her. "What did I just tell you about how easy it is to track cell phones? Location isn't the only information you can get. I didn't want to put you in any danger by possibly exposing your cell, which could be hacked."

"Oh," Kate said as she checked the mirrors before changing lanes and passing a slow-moving truck.

"I called your house a couple of times, but you didn't return my calls. Then I found out that John had been murdered, which meant that there was an imminent threat, so I flew out here immediately to try to keep the people who murdered him from murdering you."

"So that's why you said that I'm not as safe as I thought I was."

"That's part of the reason," Jack said. "Fortunately, you keep yourself pretty difficult to trace. Most of the information on you has been wiped from the internet. That's probably why the killer went after your brother first. He was easier to find."

That news gave Kate a pang of anguish on top of her sense of guilt for feeling that she hadn't been there for John.

"If you never met Everett, how can you be certain he had the same ability as my brother and me?"

"Well, the killer removed his eyes, the same as he did to John, so that's certainly an indicator. Although, like I said, I didn't think it was as strong in Everett, degree doesn't really matter to this kind of killer."

Kate swallowed at the memory. "Why would they do such a thing? Why remove the victim's eyes?"

Jack looked off into the night for a time. "They have their reasons."

Because his answer sounded so haunted, Kate decided not to press him about it. Besides, she wasn't sure she wanted to know.

"The kind of predators who kill people like your brother are intelligent, they are ruthless, and they are relentless," Jack said, still staring off into the darkness. "They will be coming after you. It's a game for them."

A game. Kate's fingers on the steering wheel trembled.

"They have my picture," she whispered.

"What?" he asked in alarm as he looked over at her.

Kate felt sick to her stomach. "There were photos of me at my brother's house, photos he had taken of me that he stuck on his refrigerator, photos on photographic paper printed from negatives. Those photos were missing from John's house."

Kate saw Jack's hands fist in his lap.

"That's why I'm here," he said at last. "You're in over your head and you don't even know it, yet. I'm here to keep you from drowning until you can learn to swim."

Her gaze briefly met his. "Or . . . what?"

"Or tomorrow will never come for you."

Kate fell silent as she drove on into the alien darkness.

CHAPTER TWENTY-EIGHT

Jack pulled out his phone when it rang. He looked at it briefly. "My editor. Sorry, I need to take this. She might have a lead on someone who needs my help."

"Sure," Kate said as she took the exit onto Harrington Road south to her house. She wondered how many people there were like her who were being hunted by predators.

As was her ingrained habit, she checked her mirrors to see if anyone followed her onto the exit. A single woman was always a target. Some of them never realized it or thought about it. Kate did. She could feel when there were eyes on her.

She watched a car in her rearview mirror with the right headlight pointed down at the ground because of body damage. She had been keeping track of it since getting onto I-90. It always seemed to be somewhere behind her. She was relieved when it didn't take her exit.

One time an SUV with four heavily tattooed men who looked like belligerent drunks had kept pulling up beside her at stoplights, trying to get her attention, trying to get her to stop. Angered that she wouldn't stop and that she ignored them, they had followed her onto the interstate, sometimes mere feet off her back bumper.

As they'd pulled alongside her, two of the men on the passenger side hung out the window, banging on the side of their door, yelling what they wanted to do with her, laughing between the taunts, telling her how much she would like it. She kept them pacing along beside her, at about twenty over the speed limit, and then at the last moment she cut off the interstate onto an exit. They sailed past before they had time to react and she never saw them again.

In her car or not, Kate always kept track of anyone who was paying too much attention to her. Sometimes it was simply men gawking. Sometimes, she worried that it might be more than that.

"Hi Shannon," Jack said into the phone. "Do you have something for me?"

There was a pause while the woman on the other end of the line explained. Kate could hear the muffled sound of the woman's voice. Even though Kate couldn't make out the words, the voice had something of a lullaby quality to it.

"I don't know, yet," Jack said. He listened in silence for a moment before answering. "Yes, I know that they have schedules. Of course I want it published as much as you do. I could send you the chapters if you like, but to tell you the truth none of it is really going to be clear until I finish the manuscript. At the moment I'm still involved in some research and I—"

He let out a sigh as the distant voice murmured away. "I know. I understand. Of course I know that they can't publish part of a book. I'll try to get back to it as soon as I can, but you know that lives are what really matters in all this."

The female voice went on, apologetic-sounding, soothing, but insistent.

"To New York? How soon?"

Jack listened as the woman gave him an explanation of something. He was nodding even though he wasn't speaking.

"All right, I understand. No, you're right, publicity does need to get a head start on it . . . I'm not sure yet. Hopefully I can make arrangements to come out in a few days. I'm in Chicago working on something . . . Of course. I'll get back to you as soon as I know. Okay, thanks."

He ended the call and slipped the phone back into a pocket. "Sorry. My editor, Shannon Blare."

"Is she causing you a problem?"

"No, it's not that," he said. "She's the one who believed in the first book and pushed for it at her publisher. My agent submitted it to her because he thought she would like it.

"Without Shannon, *A Brief History of Evil* would never have been published in the first place. In a way, she's become kind of like a silent partner in helping to find people like you. To maintain security, I'm damn near impossible to get hold of."

"That's what AJ said—that she had a hard time getting in touch with you."

Jack nodded. "I stay off the radar in order to protect the lives of people like you. Since I'm sure at least some of these predators know about my book, I don't want them to be able to use me to find those I'm trying to help."

Kate was beginning to feel like an endangered species more than a human being. Protected because she was a valuable asset.

"So you let this Shannon woman be the gatekeeper for people wanting to get to you?"

"Partly," Jack said. "A lot of people want to get in touch with me for everything from wanting an autograph, to wanting me to speak at their group, to wanting me to help them get published. Shannon acts as a stone wall for most of those people but she passes on the occasional legitimate lead. I investigate and decide if the person is someone I need to talk to.

"Despite wanting to be helpful in what I do, she is still an editor at her publishing house and that's a business. She went out on a limb selling them on the idea of a second book, pushing it purely on faith, and she is a bit nervous now because she is in the dark about a lot of the specifics."

"You mean she's afraid of losing her job?"

Jack laughed quietly. "No, Shannon Blare isn't afraid of losing her job. She's only afraid of losing face. Her family is wealthy. And by 'wealthy,' I mean crazy rich wealthy. She buys high-rises in the city sometimes because she thinks they're 'cute,' like another woman might buy an expensive handbag. She goes to work in a limo and has it parked outside all day, waiting for when she might want it.

"She doesn't work because she has to. She seems to want to be involved in books in order to make herself look cultured. I think it gives her something 'intellectual' to do to impress her friends. She only has a few authors, so she only works part-time. It's kind of a hobby for her. Despite all that, she seems genuinely interested in my ideas. I'm not sure how much she believes in what I do, but she believes enough to serve my purpose, and that's all that matters to me."

"What would make a woman like that interested in a book about killers?"

"She championed it and took it under her wing because it has that historical, highbrow flavor that seemed to fit her interest. The fact that it's about murder titillated her because the subject scandalized her wealthy friends."

Kate's knuckles were white on the steering wheel. "I don't think that murder is titillating."

"Nor do I," Jack said.

Kate gestured with a hand. "I didn't mean to include you. It's just that . . . people like that don't understand what it feels like. They haven't looked down at a pool of a loved one's blood, or felt terror because the killer is coming for them."

"I know," Jack said in sympathetic tone. "I realize that people like her don't really get it. But this is one way that helps me protect innocent lives. I can't change Shannon Blare any more than I can change the world, but she can do things that I can't. I needed the book to have a way of connecting with those like you. Shannon is useful because she felt that the book was important, from a historical perspective. She probably also wanted to impress her friends. The book needed a champion at her publisher if it was ever going to come out. She was useful for that reason.

"So, I owe her."

"And because of what they paid for the book?"

"No. The Israelis, remember? I owe her because without that book being published I wouldn't be sitting here in this car with you."

"Do you think it was all worth it?" Kate asked, trying to take some of the tension out of the air. "To be riding along in my beige car and going for pizza?"

Jack chuckled a little. "Hell yes. I can get a better car, but I couldn't find a more gorgeous date."

Kate blushed in the darkness. "So she wants you to go to New York?"

"Yes, she wants to have a meeting to discuss the new book. She's in the dark. I've been keeping that under wraps for now. She wants me to give her some guidance to help her sell the book internally and get everyone behind it.

"The publisher wants to promote it as the second volume to *A Brief History of Evil*. They want to call it part two, or something like that. Publishers love related books or a series, because they tend to sell better. Shannon wants to talk to me about this book, but more importantly she wants to talk about a series, a kind of compendium of evil as she calls it. She envisions a dozen volumes. That means that this second book is an important part of her plan."

"And you care if they sell because you want . . . what? If it sells better that helps you to find people like me?"

"Partly. But like I told you before, I'm the only one of my kind, the only one who can do what I can do—recognize those like you. I think it's important to get what I know all down on paper so that hopefully there can be wider understanding."

"Understanding of what, exactly?"

"That we've entered a nesting period."

Kate remembered AJ mentioning a term like that, but she didn't know what it meant. Kate wanted to ask him about it, but a more important question came to mind.

"You basically found me by hacking AJ's cell phone. Don't you think someone, one of these predators, might do the same with your cell?"

Jack smiled to himself. "Good catch, but no. I use burner phones. They don't have GPS."

"But records of phone calls can be traced to cell towers to give locations."

"True, but that's a higher level of hacking than getting into an iCloud account. Still, your basic point is valid. That's why I use disposable phones. I change them frequently."

"You left your number with me, on my answering machine. Couldn't that be used by these predators to find the people you're trying to help?"

"If anyone listened to my message on your machine they couldn't track me because I have already destroyed that phone and I have a new one. There is no way for them to know the latest number for me. They're all different. I encrypt the numbers and send them to Shannon so she can get hold of me.

"I also maintain a relationship with the Mossad, and they sometimes have urgent need of me. I go over there every once in a while to help them out. They always have my number. I also put the number of my Mossad contact on speed dial of each new phone I get in case I have an emergency and need to contact them."

As Kate pulled into her driveway and put the car in park, she decided to wait until they got to AJ's to ask him about the meaning of "a nesting period." It was getting late and she didn't want to hold up the Janek family's dinner any longer.

"My castle," Kate said.

CHAPTER TWENTY-NINE

Jack sat silently in the car, studying the front of her house. He looked up and down the street to each side.

"I just need to throw some things in a bag," Kate said. She thought that maybe he wanted to keep watch outside. "It shouldn't take long. Do you want to wait here? Or would you like to come in?"

Jack gave her a look. "Didn't you hear what I said about keeping you from drowning before you learn to swim?"

Kate's gaze shifted to her dark house. Her place had always been a refuge, her safe haven. She wasn't used to thinking in terms of someone stalking her. Or ambushing her.

"You mean you think the killer could be waiting for me to come home?"

Jack popped open his door. "Well, at least you're learning to tread water. It's a start."

Kate followed Jack's example and closed the car door as quietly as possible. Seeing the way he moved, the way he watched everything, heightened her sense of concern.

She hadn't left the porch light on, but fortunately the streetlamp gave her enough light to see to unlock the front door. Jack gently moved her to the side with an outstretched arm as he let himself in ahead of her. Kate flicked on the living room light for him.

As he moved through the dark house, she followed behind, turning on lights. He said nothing, asked nothing. His gaze glided over everything, taking in everything. The way he looked around made her see it all as if for the first time.

For someone who was worried that there might be a killer waiting for her, his movements were measured, but not overtly careful. She thought that maybe she had just seen too many TV shows with a SWAT team yelling and screaming as they charged though a house to clear it.

They went through the spare bedrooms, where he looked briefly in all the closets. He checked behind the shower curtains in the bathrooms. In a way, it made her feel silly to be clearing her own house in this manner, but on the other hand it spooked her. His calm confidence reassured her.

Jack looked in the utility closet in the hallway, where he found the short door to the basement. He went down alone to check it out. The basement was basically a big square space with virtually nothing except a water heater and her simple workout area. Jack returned as soon as he was satisfied that no threat lurked down there.

If there were an intruder, Kate thought, there would have been signs, but everything was untouched and exactly as she had left it.

When they finally reached the kitchen after having checked everywhere in the rest of the house, Jack tested to make sure the door to the backyard was locked.

"You've seen everything in the house," Kate said as she pointed back toward the hall. "I'm going to go pack a bag. Would you mind going out and latching the shed door? It was blowing around last night. Let me see if I can find a flashlight."

"Never mind—I've got one," Jack said, pulling a small flashlight from his pocket. "I'll be right back."

"Okay. When I'm done changing I'll open the bedroom door, so come on in when you're finished."

After Jack went out to check on the shed door, Kate closed her bedroom door and quickly changed into a pair of jeans and workout shoes. It felt good to be in comfortable clothes. She picked out a black top and tossed a jacket on the bed.

Once dressed, she opened the bedroom door before flopping her carry-on bag up onto the bed, then quickly started gathering up things she would need. She collected makeup and toiletries and put them in their proper zippered pouches in her bag. She had a routine from when she traveled for work. She folded some tops and slacks and put them in the bag along with some clothes for work. She could hear Jack come back in and shut the kitchen door.

"You can come on in," Kate shouted out toward the hall as she went to the dresser and pulled open the top drawer with her underthings.

When she started to reach in, she froze.

Jack came to the bedroom door, one hand on the doorframe as he leaned in.

"The shed door was already latched tight. I double-checked it to make sure it was secure."

Kate stood staring down into the drawer.

"Kate?" Jack stepped into the room. "What's wrong? Your face has gone white."

"There is a pair of pink panties on top," she said in a small voice.

He frowned as he stepped closer and looked over her shoulder. "So?"

"I don't like that pair of panties."

Jack clearly looked confused. "So?"

"So I keep them at the bottom of the stack in back, just in case I ever need extras for some reason. But I never wear them. I haven't worn them in years. I always intended to throw them out.

"Now, they're on the top in front."

His expression darkened with concern. "Are you sure you didn't put them there without realizing it? You've been pretty distracted with your brother's murder. Are you sure?" He reached up and clasped her upper arm and turned her toward him. "Kate, this is important. Are you sure?"

She looked into his eyes. "I didn't put them there. I don't ever put them there in front on top. Never. They were buried in the back of the drawer. Distracted or not, I wouldn't have dug them out. I wouldn't. Someone has been through my underwear."

Jack glanced around the room. "Is anything else out of place? Has anything been taken?"

Kate went back to the closet, looked through the hanging things, then the folded sweaters and tops on the shelves at the side. She pulled open drawers, checking everything.

"Nothing else looks out of order," she finally said. "Everything is here and just as I keep it." She looked back at him. "Did either of the doors to the house look like they had been tampered with?"

"No. I checked for any evidence of that."

"Then how did he get in?"

"He wouldn't need to use force or break a window. Most likely he simply picked a lock, probably the one on the kitchen door. Maybe with a bump key. A few taps and he'd be in. None of the neighbors could have seen him, so he would have had all the time he needed to get the door unlocked."

"Why would he do this? Why move one pair of panties?"

"To rattle you. The people who want to kill you are intelligent, sophisticated predators. Scared people make mistakes. But mostly they simply enjoy terrifying people.

"If you have your things packed we should get out of here and get you to AJ's house."

Kate sat on her bed, opened the bottom drawer of her nightstand, and then unlocked the gun safe. She pulled out her Glock.

"I think we had better take this," she said.

Jack shook his head. "No. Leave it."

Kate was incredulous. "What? Someone wants to kill me. They've been in my bedroom—and you don't want me to take a gun?"

"Guns have their place and there is no doubt that sometimes they are invaluable in saving your life, but guns can also get you into all kinds of trouble you don't need. If you go into the wrong place and forget you have it you will get arrested. Then you have a weapons offense linked to your name and if you need the police they likely won't be on your side."

"But I—"

"What if you're on the run and you need to get on a plane, or into someplace with security? Where are you going to leave it? Guns make people, especially police, freak out. If you shoot someone you will go to jail while they sort it out.

"Jails are full of bad people. There may even be someone there who can recognize what's in your eyes. You would be helpless in that situation, trapped in a cage with a killer like a Christian in the Colosseum with a lion. You wouldn't be able to run and you wouldn't be able to protect yourself.

"More importantly, a gun isn't always going to save you."

Kate wasn't willing to give up the idea so easily.

"I'd rather take my chances of ending up in jail for shooting a killer than be killed myself. At least I'd be alive."

"That's the right attitude, but there are better ways."

Kate was beside herself. "You came to find me because killers are after me. And yet you don't want me to have a gun so I can protect myself?"

"Of course I want you to be able to protect yourself," he said. "Like I said, guns certainly have their place, but in this situation they aren't going to help save you from the kind of killer who will be coming for you."

Upset, Kate stood with the weight of the gun in her hand at the end of her hanging arm. "What do you mean?"

He gestured to the gun in her hand. "Pretend I'm a threat. Try to shoot me."

Kate was incredulous. "What? It's loaded."

Jack took the gun from her hand, dropped the magazine onto the bed, and then pulled back the slide to empty the chamber, letting the chambered bullet land on the bed beside the magazine. He slid the slide back again, double-checking to make sure it was empty, then handed the gun back to her, grip-first.

"You couldn't shoot me if you tried, but there you go—now it's empty." He flicked a hand. "Go stand over there by the closet and I'll show you what I mean."

Kate was skeptical, but moved closer to the closet.

"I'm a killer," Jack said. "You just came home. I've been waiting, hiding inside your house. I'm here to kill you. I just walked into your bedroom, catching you by surprise. Try to shoot me."

"What?"

Jack lunged at her. In an instant he closed the distance. Kate started to raise the gun to point it at him but before she could, he slammed her up against the wall with one forearm. With his other hand he had already grabbed her wrist with the gun, holding it down before she could point it at him.

Kate blocked upward, knocking his forearm away. She spun out of his grip. Before she could twist away from his attack, he slammed her up against the wall again, face-first.

She felt something sharp at her throat. She froze, panting. His weight held her pressed up against the wall.

She didn't know how he had gotten it, but he had the cold barrel of the gun pressed against her left temple.

Jack pulled her back away from the wall enough to hold the blade up before her eyes, showing her the knife that had been at her throat. He tossed the gun on her bed.

"Rule of twenty," he said.

Kate stared at the short, stout blade in front of her face. It looked sinister.

She looked back over her shoulder at him. "Rule of twenty?"

Jack finally released her. "Inside twenty feet a knife is faster than a gun. You didn't even begin to get the gun up enough to shoot me before I got to you. Bad guys always try to get as close as they can, first, so they can attack before you have a chance to react. They want surprise on their side. You lost before you started. I already had you where I wanted you.

"You said that you've been practicing martial arts all your life. You know how to protect yourself, yet in that instant of surprise, you abandoned what you know, depending instead on the gun.

"Unless you have a lot of training and a gun close at hand at all times, you won't have enough time to use it. This is about saving your own life, not the method you use. The kind of killer who is stalking you isn't going to announce himself from a distance and tell you that he's going to kill you so that you can pull out a gun and shoot him. He's a predator, and a predator is going to sneak up and get up close in order to strike before you have a chance to react. These people are up-close killers.

"He's going to want to get close enough for you to look into his eyes before he kills you."

"But I didn't—"

"Doesn't matter. You're already dead. Excuses can't change that. A gun is false security in this situation. In your case, it's better to use your training. You have muscle memory that's already there with you all the time. That's the start of how you will be able to defend yourself. I'll teach you the rest."

Kate pulled hair back off her face as she sat on her bed. She looked down at the gun in her hand a moment before reloading it and then locking it back in the safe.

"AJ is expecting us," she said as she closed her carry-on bag and pulled it off the bed. "And I'd like to get out of my bedroom where I know a killer has been through my underwear."

"I don't mean to scare you. I only want to keep you alive."

Kate nodded. "I don't want to end up like my brother. You just keep on doing what you need to, even if I don't like it."

"I understand," he said. "Let's get to AJ's."

CHAPTER THIRTY

Kate was silent on the short drive to AJ's house. She couldn't help running everything through her mind over and over again. AJ would want every little detail.

Kate had been shaken by the realization that some guy, most likely John's killer, had been standing in her bedroom, pawing through her underwear. He had wanted to make her afraid. He wanted her to know that he could reach out and touch her. He wanted her to know that he was coming for her. He wanted her to feel violated and vulnerable.

But her initial reaction of fear had curdled into anger. He had intended her to know he had been in her bedroom to terrify her at a gut level.

Kate was long past terrified and well into seething rage.

She remembered vividly a *sifu* from California coming to her martial-arts school when she was young, perhaps twelve or thirteen. It had been a great honor for their school. Kate didn't remember the man's name. She only remembered him as a quiet, bald, firm Asian man of few words. He had smiled, but it wasn't friendly. It was judgmental.

To her, martial-arts school was an escape from a world she couldn't change. It was a time for herself away from watching over John. It was a time when she could be her own person, with her own life, and not John's sister, minder, protector.

Each student at the school had been pitted against an opponent so they could put on a demonstration of their skills; the visiting sifu evaluated them each in turn. Some of the older students received an approving nod. Some received a word or two of advice, and some a stronger criticism of the way in which they performed a particular move.

Kate went through her routine with an older boy who was more advanced. She was supposed to defend herself against his attack. She had been proud of her quick blocks and the variety of defensive moves she had used. When they were finished, she bowed before the sifu, sure she had acquitted herself well against the bigger boy.

When she straightened from her bow, the sifu looked long and hard at her. She remembered his intimidating eyes. They seemed fierce and knowing, as if they could see right through her. He tapped a finger against the base of her throat, at the top of her rib cage.

"That was disrespectful crap," he told her in broken English as he lifted his nose. Kate stood motionless in shock.

"If you are attacked," he went on, "it is because they have the advantage. For you, they will always be bigger, stronger. No one is going to help you, so don't expect any. You must do everything you can with the bad intention of hurting your enemy."

He tapped his bony finger at the base of her throat again. "You do not respect your own life. You are afraid of hurting your attacker. You should instead be afraid of him hurting you, and stop him." He leaned toward her, his mouth in a sour expression. "You are better than you have shown me. I am disappointed in you."

Kate had been humiliated. The class was dead silent at his words, and when it was over she cried on the long walk home. She made excuses in her own mind that she was only a girl and the boy had been much bigger and more experienced.

But even in that moment, she knew better. It didn't matter. Failing to do what was necessary to stop her attacker had been what mattered, regardless of age or strength or gender. The sifu had been right.

Jack's demonstration had brought back the burning shame of that lesson.

While her brother's death was horrifying, in a way it also seemed surreal. She knew it was true, of course, but she couldn't really wrap her head around it.

Knowing that it was likely the same man who had been in her bedroom, his hands on her underwear, made it suddenly real. It made those lessons relevant in a way they never had been before.

Rather than wanting to defend herself from the threat, as she had when she had been a girl, the way she had tried to defend herself from Jack—and having him easily get the upper hand over her—had caused some profoundly important internal switch to flip. She now grasped in a very real way that if she wanted to survive, there was only one way. She had to eliminate the threat.

She knew how to do it. She had been practicing those moves for years. Before, they were only theory practiced against a vague threat, and that threat didn't try to kill her as she went through routines. She had never really thought about those moves being delivered with the deliberate intent to maim and cripple.

Now she did.

"Are you still mad at me?" Jack asked.

She frowned at him. "I'm not mad at you."

"You were. I could see it in your eyes. It wasn't a look I enjoyed seeing directed at me."

"Well," she said, "I guess maybe I was a little angry. But I know you were only trying to help me."

"I'm glad you realize that."

"I shouldn't have been angry at you, I should be angry at myself for letting you get the better of me that way."

"Kate, you can't expect to know how to handle all of this. No one would. Ordinary people don't go around getting attacked. They don't expect it to happen. That's where fear and instinct step in to help us.

"Give yourself some credit for how well you've been handling everything so far. Most people would be so broken up by their brother's murder and the idea that the same person was now after them that they wouldn't be able to function. You've been keeping your head."

Kate swallowed back her emotion. "Will you teach me how to have bad intentions of hurting an attacker?"

As Jack studied her face, she deliberately looked at him only out of the corner of her eye, afraid that he would say no.

"I always hope that the people I find will be smart enough to ask me that. You're the first one who ever has. I will help you for as long as you want me to teach you."

Kate sniffled and wiped her nose on the back of her wrist as she nodded.

She finally turned off the main four-lane street into AJ's neighborhood. AJ had been right about the party. The house across from AJ's place was all lit up. As she drove past she could hear loud music.

At least, from what she'd heard from AJ and by the looks of people she saw, it was an adult party and not a bunch of drunken teenagers vomiting all over the front lawn. The street in front of AJ's house was lined with parked cars. There were no empty spots to park in.

Kate drove around the block, and then widened her circle until, as AJ had guessed, she found a parking place a couple of streets over.

Kate put the car in park and then stared at nothing for a moment. "How did he get in my house?"

Jack leaned an elbow on the armrest. "That's the wrong way to look at it."

Kate frowned over at him. "What do you mean?"

"He wanted to get in. If you'd been at home, he could simply have kicked in the door or broken a window. The point is, he would have gotten in one way or another. You shouldn't worry as much about how he is going to get to you, as what you will do when he does."

Kate grimaced. "I guess you're right."

"I think that for now the best thing would be for you to stay at Detective Janek's house. We need to have a long talk with her about a number of things, not the least of which is how to keep you safe. For now I'll feel a lot better if you aren't sleeping alone at your place."

Kate nodded as she watched the figures of people, intermittently lit by streetlights, turning to shadows as they made their way to and from the anniversary party. A few people were leaving but most were still arriving.

It was a chilly night, so both she and Jack put on their jackets. When Kate pressed the remote to lock the car doors, the chirp blended in with the distant music and voices carrying through the night air.

"I can stay at AJ's place tonight, and maybe for a few nights," Kate said, looking over at Jack as they passed under a streetlight. "But I can't stay forever. What good is running away or hiding going to do as long as these people are hunting me? Once I go back home, they will be waiting in the shadows for me. It seems clear they were even trying to get to me at work."

He considered for a moment, and then looked over at her with a sudden thought. "Why don't you come to New York with me? I need to go anyway. We could even go to Israel for a while. They would be glad to have you and maybe you could even help them in return. It would get you out of danger for now."

"I have a job."

"Can't you take some time off?"

Kate smiled briefly at an older couple going in the other direction before answering Jack. "I guess I could. But once I get back, nothing will change. They will still be coming for me."

"It would throw them off your trail for the time being. In the meantime, we can work on some measures to make you harder to find."

"I'd rather end the threat," she said as she turned up the walk toward AJ's front door.

He gave her a more serious look. "That means killing whoever is hunting you."

"I didn't start this," she said.

On the front porch, Kate glanced briefly over her shoulder at a burst of raucous laughter coming from the house across the street.

Kate knocked on the front door. But when she did, it swung inward a few inches.

The door wasn't latched.

CHAPTER THIRTY-ONE

"That's weird," Kate said. "Their door isn't shut."

She started to knock again, but Jack snatched her wrist and pulled her back away from the door.

He moved them both off to the side a little and then with his foot gently pushed the door open.

Kate's attention was caught by a mess of splintered wood. As the door swung open she saw jagged stubs of stair balusters broken off halfway up the steps. Pieces of debris lay everywhere.

Among that mass of rubble and wreckage, she saw Mike.

He lay sprawled on his back on the stairs, his legs bent back under at the knees, looking like he had fallen back from where he had been standing. He was stretched out and motionless.

The spike of a split baluster had been driven through the center of his chest. Blood completely soaked his shirt and halfway down his tan pants. He was covered with the rubble.

Kate stood frozen in place by the shock of what she was seeing. Big, muscular Mike was clearly dead.

"Oh my god," she whispered.

Jack already had his knife, the one she had seen before, with the stout, short, triangular blade, in his right hand. With his left hand he pulled Kate farther back, behind him.

"Stay here," he whispered.

Kate could hear her heart pounding in her ears. Her breath came in short, ragged pulls. In her mind, she was hoping against hope not to find what she already knew they would find. She wanted to pull everything back and not have it be real.

Jack carefully stepped over the threshold and into the house. All the lights were on. Kate ignored his admonition to stay where she was and instead followed him in.

Inside the house, it looked like a tornado had ripped through the place. Splintered furniture lay scattered everywhere. What had been a warm, welcoming, lovely home was now an incomprehensible scene of wreckage. A broken lamp, still on, lay on the floor on the opposite side of the room, the shade torn off and crushed under part of a broken chair.

Blood seemed to cover everything. The smell of it hung thick in the air.

There was so much debris and torn cushion stuffing everywhere that Kate was having trouble making sense of anything, recognizing anything. The couch was the only thing still where it had been.

And then she spotted Ryan's body in a crumpled heap at the base of the opening in the wall leading into the dining room. What was left of his head was bent back at an impossible angle. A massive amount of blood and brain matter were splattered against the fractured wall. It was clear to Kate that he had been swung by his ankles, bashing his head to kill him.

Kate saw a colorful plastic truck on the floor.

That was when she finally saw AJ among the debris.

The woman lay on her back in the middle of the shattered glass of the broken coffee table. There was so much rubble, cushion stuffing, and plaster dust all over the floor, and all over AJ, that Kate hadn't seen her at first.

AJ was naked from the waist down. Her legs were splayed open. The barrel of her gun had been shoved into her vagina and left there.

Under a layer of plaster and wood bits, her white blouse was now red with blood. Thick strings of blood lay across her face. Silver duct tape had been wound sloppily around her head, covering her eyes, but not her mouth.

Kate panted in panic at what she was seeing. She wanted to scream. She thought she might pass out.

"Don't step in the blood," Jack said quietly as he moved farther into the room. "Better yet, stay where you are."

Kate was paralyzed in place, her eyes wide, unable to look away from AJ's body. Her mind couldn't fully take in what she was seeing. She wanted to look away, but she couldn't.

She felt a tear run down her cheek. Pain bore down on her insides as she started to tremble.

Jack came back and gripped her arm. "Kate, I don't want you going back outside alone. Can you just stand there? Don't look at her. Just stay where you are. Don't step in the blood. I don't want you leaving your footprints here, contaminating the scene. Do you understand? Kate, do you understand?"

Kate nodded.

"Why don't you watch the door?" he said.

Instead, Kate slowly lifted her arm to point.

There, in the center of AJ's chest, sat her detective's card.

All four corners were folded over.

"What is it?" Jack asked. "What are you pointing at?"

"That card. That's AJ's card. She gave me one just like it."

"So?"

"She gave one to my brother, too. John was afraid of sharp things, like corners, so he always folded over the corners of pictures and cards.

"AJ told me that she had left her card with John, but we didn't find it in the house."

Jack nodded unhappily. "I guess that leaves little doubt who did this."

Tears running down her cheeks, Kate squatted

down close to AJ. She touched the woman's cheek.

"Dear god, AJ . . ."

AJ's head was turned to the side, her mouth covered in blood. Kate hoped that AJ hadn't seen the horror of Ryan being killed.

She remembered when she had been on the phone with AJ, and the woman said she had to go because there was a commotion at the front door.

It was the devil at their door.

Kate spotted a human finger lying on the floor not far away from AJ's head. She pointed.

"That's not hers."

Jack looked at it a moment. "It's a man's finger. It looks like she managed to bite off the finger of the killer."

"AJ would have fought with every ounce of strength she had. She wouldn't have gone down easily."

"There's no doubt she didn't," Jack said in soft compassion as he looked around at the wreckage of the house.

Jack squatted down and circled his arm around Kate's shoulders. He gently lifted her to her feet, even though she didn't want to leave AJ's side.

"We can't stay here, Kate. We need to leave."

"I need to get something to cover her," Kate said, ignoring him as she struggled to hold back a dammed-up flood of tears.

"We need to leave everything as it is. Don't touch anything. Don't pick up anything."

"We need to call the police," Kate said with a stifled sob.

She covered her nose with a hand, trying in vain to block the stench of blood and gore.

"No, we need to leave, right now," Jack said.

Kate looked up at him. "What? But we have to."

"No, what we have to do is keep you alive. There is nothing we can do for them, now. What happened here is over. It's done.

"Getting you involved with the police will only put you at more risk."

Kate's brow bunched. "What are you talking about?"

"There will be hours and hours of questions. They will want to know what you were doing here, what your relationship was with Detective Janek. Relatives of murder victims don't spend the night with detectives. What are you going to tell them? That you can recognize killers and you were helping AJ identify murderers?"

"But AJ would want—"

"AJ would want you to get away from here. She would know that being here could only put you at risk."

Kate looked back at AJ's still corpse. It somehow didn't look real. "We can't just leave them here like this. We have to do something for them."

"Listen to me." Jack gripped her shoulders and turned her to face him. He leaned in close. "Listen to me. There is nothing you can do here that is going to help her, now. Nothing. We need to get out of here. You need to trust me in this. I know what I'm talking about."

Kate's vision was turning watery. "Are you sure we can't—"

"I'm sure. I've been involved in this kind of thing before. You can't help what's already done. What matters now is protecting you."

"How can we do that?"

He gripped her shoulders tighter. "You have to understand something, and you need to understand it starting right now. This is about you staying alive. The police aren't going to help you to do that. If you lie to them they will catch you in that lie. If you tell them the truth, your story will seem so bizarre they will suspect you are somehow involved. At the very least, they will likely have you locked up for psychiatric evaluation."

Kate blinked at him. She tried to think if what he was saying made sense.

"There are bad people in the world," he said, "and there are good people. The police are good people. But with this business they won't understand you. They won't want to."

"You want me to leave without telling the police I was here?"

"Yes. The less information the police have on record about you, the safer you will be. You must not get involved with the police. Do you hear me? They are for the most part good people, but they are bound up in a bureaucratic system where you don't fit their official world view. You are different and you have to do things differently if you want to stay alive."

"Differently? What do you mean?"

"You need to be a ghost in these matters. You can't afford to get officially entangled in any of this. This is outside what law enforcement understands. AJ was a good police detective and she knew better than to trust them with John and you. She kept you and your brother a secret and didn't tell her own department about any of this business with either of you being able to recognize killers. Did she?"

"No, but that's not how I've lived. That's not the rules I've lived by."

"Rules are for people who lose fights. If you want to live, then you have to live by new rules—your own rules."

Kate looked around at the bloody scene of destruction, at the bodies of people she knew—people she cared deeply for.

It all seemed so hopeless.

But Jack was right. She knew he was. This was the reality she had to face.

She gritted her teeth as she looked back at

him. “We need to kill this bastard and end this.”

“If only it were that easy,” Jack said under his breath as he squatted down.

A cell phone lay on the floor near AJ’s bloody, torn panties. Jack pulled the sleeve of his jacket down to cover his knuckle, and then used it to press 911.

“Okay,” he said as he stood. “The police will trace this call and when they realize it’s a police officer they will descend on this place with an army. That’s the best we can do for AJ and her family. We need to be gone when they get here.”

CHAPTER THIRTY-TWO

Out on the porch, in the cold air, Kate stood close beside Jack, feeling hot and lightheaded and sick to her stomach. He swiped his hair back off his brow, peering out at the night as if trying to see the killer out there somewhere.

"I want you to listen to me," he said. "We need to worry about your life, now. I need you to go get the car."

Kate wasn't sure she had heard him right. "You want me to go get the car? Alone?"

"Yes. Hurry, now. Come back here and get me. Understand?"

"No. Why aren't you coming with me?"

He gripped her upper arm and leaned toward her with grim intensity. "Kate, listen to me. You need to trust me and do as I say. I know what I'm doing. We need not to be seen here. Go get the car."

Kate couldn't imagine what he planned on doing inside AJ's place. She glanced over her shoulder out into the night. When she turned back, she could see the carnage inside through the partially opened door. It was such a sickening sight that she had difficulty making her mind believe it was real. She half expected AJ to open the door and smile at her and make the whole thing evaporate like a bad dream.

But AJ was never going to smile again.

The houses were set back quite a ways from the street, with deep front yards, so none of those people across the street where the party was going on noticed Jack or Kate on the front porch of the Janek home. Older rock music was blaring. Every time the front door opened and someone went in or out, the music got louder until the door was closed again. She could hear people laughing and talking.

"Get going," Jack said. "Don't be slow about it."

Kate looked out at the night. "What if he's still out there, waiting?"

"How would he know you were coming over tonight? Besides, there are too many people coming and going for the party. He wouldn't be able to recognize you in the dark. He wouldn't be able to pick you out from everyone else. Go on, now. Hurry."

As Jack went back inside, making the order final, and a sense of urgency overcame her, Kate abandoned her objections and hurried across the front lawn in the direction she had left the car. She couldn't imagine why he was sending her alone, but she didn't want to waste time considering the grim possibilities.

She turned up her collar against the cold night air and stuffed her trembling hands in her pockets.

She walked as quickly as she could down the side-walk without breaking into a run. If the killer was still hanging around, running might draw his attention. She told herself that there was no reason to believe he was still anywhere nearby. Like Jack had said, the killer hadn't known that she was coming over.

Kate felt numb, her mind balancing on the razor edge of tipping over to panic and grief. She forced herself to block her emotions. This was no time to lose it.

She crossed the street and quickly made her way down the block. The car was another two streets over.

When she turned and looked back, she saw a tall man in a hoodie. He hadn't been there a moment ago. She didn't know how he seemed to appear so suddenly. He had his hands in the pockets of the jacket. He was following behind her.

Somehow, she was not the least bit surprised to see him.

Kate knew without a doubt that it was the man she had seen the night of John's murder, outside his house.

It was the man who had been watching her that night.

She started moving faster. When she did, the man responded by breaking into a run toward her.

Once she saw him coming for her there was no longer any doubt as to who he was, or what he intended. Kate immediately cut through a side yard between houses. She wove through a maze of bushes, hoping he wouldn't see which way she went. When she looked back she saw the man follow her in. As he ran under a light on the back corner of the house, she was pretty sure she could see that he was covered in blood.

Kate raced across a backyard and jumped a chain-link fence into the next backyard. As she ran across the back lawn, a dog rushed out toward her, barking like crazy. His barking set a half dozen dogs in the neighborhood to barking in response. It was clear that if the dog caught her he was big enough that he would likely take her down. She cut to the left to avoid the dog and slipped on the grass. Without pause she rolled to her feet and kept going, hardly missing a beat, then leaped over the fence on the far side just before the dog could grab her ankle in his teeth and kept running as fast as she could.

She snatched a quick look back and saw the man kick the dog so hard it was sent tumbling. The dog yelped in pain. A light on the back of the house flicked on. As tempting as it was to get the attention of the people who had turned on the light, she knew she dared not stop. Besides, what were they going to do against such a vicious killer? Kate didn't want them to end up dead as well.

When she looked back, the man was over the fence and still coming.

Kate raced between sheds and detached garages, taking whatever opening presented itself, trying to make sure she didn't get boxed in, always keeping in mind where her car was. She knew, though, that with as close as the man was behind her, even if she made it to her car she would never get it unlocked and have time to jump in, start it, and drive away before he pounced.

She ran as hard as she could, trying not to think of the inevitable. She had to get away. It was as simple as that.

As she wove her way through obstacles in the older neighborhood, jumping over lawn mowers, woodpiles, and a pair of rusted bicycles, she fought back her burgeoning sense of panic. She was well aware that if she let panic have control of her, she would die. She knew that her only hope to live was to keep her head. She had to find a way to get away from the man.

The thought of him catching her, and what he would do to her when he did, fueled her straining muscles.

Branches of bushes snatched at her as she raced past. She had to bat some of them out of the way. As she went past a ladder leaning up against the side of a house, she pulled it down behind her, hoping to block the way or at least slow her pursuer. The aluminum ladder banged down against the ground.

She didn't take the time to slow to look back to see if the ladder slowed her pursuer. She skidded to a stop momentarily in the alley behind a garage, looking both ways, trying to pick the best route. She quickly decided to cross the alley and go between garages, hoping that in the dark they would hide which direction she had gone.

As she burst through a narrow space left in junk piles between the garages, the man abruptly stepped out in front of her, blocking her way. He had apparently seen which way she had gone and with his longer legs raced around the garage to intercept her.

Kate skidded to a halt before she crashed into him. Panting hard to catch her breath, before he could snatch her she immediately shot away to the right, jumping one fence and charging though the open gate of another.

Now out of the alleyways and side yards, she raced across the open front yards. The light on the closest light pole was out, leaving her in a pool of darkness between distant streetlights.

The man, his shadowed form looking like he could be the grim reaper himself, raced out from between the houses, angling right toward her. In that instant, as close as he was, Kate knew that he was faster than her and she wasn't going to get away.

CHAPTER THIRTY-THREE

As the man charged in at her, he lifted his arms to tackle her. He was too close for her to escape. Before Kate had even given it any thought, she acted out of instinct. She spun around and threw a side kick into the center of his chest. The man staggered back a couple of steps, but kept his balance.

This was the man who had killed John. He had left AJ's card with the bent corners from John's house on AJ's body. It was his calling card. He wanted her to know it was him. It was a message, the same way moving her underwear was a message.

This was the monster who had butchered AJ, Mike, and Ryan.

She could see that his left hand was wrapped in a bloody hand towel. She knew that he would be missing a finger.

The injury didn't look to be slowing him down, nor did her kick. His arms were long and she had been fixated on keeping him from getting close, so he had been a little too far away for her kick to do much damage.

This was a predator. The instinct of a predator was to chase down prey. When they had prey in sight, on the run, nothing else mattered to them except taking that prey to the ground. Kate was now the prey he was after.

She knew that, as close as he was, if she ran he would be on her in a flash. He was going to keep coming no matter what.

When he rushed toward her again, she knew that she had no choice. Whatever hesitations she'd had in the past now seemed foolish. This was about her life, and whether she would willingly give it up or fight for it.

Running now would be a foolish mistake, so she didn't run. Kate instead bladed her body and covered her center. Even though there wasn't a lot of light, she could see him grin when she took a stance to stand her ground. That was what he wanted—a helpless victim that he could overpower.

Kate kept her left fist near her stomach and put the thumb of her open right hand under her chin to coil the strength of her right arm. When he closed the distance to her she twisted her weight toward him and thrust her arm out with lightning speed, adding the force of her weight to the strike, hitting his left ear with her cupped hand.

The blast of pressure from her cupped hand slamming his ear that hard blew out his eardrum. The man cried out in pain as he twisted to the side, holding the side of his head.

The pause only lasted a moment, and then he

was coming again. Kate realized immediately that it was a mistake for her to wait to see if her blow would stop him. She admonished herself in that instant not to make that mistake again.

To prevent him from pushing her into a retreat and then overpowering her, she instead drove in toward him and cleared the line of his arms. Almost right up against his chest, she threw her weight into a punch to his throat. Before he could react, she kept herself close inside his defenses and unleashed chain strikes as fast as she could, the way she punched the bag in her basement when she was angry. She had practiced those rapid-fire punches most of her life, except that now it was for her life.

She ducked under his arm when he swung at her, and punched upward with a blow to his midsection. He let out a grunt. He struck out at her again. She ducked under his arms again, came around his side, and drove her closed fist into his kidney.

He rounded on her faster than she expected. She felt the stunning blow to her face. It knocked her back, sprawling across a front lawn beside the sidewalk.

She rolled onto her feet again before he could throw himself on her. Her face stung and felt numb at the same time.

He slowed for just a moment, assessing her with those cold, deadly eyes, apparently deciding on how to change up his attack in order to put an end to her resistance once and for all.

Kate remembered her instructor's words, words that at the time had seemed like emotionless theory. Now those words were her lifeline.

Don't defend. Attack. In a life-and-death situation with a bigger enemy who intends you harm, there is no such thing as defending. There is winning or losing. Life or death. She knew that if she was to survive, she had to come at her attacker with superior aggression and violence of action. Size and pure muscle power weren't the only things that mattered. She couldn't let him control what she did. She couldn't react. She had to act.

By favoring his injured ear, he left the other side open. Without pause, she stepped into the strike. Using her fist, twisting her hips to put all her weight behind the blow, she cried out with the effort of her strike to his mandible on the opposite side of his injured ear. She heard the bone crack as the blow knocked his head sideways. As he swung back around toward her she met him with an elbow to the center of his face.

She kept it a tight, close-in fight, because she knew that was her only chance. By limiting his ability to extend his arms in a fully developed blow, she denied him his strength. She knew better than to let him back her up, because that would give him all the advantage of distance, weakening her attacks. With his longer arms, retreating would let him fight using his strength advantage and he would overpower her in mere seconds. So instead she kept getting inside his attacks, staying on the attack herself, keeping him off balance, striking right into him from up close, where she could fully extend her shorter arms to full effect.

She aimed for vulnerable places when she could. She didn't try to remember forms or proper sequences; she simply took advantage of whatever worked in that instant.

He caught her behind her neck with his wrist and drove a blow into her midsection. It was unexpected and it knocked the wind from her. She staggered back a step, but made herself reverse back at him before he could take full advantage and dominate her movements. The next time he reached out to catch her the same way, she ducked, spun, and kicked his knee, buckling him for a step so she could press in at him again.

By staying in close, she kept him from extending fully for a devastating blow, changing the dynamics to her advantage.

When the heel of her hand connected with the middle of his face, he reacted with a cry of rage and threw his weight at her. Rather than backing away or absorbing his energy, she dove in toward him, using his weight to increase the power of ramming her knee into the center of his gut. As he staggered back a step, he somehow landed a fist on the side of her head.

Trying to ignore the dizzying blow, she saw that he was still favoring his right jaw. She saw an opening. Kate struck with lightning speed, bringing her fist down to break his collarbone.

His other fist, which had been covering his ear, whipped out and caught her in the side of her head, knocking her sprawling.

Kate crawled away, determined to stay out of his reach as she fought to remain conscious.

It was hard to believe the injuries she was sure she had inflicted hadn't stopped him. He had to be running on pure adrenaline. She knew that a person running on adrenaline, like men injured in battle, would frequently not feel the pain of injuries and keep fighting.

She was running on adrenaline, too, but she was near the end of her endurance.

Kate forced herself to get to her feet. She knew that she was not going to be able to escape him.

She looked into his eyes, remembering AJ lying on her living room floor, dead. She knew that he had far worse planned for her. AJ and her family were merely the warm-up. A taunt. She was the main event.

This was not a predator who would ever give up.

CHAPTER THIRTY-FOUR

As Kate staggered back a few feet, her vision narrowed to a dark tunnel. Her muscles were spent.

She fought to hold on to her vision, to remain conscious. She knew without a doubt that if she blacked out, when she woke up she would find herself in the middle of the agonizingly painful ordeal of being the man's next victim.

Kate shook her head as she struggled to lift the leaden weight of her hands. She told herself again not to chase his arms but to concentrate on doing as much damage as possible as swiftly as possible. She needed to degrade his ability to fight more than she had already managed to do. That was all that mattered.

While he was bigger and stronger, she knew that some of the injuries she had inflicted had evened the fight to some degree, and while she wasn't sure how much, she knew it wasn't enough. She knew that she couldn't waste time wondering. She also dared not count on it to slow him. He was still dangerous in the extreme. It was up to her to decide if she was going to live.

She realized that the reality was that she had to put him down and make sure he was no longer breathing.

It was an odd kind of clarity, knowing that her singular goal was to kill this man in order to live.

There was something primal about that clarity, a kind of liberating realization that the laws of civilization no longer applied. This was survival at its simplest. Kill or be killed.

The man's eyes gleamed with murderous intent as he took the measure of her. Blood ran down his chin, dripping off in long strings.

"What do you see with those eyes of yours? What do you see, Katie girl? I think you see too much." He spit blood off to the side. "It doesn't matter, really. I'm going to bring you everlasting darkness, just like I did to Johnny boy."

The grating sound of his voice made her knees weak. She couldn't imagine the devil himself having a more terrifying voice. She remembered John saying that if she ever looked into the eyes of the devil, she would know it.

It was bone-chilling when the man smiled at her. It was as if, behind that smile, he was thinking of exactly what he was going to do to her once he had her and while she was still alive.

Before she could move, she saw a dark shadow come out of the night, flying at the killer from behind.

In a blur of motion, what looked like a leg whipped around the man's head. The torso of the shadow came up, spinning around, led by the arcing swing of the leg. A coat flew behind like a billowing cape.

As the dark shape spun, driving the killer to the ground, Kate heard a sickening snap.

The night fell silent. The killer lay still on the ground, the shadow over him with one hand balancing himself on the ground.

Finally, as the shadow rose up, Kate saw that it was Jack.

She staggered gratefully into his arms, panting, out of breath, letting herself sag under the weight of her relief as he held her up.

"It's okay," he said, holding her tight. "He can't hurt you now."

Her face was starting to throb in pain. She could taste blood and felt the warmth of it dripping from her chin.

Kate pushed away and then slapped him across the face. "Why did you make me go alone! You knew there was a killer out here and you sent me out alone like bait!"

Jack nodded, understanding her emotion. "I know. I'm sorry. But you were never alone."

"What are you talking about?"

"I was behind him every step of the way. I was watching the whole time so I could step in to end it if I needed to."

Kate slapped him again, harder this time. "You bastard. You let him attack me? You left me to fight him alone when you could have helped? I was scared to death. I thought I was going to die!"

Jack caught her wrist when she tried to slap him a third time. "I had to know what you would do. I had to know if you would fight or simply shut down and let him kill you.

"I've learned through bitter experience that I can't help people who won't fight for their own life. Some people simply give up and surrender to death. I can only help those who have it in them to survive.

"Once I saw that you were going to fight for your life, I needed to know how you would do, how you would fight, and how good you are so that I know what more I need to teach you.

"It had to be real. I needed to see it. I was doing what I had to do so that I know if I can help you stay alive. I didn't like letting you fight him alone, but it's the only way I can help you to survive what's coming for you."

Kate stood glaring at him, still catching her breath. "You needed to know how good I am? You let me think I was going to die? That's why you left me to fight him alone?"

He nodded. "You were really good, Kate. You really were."

"Then why step in now?" Kate asked, still panting to catch her breath, still angry. "Why wait until now before you helped?"

Jack gestured down at the man on the ground. "Did you see him pull out a knife?"

Kate blinked. "Knife?" She looked down at the dark mass slumped on the ground. She saw the glint of a blade not far from his outstretched right arm. With a sickening sensation she realized that that was why the man had smiled.

"I never saw a knife," she admitted.

"He deliberately distracted your attention by talking to you, taunting you, to help cover what he was doing."

Kate didn't know what to say.

"Did you notice that Mike's throat had been cut?"

Kate swallowed at the horror of that memory as she looked up at Jack. "No . . . I guess I didn't."

"Did you see that AJ's throat had been cut?"

"No," Kate admitted in a quieter voice. "There was so much blood and other things he had done to her that I . . . I guess I didn't really notice that part of it. I thought that Mike had been killed by having that big sharp piece of the baluster driven through his chest."

"No, that had been done after he was already dead, probably on the killer's way out. It was an act of spite, an act of hatred meant to demean him."

Kate's gaze drifted to the ground in shame. As an investigator, she should have paid more attention to all the evidence right there in front of her. She prided herself on catching details when others didn't. This time, it had been she who hadn't noticed critically important facts. It had been such a shock, and such a bloody scene, that she had been overwhelmed and failed to see what was right there in front of her. Still, she knew that was no excuse.

She had made a mistake. If not for Jack being there, it likely would have been a fatal mistake. The knife that cut Mike's and AJ's throats could just as easily have cut hers.

With a finger, Jack lifted her chin. "There was a lot to take in, Kate. That was something you weren't prepared to deal with. Few people ever are. Don't be hard on yourself.

"But for future reference, had you seen that their throats had been cut, you would have known that the killer had a knife and you would have been on alert for it and mentally prepared to deal with it. Bullet holes in them would have told you he had a gun. You have a chance to handle a predator with a gun as well as one with a knife if your mind is on top of the situation.

"You didn't see him pull that knife. I did. I couldn't take the chance that he would cut you with it, so I had to put him down."

Kate swiped strings of sweaty hair back from her face. She looked at the dead man again. She looked at the knife again.

"Thanks, Jack. I'm sorry I slapped you."

He dismissed it with a wave. "You were doing

good. I think that you might have been able to finish him, but I could see that the fight had gone on too long and you were running out of energy. I didn't want to allow a mistake to get you severely injured or killed after you had fought so well. You fought really well, Kate, so give yourself some slack."

The words seemed strange to hear. "I fought well?"

"You ruptured his eardrum first, which made it easier to inflict more damage. You were systematic about inflicting injuries and reducing his ability to fight."

Jack checked the area to make sure there was no one around before he squatted down. He used a finger to push the man's jaw down, opening his mouth. Kate could hear the crunch of bone.

"You knocked out his front teeth. Did you know that? You broke his mandible. It takes a blow of about forty or fifty pounds to break the mandible. A powerful blow delivered in just the right place can do that. I suspected you knew that, and that's why you went for that spot when you saw an opening?"

Kate nodded when he looked up. "Yes, I knew."

"You also broke his collarbone. That only takes about eight pounds of pressure, but you need to have just the right opening to take that shot. Again, you saw an opening, took it, and broke his collarbone."

He looked up at her. “Do you still have your front teeth?”

Kate wiped her bleeding lip and felt her teeth with her tongue. “Yes.”

“Do you have any broken bones?”

“No,” she said, finally feeling in control of her breath.

“I’d say that’s pretty much the definition of fighting well.”

“I guess I didn’t know I had it in me,” she said. “I only knew that if I wanted to live, I had to stop him.”

“I think you have more in you than you’re aware of. This is a man who just murdered an ex–Army Ranger and a trained policewoman. I think that what you did to a man like that took an avenging angel. That’s the way you fought, that’s what made the difference, and you stopped him when they weren’t able to.”

Kate didn’t think she was an avenging angel. But she did feel like something within her had changed.

“Now that I know you have that inner will to survive, I can provide you with the rest of the knowledge and skill you will need.”

Kate gestured down at the crumpled heap. “Did you break his neck?”

Jack nodded.

This was a man who not only had killed her brother, but had just slaughtered an innocent family that she cared about.

"I kind of wish I could have been the one to break his neck."

Kate looked both ways and saw that the streets were empty. She could hear the distant music coming from the party. She squatted down beside the dead man. The man's face was bloody. She was pleased to see that she had also broken his nose.

"Can I see your flashlight?"

Jack fished it out of his pocket and handed it over. Kate clicked on the light and looked into the man's eyes. They were terrifying, just like the photos of killers that AJ had shown her. Even in death, the man's eyes betrayed his evil and gave her a primal chill of fear.

"We need to get out of here," Jack told her. "But first look through his pockets on that side and see what he has on him that might help us."

Jack pulled a wallet out of the man's back pocket and without looking in it slipped it into his own jacket. Kate reached into the nearer side pocket and felt two fat cylinders of something. She pulled them out.

Each was a tight roll of hundred-dollar bills with at least a half dozen rubber bands securing it.

Kate held them up for Jack to see. He didn't look surprised. "There will be ten, twelve thousand in each roll."

"How do you know that?" she asked as Jack pocketed a phone.

"Just put them in your pocket and keep looking for what else he has on him."

Kate pushed her hand into the other back pocket and felt something flat and smooth, like a stack of irregular cards. She pulled it out. In the dim light from a streetlamp down the block, Kate was shocked to recognize the photos.

"These are photos of me." She shuffled through them, looking. "These are the photos of me that were on John's refrigerator. These are the photos missing from his house."

Jack didn't look at all surprised. "Put them in your pocket. We want to take anything he has on him."

Kate held up the photos. "This is the man who killed John. This proves it."

"He's likely the one who killed Everett as well."

"So he killed Everett, came here and killed John, then came looking for me?"

"That would be my guess."

Kate reached across the corpse and gripped Jack's sleeve to make him look up at her. "Then this means it's over. Now that he's dead, this ends it. The nightmare is over."

"I'm afraid not."

"But he's dead. The killer who did all this damage and came after me is dead. How can that not end it?"

Jack looked away from her eyes. "It's not that easy, Kate."

"Why isn't it that easy?"

"It has to do with a nesting period we're in. This isn't about catching a murderer. This is about something much bigger."

"You said that before—'nesting period.' I don't know what that means. Why don't you think this ends it?"

Jack gestured with a rolling motion of his hand, urging her to hurry. "We need to get away from here. I'll explain it all later. For now, see if he has anything else in his pockets."

Kate found some keys. "These too?"

"Everything," Jack said as he glanced over his shoulder, checking the empty street. "We need to get going. We can't risk someone spotting us with the body. We can't risk being connected to any of this."

In the distance Kate could hear the wail of sirens. "It sounds like the police will be here in a minute or two."

Jack nodded as he stood. "Let's get to your car and get out of here."

CHAPTER THIRTY-FIVE

As they reached Kate's car, the piercing wails of police sirens racing toward the scene at the Janek home were only a block or two over. It sounded like half the Chicago police force was coming to the rescue.

As was so often the case, they were not coming to the rescue. They were coming to the aftermath, after the murdering was over and done with. That chilling realization only added to the things that Jack had said, as well as what the sifu had once told her. She shouldn't depend on anyone coming to help her.

Flashing lights strobed off tree branches and houses in every direction as the police cars and ambulances raced in. Kate saw a number of people in the distance come out on their front porches to see what the commotion was all about. Fortunately, the distraction of all the flashing lights left Jack and Kate in the obscurity of darkness, and in the opposite direction from the sirens that everyone's attention was focused on.

With such a large police response it was only a matter of time before the body of the killer would be found. Forensic evidence, especially blood evidence and DNA, would show him to be the killer. Although they would have no idea how the killer had met his fate, the crimes at the Janek home would be solved.

But those murders were over and done. The killer hadn't been stopped beforehand. While it served justice that the killer would be identified, AJ and her family were gone forever; their lives, their world, had ended.

That thought brought home the significance of what AJ had been doing with John and then with Kate—stopping killings before they could happen. AJ had done that work secretly because such methods would not be officially tolerated. Jack had gone to Israel because those methods would not be officially tolerated. What had happened, had happened to the one person who had been trying to stop these killers.

Kate knew that she would remember the horrifying murder scene in AJ's house for as long as she lived. Kate thought that most of those officers who were about to discover it would never forget it, either. A police officer shot in the line of duty was tragic enough, and dead was dead no matter how it happened, but for an officer and her family to be slaughtered in such a gruesome fashion would be viewed on an entirely different level. In a way, it shook the very foundations of law and order, exposing the barbarism that was leaking through the crumbling veneer of civilization.

Expanding rules and regulations aimed to deny

reality. Officials hid comfortably behind those regulations. AJ had instead found consolation in finding a way to stop killers.

AJ had been interested in protecting her, but the police would not have been so understanding. They didn't know her the way AJ had. They didn't know anything about her.

Jack was the only one who truly understood what was going on and the danger she was in. Kate didn't even grasp the whole picture, but Jack did. Jack had been the one who was there to help keep her alive. He was the only one who could keep her alive. She was beginning to see his wisdom in getting them away from the scene and staying off the police radar.

"Why don't you let me drive," Jack said. "I don't think you're up to it at the moment."

"I think you're right," Kate admitted as he opened the passenger door for her and let her get in. She noticed for the first time that her hands were bloody. Some of it was from cuts on her hands, but she knew that a lot of it was from the man who had been trying to kill her.

Once Jack got in and closed the driver's door, he watched the cross street as ambulances raced by.

Just then, a man suddenly appeared at the driver's side of the car. With the light behind him, Kate couldn't see who he was. He seemed to have appeared out of nowhere. She didn't know if he was a cop or maybe a neighbor. Her immediate thought was that he was someone who had seen Jack kill the man and then the two of them go through his pockets, and thought it was a robbery.

And then the man tapped on the driver's window with something metallic.

Kate saw that it was a gun barrel.

"I saw what you did," the man's muffled voice said as he stood outside the car, pointing the gun in at Jack.

Kate's heart felt like it had jumped up in her throat.

The man gestured with a tilt of his head. "I saw what you did to that man back there. I saw you rob him. Now get out of the car and put your hands up." He leaned down a little and pointed the gun at Kate. "Both of you."

Jack already had his hands up. Kate followed his example, holding her hands up where the man could see them.

"All right," Jack called out, sounding compliant. "We don't want any trouble. Take it easy. I'm getting out."

With a quick look over at her, Jack whispered, "Stay where you are."

Jack kept his left hand in the air as he unlocked the doors and then leaned over and popped open the driver's door with his right hand. He looked and acted like any terrified victim of a mugging at gunpoint. Looking confident, the man waved the gun, directing him to get out.

Kate heard a soft, metallic click.

As Jack carefully pushed the car door open so as not to startle the man with the gun, it forced the man to step back a little to make room. As Jack rose up out of the seat to step out, and as if reaching for the edge of the side window like he meant to close the door, in one smooth motion he instead took hold of the gun hand of the man and twisted it sharply inward.

The man cried out from the sudden pain of having his hand turned inward in a way it wasn't meant to bend. He leaned toward the right as his hand was being twisted inward.

At the same time, before the man had a chance to struggle, Jack calmly swiped something along the exposed left side of the man's neck.

Jack stood quietly, holding the man by his bent wrist to keep him from being able to move, to point the gun at them, or put up a fight. The man's free hand went to his neck as he started to sag. Kate knew that with the way his hand was bent, if he resisted Jack could easily break the man's wrist.

Kate saw great gouts of blood pumping out between the man's fingers as he held the hand against the side of his throat. His knees buckled.

A few seconds more, and he had slumped quietly to the ground.

Kate sprang out of the car and ran around the

front. "What in the world did you do? The guy was probably an innocent bystander who saw us picking the dead man's pockets."

By the time Kate knelt down beside the man, she could see that he was no longer breathing.

Still holding the man's gun hand back, Jack clicked on his little flashlight, shining it at the man's face.

"Look at his eyes, Kate. Look at his eyes and tell me if you think he's just some innocent witness."

With a finger on his chin, Kate turned the man's head toward her a little so she could see his eyes. The blood that had been gushing out in spurts only moments before had slowed until it merely oozed. She knew that his heart had stopped.

The man's eyes were open. The sight of those eyes gave Kate an icy jolt of fear.

They were the eyes of a killer.

She looked up at Jack as he clicked off his flashlight. "What in the world . . ."

"Like I said, it's not over."

"You mean he was with that other man? How did you know he wasn't just some innocent witness who saw you kill that other guy and go through his pockets?"

"Experience, the way he moved, the look on his face, the way he held the gun. I can't see in his eyes what you can see, but looking up at him made the hairs on the back of my neck stand on end. Doesn't that ever happen to you?"

"Yes," she said, "as a matter of fact it does."

Jack had just killed two men, swiftly, and with a minimum of fuss. With the second man, he hadn't even looked like he was trying. It seemed as if he had done nothing more than step out of the car and hold the man's hand, helping to ease him to the ground.

Kate now understood what she had seen the first moment she had looked into Jack's eyes. If she had killed the first man, when she looked into a mirror would she see the same thing in her own eyes that she saw in Jack's?

Jack was already going through the man's pockets. He pocketed a few items and then stood in a rush.

"We've already spent too much time here. Let's get going."

Kate gestured down at the dead man lying at the curb. "Where did he come from? What's going on? Was he working with the other one?"

"Now is not the time. We need to leave. Get in the car, Kate."

CHAPTER THIRTY-SIX

Jack pulled away from the curb in a relaxed manner, as if he were just going out to the store to get a few groceries. Kate knew that with all the police cars descending on the neighborhood, he was trying to maintain a low profile and not attract attention. The police would soon have the entire area cordoned off as they started frantically looking for the killer. She knew that Jack wanted to be gone before they were caught up in that net.

Kate understood his reasons, but she couldn't help having mixed feelings. It went against the grain of how she had been raised, how she lived her life, and how she always tried to be completely professional in her job.

She realized that she didn't know where they were going; he seemed to be simply driving, simply covering ground to get out of the area.

"We can go to my house," she suggested.

"No, we can't."

"But we should be safe there, now."

"I wish it were that easy, but it isn't. For now it's too dangerous to go to your place. Are you forgetting the second guy who showed up out of the blue? The first guy you knew was looking for you. He killed your brother and came looking to kill you. You didn't realize there was a second man hunting you. You don't know who else might be hunting you. If there are others, and there will be, they will look for you at your house."

"I don't understand. Who was that second man? There was just one person John hit over the head and chained in his basement, and that's the guy who killed him. That guy had my photos. So who is the second guy? Who are these other people you're talking about?"

"It's complicated."

Kate's head and neck were throbbing in pain. She was rattled and losing her patience. "What's complicated?"

Jack glanced over at her after going around a corner toward a main street. "I'll need a computer to show you."

"I brought my computer. It's in my carry-on bag in the trunk."

Jack shook his head. "We can't use your computer. We need to use a computer that can't be traced to us."

"Traced?" Kate wiped both hands back across her face. "Who would trace it? How would they? You mean you think these predators could somehow track me through my computer?"

"In this case it's not the people intent on murder I'm concerned about. The government traces everyone who goes where I need to take you online. We need to use a computer that can't in any way be linked to either of us."

"I sometimes work with the government," Kate said. "They already know all about me. I have a security clearance. I learned about your work for the Mossad from them. Maybe I could get my contact to help us."

Jack shook his head emphatically. "No. This is different."

"Why? What is it you need to show me?"

"I need to take you into the darknet and show you the face of evil."

Kate had only vaguely heard about the darknet. Brian had mentioned it in passing once or twice, but she had no idea what it was. As unnerved and shaken as she was, she tried to think of a way that wouldn't link them to a computer.

"I've heard Brian at work, my computer expert, say that hackers sometimes use college computer labs as a way to use a computer without anyone being able to tie it back to them. Our computers at work are under continual attack. Brian says they sometimes try to hack into KDEX from school computer labs or internet cafés.

"I think we could bluff our way into a college computer lab. Once we're in there, we watch when people are about to leave and then I could sweet-talk some guy into letting me get onto a computer before he logs out."

"College computer labs are a risky way to do what we need to do. There are too many ways to get caught."

"Not if we're careful."

"And how would you explain a surveillance video of us going into a college computer lab? Those places are monitored, and if anyone checks into us for some reason, we have no legitimate excuse for being there. We couldn't explain what we were doing there.

"That alone is a big red flag to the police. Once they could see what computer we were on, they would look into what the computer visited. The government would get involved. If you want to stay alive, for now you need to be invisible."

Kate couldn't imagine that Brian didn't know the best way to be clandestine with the use of a computer. She didn't know if Jack was just paranoid, or if he had legitimate reasons for his concern. So far all of his warnings had proven well founded.

"So then what do you suggest?"

"I have a way that no one will know what we're doing and it's a lot simpler," he said.

"Like what?"

"I'll show you tomorrow. Right now we need to get you somewhere safe. Do you know a nice motel not too close to here?"

"Sure. Lots of them." Kate looked at her bloody

hands. Her face hurt in earnest. Her lip was throbbing. "I must look a mess."

Jack stole a quick look over at her. "I think you look beautiful, but we do need to get you cleaned up and I need to get a better look at those wounds. They need to be cleaned and treated. We need to get somewhere safe and alone where you can get cleaned up before anyone sees all that blood on you."

Kate flipped down the sun visor and opened the lid on the mirror. "Jeez," she said under her breath at the sight of herself in the mirror. He was right. If anyone saw her the way she looked, they would probably call the police thinking she was an abuse victim.

Kate pointed off to the right. "Go that way at the intersection."

Jack drove for a time in silence. He seemed preoccupied. Kate certainly was. She was still unnerved by how easily, how casually, how quickly Jack had killed the man with the gun. If she hadn't been paying attention, she would have thought that he was merely getting out of the car and had done nothing more.

She was even more unnerved by what would have happened had Jack not been there, and that man had her at gunpoint. By the look in his eyes, her fate would have been no better than it would have been in the hands of the first guy.

Kate stared ahead out the windshield, watching

the sparse traffic. "How did you kill that last man so quickly? What did you use to cut him?" she finally asked. "And what was that sound I heard just before?"

"You heard that?" When she nodded, he said, "Good observation."

Jack held up his right fist. She could tell he was holding something, but she couldn't see it. He flicked his thumb and a blade popped out of his hand as if by magic, accompanied by the soft metallic click she had heard before. The blade wasn't very long—it was so short it was almost triangular-shaped, kind of like a box-cutter blade, but a little longer. It was the same blade he had put against her throat in her bedroom.

"Like I told you, inside twenty feet a blade is your best bet."

"But it's so small. . . ."

"The guy's dead, isn't he? It doesn't take a big blade to cut the carotid artery. That cuts blood to the brain. The person loses consciousness in seconds. Death follows quickly. The fight is over."

Kate stared out the window again, feeling a little sick.

"That's what you want to teach me?"

"I want to teach you to stay alive. The world is becoming a treacherous place, Kate. I just want to give you a chance to be safe."

She rode in silence for a time before asking him another question. "What are we going to do?"

"Go to a motel, let you get cleaned up, give you some first aid, and then you need to get some rest."

"No, I mean what are we going to do after that? In general. Longer term," she said, staring out the side window at the dark businesses along the street. "You said the threat isn't ended. I presume you mean that there will be more men like those coming after me."

"I'm afraid so. Has anything else suspicious happened lately?"

"There was a man arrested near where I work," she said. "He attacked a woman a few days before I got back to town. He hit her in the side of the face just for the fun of it. She died.

"When they arrested him, he had a piece of paper in his pocket with my name on it. From his description, he wasn't that second man. Besides, I'm pretty sure he's in jail. With everything that's happened, it seems pretty clear he was coming to kill me as well.

"That makes three men—that I know of—hunting me. How do I end this? How do I make it stop?"

Jack shook his head. "I'm sorry, Kate, but I don't know yet. We need to get more information. Let's take it one step at a time, okay? Tonight we get you some rest, then tomorrow I need to get onto a computer to find out how serious the threat is in your particular case."

"That killer had my photos on him."

Jack nodded. "That's part of the reason I need a computer that can't be traced to us."

There were so many thoughts crashing around in her head that Kate decided she didn't need any more confusing or frightening things to think about, so she didn't press him. Instead, she simply gave him directions of where to turn to get them back onto the interstate.

She figured he wanted to be a good distance from the scene of the murders. The interstate was the best way to cover ground quickly and get them farther away. After a time she finally had him take an exit to a nice motel in a good part of town. He pulled up under the portico and put the car in park.

"I'll get us a room."

"Us?" Kate gave him a look. "We're staying in the same room?"

He looked suddenly embarrassed. "No, I didn't mean . . . I'll get us adjoining rooms, okay?"

Kate realized that she really didn't want to be alone. Jack's calm presence helped her to keep herself under control. She was afraid that if she was left alone she would break down in tears and not be able to stop.

"Twin beds would be okay," she said.

He smiled. "Sure. That works. But if you'd rather—"

"No, that's fine. To tell you the truth, I'd really rather not be alone right now."

Jack looked sympathetic. “I understand. Sit tight. I’ll be right back.”

Kate watched him go inside the well-lit reception area. It occurred to her that one would never know by looking at him that he had killed two men that night. He was calm and polite. He didn’t look aggressive or dangerous. He looked like a nice guy.

As the woman slid a sign-in sheet across the counter, Jack took ID out of his wallet and then bent to fill out the form. Kate scanned the motel parking lot. She looked carefully at everyone, at every movement. She checked the shadows and doorways.

The world had changed. She had changed.

Jack returned to the car and handed Kate an envelope with receipts, restaurant ads, and an electronic room key.

“With your concern about security and secrecy and staying off the radar, don’t you think that registering at a motel is rather risky?”

He put the car in gear and drove on into the side parking lot. “Not considering that I signed us in as Mr. and Mrs. Weldon. We’ve just come down from Milwaukee for a few days of sight-seeing and shopping. I requested a nice suite because it’s our fourth anniversary. The lady thought that was sweet and gave us their best room.”

“But they need ID.”

"I gave them ID. I told you, Kate, I know what I'm doing. I've been doing this kind of thing for a long time now."

She had no idea how one would go about getting a fake ID, but she supposed that maybe the Mossad was able to supply him with those sorts of things.

"How many of the people you've tried to help have ended up dead?" Kate asked.

After he parked near the dark end of the lot, not far from a back entrance, he sat for a time, staring off at nothing.

It was a pretty blunt question. She hated for it to be so harsh, but that was the way the investigator in her asked questions. If you wanted to know the truth, you sometimes had to ask tough questions.

Kate had to look away from the anguish in his eyes. She hadn't intended the question to be hurtful.

"I'm sorry. That was a terrible thing for me to ask."

He put his fingers under her chin and turned her face back to look into her eyes. "Considering your position, it's a perfectly reasonable question to ask."

She stared back into his eyes a long moment. "You don't need to answer. It's just that—"

"Too many," he said. "I try as hard as I can to help people with your ability, people who are able to do what you can do. Despite how hard I try, too many have been lost. Most never come to understand their place in all this. Most don't want to. That makes what I do pretty discouraging at times.

"Each one of those deaths cuts my soul. With each of them, a part of me dies, too."

She looked down at her hands. "I'm sorry, Jack."

"But you should know that most of those were not like you."

She looked up at him. "What do you mean?"

"They weren't avenging angels. They didn't have what it took to live given their unique ability. And they weren't protectors."

Kate frowned. "Protectors?"

"Protectors of mankind. Most were simply victims who had a talent they couldn't accept or use to help them survive. Having the special vision like you have didn't help them to survive. Survival is ultimately up to the individual, not their vision.

"You do more than survive, Kate—you protect others. That's really rare, even among your kind."

"Where are you getting all this? I'm no protector. You're the one who protected me, remember?"

"That's different. You helped AJ identify killers, didn't you?"

"Well, yes, but—"

"That's what a protector does. She doesn't simply run from killers, she turns and faces them. She wants to stop them.

"The woods are full of wolves. Your inherent nature is to protect the flock from those wolves. You, Kate Bishop, are part of mankind's never-ending struggle with itself."

"You talk in riddles a lot, Jack Raines."

He showed her a brief smile. "Sorry. That's why I'm writing the second book, but since it isn't written yet, tomorrow, after you're rested, I'll try to make it more clear for you. And then you can decide for yourself."

"Decide what?"

"If you really want to survive. Sometimes even I don't know if I want to."

CHAPTER THIRTY-SEVEN

While Kate waited in the car, Jack went by himself to casually check the entrance. Except that as she was getting to know him a little better, she recognized that he was anything but casual as he looked for potential problems or people who could possibly see Kate and end up causing them trouble.

Once satisfied, he returned to the car and opened the trunk, taking out both their bags before opening her door.

"I didn't see anyone. The place looks pretty quiet. Turn your collar up and keep your head down. Let your hair fall down around your face. I don't want anyone seeing you before you have a chance to clean up."

She knew that he really meant "before you clean off all the blood." She knew that she had a lot of the killer's blood on her. He'd had a lot of Mike's, Ryan's, and AJ's blood all over him as well, and as she'd fought him up close a lot of their blood had gotten on her. The thought of it sickened her. More than anything, the weight of grief was crushing.

Kate took the handle of her carry-on from Jack, rolling it behind her as they left the relative darkness of the parking area for the well-lit rear hallway. Skinny columns separated the hall from an atrium with a koi pond. Real plants and flowers grew around the pond, making it an oasis of sorts among the artificial grass.

The humid air carried the sharp smell of chlorine from the pool. On the other side of the atrium a small group of people, talking and laughing, moved down the hallway. They were self-absorbed, possibly drunk, and didn't look her way.

After the events of the night, the civilized normality of the motel was jarring. She felt as if since leaving her office with Jack she had gone through the looking glass into some kind of alternate world where she no longer knew the rules.

Once Jack checked the hallway around the corner, they took the elevator up to the second floor. A man and woman at the far end of the hallway were letting themselves into their room. Given the distance, and her black top, Kate doubted they would be able to make out the blood all over her. She kept her head down as Jack inserted the key card in the slot.

At the click, he opened the door and went in first. Kate was getting used to him checking things out, so she stood just inside the doorway until he was satisfied and tilted his head, signaling for her to come in. She was tempted to ask him how in the world a killer would have known the motel she would pick out and the room they would be given, but decided to let it go.

It was a comfortable-looking suite done in soft yellows and mellow tans. Beyond double French doors was a sitting room with a TV. There were two bathrooms, and in the bedroom portion two king-size beds. Even though there were two beds, it felt a little awkward to know that she was going to spend the night sleeping in the same room with him. This was a man she had only met that day.

The thought of the alternative was more unnerving.

Jack gestured to the larger of the two bathrooms. "Why don't you use that one and get cleaned up so I can take a look at you."

Before getting into the shower, Kate put her top in the sink to soak out the blood. Surprisingly, it was only on her top and not on her jeans. She was dead tired, and her neck and shoulders ached, but it felt good to stand under the shower and let the water beat against her skin. When she looked down, she saw that the water spiraling around the drain was red, like in the movie *Psycho*. By the time she washed and rinsed her hair twice, the water was finally running clear.

After she got out and toweled her hair, she washed the top soaking in the sink and hung it over the shower curtain to dry. She used the hair dryer belonging to the motel, rather than unpacking her own.

Inspecting her face in the mirror, she thought she looked a little like an abused woman. Her lip was swollen around a cut to the left side. There were a few abrasions on her cheekbones. Fortunately, she had prevented the killer from having enough distance to be able to pile-drive his fist in at her, so most of the rest of it was bruising she thought she could tone down with makeup.

Considering how hard the blows had felt, she was actually surprised she didn't look worse. The way those blows had snapped her head back left the muscles in her neck tight and sore. Had he ever connected using his advantages to the fullest, he would have probably killed her the same way Wilma had been killed.

Kate put on her nightshirt and the white guest robe. She tied it around the waist before going out. Jack was waiting on the couch in the sitting area. He had a first-aid kit out, no doubt one he had in his carry-on.

He gestured to the couch beside him. "Come sit. Let me take a look at you."

Kate sat on the couch beside him and tucked her legs under herself. The room was dimly lit by lamps on end tables.

Jack put his big hand on the top of her head and tilted it back for a better look. He gently pulled her lip down with a thumb, then put something on a gauze pad and pressed it to her lip. It stung like crazy. He got another and cleaned the scrapes on her cheek.

"All in all, you look in surprisingly good shape."

"If you say so."

"Anything I can't see that I should know about?"

Kate shook her head.

He put antiseptic ointment on another gauze pad and gently rubbed it into the cut on her lip. "Nothing needs stitches. That's good. You can't really bandage your lip, so we'll just have to put some ice on it and let it heal on its own. I think it will be fine."

Kate hardly heard him. In her mind, she was seeing AJ lying on the floor, silver duct tape wrapped around her head to blind her, half naked, covered in blood. She would never be fine.

Kate swallowed. "Why did he put duct tape around her eyes?"

There was no doubting who she meant. Jack didn't answer.

"I want the truth," she added. "Don't say you don't know. You know."

Jack looked at her a long moment. "To add to her terror," he said in a soft voice that somehow made the words more horrific. "He probably wanted her to hear her son screaming for her, but not be able to look at him for the last time. To have her know that her son couldn't see his mother."

"And why didn't he put tape over her mouth?"

Jack didn't shy away from the question. "With the party going on across the street, he knew that no one would hear her. He killed her husband immediately, then surprised and overpowered her. He didn't put the tape on her mouth because he wanted to hear her beg for her son's life."

Kate was having difficulty breathing. She knew how much AJ loved Ryan.

"He killed her husband first so that he could take his time on her. He must have known that you were going to be coming over. He wanted it to be as gruesome as possible for your benefit. He left the card with the bent corners for you to see so that you would know that he was also the one who had killed your brother."

Kate lost it.

She broke into sobs, unable to stop imagining AJ's horror, her pain, her terror, her agony.

She felt a mountain of guilt that Mike, Ryan, and AJ had died just so the monster could strike horror and fear into Kate. Had Kate never gotten to know AJ, she and her family would still be alive. Kate had brought the devil into their lives.

"It's not your fault," Jack said, seeming to know what she was thinking.

She knew it was. Even if it wasn't intentional, it was her fault. All the connections with Kate had brought the killer into AJ's home.

As Kate gave in to the crushing weight of grief, Jack put his arm around her shoulders and gently pulled her over against him. Kate buried her face against his chest as she wept uncontrollably. She had no strength left to hold back her tears. He put his hand on the back of her head and held her, letting her cry, not trying to get her to stop.

It wouldn't have done any good. Kate couldn't be stopped at that point.

Everything that had happened seemed to come falling in on her. All the people around her who had been murdered because these predators wanted her.

Wilma had died because the killer couldn't get to Kate. John had died because Kate hadn't been there. Now AJ and her family had been slaughtered because Kate was in their lives.

Jack reached back and turned off the light on the side table.

He hugged her with wordless sympathy and sorrow for what she was feeling. Kate had only just met him, and he was the only one in the world who could understand her helpless agony. In a world gone mad he was the only one she could turn to.

Her fingers clutched his shirt, her face pressed against him, as she wept in choking sobs. She wanted out of the nightmare. She wanted AJ's family to be alive and well. She wanted Wilma to be thinking about retirement. She wanted John to be alive and living his life.

Even though the man who had slaughtered AJ's family was dead, it wasn't enough. It wasn't justice enough for what he had done. Beautiful lives had been snuffed out in the most horrific manner by a worthless human being, and he got to have his neck broken and die in an instant. It wasn't fair. His useless life was not a fair trade for their priceless lives.

Kate didn't know how long she cried in Jack's arms. She didn't try to stop. She wouldn't have been able to, yet her sobs slowly lessened and, in her exhaustion, finally died out. She lay where she was, against him, not wanting to move.

In that moment, she was a helpless child in the comforting embrace of someone strong and good.

It had been a very, very long time since she'd had anyone comfort her, since anyone had let her give in to her fear and anguish and just held her.

At last she had to turn and snatch some tissues from the end table. She blew her nose and wiped her tears.

Jack didn't say anything. Not saying anything was the kindest thing he could have done for her right then.

Oddly enough, she didn't feel embarrassed that she had given in to her grief in front of him. That he understood and simply held her made her feel closer to him, on a human level, rather than the guy who wrote the book with all the bad reviews who had come to tell her that there were crazy people trying to kill her.

Her cut lip ached. The blows the man had managed to land left her face hurting and her neck sore. Her arms ached. On top of that, she was flat-out exhausted, both mentally and physically.

She finally looked up at Jack. "I think I'd like to get some sleep."

"I think that's a good idea."

Jack finally got up and retrieved a pill bottle from his bag. He returned and shook a pill out into his hand.

"Here, why don't you take this?"

"What is it?"

"A Valium."

Kate shook her head. "I don't want to take a tranquilizer."

"It's really a muscle relaxer. It's a low dose—only five milligrams. It will help you sleep."

Kate stared at the pill for a moment. "Thanks, but I'm so tired I think I'll sleep fine without it. I don't like my head to get foggy from medications."

"I understand," he said as he put the pills away.

It occurred to her that with all the horrors he

must see, with all the things he dealt with, he probably needed to take those pills himself sometimes to dull the pain of it all.

Kate shed the robe and crawled under the covers. Jack turned on a smaller light in the bathroom, closed the door most of the way, and then shut off the light in the bedroom before taking off his shirt and shoes and lying down on the other bed.

Kate tried to close her eyes but they kept coming open as her mind raced. She wondered if maybe he had good reasons for offering her a Valium and she should have taken it. After a time she turned on her side, toward him. His fingers were locked together behind his head as he stared at the ceiling.

She watched him in the near darkness for a time.

"Are you asleep?" she whispered.

"No. What is it?"

"Can I ask you a personal question?"

He shrugged. "Sure."

"You seem to know all about me, but I don't really know anything about you."

"What do you want to know?"

"Well, do you have family? Do you have kids? A wife?"

He simply said, "No."

She thought about it a moment. "What about a woman in your life? Aren't you involved with anyone? Isn't there a woman somewhere waiting for you? Someone you love. Someone who loves you?"

He was silent for a long time before he finally answered.

"I can't afford to become involved with a woman."

"Because of what you do?"

"Yes."

"So you don't go out with women for fear of becoming involved?"

He nodded without looking over at her. "It's hard for me to explain. I suppose that seeing a woman socially is an intimate taste of what I know I can't have."

"But you must have been in love before."

"I'm afraid not. Not even close." He looked over. "Have you been in love?"

"No," Kate admitted. "A few times guys have told me they loved me, but it was pretty clear to me that they were just trying to get laid. Other than a crush or two in high school, I guess I've never really been in love.

"Sometimes life gets kind of bland and empty without someone. You know? Without at least the hope of finding the right person, existence would be pretty desolate, don't you think? I think that someday I'll find the right guy and fall in love. You will, too."

After a quiet moment, he said, "That can't ever

happen. I've had to come to terms with the fact that I can't bring a woman into my world."

"But why not?"

"How could I care for anyone when I know that doing so would endanger her life?"

"That's right now," Kate said. "Maybe things will change."

"I'm afraid not." He reflected silently for a moment. "I know it probably sounds strange coming from a guy, but to tell you the truth, it's pretty damn depressing sometimes, never to have had a woman say she loves me, and to know that I never will."

Kate thought that was about the most disheartening thing she had ever heard. It seemed to suck the meaning out of being alive, out of being human.

"But you—"

"You need to get some sleep, Kate. Tomorrow I'm taking you to a very scary place."

CHAPTER THIRTY-EIGHT

"This is the scary place you wanted to take me?" Kate asked, looking around the big parking lot. "An electronics store?"

"The store itself isn't the scary place. Think of it as a doorway."

"A doorway." She shot him a skeptical look. "A doorway to what?"

"To Onionland."

Kate shielded her eyes with a hand as she squinted over the top of the car at him in the bright sunlight.

"Onionland? What's Onionland?"

"The place where bogeymen hide."

His tone was sobering enough that she knew that there was something very serious behind the vague response, and that she was finally about to get to those answers.

Cars jockeyed for parking places or waited for people to pull out of spots in a lot busy with Saturday shoppers. People with jumping kids rolled out of the store with shopping carts loaded with new game systems, TVs, and computers.

Kate wondered if it wouldn't be better to come back on a weekday, when business was slower. But she also wanted answers about the dimension of the danger they were in. Considering what had happened the night before, waiting didn't seem like the best option.

She had thought that killing the man who had murdered John, AJ, and her family and had been hunting her, to say nothing of killing the man who had come out of nowhere, would mean that it was over and she was finally out of danger. Jack had discouraged that notion, saying he needed to show her. Considering her newfound ability, she was apprehensive that it could never really be over.

So, she guessed she was going to this Onionland place to meet the bogeymen.

Jack leaned closer as they walked toward the entrance. "Listen, Kate, this is going to be hard."

She looked over at him. "What do you mean?"

"For one thing, this is an electronics store, so there are going to be lots of TVs on display in here. You're going to see reports on the murders last night all over those TVs."

She looked away from the concern in his eyes and nodded. "I understand. I'll be okay."

As horrified as she was by the death of AJ and her family, she knew that she couldn't let herself become trapped in a yesterday that she couldn't change, or she would be lost. She needed to focus instead on the problem at hand and what she might still be able to change.

"Seeing the news about the murders isn't going to be the worst of it," Jack said.

Kate took a deep breath. "What could be worse?"

"I'm taking you to the underworld."

"The underworld." She made a face at him. "Do you have to talk in riddles all the time?"

"The riddles are about to end. To do that, I need to bring you face-to-face with things that most people will never see and wouldn't accept if they did. You need to see the reality I'm dealing with, the reality I'm trying to protect you from, the reality you're going to have to deal with if you want to live."

"Why wouldn't I want to live?"

"You'd be surprised. Some people with your ability that I try to help simply can't handle it and give up a level of control over their own fate."

Kate scanned the crowds funneling with them toward the store entrance. She wanted to live and was determined to face whatever she needed to.

"I need you to keep in mind that we don't want to attract attention to what we're doing," Jack said.

"Meaning?"

"Meaning we need to blend in. There are cameras everywhere, so if you lose your cool, it will be recorded. We need to look like nothing more than a couple out Saturday shopping. So stay as calm and collected as possible, no matter what you see. After last night I have faith that you can handle this."

"I understand," Kate said as they went through the glass doors into the store.

Despite how tense she felt, she consciously tried to act casual. She didn't rush and she didn't make herself obvious by looking around at everyone. She knew that they were there for a very different reason than every other ordinary person she saw.

Mere days ago she had been a relatively ordinary woman living in the ordinary world—going to work, going to the grocery store, caring for her brother—but now she grasped that she was living in an unfamiliar world she didn't yet understand. It was disorienting not knowing the rules of this strange new world she found herself in.

Every face that turned her way seemed to momentarily elevate her heart rate. She scanned every pair of eyes that turned in her direction. They all looked so ordinary that it made her almost doubt her newly discovered vision. Almost.

Inside the store, crowds churned through the maze of aisles made from shelves and tables in the vast, open warehouse space. Off to the far left she saw a wall of TVs. Jack was right: most of them were showing the news. Kate recognized AJ's place, surrounded by yellow tape. Reporters stood outside the tape barrier speaking on camera, or interviewed neighbors by the looks of them. She was glad that she couldn't hear what they were saying over the store music.

While the murders of a police detective and her family were the lead story, it was only one of a number of murder reports. She saw a parade of bodies lying in the street or on sidewalks, all lit by strobing police lights. It had been a busy night for killers.

Shoppers roamed down row upon row of shelves lined with merchandise, from copy machines to cell phones to a wide variety of speakers and sound systems. There were aisles of supplies with everything from reams of paper to pens to hard drives. Banners hung down announcing sales. Computer boards and video cards were mounted on a display high up against the end wall. Below it were shelves with numbered bins corresponding to the parts on display, and one aisle was dedicated to empty computer cases for people who wanted to build their own systems with the parts.

Jack led them on a meandering course, stopping momentarily to pretend to look at WiFi routers and portable hard drives so as to make them blend in with the rest of the shoppers, until they arrived at a long white counter dividing the computer portion of the store. On each side of the counter, sample computers were set up for shoppers to examine. Near the end of the far side were desktop computers and monitors. The side they were on had dozens of laptops, all open, most of them running.

Jack looked at a few of them, checking the price, acting mildly interested as if he were just another shopper.

A young man in a dark blue shirt and tie intercepted them as they moved along the counter. "Can I help you find anything in particular?"

"Thanks," Jack answered casually, "we're just looking at laptops. Are these here last year's model that I saw advertised on sale?"

The man gestured to the ones in front of Jack. "You found them. These are all last year's models. There are some great deals here if you're not the kind of person who wants the latest and greatest. We still have most of them in stock."

Jack nodded thoughtfully as he gazed over the display, looking like he was in no hurry to find just the right bargain. "Okay, thanks. We'll check them out."

"I'll leave you to it, then. Just come find me if you need any help."

"Will do," Jack said.

It was obvious that the young man was overwhelmed with a store full of customers and too little help, so, his duty done, he was glad to leave Jack and Kate to peruse the computers on their own.

Kate had watched the salesman's eyes. She

remembered the story AJ had told her about the unassuming Edward Lester Herzog and the women customers he had murdered and cut into pieces. Herzog had worked in an electronics store, probably something like this one. John had identified him as the killer for AJ.

This salesman probably looked something like Herzog had. It was easy to see why he wouldn't have struck fear into the hearts of the women he had murdered. Not all killers looked scary.

Jack worked his way down the counter toward the center of the long display and finally came to a stop before one of the open laptops. Customers checking out other computers were at least eight or ten stations away.

"Stay on the lookout for anyone with the kind of eyes only you can see," Jack said in a quiet voice without looking at her.

"Like you needed to tell me that," Kate said.

Jack smiled as he played with the cursor on the laptop, moving it around, opening and closing a few windows.

Still without looking over at her, he said, "There are cameras in this store. The computers are cabled down so they can't be stolen. A lot of the stuff on the shelves is pretty expensive, so most of the cameras are aimed at the aisles and the shelves of things that can be shoplifted.

"Don't be obvious about it, but look up and you

will see the cameras that arc watching over these computers."

"I only see cameras on the other side at each end," Kate said. "There are another two behind us, also at the ends."

Jack nodded, still playing with the computer, opening a browser window. "The store has a low margin. They can't afford to waste money on expensive surveillance cameras, since all they really want to be able to do is see if someone takes something off a shelf and stuffs it in their shirt or down their pants. For that purpose, less expensive, low-resolution cameras are good enough."

"What's your point?"

"These computers are secured with cables so they can't grow legs and walk away. That means it's not as important to spend money on expensive cameras to watch over them."

"Okay," she said, not really knowing what he was getting at.

Kate noticed a paunchy man down the aisle a ways looking at her. He was wearing overly baggy jean shorts and flip-flops. She didn't know if the man was looking at her because she was a woman, or because maybe he thought they looked suspicious for some reason. She was well aware of how men's eyes lingered on her. She partially closed and then opened the lid of the computer beside Jack's to make it look as if she were a customer checking out the merchandise.

The ogling man looked away when a pregnant woman with a young girl arrived at his side. He took over the helm of their shopping cart as they wandered on down the aisle. He didn't look at Kate again once his wife arrived. That alone solved the mystery.

"Since there is only a camera at either end," Jack finally went on, having also noticed the man, "that means that at their oblique angle they can't see what's on the screens of the computers in the center where we are. They won't be able to see what I'm going to show you."

"That's why you wanted to use an electronics store?"

Jack nodded. "Unlike going into a computer lab at a university, we fit in here with other shoppers. Unlike a computer lab or an internet café, the cameras aren't watching as closely and aren't able to see what we're doing or what's on the computer screen. There is also considerably less supervision. Most important, we won't require a credential to access the internet and every one of these machines auto-erases itself back to a clean demo mode on restart."

"I see what you mean," Kate said. "So what do you want to show me?"

Jack looked at her out of the corner of his eye. "Do you remember when you were little, and you were afraid to go down in the basement because you thought there might be monsters hiding down there?"

"As a matter of fact, I do."

Jack had his left hand near the side of a computer. He turned it up a little to let her see the thumb drive resting in his palm.

"This is the key to the basement door. I'm going to take you down there so you can see where the bogeymen live."

CHAPTER THIRTY-NINE

Jack covered the thumb drive from view with his hand as he plugged it into the USB port on the side of the laptop.

"The internet that people know," he said, "the internet they use a search engine to navigate, the websites, social media, the places they go to buy shoes, to listen to music, to watch videos, to pay bills, to do their banking, is only a very small portion of the web. There is probably a hundred times as much material that can't typically be accessed because it's blocked from search engines. That hidden part of the web contains databases, archives, medical records, scientific reports, government resources, and password-protected company websites that use nonstandard protocols and ports. That's the deep web."

"That's where the bogeymen live?"

"No. Where we're going is the vast layer beneath that. It's even more obscure. It's called the darknet." Jack casually glanced both ways. "Stand closer to me to block the screen so if anyone walks by they can't really see it."

Kate moved shoulder-to-shoulder with him, watching as he restarted the computer. When it came back on, it loaded a black screen that looked outdated.

“Why are you restarting from your thumb drive?” she asked.

“I don’t want to use this computer’s operating system for where we need to go. To prevent kids from installing remote administration tools on these computers, this store might be using monitoring software that could follow a glowing trail of bread crumbs from what we’re doing.

“We need to stay anonymous,” Jack said. “So instead of using this computer’s operating system, I’m running it on an operating system called Tails.”

She was momentarily tempted to think he was joking, as if he didn’t want to be tailed, but she remembered all the strange acronyms Brian in the computer department at KDEX used.

“What’s Tails? I never heard of it.”

“Not important, but if you really want to know, it stands for The Amnesic Incognito Live System.”

“Seriously? Amnesic? You mean it forgets where it’s been?”

Jack flashed her a quick smile. “And incognito; concealed identity. Plug in the USB, restart, and the computer is being run from the Tails operating system rather than the system installed on the computer. Tails doesn’t store data locally. Once I pull out the thumb drive there is nothing left behind to find.

“To get into the darknet you need to run Tor,

which I also have on this thumb drive. Tor stands for The Onion Router," he said before she could ask as he opened the browser. "Unlike the places you're used to going that end in dot com, most of the addresses in the darknet end in dot onion. You need to use the Tor browser to access those addresses. Hence the reason the darknet is sometimes called Onionland."

Kate pressed her fingers to her forehead. "I'm getting a headache from this stuff."

"I'm not trying to give you a headache, but it's important for your longevity that you begin to understand how some of these super-predators operate in order to help you understand the extent of the nesting phenomenon."

"Nesting phenomenon?"

"Yes," he said without explaining. "Some of the most dangerous people hunting you want anonymity, too, so they are hiding in the darknet. If you want to stay alive, you need to know what they're doing and how they're doing it."

Kate gestured at the screen. "You mean they do all this?"

"The smart ones do. And it's the smart ones who are the most dangerous."

"So bad guys developed the darknet as a way to hide?"

"Actually, it was developed by the US Navy, primarily for ultra-secure communications."

"So it's more secure than the regular internet?"

"As far as anonymity, yes. Instead of data going directly through known, traceable points, the darknet uses layers of relays, like the layers of an onion. Each node only knows the identity of the next relay—not the point of origin or the destination—and those handoffs among relays are in constant flux as they're bounced all around the globe.

"In addition, each hop is encrypted. No one can track you down, no one can find out who you are, no one knows where you've been, and no one knows what you are doing. You are anonymous and what you do on the darknet is unknown, unless you disclose any of that information either deliberately or unintentionally.

"The darknet was eventually released into the public domain to enable people in countries with repressive regimes to communicate and remain anonymous. Were those governments to discover who these dissidents were, they would be thrown in prison or executed."

"Well, that all sounds like a pretty good thing, then."

Jack cast her a look. "That side of it is, but when no one can be identified or traced, it also becomes a perfectly secure place to conduct illegal activity.

"In the darknet criminals are anonymous. Law enforcement doesn't know who they are or what they're doing. Search engines work by using spiders—algorithms that crawl through web servers and follow every link down every possible avenue of the web. The structure of the darknet makes that impossible, so there are no search engines down here. Tor simply gives you a connection into this underworld—a stairway down into the darkness."

"Then how do you find anything?"

"It's not easy. Webpages there are alpha-numeric, so you can't look for sites based on their names. In a lot of cases you need to know the specific address of where you want to go. There are also a few popular directories and star reviews of sites that sell illegal items, like drugs. They provide links with headings like 'Good source for drugs here' and 'A-plus forged documents.' They read like a terrorist's private phone book."

"If it's so secret, then why couldn't we just have used my computer?" She glanced around. "Then we wouldn't need to be sneaking around doing it here."

"Because if it's illegal you can buy it there. You can buy everything from young girls to uranium. You can hire a hit. You can buy and sell everything from counterfeit driver's licenses and passports to security passes for nuclear sites.

"Anonymity makes it a thriving underworld of illegal activity. More and more it's becoming a meeting place for hackers to join forces. It's the originating source of sophisticated hacking attacks against everything from banks to military installations to infrastructure to insulin pumps."

"And KDEX, the place where I work," Kate said. "We're under continual attack from hackers."

Jack nodded as he glanced around. "The thing is, because there is so much illegal activity taking place on the darknet, the government and law enforcement agencies obviously want to know who is using it and why.

"All of this makes the activity on the darknet a national-security threat. Tor is considered a major tool of subversive, criminal, and terrorist activity, so the NSA has packet collection and inspection systems at every level of the regular internet. Simply using a normal search engine to look up information about the darknet, or using key-words in emails or texts, triggers tripwires at the NSA and they grab all of the data associated with you. They grab everything—mobile phone GPS tracking data, your cloud data, your travel, instant messages, emails, photos, the content of social media. All of it. Programs sift through that massive volume of material to come up with a threat analysis based on your patterns of activity.

"From that they generate a smaller list of suspicious activity for more focused investigation. Auditors review all of that material, including listening to recordings of all your phone calls, reviewing your text messages, and reading all your emails. If they find evidence of any kind of criminal activity they share it with other agencies—DEA, ATF, police departments.

"You don't want to get caught up in that net.

"A lot of very bad players also want to know who is using the darknet. Beyond the ability to scam people out of their money—say, people wanting to buy illegal guns—imagine the blackmail potential."

Kate lifted her hands in frustration. "So then it's not so safe."

"Well, the problem is, by using your own computer, they know who you are and they know that you're going on the darknet, but they don't know where you go or what you do there."

Kate ran her fingers back into her hair. "This is so confusing. They know you're going there, but yet they don't?"

"I know that it's a lot to take in all at once, but for a start I need to you understand the big picture."

"I'm trying," she muttered.

"Think of it this way. Imagine that there is a really big office building. That's the darknet. In that building you could go to a room to conduct top-secret government business; or into a room to have a political discussion with dissidents about overthrowing the government of Iran; or a chat room on racist topics; or a room to launder money; or a room to buy child porn; or a room to buy drugs, or guns, or to hire an assassin.

"The government wants very much to know about those illegal activities going on in some of those rooms, but they can't see where you went in that building and they don't know who's running the rooms. What their packet-collection software does do is to act kind of like an FBI stakeout sitting in a car across the street, watching the building with binoculars."

"What good does that do?"

"It sends up a red flag. They knew you went in there. Is it a threat to national security? Knowing when you go onto the darknet—those FBI agents on stakeout watching you go into the building—becomes one element in the three-dimensional software that I mentioned before used to analyze everything electronic in your life."

Kate took a quick look around. "So they would know that you're logged in here, going onto the darknet right now?"

"Yes, but because of the kind of operating system and software I'm using, and the fact that I'm using that software on a machine in a store, not my own computer, it makes determining who we are extremely difficult. We're adding layer upon layer to hide ourselves from their tracking systems. It would be unprecedented investigative work and gobs of resources just to determine that it's Jack Raines standing here in this store going onto the darknet. And they still wouldn't know what we're doing.

"Not even recordings on the store's cameras will tell them anything other than that two rather fuzzy figures were looking at computers on sale. When we leave, the computers will still be sitting here. As soon as I pull out this thumb drive, everything is gone off of it. If they followed us and came in here and went through this computer, there would be nothing on it to find. Some stores use desktop auditing software that captures screen images of what customers are doing, but we would have to be running the computer's regular operating system. Because we booted into this thumb drive, using Tails, those tools aren't running."

"Jeez, Jack, you are one sneaky character."

"That's why I'm still alive. You need to understand that government agencies that would be tracking you would be doing so to try to protect national security, and while that's all well and good and you're not actually doing anything wrong, law enforcement agencies don't know that and wouldn't understand your ability. It might as well be voodoo. They wouldn't want to believe you, so they wouldn't try. They would think you were only making up excuses to hide something dangerous."

"What is there for them not to believe?"

"Well, for instance that you and I killed two men last night in self-defense. Yes, we might be able to prove it, but how many years would that take? We would have to prove your ability, prove everything that's happening, get everyone to believe that there is an entire hidden layer of super-predators hunting people like you. Do you think they would believe that? Why would they want to? There are plenty of officials and prosecutors who are only interested in a conviction. You could easily become an innocent person sent to prison for murder."

"Oh," she said with sudden realization.

"Modern forensics are incredibly good. Your safety depends on making sure no one has any reason to look at you in the first place. Getting on the radar of any agency or police force would only result in your life becoming tangled in all kinds of complications. They can turn your life into a living hell.

"Cops are the good guys—just look at AJ. But even AJ was smart enough not to tell her department about what she was doing with John, or what she knew about you. She was protecting you. She had very sound reasons for doing that."

"I think I'm starting to see what you mean."

"Good, because if for some reason you get on the radar of law enforcement, or are connected to anything from last night or what we're doing right now, while you're being questioned, interviewed, hiring lawyers, trying to get yourself out on bond, and having everything in your life turned upside down and picked apart, the predators who don't follow the rules will be hunting you from the shadows, waiting to catch you.

"In the darknet, digital information about everyone is a commodity. All law enforcement agencies have already been hacked and all of their data is for sale, here on the darknet, for these super-predators to buy.

"Your digital life is naked here, in the darknet."

"That's a pretty scary thought," she said.

"It is," he said. "But that's today's reality. It's worse for you because you are not like ordinary people. Your safety depends on you staying as invisible as possible—including from the police—in order to stay invisible to those hunting you.

"I realize that you didn't bring this on yourself, but that doesn't matter. There is only living or dying. Those hunting you don't follow civilized rules. To survive, you are going to have to avoid a lot of the rules you've lived by up until now. You need to learn how to stay alive. That's all that matters.

"There are no rules for you from now on except not to harm innocent people and to stay alive yourself."

Kate ran the fingers of both hands back into her

hair. "My god, Jack, I don't know how I can live like that."

He put a reassuring hand on the back of her shoulder. "I'm sorry, Kate. This is what I meant about the people I find not wanting to believe me. They can't accept the truth. They can't deal with it.

"There are only so many people I can help, so I have to focus my efforts on those who are willing to face reality. It's not easy, and it may not be right, or fair, but it's the only way I know of that you are going to be able to stay alive.

"I needed you to understand how this darknet underworld functions so that you can use it as a tool to help you stay alive. The advantage is that the bad guys don't know that I found their room in that building. They don't know that we can watch them."

"The hunters become the hunted?"

"That's part of how you stay alive. You have to become the huntress."

Kate regarded him for a moment with a sidelong look. "You mean I'm going to have to kill them before they can kill me."

Jack shrugged. "You may have to. You need to know how this works so that you have an advantage.

"I'll eventually give you a thumb drive like this one so that one day when I'm no longer around you can do this on your own to find out what they know. It won't tell you everything, of course, because only some of them know about this site. By nature they tend to be loners, but it will still be a useful tool. Maybe it could even help you to find others like yourself so you can help each other."

Kate suddenly felt a flush of panic at the thought of Jack not being there to help her in this alien world she found herself in. The thought made her feel vulnerable and alone in defending herself against things she couldn't yet understand and or even imagine. How was she going to defend herself against these predators by herself? How was she going to be able to live her life and stay one step ahead of unseen killers who were out there hunting her?

But Kate couldn't help thinking, too, about all those reviews saying Jack Raines was a fraud.

Was she getting caught up in what were elaborate delusions? Was this all just Jack's crazy paranoia, him imagining conspiracies where there were none? Or even seeing things just because he wanted to be in a cloak-and-dagger world? Was the night before simply a series of weird, chance events that were only sucking her deeper into his grand illusions?

Some of it was obviously true, but was she being gullible to believe all the things he was saying?

A lot of the professionals who had posted

reviews of his book had cautioned against falling for his phony "expertise," saying that he didn't really know what he was talking about. They said that he gave the real experts a bad name.

But on the other hand she desperately wanted to believe him, not because she wanted it all to be real, because she didn't, but because she wanted Jack to be real. She had never met anyone like him, and she wanted more than anything for him to be everything he seemed to be, everything she wanted to believe a man could be.

Kate took another deep breath. "So what are we doing in Onionland? What's hiding down in the basement? What is it, exactly, that you want me to know?"

"It was a lot of trouble to find this place," Jack said.

Kate caught the look in his eyes. "Are you saying that you killed people for this information?"

He lowered his voice as he leaned down a little closer. "I'm trying to keep innocent people like you alive."

She got the point.

"So what's this place you found?" Kate finally asked, suddenly hesitant about what he was going to show her.

Jack typed in a web address. It was alphanumeric, rather than a name.

"Do you have a good memory?"

"Pretty good," she said. "I'm good with facts and figures. It's part of why I'm effective at my job."

"Then memorize the address I just typed in."

Finally, after a long delay as the request skipped from relay to relay all around the globe, a black page with white lettering came up.

It said *Welcome to SCAVENGER HUNT*.

CHAPTER FORTY

Scavenger hunt? Scavenger hunt for what?" Kate asked.

Jack clicked to enter the site. It opened to a rather crude page with a list of names on the right side. The name John Allen Bishop immediately seized her attention. There was a check mark after his name, and underneath it said, "50 bitcoins."

Kate intuitively grasped why John's name was listed there. "How much is fifty bitcoins?"

"At today's exchange rate? Roughly twenty, twenty-five thousand dollars. Somewhere in there."

Kate glanced over at Jack. "That guy, the one with my photos in his pocket, had two rolls of hundreds. You said it looked like it was about ten or twelve thousand in each roll."

Jack nodded as he clicked on John's name. "I hate to do this to you, Kate, but you need to see what's going on here."

When the new page for John opened, the first thing she saw was a photograph of a mutilated human eyeball lying on a hardwood floor. Below that picture, she saw a photograph of John crumpled on his side in a pool of blood in his living room.

Kate stared in horror. The reality of the photo was worse than she had imagined. It made her worst fears real.

Under the photos, it said, "Scavenger hunt successful. The item has been removed from competition. The lucky winner has been paid."

Kate glanced around to make sure no one was looking at the screen.

"What is this site?" she growled in a low voice.

"It's a site frequented by killers who know about it. It's an information source for predators interested in the project—a scavenger hunt—aimed at eliminating those with your kind of ability. The fewer of your kind there are, the less the risk to them, the easier it is to prey on others at will."

"You mean, like what you did in Israel made it harder for terrorists to slaughter people, so they would want to kill people with my kind of vision that you were able to find?"

"Exactly. Because they are obsessed with killing, some serial killers manage to find this site. Not all the killers who come here know anything at all about people with your ability—only those super-predators who can recognize it in your eyes do—but the competition of this kind of scavenger hunt appeals to them. It makes them feel like they're part of an exclusive club."

"In other words, take part in a hunt to murder people."

"That's right. Some want to prove they're better than any of the others who come here by being the one to claim a victim."

"Who is paying to have people like John murdered?"

Jack exhaled unhappily. "I don't know. I wish I did because then maybe I could end this sick scavenger hunt. It wouldn't end what is happening or save the world, but it would help some of the people like you stay alive."

"Why would anyone create a site like this? How in the world can this even exist? Why would anyone go to this kind of place?"

"Those are questions born of your nature, your perspective on right and wrong. These people don't think that way.

"Evil, mental illness, belligerent passion, lethal anger, combative personality—whatever you wish to call it—exists in the nature of mankind. It's a part of mankind most people don't see—or don't want to see. This kind of person often idolizes evil, revels in it, seeks it out. It's a mistake to ignore this kind of thing because it's so offensive or because you don't want to believe that there are people like this.

"Any number of serial killers study other serial killers, as if they were role models, heroes to emulate. Most psychopaths don't experience anxiety. They have little to no fear of getting caught. With that deadened sensitivity, killing provides excitement they can't otherwise achieve."

"In other words, they get off on it," Kate said.

"Exactly. Killers want to be killers. They take pleasure in acts of torture and murder. They are obsessed with it. They are frequently sexually aroused by the things they do to victims.

"This site is a place where they not only share their tastes, but where they sometimes share information. There's a chat room deeper into this site, for example, where they discuss sex acts with the corpses of their victims."

"My god," Kate whispered, half to herself. "You've got to be kidding."

"Unfortunately, I'm not. This is a glimpse under the façade of civilization at the darkening nature of mankind. It's a peek at the cancer within mankind. It reveals a true, inner hunger for violence against anyone and everyone."

"But that's just criminals."

"You think so? While the darknet helps facilitate all of this, just think of how the internet—the internet you ordinarily see—is filled with hatred. The internet is awash with hostility for a particular politician, actors, famous personalities, or even another girl in school.

"And that's the regular internet. The darknet is an order of magnitude darker. It's like looking into the mind-set of what it means to be human beings."

"Not all of them," Kate said. "Not everyone."

"Not everyone," he agreed. "But more than you realize."

Kate wasn't willing to concede the point. "There are a lot of wonderful people out here in the world who go onto the internet to express sympathy and support for others. There's places devoted to helping others in need. There isn't only darkness, there's a lot of light as well."

Jack nodded. "It all makes up the nature of mankind. It's all part of the struggle for what we will be."

Kate watched a couple of teenage boys busily discussing a gaming platform walk past before returning to what she needed to know. "So what's this business with bitcoins?"

"That's the currency of the darknet. For all practical purposes, it's untraceable. That's why these killers are paid in bitcoins. Transactions on the darknet for everything from drugs to hiring a hit on someone are done with bitcoins. There are sites where you can exchange them for cash. The exchange rate fluctuates similar to any other currency."

"If this guy who was chained up in the basement then killed John and took photos of it on his phone," Kate asked, thinking out loud, "then how come he couldn't call for help in the first place? AJ said he was chained up there for about three weeks."

"You said that you thought your brother

recognized this guy as the 'devil,' surprised him somehow, knocked him out, and chained him up. John undoubtedly took the guy's phone. Once he escaped and killed John, he probably found his phone, then took the photos and uploaded them to prove he had completed the murder so he could collect the reward."

"I guess," Kate said with a sigh. "Can one of these predators tell by the photo of the eyeball that John has the ability to recognize them? Can you tell?"

"No. That can only be done with a photograph on photo paper printed from a negative."

She gestured angrily at the screen. "Then why take a photo like that?"

Jack took a moment before answering. "I think the guy was being funny."

"Funny? That's funny?"

He put a hand on the small of her back to remind her to calm down.

"The photo of the eye he cut out was most likely an outburst of his anger at John, but it was also a kind of statement, saying that he could see John's special vision and he had defeated it."

"I still don't see how—"

"Kate, these are sick people. They're predators. You can't think of them through the lens of your sensibilities. They aren't like you and me. They get off on this kind of stuff.

"Some of them torture their victims for days.

They upload videos of the torture scenes over a period of time before they eventually kill the person. They want their audience here to see it as it's taking place."

Kate was stunned. "They post videos of torture? You've seen them?"

He didn't look at her. "This photo of John is enough for you to understand what's going on here and what these people are like."

Kate was sure that he was right. She had to look away from the still photo of John lying in a pool of his blood. She couldn't imagine how horrific a video would be. She couldn't imagine being tortured, helpless, and having it videoed so others could watch.

"Are any of the other victims like John? People with the ability like I have to recognize killers?"

Jack's brow twitched at the question. "All of them are. This is a site devoted to eliminating people with your ability."

Kate lifted her hands and let them drop. "But how do they find out about people like John, like my uncle?"

Like her.

"Sometimes one of them will spot a person with that kind of vision and stalk them. Rather than kill them right away, they keep track of them while they research the family to find others with the same unique vision.

"It's likely they somehow found out that your uncle had that ability, did research on his family, and added John to their list of targets. As they find out about people with your ability they share that information here."

"What if the relatives they research don't actually have the ability?"

Jack looked back over his shoulder at her. "They're killers, Kate. Everyone they kill, ability or not, is an innocent. A lot of killers seek out a specific type of victim. Hair color, physical build, age, that kind of thing. But your vision, your ability, is a universal target for their hatred. If a relative they kill doesn't actually have the ability, they don't care. Their view is better safe than sorry.

"Without knowing it, they are culling the human race of what in their view is an unwanted trait—like wolves hunting sheepdogs. Over time that changes the balance of human nature."

He went back to the first page that listed names. "Most of these people are dead. See there, after their name? The ones like John with a check mark have been killed and the bounty paid."

Kate felt sick. "Did you know any of those people with their names checked off?"

Jack deliberately didn't look at her as he leaned in on his arms, staring at the screen. "Yes."

"Were those people you tried to help?"

He stared at the screen for a moment longer. "Yes, I tried."

He tipped the screen down as a heavyset woman in a flower-print dress walked by, looking over each of the laptops on display, seeming a little miffed that they were hogging one of them. She leaned in deliberately to look at the price of the computer they were using. When Jack and Kate remained where they were, she moved on. Once she was past, Jack lifted the screen again.

He pointed. "This is what I came to see. I had been hoping it wouldn't be here."

CHAPTER FORTY-ONE

Kate saw a list with the heading "Active Scavenger Hunts."

She scanned the list of eight or ten names and blinked in recognition. "That's my name."

"Remember what I told you," Jack cautioned. She realized she had been a little louder than he would have liked.

Kate glanced around. "Sorry."

Jack watched her a moment to make sure she was going to remain calm before he turned back to the screen.

"It's been a while since I visited the site. I wanted to know if they had found out about you. Unfortunately, it looks like they have and they've added your name to the list. Most likely because you're related to Everett and John."

"Great," Kate said under her breath.

He clicked on her name and another page opened.

Kate was stunned to see that the photos that had been on John's refrigerator were all posted there. She pulled out the photos in her pocket, the photos she had taken from the pocket of the man she had fought, the man Jack had killed.

They were the exact same photos. All of them had been uploaded to the Scavenger Hunt site.

Kate held up the stack, showing them to Jack, unable to find words.

He nodded in sympathy for her silent anger.

She glanced around, checking the people wandering the store, then pointed at the price for her life under her name.

Two hundred bitcoins.

"That's nearly a hundred thousand dollars," he said.

"Why so much more than for John?"

Jack clicked the back button so she wouldn't have to look at the photos of herself meant to help killers identify her. "It's a reflection of your ability. A reflection of how much they want you dead." He gestured at the page with the names. "No one else is bringing that much of a bounty."

"Some honor," she said.

The prices ranged mostly from twenty to seventy-five bitcoins. The highest she saw was one hundred, for a man named Philip Morgan. There was a check mark after his name. Underneath, it said, "Scavenger Hunt ended."

"Where do they get this reward money?" she asked.

Jack shrugged. "They aren't simply killers. Most are into all kinds of crime—robbery, cybercrime, drug dealing. They see people like you as a professional liability. This is pocket change for them. In Israel the terrorists had all the money they wanted for rewards to kill those like you."

Kate reached in and clicked on her name to take her back to the page with her photos. She scrolled down the page where there was information about her.

“That’s my Social Security number. And my address. That’s my cell phone number and my license plate number. There’s the address where I work, even the floor.”

She looked back at Jack. “Brian, one of the IT guys at work, said that he had gone to a lot of effort to keep information about me off the internet. He had been trying to protect me, the same as he did for other executives. He said he wanted to make it difficult for anyone I’d fired who might want to retaliate to find out any of my personal information.”

“Personal information is a commodity on the darknet. There is no longer any such thing as data security. That’s an outdated concept. Hackers routinely break into every company, store, agency, even the IRS, and scoop up all the personal information. They steal information on hundreds of thousands of people at a time, every hour, every day, seven days a week.

“If you work for the government, have health insurance, have a bank account, a credit card, a driver’s license, have a mortgage, shop online, have email, are employed, visit social media, register a new appliance, own a car or home, then your personal information has already been stolen and your digital life is for sale somewhere on the darknet.

"Large criminal organizations have sophisticated data-mining departments that sort all that information, slice it and dice it, in any way their customers want. You can buy identities by the dozen or by the tens of thousands, complete with account numbers, passwords, and your mother's maiden name.

"Everyone's digital life is available for sale on the darknet. People have no idea how easy it is for bad guys to get access to this kind of personal data.

"Your information would have revealed that you do security audits and have a security clearance. That makes you a much higher-value target. It's easy to kill someone like John. It's a lot harder to kill someone who deals in security issues. Your security job is an indication that you have above-normal intelligence, which means you are likely to have a more highly developed ability. A higher ability is a larger danger to them, so that makes you a higher-value target.

"You said that a man was arrested near your office and he had your name on a piece of paper in his pocket?"

"That's right."

"He most likely got your name and where you work here, on this site. By how amateurish he was, he was probably a lurker on this site and didn't really understand its broader purpose. He probably simply got the bright idea that he could make a lot of money and have some excitement doing it. He was undoubtedly coming to kill you."

"And he killed Wilma instead . . ." Kate said.

"Like I said, an amateur. A super-predator who can recognize your ability by your eyes would have plotted to capture you so he could have done whatever he wanted with you."

"Can you change it?" Kate asked, feeling a crushing sense of vulnerability. "Can you go in there and change this information to make it harder to find me?"

"No, unfortunately there's no way for me to do that," Jack said. "Wish I could, but I don't have the site credentials to do that sort of thing."

"So then they know everything about me. They can find me."

"If you continue your standard patterns, I'm afraid so. That's why it was so important for me to get to you first so I could help you."

"Help me? Good god, Jack," she said as she gestured angrily at the screen, "how the hell are you going to help me if some psychopath can find me this easily?"

"Kate," he said, speaking softly to get her to do the same, "I can't change the world. The only thing I can do is show you what's really going on and then teach you what I can so that you can better protect yourself. Last night you proved that you have it in you to do what you must to live. You didn't give in to being a victim. You fought for your life. Whether or not you choose to defend yourself in the bigger picture, or how you choose to do it, is up to you."

He wiped a hand back across his eyes. "I can't make this all go away, Kate. I wish I could, but I can't. I'm only the messenger."

"I'm sorry." She laid a hand on his arm. "I know this isn't your fault."

He showed her a sad smile as he started to reach for the thumb drive.

"Wait," she said, grabbing his wrist. "What's this?"

She moved the cursor to a small box on the left side that said, "Book reviews. Earn extra money."

"It's not important," Jack said, making a dismissive face. "Just more of their hostility."

Kate clicked on it anyway. It slowly opened a page that had a picture of Jack's book. Beneath that was the back of the book, showing a photo of Jack standing with his arms folded, leaning a shoulder against a tree. In an unusual twist on the typical author photo, his face was in shadow just enough to be unrecognizable, except that Kate could recognize him by his body language.

Kate read the copy under the book. It explained that the Scavenger Hunt site was paying one bitcoin for each negative review of the book planted on sites like Amazon.

Reviews had to be posted on the Scavenger

Hunt site first to prove they originated with a member of the site, and then that same review had to later appear in the reviews section of online book retailers. If it did, it would earn a bitcoin.

Kate clicked on the link to the reviews. When the page opened she scanned down the long list. With a sense of icy recognition, she saw that they were the reviews she had read the night she had met AJ. Under each review it said, "One bitcoin awarded."

She scrolled down and at the end there was a section with directions on writing an effective negative review. It advised saying that you were a law enforcement professional, or a criminal profiler, or some kind of authority figure on the subject. It gave pointers on how to be dismissive of the book, giving key words to use. Kate recognized all the pointers as having been used in the reviews she read.

She felt sick to her stomach.

She felt her face turning red at the memory of how she had been swayed by those reviews. She prided herself on being a levelheaded investigator able to see through false narratives . . . and yet she had been duped. Worse, duped by calculating, corrupt people with an agenda.

"These people don't like the public to know about them, so they try to discredit the book." Jack gestured to the screen. "When they post these bad reviews, it encourages others to join in. The internet gives people a way to act out while remaining anonymous. It gives them keyboard courage, much the same way hiding behind white pointed hoods gives members of the Ku Klux Klan courage.

"Terrorists have embraced the internet because it's a perfect environment to incubate hatred and slaughter. It's all the same base mechanism at work."

She looked back over her shoulder at him. "But this isn't fair. Can't you do something about it?"

"One of the things you need to learn in order to stay under the radar is never complain, never explain."

"But this keeps you from making a living."

"The Israelis, remember? I do this because it's a calling. I have my own reasons for this book and for the new one I'm working on."

"But if the book sold better," Kate said, "you could find more people like me."

He suddenly looked tired and a little defeated. "I'm only one person, Kate. As far as I know, there's no one else with my ability, no one else like me who can recognize those like you. As it is, I have more people to help than I can handle. Most people I do reach don't want to hear what I have to say. The book helps me reach others, like it did with AJ, and that led me to you. The simple truth is I can't help everyone.

"This is all connected to something much larger.

This is a speck of dust in the mountain ranges of history. The darknet is a part of that connection. I have to keep my focus on what small part I can play in it. In that context, the reviews are irrelevant to my purpose.

"Much like the industrial revolution changed mankind forever, the internet—and the darknet in particular—represents another paradigm shift in the delicate balance of mankind, but this time it is accelerating nesting events in a negative way.

"I can't save the world any more than you can. You need to have the right mind-set—survival. This is but one nesting event among many in the great span of time, but one that is monumentally different.

"This time, it may be an extinction-level event."

Jack pulled the thumb drive out of the computer.

"I don't understand all of the connections you talk about, or how I fit into them," Kate said. "I don't understand what you mean about nesting events."

"Of course you don't. I haven't explained it to you yet."

"Don't you think it's about time you did?"

He peered at her for a moment. "Are you hungry?"

"Starving."

"Okay, let's get something to eat and I'll explain it."

Kate had the feeling that her view of the world was about to again shift under her feet.

CHAPTER FORTY-TWO

Kate dropped her purse, her jacket, and a sack of disposable cell phones they had bought at the electronics store on the bed as Jack went into the sitting room and put the plastic bags with their dinner down on the coffee table in front of the couch.

They had stopped at a Chinese restaurant and gotten takeout. As hungry as they both were, they didn't want to have a conversation while someone was sitting in the next booth. He thought it would be easier to talk if they were alone, so they decided to have a mini buffet in their motel room.

For the most part they had both been silent in the car on the way back to the motel. She wasn't sure why Jack had been so quiet, but Kate hadn't really wanted to talk. Her thoughts were in a whirlwind after everything he had shown her. She was still trying to digest it all. The whole concept of the darknet was a disturbing revelation in and of itself, to say nothing of the Scavenger Hunt site.

Seeing the photos of herself with a price on her life was chilling, but even more than that, it made her angry.

Kate checked herself in the bathroom mirror and, satisfied after ordering her hair a little, went back out into the sitting room.

Jack had been setting the containers out on the coffee table. When he turned back to her, Kate confronted him.

She took a deep breath. “I’d like to apologize.”

“For what?”

“I read those reviews of your book before.”

“You did?” He set down two bottles of water. “When?”

Kate opened her hands. “The night I met AJ. She told me about your book, and how it might help me understand the changes I’m going through. After she left, I went online intending to order a copy, but then I read the reviews and I didn’t.

“After everything you’ve done for me you especially don’t deserve me believing that such lies were true. I’m ashamed to say they influenced me.”

He smiled a little. “Ah. That explains a few things.”

She scrunched up her nose. “Can you forgive me, please? I feel terrible for how I treated you because of it.”

He dismissed it all with a self-conscious gesture. “Don’t give it a second thought. We have much bigger things to worry about. Forget about it. Really, I mean it.”

Kate smiled and put her arms around him in gratitude, laying her head against his chest as she hugged him tight.

The embrace had been unplanned. It wasn't like her to give hugs. But it felt right.

Actually, it felt more than right.

She was relieved to have cleared the air.

Jack put his hands on the back of her shoulders, holding her as she hugged him. "It's okay, Kate. Don't give yourself a hard time about it. It's just words."

She was relieved that her own impressions of him had been right all along.

"Sorry," she said again as she separated herself from him, a little embarrassed that she had hugged him out of the blue.

He gently grasped her by her upper arms as he also held her in his gaze. "It's all right, Kate. We're good, okay?"

She suddenly sensed a shadow of something in him, a hint of sorrow about something, a reluctance, passing across his eyes.

All of her instincts as an investigator, her intuition about people, and she supposed her newly discovered inner ability kicked in and came together in an instant.

It suddenly hit her.

"One of the women on that list meant something to you. You cared about one of those women who was murdered, didn't you?"

He straightened. "What makes you say that?"

"I find connections and put things together. It's what I do. I'm pretty good at it."

He nodded. “I guess you are.”

“I’m sorry.” She turned up a hand. “I’m sticking my nose in where it doesn’t belong. I’m sorry. I know—I seem to be saying ‘I’m sorry’ a lot all of a sudden, but I’m sorry.” Her own words felt incredibly awkward to her. She realized that she had inadvertently stepped into a very dark place. She couldn’t seem to make herself shut up. “Really, I am. I’m sorry.”

Jack was still looking at her, looking into her eyes that way that made her feel like he was looking into her soul.

“You have no need to be sorry,” he said in a quiet tone. “You find answers. Like you said, it’s what you do. You have sound reasons for wanting answers to fill in the blanks of things that are so new and confusing.” He put his hand behind her neck, holding her head for a moment as he looked at her. It was a gesture of reassurance. “If I expect you to put your life in my hands, you deserve to have answers to your questions about me.”

His beautiful eyes, the way his gaze stayed fixed on her, made her feel weak.

“When I came back into the country I landed in New York,” he finally said as his hand dropped away. “I stayed in the city for a while. I found her by chance one day. It was her eyes. They took my breath away.”

He flashed a brief, self-conscious smile. “It’s

rather hard to walk up to a woman and tell her out of the blue that you know she can recognize killers."

"Is that what you did? Tell her that right off?"

His achingly sad smile returned. "We were both standing at the curb, waiting to catch a cab. I couldn't stop looking at her. She noticed, of course. I realized that I had to be making her nervous, so I told her that she had remarkable eyes. She said that wasn't a very original line and challenged me, asking what was remarkable about them. She thought she was putting me in my place by putting me on the spot.

"Without a second thought, I said that with those eyes of hers she could see evil. Her face turned white and I knew in that instant that she knew all too well what I was talking about.

"She agreed to share a cab ride with me. In the cab, she asked if I was talking about 'Sid.' I told her I didn't know, and asked who he was. She said it was just a guy who worked in her building, and then she dismissed it, saying she didn't want to talk about it. I could tell that she meant it, and if I pressed her I'd lose her, so I didn't.

"I had worked with a number of people—like I told you before, it's my calling in life. I'd just spent five years in Israel helping to find men and women like her, working with them, helping them. It was exhausting and I was burned out.

"I had already done a lot of research, and I was

beginning to have a handle on the whole picture, beginning to see how it all fit together. Yet there are things going on that I can't explain."

"Like what?" Kate asked.

"Well, for whatever reason, I'm finding people like you more often than chance would suggest is to be expected. Same thing with your kind and killers crossing paths. It shouldn't be happening as often as it is. The odds of these encounters are far too remote—like your chances of winning the lottery. Yet it's happening.

"I suspect that it may be something unique to nesting periods.

"Chance or not, I couldn't let her get away from me. That first day in the cab I talked her into dinner, putting her at ease by promising not to mention her eyes. After that we had a few long walks in the city, met for lunch a couple of times.

"I could tell by her eyes that she had already crossed paths with a killer, and I knew she would again. I also knew how vulnerable she was. I wanted to help protect her and I wanted to teach her how to protect herself. I just didn't know how I was going to do that.

"She was one of those rare and wonderful souls whose smile brightened everyone's day. She was open and innocent and grinned at people all the time. She was a special person. People who met her instantly liked her.

"At the same time she was also one of those

fragile creatures that just didn't have it in her to fight back. She was petite, delicate, a wisp of a woman, physically, with short blond hair. Despite how delicate she was physically, she was a force of vibrant personality, but she wasn't a woman of imposing presence like you.

"She saw darkness in the world and tried to overwhelm it with sunshine. She didn't like me talking to her about danger. It frightened her when I did, so I had to back off, hoping that at some point I would be able to start to ease her into the subject so I could help her to be safe.

"Having that kind of vision is one thing. Fighting to survive is something else entirely. I've found that they are only rarely present in the same person, as they are in you. What you did last night fighting that killer was quite remarkable, not just your physical ability, but your inner strength as well. That part is so key that without it, physical ability is next to useless.

"Anyway, before anything could really come of it . . ." He paused to swallow. "Before anything could come of it and I could convince her of the things she needed to do to start to protect herself, she vanished."

Kate touched his arm. "I'm so sorry, Jack."

He pulled his lower lip through his teeth. "The guy posted torture videos of her on that site. Every day for a week. She lasted a little over a week."

"Dear god . . ." Kate, her eyes widening, put both hands over her mouth.

"Seeing that kind of changed me, you know? It made me kind of ruthless in how I go about what I do. It's also the reason I wrote the book.

"I've always had this ability for recognizing people who in turn had the ability to recognize killers. Somehow I'm drawn to them. I wish I had their ability, but I don't.

"Throughout my life I've run across a number of people with your vision. I have an inborn drive to protect them. I guess I'm kind of like a shepherd dog—I want to protect the innocent from the wolves. Too often the wolves take them.

"After . . . after she died, I had the idea of using a book to help bring some of those with the ability to see evil out of the shadows so I could help them."

"So you wrote the book because of her?" Kate couldn't muster the courage to ask her name. She didn't want to make him say it out loud.

He nodded. "I had been doing research and I had already started, but after she was gone I really devoted myself to it. I wrote just enough into the book so that those who had the vision you have, or who knew of them, like AJ, would grasp what I was saying and hopefully contact me. I didn't want to hear from a lot of curious people, I only wanted the special few to seek me out. The effort it takes to get in contact with me is a kind of vetting process in and of itself. It shows a certain sense of inner will.

"I wrote the book because of her. So, in a way, even though I couldn't save her, she helped me save others.

"I dedicated it to her, to 'R.' I didn't want to use her name, Rita, because I didn't want the killer to recognize it."

"Was he ever caught?" Kate asked in the dragging silence.

"No," Jack said, shaking his head. "He still visits the site I took you to. I recognize his postings. He's still out there, hunting people like you. I suspect he killed another woman—same build as Rita, slight, with short blond hair—but I can't be certain."

"So . . . were you and she . . . close?"

"No," he said, suddenly realizing what she was asking. He gestured to help dismiss the notion. "I never really got to know her all that well because we had only met and we had precious little time together. We never had the chance to get to know each other. She had a sunny disposition and was open and cheerful to everyone, but only up to a point. Beyond that, she was actually pretty cautious and private.

"She was just so special, though, that I thought maybe someday, something might come of it, that a real relationship might develop, you know? But it never got that far. Just . . . all of a sudden . . . she was gone.

"When she disappeared, I frantically tried to find her. I managed to hunt down the sweaty little goon named Sid she had mentioned when we first met. His main job was operating a floor buffer in the building where she worked. I knew the instant I saw him that he knew something. When our eyes met, he turned and tried to leave, but I stopped him. He put a hand in front of his mouth when he answered my questions. He touched his eyes a lot. He offered rambling answers to things I didn't ask. He tried to tell me everything except what I wanted to know.

"So I took him somewhere we could have a more private conversation. Because when I first mentioned her vision, Rita had asked if I was talking about Sid, so I knew that even if I couldn't see it in him, she recognized that Sid was a killer.

"He insisted that he had nothing to do with Rita's disappearance, but when pressed, he admitted that on occasion he had been with this guy, Victor, when Victor 'got into his crazy-shit moods about women.' He said he owed Victor a favor—Victor generously provided Sid with date-rape drugs. So, knowing Victor's type and to repay him, Sid tipped Victor off about this woman in the building where he worked. Rita."

Kate squeezed his arm. "It's okay, Jack, you don't need—"

"Sid was how I found the Scavenger Hunt site.

"He hadn't been with Victor when he took Rita,

and didn't know where he would have taken her. He said he met up with Victor in a bar from time to time. That's all he knew. I haunted the bar and put out generous offers for anything on Victor, but nothing ever turned up."

Jack stared off into the distance. "I went back to where I had Sid tied up and started to cut off his fingers, one at a time, each time asking him again where I could find Victor. After three fingers he finally gave me an address of a flop-house. But Victor had long since moved out.

"When I went back to Sid, I started in again, asking him after each finger where I could find Victor. Sid was in tears by then, of course. His skin was cold and pallid, his breathing irregular. I could see the carotid artery in his skinny little neck going a mile a minute. At that point he would have given over his mother if I had asked. I told him he had better think real hard and come up with a place I could find Victor.

"Sid was afraid of Victor, but he was more afraid of me. After I cut off one of his thumbs, he said that the only thing he could think of was this website Victor liked to go to, called Scavenger Hunt. He rattled off the site address over and over, like a prayer for salvation. I recognized that it was on the darknet.

"I went to the site. That's when I found the first two videos of Rita that Victor had posted. They were torture videos. At the end of each one he leaned in to the camera—he was wearing a stocking mask with eye holes cut out—and said, 'This is Victor, signing off until the next installment of fun time with this little bitch.' "

Kate felt the hairs on the back of her neck stand on end.

"I called my contacts in the Mossad and asked them to help me find something, anything, about the Scavenger Hunt site. I knew that she was still alive and I might be able to save her if I could get to her in time.

"But the site was down in the darknet, where the bogeymen hide, where monsters like Victor hide. As much as I know my Israeli friends desperately wanted to help me, they couldn't. They knew what kinds of things I dealt with, and what was at stake. I had helped them save lives. I know they would have done anything in the world to help if they could have, but they couldn't. That's how anonymous everyone is in Onionland.

"Victor posted a torture video of her every day for a week. He had her in a dark room, tied to a chair, with a light on her so she was all you could see. Her legs were bare. As horrific as the things he did to her were, it was clear to me that he didn't want her to die, yet. He wanted to keep her alive, keep the game going. He wanted her to be terrified. That's what these kinds of predators get off on—control and terror. After that, they gorge on the final act of killing.

"Then in the next video, he wrapped a tourniquet tightly around her left thigh—she had slender legs—and used a hand saw to cut her leg off just above the knee.

"He didn't gag her. He wanted everyone watching to hear her scream.

"In between her screams, she would say over and over, 'Jack, please help me!' "

Kate could feel her knees trembling.

"The next day he put on a tourniquet and cut off her other leg. By then she was delirious and I could tell that she had given up all hope. The only mercy was that I could see she was going into shock.

"I watched Rita die in that last video.

"My Israeli friends did the only thing they could to help me. They made Sid's corpse vanish.

"Victor still visits the Scavenger Hunt site. I recognize his postings, the phrasing he uses. He's still out there, still hunting people like you. The only way to stop people like that is to kill them."

Kate was frozen in shock at the story. She could hardly breathe.

Jack seemed to finally come out of his distant daze and looked down at her. "She's gone now. I don't know if anything would ever have come of us. We never had a chance to find out.

"Her suffering is over. I try to find comfort in that." For a moment he searched for words. "I wish I could have buried her, you know? It would have at least been something to have been able to lay her to rest. But her remains were never found.

"Sometimes I lie awake, staring up at the ceiling, and I see her. When I sleep, she's there in my nightmares screaming, calling my name, begging me to help her.

"The Valium helps me sleep without remembering the dreams. It's a blessing not to remember your dreams. You know?

"I always figure that if Rita and all the rest I've seen becomes too much for me to take anymore, I can always use the whole bottle and just . . . go to sleep and not ever have to dream again."

Kate, her vision watery, pulled him into an embrace, where he found comfort for a moment before separating.

"I guess that's why I can seem so cold. I don't mean to be, but in the world I deal in, I can't sugarcoat anything. If I do, I'm only hurting the people I want to help. Life and death are cruel and hard. I feel a sacred duty to at least give the people I find the information they need to survive. The rest is up to them."

He stared off into the distance again. "But I can still see her eyes. Rita had the most remarkable eyes. They were the eyes of an angel. I had never seen eyes like that before, and never again since—until I met you."

He looked down at Kate. "That's why when we first met I was stopped in my tracks when I looked into your eyes. You have eyes like hers. You, too, have the eyes of an angel.

"Except that in you it's more. You have the eyes of an avenging angel."

Kate, her chin trembling, pulled him back into the embrace, where she hoped that he could for a moment pause time and find a brief bit of comfort in her sympathy and understanding.

After those moments of time suspended, she pulled back and wiped the tears from under her eyes. She wasn't sure she was going to be able to speak, but she forced herself to find her voice. She knew what he needed to hear, what would help him more than anything else, what would be his anchor in the storm of a world sliding into chaos.

"Jack, I want to live. . . . Will you please help me? Teach me what I need to know?"

He smiled as he ran a hand down the side of her head. "Sure, I can do that."

She nodded her gratitude.

"Why is it," she asked, "that so many people around us, good people, people we care about, are being murdered like this?"

This time, he pulled her into a reassuring hug. "I'm afraid that we have the misfortune to have been born into a very dark moment in the long history of evil.

"But I'm going to teach you to survive."

CHAPTER FORTY-THREE

In the solitude of the bathroom, Kate stood in front of the mirror as she ran cold water. Tears tinted with mascara dripped into the white sink to spiral down the drain. She put a washcloth under the running water and wrung it out.

With trembling fingers she pressed the cold washcloth over her face, muffling her sobs. Every moment seemed to be worse than the last. Every day darker. She felt as if she were slowly descending into hell.

It was more than she could take. She wanted it to end. She wanted out of the corner she felt trapped in.

She didn't know how Jack could stand it, how he could not swallow that whole bottle of pills and just go to sleep forever.

By sheer force of will, Kate composed herself. She wasn't helping herself, and more importantly she wasn't helping Jack, by giving in to weakness. She needed to be strong if she was going to survive. He wanted to help her, but he needed her to be strong if he was going to be able to do that.

She stifled her weeping and washed off her makeup. She rinsed out the mascara and then put the cold washcloth against her eyes again, trying to get some of the redness to go away.

"Are you okay in there?" she heard him call from the other room.

"Yes," she answered. She sniffled. "Be right there."

When she came out she said, "My mascara was running. I had to wash it off."

"You don't need it. You're beautiful without it."

He gave her a brave smile that even made it into his eyes. She didn't know how he was able to do it. She returned the smile. She didn't know how she managed to do it herself. Two people offering the comfort of a smile in a grim world gone mad.

"Here," he said, returning from his carry-on bag.

He seemed composed. Maybe because she had given him a purpose. But then again Jack always seemed self-possessed.

He handed her two small knives.

"These are kind of . . . cute," she said, trying to brighten the gloomy mood a bit. She looked up at him. "But seriously, I can protect myself with these?"

"It's not the weapon that matters as much as the person who uses it. A plain old rock can make a deadly weapon."

"Why are you giving me two?"

"You have two hands, don't you?"

Kate looked at the knives. They had simple

textured sides to keep the fingers from slipping. Each knife had a clip along one side. They fit the palm of her hand nicely, yet they were so small she didn't see how they could be effective.

Jack pulled the knife out of his pocket. It was exactly the same as the two he had given her.

"One of the important features of this knife is that you think it's cute."

Kate was baffled. "Why is that an important feature?"

"Because it doesn't look threatening. A big, wicked-looking knife will scare people. Scaring bad guys is all well and good, but it's important not to scare the good guys."

She wiped her nose with the back of her hand. "Okay . . ."

"If the police should happen to see a big knife—in your hand or in your purse or find it in your pocket—alarm bells go off in their heads. You just made yourself a potential threat to their safety. They are instantly on alert and instantly suspicious of you, much the same as if you're carrying a gun.

"It may not be fair, but that's the new reality you have to deal with. Fair isn't one of the rules. The police are under constant assault from all sides and second-guessed in everything they do. They are increasingly vulnerable on the streets. They rightly feel that no one has their backs.

"A big knife makes them view you as yet

another potential threat and they will treat you that way. Even if you cooperate, it's to their personal advantage to go all bureaucratic on you."

He showed her the knife in his hand, pointing to the clip.

"Always keep it clipped on your pocket so it's right there just inside. That way it's easy to get to. You won't have to remember where it is. It's not going to be a million miles away in your purse in those brief seconds when you need it to live. You won't have to fumble around looking for it. Having it in the same place every time and pulling it the same way every time develops muscle memory. That gives you one less thing to worry about in a deadly situation."

Kate nodded "Okay, I get it."

"To open the blade you hold it like this, in your palm. Press your fingertips against the side to hold it tight against the heel of your thumb, leaving the top of the blade clear. See this metal stud on both sides of the back ridge of the blade?"

Kate leaned in a little and looked, then looked at her own knives. She saw what he was talking about. "What do they do?"

"It's a thumb stud to assist in opening the blade," he said, "so that you can open it with one hand in an instant. Use your thumb on the stud to flick the blade past its resistance point and it pops right open. Watch."

The blade snapped out so fast she could barely

see the movement. She recognized the soft metallic click she had heard the night before when he had gotten out of the car for the gun-wielding killer.

Both the top of the blade and the sharpened bottom edge tapered in very slight arcs to a wicked-looking needle point.

"The blade can't be more than two or three inches long," she said, looking at the knife he was holding. "That doesn't seem long enough to be an effective weapon."

"You don't need the blade to be longer than that," he said. "A longer knife is certainly deadly, but if a bigger knife, then why not a sword? It's a matter of what's practical. A bigger knife is deadly, but in some ways harder to handle, which means more opportunities for mistakes. If you make a mistake when you need a knife the most, you will die.

"A big knife is also harder to carry and to hide. In some places knives over a certain length are illegal and will get you in trouble. This one is so small it rarely raises any more suspicion than a nail clipper would. That's because people don't understand what you can do with this."

"What you can do? How am I going to defend myself with this little thing?"

"Well, for one thing, a bigger blade creates more drag so you can't necessarily cut as easily."

She looked up at him. "Wouldn't a bigger blade

give me a better advantage? More reach? More power behind it and the ability to stab deeper?"

"How do you peel a pear?"

Kate's brow twitched at the question. "I hold the knife in my fist, like this. Then I put my thumb against the pear and pull the blade toward my thumb, but holding it like this, so it won't slip and cut my thumb."

"You do it the right way—cutting the skin off the pear with the heel of the blade, right up next to the handle. You do it that way because it gives you more precise control. Would a twelve-inch kitchen knife make it any easier to peel the skin off the pear? Would you use the pointed end, out near the tip?"

"Well, no, that would be awkward. But if a two-hundred-and-fifty-pound guy is lunging at me, what do you expect me to do with this little thing? Peel his scalp like a pear?"

"No, I expect you to do the same thing as when you peel a pear with it: control the blade to make precision cuts."

Kate cautioned herself to douse her alarm and listen to what he could teach her. Jack obviously knew what he was talking about.

"All right, what do I do and how do I do it?"

"You already understand the basics because of your martial-arts training. If you had had this knife when you fought that guy last night, the fight would have been over in the first few seconds. You got in that first strike against the side of his head, largely because you surprised him. It was effective, but not lethal. However, it was a perfect killing strike you can use with this knife."

Kate frowned as she looked from the knife back up at him. "Okay, how?"

Jack put his finger on the side of her neck below her ear and drew it around and down toward the front of her throat.

"Your hand was already there, at his ear. With the knife, instead of worrying about punching his ear, you thrust out the same way, then pull the blade back toward yourself, cutting the carotid artery at the side of his neck."

He held the side of her head with his left hand, and put pressure against her neck with the fingertips of the other. "The carotid artery supplies blood to the brain." Kate almost immediately felt herself starting to get light-headed.

"See?" He released her. "If you sever the artery, that denies blood to the brain and the person will be unconscious in a matter of seconds and dead soon after. The jugular is there as well, so you're likely to get that as well. The jugular returns blood from the brain, so cutting it, too, speeds the loss of blood from the brain. It's remarkably fast. Remember the guy with the gun last night? Remember how quickly he went down?"

"I remember," Kate said.

"There are also vital muscles and tendons in the

neck. With a small, razor-sharp knife like this, you can slice faster, cleaner, deeper, and easily sever those tendons. Even if you miss the carotid artery and sever muscles and tendons in the side of his neck, he won't be able to hold his head up."

"What if you don't have an opening to go for the side of his neck?"

"Point your finger at me, like you're pointing a gun at me."

Kate did as he asked, imitating the way AJ had done it.

"Block the gun to the side, like this, the same way as you must have practiced for most of your life. You already have the muscle memory for that, right?"

Kate nodded. "Sure—it's a pretty basic move."

"Once you block the attacker's hand off to the side so he can't shoot you, then you can do a variety of things. For example, as you block, bring your other hand down in a fast strike with the knife, slicing the inside of his wrist.

"That cuts the tendons so his dominant hand won't work. He won't be able hold up the gun to pull the trigger, so you have effectively disarmed him. Secondly, you will have cut the arteries in his wrist and he will begin to bleed out. It's not fast like the carotid artery would be, but he is going to start to lose a lot of blood. Don't forget, cutting those arteries in the wrist is a tried-and-true suicide technique, so it's going to be a dangerous wound unless the bleeding is stopped.

"When people see themselves bleeding profusely, it tends to freak them out. Unless they're on drugs, of course, or a psycho.

"Either way, once you've done that, then it's easier to kill them as quickly and efficiently as possible. What do you usually do when you block a gun hand like that?"

"Well," she said, demonstrating in slow motion, "if the guy is bigger, like you are, I would punch up with my right hand into his throat."

"Good. Do that with this knife in your fist and you will cut his windpipe. If your knife slips off to the side, you'll likely cut the carotid artery. Either way, he's going down. The fight is over in the first few seconds."

"What if he doesn't have a gun and instead he simply hunches as he lunges in at me to power me to the ground?"

"Use a strike you already know how to do. Two quick jabs and in a matter of a second or two you've permanently blinded your attacker. Blinding them right off makes you the one in control of the fight, and in control of how you finish him.

"If you need to, the blade is long enough to slice open their abdomen, unless the attacker is really obese. Do that and their intestines spill out across the ground. Then they, not you, are going to be the one who is panicking.

"If you have to duck low, stay close like you already do and sever the femoral artery on the inside of their thigh. That will make them lose massive amounts of blood in short order. It's a lethal strike.

"If they knock you to the ground, spin around and cut their hamstring to cripple them. Cut the other one and they'll be on the ground. This knife is razor-sharp and ideal for that.

"You know how to fight, Kate. You know all the vulnerable parts of an opponent. You proved that last night. You simply need to add a blade to the moves you already know."

Kate looked at the little knife in her hand in a new light. It suddenly was a legitimate deadly weapon. The things Jack was telling her fit right in with what she already knew. She never really thought of martial arts as primarily a lethal discipline. The things Jack was explaining turned it into one.

"We'll practice to get you used to the most effective moves," Jack said. "Maybe we can use lipstick so you can make a mark where you would have cut me if you were holding a knife."

Kate was calmed by how clear Jack made the lessons. It wasn't as foreign a method as she had imagined. "That sounds straightforward enough. It certainly would have ended my fight with that guy last night a lot quicker."

Jack nodded. "Every second a fight goes on is a

second your attacker could do something just as deadly to you. They could shoot you. They could throw you down on the concrete and split your skull open. That guy last night had a knife he pulled at the end. You were tired and it was showing. You didn't even see it. He could easily have stabbed you.

"Just remember, there is no ideal method to defend yourself." Jack tapped her forehead with a finger. "That's your best weapon.

"It doesn't matter if you stab a killer intent on murdering you, or if you shoot him, or you split his skull with a tire iron, or you run him over with your car. It only matters if you live and he doesn't. There are no rules.

"And, remember, there are always bigger, more deadly weapons. You have a knife, he can shoot you from across the street. You have a gun, he can throw a hand grenade at you. You have a hand grenade, he can nail you with a sniper rifle from a mile away."

"That's not very reassuring."

"I'm afraid that's just the way it is. All you can do is be prepared and do your best. One thing to keep in mind is that these predators who are hunting you want to get up close, so on balance this knife is a good way to defend yourself.

"Keep in mind, too, that you can't always depend on being able to recognize a killer by looking at their eyes. You may not always be able to see their eyes. It may be dark. They may be wearing sunglasses. They may have seen you first and so they don't give you a chance to look at their eyes."

"The guy last night was like that," Kate said. "I saw him at my brother's house, after the murder, but I never saw his eyes."

Jack nodded. "That's what I mean. Keep in mind, too, that serial killers often try to present themselves as nonthreatening. The better he is at killing, the better he is at putting people at ease first. They can be charming, and if you can't see his eyes you may have no way of realizing the threat.

"Because of who you are, everyone is a potential threat. Don't let them have that element of surprise. Your advantage is in seeing evil first, if you can. Your safety is in ending a fight as quickly as possible.

"For example, that woman, Wilma, where you work? One punch ended her life. If you let a killer get in that one blow, it could easily be over before you have a chance to fight back.

"Your best defense is to be polite, be professional, and have a plan to kill everyone you meet."

Kate sighed as she realized he was giving her the only real advice he could give her. But it was discouraging to have her world turned upside down in a way she could never have imagined.

"In the meantime," he said, "I want you to practice opening those blades until you have calluses on both thumbs and you do it all night in your dreams."

"Got it," Kate said. She did feel a little bit more empowered.

Empowered or not, the idea that people wanted to kill her, and they had posted photos of her, was intimidating.

She flicked open the blade of the knife in each hand. It was a little awkward, especially with her left hand, but it was easy to tell how far a little practice would go.

Jack smiled his approval. "Good. Just be careful not to cut off one of your fingers."

Kate didn't think he caught the irony of what he'd just said. She didn't want to remind him of it.

"I'm sorry that I'm pushing this on you so fast, when your brother hasn't even been buried yet, to say nothing of AJ and her family just being murdered."

Kate nodded. "I understand. It's all right. You just keep pushing me. In a way, it gives me purpose and that keeps me from dwelling on grief."

Jack smiled and gestured to the sitting room. "How about we eat before the food gets cold? You gotta eat to live, right?"

"Right."

CHAPTER FORTY-FOUR

Jack opened the square white containers and set them out on the coffee table. Kate tore the wrappers off the plastic knives and forks.

"I wish I'd had the chance to read *A Brief History of Evil,*" she said as she stabbed a pot sticker with a plastic fork. "Maybe you can fill me in."

As she dipped a pot sticker in a cup of sauce and then took a big bite, Jack took a few pieces of shrimp tempura.

"Well, at this point it wouldn't do you a whole lot of good. You're well past that book and into needing to know about my next one."

"What's it going to be called?"

"*A Long History of Evil.*"

Kate paused a moment at such a chilling title. "So is it about evil down through the ages?" she asked before putting the other half of the pot sticker in her mouth.

He watched her a moment, apparently considering how to explain it. "You and I both want the world we live in to be a civilized place, a safe place of law and order. We want to live our lives in peace and for corruption to be stopped."

"What's wrong with that? I think most people would want the same thing."

"What's wrong with it, is that despite how much most people would like it to be that way, that doesn't always fit with man's fundamental nature."

Kate shrugged as she chewed. "There are times when things go wrong, and times when the world is doing better. I get it."

Jack made a face. "No, I don't think you do, not in a complete way, a way that makes the connections from historic eras all the way down to the Scavenger Hunt site and guy who killed your brother. That's what the new book is about."

That was too inclusive to make any sense to her. "So what are the connections you're talking about?"

"There are long eras when good is on the ascendancy, times of enlightenment when knowledge is expanding and lives are getting better. Then there are the opposite kind of times, when hard-won enlightenment fades as forces gather to bring darkness in around mankind. Those times are grim and life is harsh.

"There is great power behind the movement of these historical periods, so they endure for thousands of years."

"So that's what your new book is about?" Kate asked. "The history of mankind going through these long periods of good and bad times?"

"No," Jack said. "It's about the hidden force behind that pendulum, what drives it, what makes it tick."

Kate didn't follow what he meant. "So, the book is going to be about . . . what?"

When Jack finished a shrimp, he waved the tail for emphasis. "Basically, it's the story of how the mechanism of murder drives historical trends."

"So it's a history book? The history of murderers and the part they played in the world during different times?"

"Not exactly. You're thinking in terms of result, while I'm talking about causation." He frowned up at the ceiling as he appeared to consider where to begin.

"It's not about the people who murder," he finally said, "but about why they murder."

"My brother used to call those kinds of people the devil."

"There is no devil," Jack said. "We are the devil. The devil is us."

Kate paused. "What are you talking about?"

"What do a serial killer; a man who murders his children and wife because he finds responsibilities intolerable; an armed robber who shoots a store clerk; a nurse who murders elderly patients; a dictator who orders tens of thousands, or hundreds of thousands, or millions of people to be executed; a guy who shoots his neighbor over a boundary dispute; a gang member who shoots a member of another race for an initiation; government officials who cause countless deaths because they want to protect a pharmaceutical industry; people who are making a product that they know is resulting in deaths; a terrorist who opens up with a machine gun, slaughtering women and children; a man who kills another man in a bar fight; a motorist who in a rage shoots a woman for cutting him off; a wife who poisons her husband with antifreeze for his life-insurance money; and a twelve-year-old girl on social media encouraging another girl to kill herself . . . all have in common?"

"Jeez," Kate said, staring at him, transfixed, fork in hand. "I guess they all involve people being killed, but the causes of those killings are wildly different."

"It only seems that way. In order to understand why, first you need to understand that humans—*Homo sapiens*—have virtually identical DNA. A small group of chimps has more genetic diversity than all the billions of people alive today."

Kate frowned as she put one of the throw pillows behind her back for support. "How can that be?"

"It came about because of several pivotal periods in our history, history that can be traced back through both our DNA and our mitochondrial DNA."

Kate swallowed a bite of pot sticker as she held up a finger to stop him. "What's mitochondrial DNA?"

"Prehistoric organelles within all our cells. The

cell provides a protective environment for them. Mitochondria create ATP—molecular energy—at a cellular level, so the relationship is symbiotic. Without them, we couldn't have developed into who and what we are today. Chinese philosophy has always called this life force 'chi,' but it's simply a chemical reaction that provides energy to cells.

"Over hundreds of thousands of years, those organelles lost much of their own DNA material because living within the protection of the host cell it was no longer needed. While our cells have something like twenty to twenty-five thousand DNA gene pairs, mitochondrial DNA contains only thirty-seven genes.

"Only the mother's mitochondrial DNA can be passed down to her offspring, so through it we can trace the female side of humans back through history."

"Okay," Kate said, trying to be patient, "what does that have to do with lack of genetic diversity?"

"All of our mitochondrial DNA—the female side of our ancestors—can be traced back through mutation rates to roughly about two hundred thousand years ago, to the time of the skeletal remains of a female pre-human known as Lucy. She—or those like her—passed on their mito-chondrial DNA to all of us. They were the female component of our ancestors.

"That mitochondrial DNA evidence shows that there have been several critical times in our history when the ancestors of humans nearly became extinct.

"For example, roughly seventy thousand years ago, the eruption of Toba, on Sumatra in Indonesia, put nearly three thousand times as much ash into the atmosphere as Mount Saint Helens. It dimmed the sun for six years, leading to the complete disruption of the environment and all living species.

"It's estimated that the pre-human population of the world fell to perhaps no more than two thousand individuals. Inbreeding of this small population narrowed genetic diversity.

"Then, about sixty thousand years ago, a male, a product of this natural selection of survival of the fittest, gave this relatively stable pre-human female DNA a mutation of the Y chromosome that started the rapid cascade of human evolution.

"Somewhere between twenty and forty thousand years ago, it's believed that this human population fell to as few as twelve hundred individuals. But these were now human individuals. They were like us."

"Wow," Kate said, trying to imagine such a world, "so at one time there were hardly more than a thousand people?"

Jack flourished a shrimp for emphasis. "Yes, but that dramatically overstates the reality of the situation. It was actually much more dire than it sounds. Remember, out of that total were those too young and too old to breed. With such small total populations, there may have been no more than forty breeding pairs—for the entire human race.

"We were an endangered species on the brink of extinction.

"But even that overstates the grim reality. It wasn't like what we think of today, where a couple comes together for whatever reason, and there were forty pairs of people, forty couples reproducing. That's not the way it would have been.

"This would have been a very hostile world of primitive groups struggling for survival, much like a wolf pack. In such a near-extinction period, where only the most cunning, the most brutal survived, the dominant male would have controlled most of the females for breeding rights. It is only those few males, or perhaps even one, who was the father of all future people."

"So how does this handful of males, or even a single male, become dominant?" Kate asked. "What did they do to win the females?"

"Now you've reached the central connection to everything.

"You see, to compete for scarce resources, and to compete for breeding rights, males benefited by killing off their competition—both to maintain breeding dominance and as a source of food. There was no benefit to allowing other males to exist to threaten what meager food was available, or to vie for the small number of breeding-age females. Killing also produced a food source for the dominant male and his breeding females so that they would live to produce his offspring.

"Killing became an essential component of the genetic makeup.

"So, these few males with a genetic mutation for murder had a survival advantage. They murdered their competition. Whatever the total population might have been, most would have been females, with these few males exerting their breeding rights.

"For those few males, killing was the prime means of survival. It was in fact their key survival advantage. Their dominance through murder took them to the top of the food chain. They passed that genetic trait on to their offspring.

"Those few offspring interbred, helping to hard-wire that genetic makeup into our DNA, resulting in the lack of genetic diversity we see today.

"It is often said that the people alive today are the descendants of this single mitochondrial Eve, or more likely a very small number of these inbred pre-human females at the time of a population bottleneck, with the unique mutation of DNA introduced by one of those dominant males that bred with her. Their descendants started the rapid cascade of human evolution and population growth that came of their genetically superior offspring.

“We are all descendants of this primitive king, this primitive killer. He was father to all of us.

“In other words, we are all the children of these same few breeding pairs, this homogeneous ancestral population, these same few dominant killers. Lucy’s mitochondrial DNA, our first mother, combined with the Y chromosome of that dominant male, our first father, made us who we are today.

“We all—white, black, Asian, whatever—are descendants of that handful of human ancestors. We all carry the same basic structure of their DNA. We are all them.

“And murder is baked into our DNA.”

CHAPTER FORTY-FIVE

Kate wiped a hand across her face, her meal momentarily forgotten.

"If our genetic diversity is so narrow, and this gene for murder is carried in all of our DNA, then why are there so many good people? Why are there people who volunteer to help others, become doctors, befriend a lonely person online, let a car merge in front of them without going all homicidal, are happy for others, help a stranger who is hurt, help a lost person, love their friends—find and help someone like me the way you did—and countless other benevolent acts?"

Jack laid one arm along the top of the couch as he rested the ankle of one leg on his other knee. "That's the other side of the human equation that came from the development of a rational brain and lifted us up from the murderous muck.

"All of those good qualities grew out of the same survival mechanism. Therein lies the source of our eternal struggle between light and dark.

"Not every wolf is the leader of the pack. Some help rear the pups, some help hunt, some help protect the pack's territory. Not everyone was as strong or cunning as the dominant alpha males and females, so while they didn't have mating privileges until later when the population grew, they developed other survival mechanisms."

"Like running faster?"

"Sure. But you couldn't always run. People learned that they could survive and have better lives if they formed alliances, if they worked together rather than always trying to kill each other off.

"An entire village couldn't always run away and hide. So, if you know that potentially dangerous males are jealous of the food you have—say your tribe just took down some large game and had a windfall of meat—you invite them to share it with you to defuse their murderous intentions. In a fight they might take it all, so why not share some of it in order to avoid a fight?

"It's the same with acts of kindness. These traits proved to be successful survival mechanisms—defenses—to prevent being murdered in the event that you aren't strong enough to kill the other guy. Since these tactics were successful, they were passed on to offspring, helping man's rational mind to develop.

"Don't forget, a dominant male isn't going to go around killing every single person he can find. It's to the advantage of those less strong to be nonthreatening or helpful.

"But murder was now hardwired into humans, so even if you weren't strong enough to vie for dominance directly, you could develop cunning ways to kill stronger competitors for scarce resources. You made spears, knives, and clubs. Rather than sheer brawn, you used your brains to help you survive and kill if necessary. You formed alliances to kill others.

"When necessary you were kind and generous to placate a potential enemy, or simply in the hope that he would leave you alone, like when you're kind to a belligerent coworker in an attempt to inoculate yourself from being stabbed in the back. Stabbing a coworker in the back is a metaphor derived from the inner recognition of the ever-present potential for murder.

"All of this became the struggle that has been going on throughout our history. Murderers turn to murder to get what they want, but if they can get what they want without putting themselves at risk of injury, then that becomes a viable alternative. In other words, they learn to get what they need to live without always turning to murder.

"It's in the best interest of the weaker to offer kindness or booty to dominant killers as a way to survive. Any number of nations throughout history paid tribute to keep murderous invaders at bay. Not ideal or fair, but it avoids bloodshed.

"So, placation becomes part of that eternal tension between predator and prey. For crying out loud, there are cities right now, faced with withering crime, that are actually paying criminals they let out of prison not to kill people. This is civilization?

"Turning a blind eye is another way people try to get by in the face of evil, letting evil get away with a little in the hope that they won't become more violent. Victimhood becomes a survival strategy, as in 'Take what you want, just don't hurt me.' In this way, weakness and placation become a workable countermeasure to murder, so that becomes part of our nature.

"These tactics can't eliminate evil, but simply keep it at bay, so the fundamental genetic trait remains in our DNA. That leaves both good and evil always at odds. Sometimes those tactics work better and civilization flourishes, sometimes it only emboldens evil and you have wars and dark ages."

Kate couldn't help thinking of the way Jack said that Rita tried to counter the darkness in the world with sunshine. She was doing what Jack described. And she had still been murdered. Through the long perspective of history, Jack already saw the whole depth of her weakness and vulnerability. It must have torn him up inside to see the history of mankind played out with that one fragile woman facing a world of predators.

It was the same way with all the people he tried to help who instead turned a blind eye to it all. But in their case, it turned out not to be a viable survival mechanism.

"Jealousy and hate are important ancillary components to the murder gene in our DNA," Jack added as he ate a forkful of vegetables from a container.

"They are?" Kate picked up an egg roll. "What worthwhile purpose could jealousy and hate serve?"

"The emotion that manifests itself because of hunger is 'want.' Hunger, after all, is potentially a life-threatening event. 'Want' curdles into 'jealousy' that others have food and you don't. You are hungry. They are not. Jealousy stokes the drive to kill to get what you need. Your genetic makeup has already programmed you to turn to murder to survive. Jealousy therefore binds itself to the act of murder.

"Another male has breeding females and you don't. You hate him for having breeding females. That hate easily supports your internal justification for murder. It reinforces and gives support to your decision to kill the other male to get the females he has. Look at how common it is for men to fight over women and ultimately kill over them. A woman who rejects a man for another becomes an object of jealousy. Jealousy puts her in mortal danger."

"Most people usually get a divorce," Kate objected. "It may be bitter, but it rarely results in murder."

"No, like I said, we also have that reasoning side

that is responsible for all the achievements of civilization. But as mankind developed, brutality was self-perpetuating. Killing was a tried-and-true way for the most brutal to have food and breeding rights. The killers were the ones who survived to breed and in that way were able to produce offspring, so that trait of brutality was passed on to successive generations. Brutality became part of our genetic fabric."

"So that's what made it possible for you to kill those two men?" Kate asked in direct challenge.

"Absolutely. It's the reality we sometimes face: kill or be killed. We all carry that latent potential. You carry it as well. That potential is not merely to take what others have, but also to kill in order to defend yourself or your loved ones.

"But we are also reasoning creatures. Reason helped us figure out the world around us and that, too, helped us survive. So we developed competing survival mechanisms. Our intellect usually overrides that urge for murder because it provides less dangerous solutions to getting what we need.

"Even so, we all still have that hardwired DNA for killing.

"Because those inner forces of light on one side and darkness on the other are balanced on a razor's edge, it creates the back-and-forth of ages of enlightenment and dark ages in arcs of thousands of years. An age of reason allows mankind to make great advances that better our conditions. But when the evil side is allowed to establish nests among civilized men and grow unopposed, it finally becomes so strong, so widespread, that savagery once again ascends, bringing on another dark age.

"That struggle is the history of mankind, the history of us. From bad times to good times and back to bad times again."

Kate shot him a skeptical look. "But those dark ages are past history. We've mostly outgrown that savage side of our nature."

"You think we're so civilized now? So much more highly developed, now? Tell me, what are most video games?"

"I don't know," she said. "What?"

"Practice at killing people. From first-person shooter to war on an interplanetary scale, they are all ways to rehearse killing. Why are such games so successful? Because they feed mankind's inborn genetic drive to kill. If not, why else would people enjoy practice at killing?"

"But that's just the people who play those games," Kate objected, feeling helpless against the tide rising in around her. "It's not everyone. Just a certain segment of people."

"What is the central theme of books, movies, TV? Murder. Murder is central to everything we do because murder is part of our genetic makeup. In societies that don't have those kinds of entertainment, what do they do? They live by a more primitive and intimate association with murder. There are many places where women are stoned to death for 'crimes' like adultery."

He leaned toward her, fire in his expression. "Stoned to death. Murdered by the community. The whole community takes part in the murder. It excites the crowds because it's linked to our genetic makeup and the breeding rights of dominant males. Women who violate those primitive laws of nature by choosing who they mate with are eliminated.

"Killing has a long history of being public. Executions were attended by great numbers of people. Christians were fed to the lions. Gladiators fought to the death before cheering crowds. Witches were burned at the stake. Look at how people are slaughtered by the thousands in the Middle East for the crime of being the wrong religion. Islamic children are taught to carry out executions. Murder is a central part of their upbringing. This is a civilized world?

"Infants have the ability to fear before they are taught anything. Why? No one teaches them fear. They are born ready to fear other humans, because humans are by nature predators, killers. We fear other humans from birth.

"What do parents tell their children? 'Don't talk to strangers.' It's a part of the long human struggle between both sides of our nature—

predator and prey. In dark times it was common to murder all the children of an enemy people in order to eliminate them growing into a threat. Preemptive killing.

"Your ability to recognize a killer by looking into their eyes is a development of that inherent fear of human predators. It's the same thing, but fully developed."

Kate picked a small piece of meat out of her egg roll and put it in her mouth. "I can understand an infant being afraid of strangers, but I don't see how I could have developed this ability I have from that."

"Some people are better at art, or music, or dancing, or running, or math, or whatever." Jack circled a finger in front of her. "You have your own unique, inborn skill set.

"Over tens of thousands of years of evolution we learned the many clues that add up to threat. Our mind does it without conscious thought. Those instincts help to keep us safe.

"In your case, a genetic mutation gave you a higher ability in that particular area, one which others lack. You are able to see killers for who they are. They evolved a counter-mutation that helped them survive. They can see those like you."

CHAPTER FORTY-SIX

Kate took a drink out of her water bottle. He still hadn't gotten to the central issue she wanted to know about, so she asked him.

"So what are nesting events? I kind of get the general idea simply from the context, but I don't know exactly what they are or how they fit into this whole history of good and evil."

"The struggle of the light and the dark, conveyed through gods and demons, has been part of mankind's history for eons. They're an expression of what we can't see, a way of understanding the struggle within us all.

"We are god, as it were, and we are the devil."

Even as he said it, a wider understanding was beginning to dawn on her.

"What I did for the Mossad was to fight against darkness," he said, "against those who lust to kill, but it was only one place. What is happening there is merely a sign of what long ago began to happen in the whole of the world because that same mechanism is connected to all of mankind. It's not isolated to one area or one type of people. It's a universal connection.

"That's why I'm writing *A Long History of Evil*—to explain those connections and how they are all interrelated, how they all lock together into the puzzle that is our story."

Jack leaned in and picked up a container. He took a bite of chicken and chewed for a moment. The silence in the room seemed oppressive. She felt a certain sense of dread at the way concepts were coming together in her mind. Connections she had never considered before were clarifying.

"In some rare ancient books they described the growth of evil as 'nesting events,'" Jack said. "They considered nesting events to be the bellwether of change, the manifestation of a new dark era revealing itself. They tended to express these ideas in religious terms, such as demonic influence and the like, but the concept is primal.

"Life in those early times was as short as it was brutal. Death could come at any moment, on any day, swarming out of the woods around them, coming to slaughter them. Because of that, I think they were more attuned to the subtle indications of gathering danger. They saw the signs, heard the whispering hints of death approaching. They called these signs 'nesting events.'

"These movements between ages of expanding enlightenment and devastating dark times have centuries of momentum driving them. Change comes about over long periods of time as momentum gathers and picks up strength. These are swings that involve centuries and even millennia. Our lives are too short to perceive the changes.

"Rome didn't fall in a day. It began to crumble slowly. It took hundreds of years of hit-and-run invasions by a succession of savage peoples made possible by the rot of the character and drive of the Roman people themselves. At first, tribute held the forces of destruction at bay, but eventually brutality won out. The knowledge and advancements of mankind were lost as a great city crumbled.

"Don't get me wrong, Roman rule was no picnic, and it was often accompanied by brutal domination, slavery, and a murderous reign of successive despots, but it was a time of an expansion of knowledge and glorious compared to what followed when it fell.

"That's the history of mankind—a continual struggle between civilization and savagery. People alive today think that we've gotten beyond that, that we've reached equilibrium, that civilization has firmly established itself and mankind is advancing toward an ever better future.

"But what they don't understand is that evil, too, advances, develops, and grows. Evil, too, is always thinking.

"I've discovered in the course of my research that as the pendulum swings back from ordered civilization toward a darker age, the gap between predator and prey narrows. They begin to intermingle in new ways. You are a part of that phenomenon. You are given rise because of it."

"I'm the light born to fight the darkness?"

"In a way. Nature seeks balance. When evil rises, so do those who are meant to be the balance."

"Good grief, Jack, I'm no savior."

"No, but you are a part of how mankind evolves.

"During nesting periods there is an ever-increasing unwillingness to enforce law and order on every scale, from neighborhood gangs to international terrorists. It's that primitive trait for tolerance and placation at work. That creates the perfect environment for nesting events to spread.

"Even in the best of times pockets of evil survive. When the time is right those nests grow stronger. When the environment is right, it begins to spread out and establish new nests."

"This nesting of evil spreads?"

Jack thought for a moment. "In the ninth century, the Vikings were a horror show. Their brutality was as horrific as it was pointless. They liked to grab children by the ankles and bash their heads against walls.

"Just like what that killer did with AJ's son.

"With the Vikings, it was slaughter for the sake of slaughter, for the sake of killing any but their own kind. They spread out, going to new places, conquering new territory, taking women for breeding.

"That was a nesting event spreading."

"Sure, maybe in the ninth century," Kate said, "but in this day and age—"

"What do you think Islamic terrorists do with Christians or Jews they capture? Do you think they treat them in a 'civilized' or 'humane' manner?"

Kate didn't have an answer, or at least not one she wanted to voice out loud.

"We are supposed to be a modern, civilized nation, and those bad things only happen in other parts of the world. Cities here, in our country, are supposed to be centers of culture. But look at how gangs have infected our cities. Over a period of a handful of decades, that evil has spread to all of our cities. All of them, now, are infected with nests of this new evil. All of them are rotting from within.

"That's a nesting event, right here, right now.

"For many people cities have become a nightmare place to live, like the dark ages, where predators run wild and kill indiscriminately. That's an uncontrolled nesting event.

"We have stood by, impotent and unwilling to do anything as North Korea gets nuclear weapons. That is a nesting event.

"Iran has sworn to wipe Israel off the face of the earth and to destroy America, and what do we do? We help them get nuclear bombs so they can do it.

"That is a nesting event.

"Those things and many more, small and large, are all nesting events, their tendrils connected by the very nature of our genetic makeup. We increasingly are unwilling to put criminals in jail to protect civilized people. We insist that it is unfair for any number of reasons and instead allow them to roam free to prey on the innocent. The average sentence served for murder today is, what? Seven, eight years? Something like that. For murder. That is a nesting event—allowing predators to live among us.

"Evil does not remain a primitive force, the way we think it does, but networks in completely new and unexpected ways to multiply its power. Terrorists, for example, have learned to link together on social media and in the darknet. They stay ahead and out of reach of civilization. That is a nesting event.

"Nesting evil depends on the benevolence of good people to do nothing, allowing it to grow. It depends on both fear and ignorance to gain strength. In the face of such growing evil, most good people are simply trying to live their lives. They turn to those in charge, who in turn urge tolerance and understanding—the traits that our ancestors learned as a way to placate murders. In so doing, the murderous nature of mankind is allowed to become dominant.

"Nesting events take on many forms. When civilization ceases to be ruthless in eliminating the nests of evil growing in its midst, then evil becomes ruthless in eliminating civilization.

"Remember our excursion into the darknet?"

"It's not something I will ever forget," Kate said.

"Bring me your computer and I will show you a nesting event in real time."

Puzzled, Kate set down her food and pulled her laptop out of her carry-on. She opened it on the coffee table.

"Okay," he said when a browser finally opened. "Now type in 'torflow dot uncharted dot software.' "

A page opened, and a sinister-looking map of the world appeared. The seas were dark, and the landmasses black. There were particles of light flowing from place to place.

Kate was mystified. "What the hell is this?"

"I'll show you. There's a graph along the bottom. Click on the left side, at the beginning."

The bar graph started in 2007. Kate clicked on the far left. There was suddenly much less activity on the map.

"Each of those specks of light is an enormous packet of information flowing from place to place on the darknet. Now, click on the far right. That's the present time."

When she did, the world seemed to erupt with rivers of light, flowing in massive streams all across the world.

"This is a visualization of what is, for the most part, criminal activity. Each one of those thousands upon thousands of light particles represents enormous packets of information. What you are seeing is people buying drugs, buying guns, buying nuclear material, buying stolen identities, hacking intellectual property, buying human slaves, buying hits, buying forged documents, organizing terrorist attacks, hacking into everything from government sites to every company in the world to nuclear plants to oil rigs to aircraft to insulin pumps. Much of this is gigantic streams of data being siphoned from malware-infected machines and ferreted away to criminal syndicates.

"Notice where most of the activity is taking place in the world? This is evil gorging on civilization.

"Among all of this vast amount of activity, taking place every minute of every day on the darknet, is a tiny little site called Scavenger Hunt. A killer uploading your photos would be impossible to see on this page because that amount of data is so small in relation to all of the criminal activity taking place.

"What you are seeing is evil nesting, world-wide, in real time. This is a nesting event that is running out of control. This is beyond the reach of any law enforcement or the forces of civilization. You can see from that bar graph at the bottom how this nesting event, once incubated in the darknet, has exploded in just a few years."

Kate stared, her eyes wide, at tiny specks of light so small they were hard to see individually, yet there were so many and they flowed in such dense masses they formed rivers of light that entirely blanketed some countries. The specks of light streamed from place to place around the world, city to city, going from relay to relay, forming webs of light engulfing whole countries.

The scale of it all was nearly incomprehensible.

"Jesus Christ," Kate said under her breath.

"More like Lucifer," Jack said.

CHAPTER FORTY-SEVEN

Kate stared, transfixed at what she was seeing, at what it represented. Such evil was difficult to comprehend.

Jack gestured toward the computer screen with the container he was holding. "Like I said before. You can't save the world."

"I believe you," she said under her breath, still unable to look away from the sight.

"This is a partial glimpse of the formation of what may be an extinction-level nesting event," Jack said.

"People go on social media all the time to express hate." He gestured again at the screen. "Here, in the darknet, you can see that same kind of hate and envy put into action. Mankind has never before had such a perfect vehicle for spreading evil.

"Think we live in enlightened, civilized times? This is a real-time depiction of the Huns coming over the barricades."

Kate looked from the screen to Jack. "So how does all of this become an extinction-level nesting event?"

Jack picked with his fork at the food in the container he was holding. "Remember how I told you that appeasement was a mechanism to counter the aggressive nature of others? We promised the North Koreans food—booty—if they wouldn't develop nuclear weapons. They developed nuclear weapons anyway.

"The result of appeasement is a rogue nation willing to use a missile to explode a nuclear weapon in the atmosphere over the West Coast. The electromagnetic pulse would wipe out most of our electrical and technological infrastructure, effectively sending us back to preindustrial times.

"In the insanely deluded notion that defending ourselves was immoral, we long ago denounced missile defense systems. So now we're naked to an attack from a country as small and backward as North Korea. They have the potential to destroy the United States and start a world war. All because we allowed a nesting event to take hold.

"In a deal with the devil we let Iran have nuclear weapons. This, after making that same mistake with North Korea.

"Their leaders have told us in every way possible that they intend to wipe Israel off the map and that we are the great Satan and they will destroy us. To appease them, we gave them nukes.

"China and Russia don't really want to get into a nuclear war because they know they, too, would die.

"Iran likewise knows that nuking Israel will start a catastrophic nuclear world war. But they think their purpose on earth is to start an end-times war. They may decide to die in such a war. We gave them the means.

"So, if you're Israel, and you know that Iran has vowed to kill you, and they have for years been sending rockets into your country and continually carrying out terrorist attacks killing innocent women and children to prove that they mean what they say, what do you do? Does the killer DNA in you decide that you need to kill Iran first? After all, that is the purpose of that genetic killer configuration: survival.

"Once nuclear weapons are used, there is no stopping it. Every country is going to feel they have to strike. Do you know the result of such an event?"

"Nuclear winter," Kate said.

Jack nodded. "An extinction-level event."

Kate studied his face. He looked down into the container, stabbing something with his fork. He had spent years in the Middle East. He had worked with the Mossad. She wondered how much he knew. Whatever he knew, his expression didn't betray it.

"Is that what you think will happen? Nuclear war as the final result of man's murderous genetic nature?"

He finally looked up into her eyes. "Actually, no."

Kate was surprised. "No? But you said that this nesting period was an extinction-level event."

Jack chewed for a moment and then gestured to

the computer screen with his fork. "There's your extinction-level event, right there."

"I don't follow."

"Nukes mean that everyone dies. Sure, there are people crazy enough to do it, but what did I say about our genetic code?"

Kate frowned. "You mean that murder is hard-wired into us?"

"Right. Murder. Not suicide. Murder. The purpose of murder is to be the survivor, to have all the spoils from killing."

Kate looked at the computer screen. "So then how does this fit? How is this an extinction-level nesting event?"

Jack waited until she looked back at him. "Not nuclear winter. Cyber winter."

"Cyber winter? I'm not sure I follow."

"Everyone around the world is preparing for cyber warfare. It's not merely countries like China and Russia preparing cyber attacks, it's North Korea and all of the Islamic world. Terrorists are preparing to unleash a new kind of terror. Hacktivists, lusting for anarchy, want to bring down Western civilization. The thing they all have in common is that they all want to be the ones left alive.

"Military hacking all over the world is staffed by massive organizations, larger than any nuclear program. They've been hard at work, planting routines in everything electronic.

"It's like nuclear war in that once it starts, life as we know it will cease to exist. The power grid will be wiped out in the first microsecond. No electricity. Not anywhere. Elevators will stop. Traffic lights will go out. Streetlights will go dark. Refrigeration shuts down. Gas stations won't work. ATMs won't work. Cell service? Nonexistent. Landlines will be out. TV, radio? Gone. Stock exchanges will be fried. Banking will disintegrate under the load of attacks unleashed against them. Trillions of dollars will evaporate into cyberspace.

"Air-traffic control will be wiped out. Hacked aircraft systems will fail. Planes will fall out of the sky like leaves dropping. Those crashing into cities will start massive fires. Hacked water systems will shut down. Pressure will fall. Without any form of communication, any fire and rescue will only be able to respond by seeing the fires, but they will have no water pressure to fight those fires.

"Hospitals will lose power. Their backup generator systems have already been hacked and once the attack begins, all of their equipment will go dead.

"Dams? All the sluice gates will open wide and in the darkness everything below the dams will be swept away.

"Police dispatch? Gone.

"How long do you think before the looting

starts? One night? Two nights? The fires they start will burn for weeks.

"There will be complete disruption of transportation, including food supplies. How long before all the store shelves are looted and empty?

"The world we know will be gone. The night will be dead silent except for the sound of gunfire from roving gangs who will own the streets.

"Policing will be crippled and evaporate in short order. Criminals and gangs will be the new warlords. The strongest will be in charge. Those who kill anyone in their way will be the new rulers. Men resisting the criminals and gangs will be slaughtered. Rape will be an epidemic. Women will become property. Slavery will be back in full force.

"Killers and thugs will be in their element. Good people will be out of theirs.

"With chaos running rampant and communications a thing of the past, there will be no civil authority left to restore any systems. A good many of the people who knew how to make things work will not survive long. All the systems that our lives depend on will likely never be brought back to life. Just like Rome falling, in an instant, our way of life will be gone. Our knowledge lost.

"Foreign hackers in China, or Russia, or Iran, or some hacktivist haven will be grinning ear to ear.

“That’s cyber winter.

“Right now, all over the world, there are vast numbers of people working to bring this about. Hack routines are already in place and ready to be launched with a keystroke. Unlike a nuclear attack, this kind of attack would destroy us and leave them intact.

“If Iran were ever to nuke Israel, we would likely turn the Mideast to glass. What will Russia do? What will China do? Do bombs start going in every direction, trying to kill before being killed? In that scenario life on earth would end.

“That’s what everyone expects. That has been our fear for half a century, way back to ‘duck and cover.’ That has been the stuff of countless movies and books.

“It’s mankind’s collective bogeyman.

“That’s what everyone expects.

“That’s why it will never happen.”

Jack gestured at the computer screen again.

“There is the extinction-level nesting event in process. Look at it—it respects no boundaries. It’s everywhere. The globe is its nest.”

CHAPTER FORTY-EIGHT

Jack waved his finger before the computer screen. "An infinitesimal fraction of one of those dots flying around in cyberspace is the photos of you uploaded by the predator who killed your brother and AJ's family being viewed by killers as we speak. You are now targeted from inside that dark world. You are caught up in a nesting event that is growing by the day.

"For you, the extinction-level event has already begun."

Kate sat in silence, overwhelmed by the enormity of it.

"I'm just one person who can recognize a killer by his eyes," she finally said, almost as if pleading for her life.

"If the world doesn't come totally apart—and it very well may not—then it will continue to limp along much as it has been, much like the world you grew up in, but getting gradually worse all the time, with criminals coming more and more to dominate our everyday life, with gangs growing, with terrorism spreading. Things will gradually get worse, but most people will be numb to it because the decay is so gradual they will hardly notice, too busy on social media expressing their hate and outrage at whatever has their attention for the moment.

"That's typically the way these great movements of history work.

"But make no mistake, the world is in the slow process of descending into a new dark age. It will take a lot longer than our lifetimes to hit bottom, but every day of the rest of our lives will be just a little bit worse, a little bit more unfair, a little bit more dangerous, a little bit more unjust. That's the inextricable movement of the pendulum.

"Meanwhile, predators will continue to hunt you. You can't change what the world is going to do; all you can do is live your life—if you want to live badly enough.

"If you aren't able to hide well enough, which I don't believe you can, that means killing those who come after you. It means staying off the radar of the police and an increasingly invasive government in order to stay as safe as possible.

"It means hopefully falling in love one day and sharing your life with someone. Maybe having kids. It means surviving and doing your best to enjoy the good things in life and raise a family. It means making the most of the world you were born into, the same way people have since the dawn of time."

"Except that I'm going to have to kill people if I want to live."

Jack gestured with his chin toward the door. "There are people going about their lives right now who are going to be murdered tonight. Perhaps by someone who kills them to steal twenty dollars. Perhaps by a hit-and-run drunk. Perhaps by a random bullet coming out of the night to blow their brains out.

"The point is, people die every day. Yes, super-predators have made you a target, but we could walk to the car and be killed by a mindless crackhead. We could be killed in a car accident. You could have a brain aneurysm and die in your sleep tonight."

"Jeez, Jack, you really know how to sweet-talk a girl."

"I'm just saying don't think of your life as unfair, or yourself as a victim. You can't appeal to some higher court to get a different life. Your life is a glorious gift, as is your ability because it will help you spot danger a normal person wouldn't see coming. Better yet, your ability could help save the lives of other innocent people. That's a good thing.

"It's your life, so if you want to live it, then you have to do what you can to protect yourself and live to the fullest."

"Okay, okay, I get it. Wear my seat belt and have a brain scan."

Jack smiled. "For you, it's more complicated than that. But it's still your wonderful, incredible, beautiful life. It's the only one you get. Live it, Kate. Fight with everything you have to keep it."

Kate felt sick. "I know, but I feel kind of trapped in a corner, with no one to help me."

Jack lifted a hand as if to volunteer. "You have me to help you. I'm not going to let you face this alone unless you want me to. I'm the one person who understands all of this and knows what you're up against."

"Thanks, Jack," Kate said as she dug around in the bottom of the container for another piece of chicken. "And I guess that I'm better off than a woman living in the dark ages, under constant threat from marauding savages. In a way, I guess I'm better equipped to defend myself than those women ever were."

Or Rita was. Or AJ. Or John. Or even Mike.

"So," Jack said after eating in silence for a time, "that's the central thesis of *A Long History of Evil*, that people don't primarily kill for territory, religion, mental illness, gangs, greed, sex, passion, or money, but because they have an inborn genetic mandate for killing, and those things are simply the external excuses—explanations that society attaches to acts of evil in an attempt to excuse it rather than crush it.

"No one understands what underlies all of those reasons for murder. Rational, civilized people are locked in a never-ending struggle with an evil that sees killing as a means to an end."

"Does your editor know that this is what the second book is about?"

"No. I've only given her vague hints to keep her interested. I haven't told anyone but you the whole concept."

Kate ate a shrimp as she watched his face for a time.

The connections were all becoming clear. She saw at last how girls on social media urging a more sensitive girl to kill herself were no different than a woman putting her baby down in its crib, strapping a bomb vest around herself, and walking into a crowded mall to murder as many people as she could.

Murder was hardwired into both of them.

They were all the same, all driven by their fundamental nature.

"What's behind all of the things that are happening to me?" Kate finally asked. "Why do people like me and super-predators seem to be encountering each other when the odds against that happening are so astronomical?"

Jack let out a deep breath. "From my research, I've come to believe that what you can do is an indirect outgrowth of nesting. The incredibly complex mechanism of nesting, which has evolved over tens of thousands of years, has caused some people like you to develop in parallel with nesting events. You're tied to them."

Kate made a face. "I'm just one person. Like you said, I can't save the world."

"No, but think about it," he said. "Two men who are part of the nesting event we are being drawn into died last night. You lived. Those two killers are dead. They died because you can see them for who and what they are. You drew them to you."

Kate raked her hair back. "Wait a minute, are you saying that I'm like a bad-guy magnet? That in the scheme of things I'm expected to be some kind of avenging angel—an angel of death?"

Jack fixed her in a hard gaze. "It makes no difference to the world that Rita died. Fifty years from now, a hundred years, or a thousand years, no one will even remember that she once lived. Had she lived, her life would have only been one tiny star in all the darkness and then she would have passed and been forgotten anyway. It was up to her to appreciate her own life enough to fight for it, but she didn't have what it takes to do that. A lot of good people don't.

"That's just the way it is. We are part of mankind, we are part of history, we are each a part of what determines the direction the continuing evolution of mankind will take.

"What matters for you to understand is that in times of nesting, for whatever reason, killers will more often cross the path of those like you, sometimes when you least expect it. Your choice is what to do about it."

"I don't want to lose my life," Kate said quietly into the ringing silence. "I want to live."

"Good. That's where it starts and ends. That's what matters. It's all that matters."

CHAPTER FORTY-NINE

Since you want to live," Jack said, "we need to talk about what to do next."

"Okay, what do I need to do?" Kate asked.

"You need to get off the X."

Kate picked up her container of moo goo gai pan again and sat sideways on the couch, tucking her legs under herself. "I don't know what you mean."

"When you're marked for death, and you're standing on the spot where people are aiming, you are standing on the X. The best thing you can do to improve your odds of living is to get off the X.

"When someone is shooting at you the most important thing you can do is move. If you stand still you're going to get shot. Moving targets are a lot harder to hit. That's getting off the X."

"Well, anyone would move if someone was shooting at them."

"No," he said, "you would move, I would move, but more people today than you would think, wouldn't. Or at least they wouldn't move effectively. Willingly standing on the X is a phenomenon associated with nesting events."

"Seems hard to believe," Kate said. "I think anyone would move."

"Really? Well, right now, the way you're living, you're standing right on the spot where the lunatics are aiming. It's like you're waiting for a killer to come get you."

"You mean you think I should move?"

Jack took a bite of shrimp tempura. "That would help, but it's really a bigger issue than that. Defending yourself is all well and good, but staying in a place where they've posted information on you, like where you work, your license plate number—all kinds of personal information—puts your whole life on the X."

He gestured with his fork. "Have you gotten any strange calls on your cell phone, or your home phone?"

Kate thought a moment. "No, not that I can think of. Just a few of those calls where you say 'hello' a few times and no one answers so you hang up."

"That was very likely a predator on the other end of the line, wanting to know what your voice sounds like, that kind of thing. He got your number off the Scavenger Hunt site. He was probably testing the number."

That thought ran a chill through her. Kate hadn't considered that possibility. She thought they were simply telemarketers or robocalls.

"Any serial killer, super-predator, or simple opportunist who happens to come across the Scavenger Hunt is liable to think to themselves,

'I'd like to kill Kate Bishop and collect all that money. Let's see, where does she live? Where does she work? What does her voice sound like? Is she home in the evenings?'

"Traveling for your job probably saved you more times than you know. It got you off the X without you even realizing it."

Kate held up a hand. "Okay, I get it, but I can't just up and leave. I have a job, a mortgage, responsibilities. I have to earn a living." She circled a finger over her head. "Motel rooms don't come free."

Jack twisted to the side and took the pad of paper and pen with the motel's name off the side table. He wrote something down, then tore the paper off the pad.

"Put this in your pocket. Enter it in the burner phones later. Keep it with you always or keep it in a safe place where you can get to it. When you have some time, memorize it."

Kate took the paper when he leaned in and offered it. She held it up, looking at the string of numbers. "What is this?"

"It's a numbered bank account. Just call the phone number I wrote down with it and tell them how much you want and where to transfer it. They will ask for an account number. That's it, there, along with the password to the account.

"Use it whenever you need money. Take as much as you need. There's more in there than you're likely to ever use—unless you buy a private jet or something. As time goes on, the amount will grow and you will probably even be able to afford that, too."

"What are you talking about?" Kate was baffled. "What is this? Where did it come from?"

Jack lifted an eyebrow. "If you really want to know, it's a fund I set up."

"A fund," she said, suspiciously. "Where does the money in this fund come from?"

Jack's gaze held hers. "From very bad people who died while trying to kill good people like you and me."

Kate finally used her teeth to pull a piece of chicken off the fork. She chewed as she thought about it.

"You mean like those two rolls of hundreds we took off that guy last night?"

Jack nodded. "That's right. It was a reward he was paid for killing your brother. I also have the guy's phone. If he has any bank accounts, I'll drain them. A lot of these killers are involved in other things, like drugs and any number of other criminal enterprises. Some of them have had a lot of money. Millions. I think it's only right that the money should go toward helping people like you stay alive. It's not easy living the way I suggest. This helps make it possible."

Kate wasn't sure exactly how she felt about such a notion. She stared at the string of numbers and the code word "Scavenger" for a moment. She didn't know that she liked the idea of spending money paid out for her brother's murder. It seemed like she would be using blood money.

"Money is just money," Jack said, sensing her reluctance. "Don't try to give it meaning it doesn't have. Money is neither good nor evil. It's not alive. It doesn't have a brain. It doesn't decide to kill people. It's just money. It was taken from evil people so they can't use it for evil. Now it's used for good—for helping people."

"I suppose," Kate said, not able to think of any good argument against the idea. She had bigger concerns. "But still, this city is my home. I don't know that I could live on the move all the time like some kind of drifter."

"I'm not saying you have to move around all the time. How you want to live your life is up to you. I'm only telling you that your chances of survival are improved greatly if you get off the X. I can't live your life for you, Kate, or tell you what to do. All I'm able to do is give you the best information and advice I can and then it's up to you to decide what you want to do.

"But let me ask you this. Are you going to be able to get a good night's sleep, knowing that your home address is posted on the Scavenger Hunt site?"

"Well I—"

"Knowing that the man who murdered your

brother had been standing in your bedroom, pawing through your underwear? Touching it, putting it up to his nose and smelling it? The same man who then slaughtered AJ and her family?"

A chill ran through her at the thought. "For sure I'd sleep with my gun under my pillow."

"I would hope so. That's one place where a gun would be a great defensive weapon and not a liability. If you get a secret vacation cottage or something, keep a gun with you there, too.

"Life is ultimately terminal," he said. "You could move across the country tomorrow, and the moment you landed you could be hit and killed by a bus. There are no guarantees in life, except that one day we all will die. It's up to us to decide how to live with the time we have.

"But my advice is that we should leave town," he said. "At least for a while. Why don't you come to New York with me? I need to go there anyway to meet with my editor. Come with me."

Kate stirred what was left of her moo goo gai pan as she considered.

"Monday is John's funeral," she finally said in a quiet tone. "I need to go to his funeral."

"That wouldn't be very wise. It's likely that some of these killers are going to know about the funeral. They are going to know where it is and when it is. Talk about standing on the X.

"They will have seen your photos so they know what you look like. You don't have any idea who they are unless you can see their eyes. They could drive by in a car with tinted windows and gun you down. They could be wearing sunglasses. They could simply spot you and then stay out of sight to surprise you."

"I need to go," she said.

Jack was growing impatient. "Why do you 'need' to go? After everything I've told you? How is it going to help anything?"

Kate's eyes lowered as she answered, not wanting to see the look she knew would be on his face. "What was it you said about Rita? You wished you could have buried her? That it would have at least been something to have been able to lay her to rest?"

Jack didn't say anything. The room turned dead quiet. Kate didn't look up at him.

"I'm sorry," she finally said. "I don't have any right to bring that up."

"No," he said with a sigh. "You have a point. I was only thinking of how best to keep you safe, that's all. I wasn't thinking of what it meant to you . . ."

"You'll go with me?"

"Of course I will—if you want me to."

She looked up at him from under her hooded brow.

"Sometimes safety isn't in running."

Wrinkles bunched between Jack's eyebrows as he watched her. "What do you mean?"

"You've been teaching me to defend myself, right?"

"Right."

"Well, what are you teaching me to defend myself from?"

Jack squinted with a puzzled look, as if he wasn't sure she was suggesting what he thought she was suggesting.

"What are you getting at?"

"These people aren't ever going to stop, are they?"

"I'm afraid not."

"So instead of waiting for one of those random, unexpected times when one of them shows up out of the blue and surprises me, catches me unaware and maybe unprepared, and I suddenly have to try to defend myself or be murdered, why not instead put them on the X."

He was still frowning at her, as if he still wasn't sure she meant what she was suggesting.

"Put them on the X?"

"Sure. You said that any of the predators who read about the funeral on the Scavenger Hunt site will likely look for me there. If they do, and we're expecting them, if we know they will be attracted to me at that time and place, that puts them on the X."

"There is no way for us to know how many of them there are. There could be several who visit the site and know you will be at the funeral."

She dismissed his objection with a flick of her hand. "Every one of them who dies is one who doesn't make it up the food chain to come after me later."

Jack finally bit off a piece of shrimp and chewed as he watched her. "I've never helped anyone before who thought to switch roles on them like that. Turn the hunter into the hunted. That's always just kind of been my specialty."

"Seems pretty obvious to me. You and me working together increases our chances. They can't come to kill me if we kill them first."

His expression was unreadable. "We're talking about killing human beings. Not in the desperate act of self-defense, but deliberately. Are you prepared to do that?"

"If I think about my brother's body lying there in a pool of blood, his eyes carved out of his face, if I think about AJ half naked, lying there in a pool of blood, if I think about her husband Mike sprawled on the bloody stairs, if I think about her son Ryan's brains splattered against the wall, if I think about what that Victor character did to your friend Rita, another woman with vision like mine . . . if I think about those photos of me on the Scavenger Hunt site, with all my personal information posted there so that a killer can hunt me down and murder me for a reward, if I think about what it felt like to realize that a killer had been standing in my bedroom fondling my underwear, and if I think about what it felt like to have that guy coming after me in the dark, intent on killing me, then yes, you bet I'm prepared to do that."

"Avenging angel indeed," Jack said quietly.

CHAPTER FIFTY

"I'm not an avenging angel," Kate said as she set the nearly empty container on the coffee table. "I'm just a person who wants to live. I'd like to die of old age, not . . ."

"I understand," Jack said quietly.

"So, you'll teach me, then? You'll teach me what I need to know to stay alive?"

"I already told you I would. You need to practice getting those blades out, getting those knives opened in an instant, but in the meantime it's still early. If you'd like, we have time to practice some moves you need to know in order to use those knives effectively."

"I've got some extra lipsticks. We can use them, right?"

"Perfect," Jack said.

Kate got up and went to her suitcase to retrieve several tubes of lipstick while Jack pulled something out of his own suitcase and handed it to her.

"Keep this with you along with those knives."

She looked at what he put into her hand. "A little flashlight?"

"It's less common to be attacked in broad daylight. It can happen, but predators prefer the cover of darkness.

"This may be little, but it's a damned expensive

little flashlight. It turns on with a push of the button on the end and puts out a high-intensity beam. Turn it on suddenly in the dark and you can light-blind an assailant. Blinding someone, even if it's only with light, gives you an advantage.

"If you're inside, say it's night and you're in bed. You wake up to the sound of someone coming into your bedroom. Grab your gun, turn on this flashlight, lay it on the bed pointed toward the door, and then roll off to the side and take aim. The light will draw his attention and it will be so bright he won't be able to see where you are in the room.

"The surprise of bright light like this will make a person freeze for an instant. In that instant they are the one on the X. Pull the trigger. Don't give them the opportunity to make a move toward you. You might only get one shot. Take it."

Kate nodded as she stuck the flashlight in a back pocket. She opened two tubes of lipstick and held them the way she would the small knives. "Okay, what do you want me to do?"

"Well, the first thing that you need to keep in mind is your goal. You want to put the guy down as quickly as possible and in a way that he doesn't ever get up again.

"Sounds obvious, but most people who get in a knife fight are running on adrenaline and frantically thrashing and slashing. They can certainly kill you that way, but unless they get you down and really go at stabbing you, they oftentimes end up inflicting a number of wounds that may be serious but aren't necessarily life-threatening—as long as you get away from them in time. Unless they're practiced killers, they will often try to fight with brawn, like the guy you fought, even with a knife.

"You can't afford to fight like that. You don't have the strength they will have, and you can't afford to slash it out with them. A big guy can take more injuries than you can. If they have a gun, you need to deal with it immediately. If they have a knife, that's a different kind of problem and you may have to deal with that in a different way.

"If they want to grab you like that guy outside AJ's house was trying to do, you can't afford to let him get in a blow or to get you on the ground where he will be in charge of what happens, because it won't be pleasant. Don't forget, your friend Wilma was killed with one punch. Even if it doesn't kill you, or do a lot of damage, it could knock you out or knock you senseless and then you're at his mercy.

"You want to fight in much the same way you did, the way you trained. You're doing the same things—going for vulnerable spots, but with a blade.

"You need to always keep in mind what it is you need to do. It sounds obvious, but it's hard to remember in a lethal encounter. You need to keep your targets in mind." He touched both sides of his throat. "The carotid artery is probably the fastest way to put a person down, and it's lethal."

Kate grasped the lipstick tubes as if they were knives. "I guess I know what you mean."

"It's like going to the grocery store. You don't walk around and randomly pick out things and throw them in the cart. You have a list of the things you need. Think of it that way.

"You have a list of targets on the guy that you want to cut. And, just like when you're in the grocery store, if you see something along the way that's not on your list but it's useful, take the opportunity when it presents itself. Make the hit hard and fast so you can then go back to the kill zones.

"Keep uppermost in your mind that cutting him isn't necessarily the goal. To stop him you want to bleed him to death, so you want to slice big arteries. If you need to, at least disable him. Slice tendons at the inside crook of his elbow and his arm will be useless. Make a quick jab into his eyes, then you can get in and sever an artery."

Jack unbuttoned his shirt. "I don't want lipstick on my white shirt," he said as he pulled it out of his pants and tossed it on his bed.

Kate hadn't been expecting that and the sight momentarily stopped her. It was distracting, to say the least.

He pointed a finger at her, like he was pointing

a gun at her. Before he could tell her what he wanted her to do she knocked his gun hand off to the side with the back of her left fist and immediately slashed down the inside of his wrist with the lipstick in her right hand.

As he leaned toward his gun hand the way an assailant in real life would have, Kate immediately thrust a hand in toward his throat, aiming for the jugular. He blocked and trapped her arm under his. He spun around and slammed his back into her before she had time to react, and swept a leg around, taking her feet out from under her.

Kate blinked up at him. He had her pinned with a knee in her abdomen.

"Pretty good," he said. "You disabled my gun hand by cutting the tendons. Unfortunately, I could have just killed you in about six different ways."

"How did you do that?" Kate asked up at him.

He stood up and extended a hand down to help her up. "Because in trying to use the knives you were forgetting what you know. You were trying to fight in a different way. You need to remember to fight the way you know."

"What do you mean, I'm forgetting what I know?" Kate asked when she was on her feet again.

"When you slashed the wrist of my gun hand, what did I do?"

"You flinched back and—"

"I wasn't flinching back. I was getting fighting distance to disadvantage you. You have shorter arms. I made you stretch to go for my throat. That let me capture your extended arm because you weren't controlling me; by gaining distance I was controlling you."

Angry at her herself, Kate made a face. "You're right. I know better."

"Then do better. Here I come again."

Jack lunged at her to capture her in his arms. She slashed his abdomen, then as he looked down at what she had done, she drove the lipstick knife up under his chin and pulled it down, leaving a nice red trail down his neck.

Jack smiled. "Good. That was good. Again."

This time when he lunged at her, she wasn't exactly sure how he did it, but he slipped around her and held her up against him with one arm around her middle, and his finger at her throat, as if holding a knife.

Kate didn't move. She really didn't want to move. She found him distracting to the point that she could feel her face turning red.

"Don't be embarrassed," he said at seeing her red face. "I kind of tricked you into that move."

"Yeah, I guess you kind of did," she said as he released her. She didn't really want him to let her go. With all the frightening things she was learning, she ached for something as simple as being held.

Kate reprimanded herself for letting herself be distracted. She reminded herself to put her mind to what he was teaching her. This was life and death and she couldn't afford to be a bad student. A bad student was a dead student.

For the next several hours, they sparred back and forth through the bedroom and sitting room. He coached her on what she was doing, refining her techniques. He showed her how to make moves to get the knife where she wanted it and how to make a cut instead of delivering a blow.

They moved the coffee table aside to give them room. He had her put the lipstick tubes in her pocket, then pretend to walk past so he could attack her from behind. She had to throw him off her and pull her lipstick knives from her pockets to counterattack.

At one point, he had her lie in bed as if she were asleep, leaving her knives on a side chair to simulate them being with her clothes. As she lay there, pretending to be asleep, he jumped on her, planting his knees on both sides of her to hol her down under the bedspread. He looked down at her, his face mere inches away.

When she didn't move, he said, "How are you going to get out of this?"

"Well, I could show you, but I think you'd be sorry."

"Okay, I get the point." Jack smiled. "But I'm

afraid that your legs are trapped under the blanket. Try it."

She did, but she didn't have any slack in the blanket, so she couldn't move.

"You can't use your knee the way you would like. You don't have your knives on you. What are you going to do?"

Kate momentarily gave thought to kissing him. That would certainly surprise the hell out of him.

She thought better of it, though, and instead elbowed the inside of his arm at a pressure point to make his arm fold. When he lost his balance she was able to flip him on his back, reversing their positions. She simulated strikes to his face and throat with her elbow, then dove for her knives. As he threw himself on her, she marked his carotid artery with a nice red lipstick stripe.

He praised her moves, which pleased her, then had her start again with another scenario. Over and over he attacked her and she tried to cut him in a lethal way.

Before it was over, they were both sweating. Strings of hair stuck to her face as she panted.

Jack went to the thermostat and turned it down. "I guess I should have thought of this before," he said as he, too, panted.

"You're hard to kill," Kate said.

That made him laugh. She liked his laugh. She remembered AJ saying how much she liked his laugh.

"How about we call it a night. I'd like to take a shower."

"Me too," Kate said, still catching her breath.

"Tomorrow is Sunday. We have all day to practice."

Monday was John's funeral. "Only if you promise to be harder on me tomorrow. I think you were holding back tonight."

Jack only smiled. He gestured toward the bigger bathroom. "You take that one. I'm pretty tired. I'm going to take a shower and get some sleep."

Kate offered him a smile. "Sounds good."

By the time Kate finally finished showering, washing and then drying her hair, and putting on a nightgown, all the lights in the bedroom were off. The room finally felt nice and cool. Only the other bathroom light was on and the door was mostly closed to provide enough light not to fall over furniture.

She saw that most of the burner phones had been taken out of their packages. They were lined up on the nightstand between the beds. Jack was sitting on the edge of the bed programming numbers into one of them.

He looked up when she came out. "You'll have to put all the numbers you need in a few of these. You're going to have to get rid of your cell phone."

Kate remembered him explaining how he had hacked AJ's phone. She hated to have to get rid of her phone, but she understood the necessity. She supposed that as long as she could make calls, that was all that really mattered. She could give people at work a new number.

She could see him looking at her in the near darkness. If he wanted to say something, he must have thought better of it.

He had his shirt off, and the lipstick was all washed off. He wasn't sweaty anymore.

As Kate crawled under the covers, out of the corner of her eye she saw him take a blue pill off the nightstand and swallow it with a drink of water. Kate knew that it was one of the Valium he took so he could sleep.

That thought made her feel profoundly sad. What kind of world must he have to endure? What kinds of things must he have seen? How many people had he tried to help who only ended up being murdered because they wouldn't listen to him? How could he stand knowing what was coming for them, and have them ignore him?

Kate lay awake, listening to him breathe. She was having trouble sleeping herself. The mock battle had her keyed up. Within thirty minutes she could hear his even breathing as sleep took him.

She slipped out of bed and sat on the edge of his bed.

Looking down at him asleep, she thought that he was the most perfect man she had ever met. She had never had the kinds of feelings for anyone she was having for him.

But she knew, too, that the things he had seen, the things he had been involved with, made him put a defensive wall up around himself. She knew he was reluctant to let himself get any closer to her. It was his barrier against any more pain.

She kissed the end of her finger and then touched it lightly to his forehead.

"No bad dreams tonight," she whispered. "Just good dreams."

She crawled back into her bed, lying on her side, watching his even breathing until she fell asleep.

CHAPTER FIFTY-ONE

Kate idly smoothed the fabric of her black dress against her leg as she sat in the front row of the service while a minister spoke of God's plan and the eternal peace awaiting John. She wasn't really listening to him talk passionately of a mindless tragedy that had taken a gentle soul. Knowing what she knew, it sounded like ignorant babble to her as she stared at John's closed casket and wondered who might be behind her somewhere, watching her with murderous intent.

Jack was somewhere behind her, too, watching her back. She felt better knowing that he was there, protecting her while she took care of John's final journey. John had liked going to the cemetery to visit the graves of their parents. Now he would be laid to rest beside them.

Kate didn't really think that a stranger, a killer, would be among the gathering of people from the Clarkson Center, where John had worked. She couldn't recall all of their names, but she recognized their faces. Since she knew all of her coworkers from KDEX who were there in attendance, a stranger would have stood out in the silent audience. It was not a likely place for an ambush.

What worried her was what would be a good

place for an ambush. For all she knew, there could be a killer with a rifle set up in a distant building, waiting for her to walk out of the mortuary so he could drop her with a single shot. He wouldn't need to cut out her eyes for proof. Such a murder would make the news and he would have all the proof he needed to collect his reward.

As she stared at the dead-looking bronze metal of the casket, she knew that somewhere there were preparations being made for AJ's funeral, along with those of her husband and son. It was hard to believe that AJ was gone. Kate wished so much that she had had the chance to talk about Jack with her, to have her meet Jack, to listen to her laugh, or make a wisecrack.

AJ had died because she knew John and Kate. She had been an inconvenience for the hunters, and so she had been murdered.

Events were moving so fast that it didn't seem like Kate's emotions could keep up. She knew, though, that she couldn't let herself dwell in that sorrow or she might not see what was coming for her.

Kate's shoulders were a little sore from knife training the day before. It had been a long day of practice in their motel room. There were fleeting moments when it was fun sparring with Jack, but then the purpose of it all came rushing back in and it became a grim, determined effort.

At first, compared with the ways she had trained

her whole life, it had felt confusing and awkward. Somewhere in the afternoon, though, it had come together in a way that fit naturally with what she already knew. Using knives rather than her bare hands became the new normal. The knives felt right in her hand. Even though she needed more practice, the blades were sometimes snapping out with hardly more than a thought. By the end of the day, it was hard to imagine defending herself without the knives.

What she had learned from her fight with John and AJ's killer was that while she could fight pretty well, it wasn't good enough. If that man had been any better or it had lasted any longer, it could easily have ended badly.

Kate tried to bring her mind back to John's service, rather than dwelling on killers and fights. To either side of the casket were stands with beautiful sprays of flowers. Some were from the people where John had worked, some were from people Kate worked with. It was comforting to know that there were people in the world who cared, good people who had overcome their primitive killer origins and were guided by their better nature.

But her newly discovered ability set her apart from those good people in ways she would never have expected. The good intentions of friends or even law enforcement would be trailing so far behind where she was on the scale of understanding that they could only drag her down so that harm could reach her.

Kate reminded herself that there were cops like AJ that she might be able to confide in. There was also Jeff Steele. He was more than merely a contact with army intelligence. She wasn't sure, though, if he would understand any of this business with killer DNA or her ability to recognize it.

When the minister finished speaking, hushed conversation slowly welled up in the room. People stood, then started toward the front to greet Kate and give her their condolences. A lot of them hugged her and told her how sorry they were, or what a good and decent man John was. One woman with two missing front teeth told Kate a funny story about John mistakenly going into the women's bathroom at work. Kate pretended to laugh. She let a number of people take her hand for a moment as they told her how sorry they were. It was a difficult duty to endure. She did it as stoically as possible.

Theo gave her a knowing smile as he put a hand on her shoulder. "I hope that you will reconsider and take some time off. We can get by without you for a while."

Kate forced a smile. "Maybe I will. We'll see. Thank you so much for coming. It means a lot to me. It really does."

A couple of young men in black suits began

gently ushering everyone toward the side entrance as a few other of the staff waited, apparently to take the casket out to the hearse.

Jack, wearing a crisp black shirt, found her and gave her a silent nod to say that everything seemed clear.

Bert spotted Kate and Jack standing together. The burly security officer came up to give Jack a wink. "I'm glad to see you both together. You make a great-looking couple."

Kate didn't have to force a smile. "Are you breaking up our engagement?"

Bert grinned. "I bow to the better man and give him my blessings."

Jack smiled self-consciously.

People shuffled out to their cars, most of them to go home, but a few followed instructions from the people at the funeral home and joined the line that formed up behind the hearse to go to the cemetery. Kate was relieved when she was finally alone in her car with Jack. It was painful to have to greet people, to listen to them say how sorry they were about her brother. She wanted it to be over.

The whole time she couldn't help but think of all of the times in her life that she had been John's guardian, watching out for him, helping him, protecting him.

But she hadn't been there to protect him the day a killer had ended his life.

"How are you doing?" Jack asked.

As the hearse started away, Kate shifted the car into drive and pulled out behind it. "I'm okay. What John had of life was a good life for him. A lot of people like him don't get the chance to live as fully as he did."

And, Kate thought, none of them ever had the chance to help save the lives of others the way John did with AJ. There were people alive who never knew that if it were not for John and AJ, they would have encountered a killer.

On the slow drive to the cemetery, it started to rain. Streetlights came on. They rode mostly in silence, Jack leaving her to her thoughts.

After they wound their way through the cemetery and finally came to a stop at a grave site, everyone trotted through the rain to gather under a temporary tent. John's casket was placed on a stand beside the place where it would be buried. People huddled around as the minister said a final prayer.

Kate didn't really hear him. She was thinking about things all the people gathered around would never be able to imagine.

Kate remembered her last phone call with John. He had said that he went to take flowers to their parents' grave, and someone had been watching him. Now she knew he had been right.

She continually scanned the cemetery, looking for anything suspicious, anything threatening.

Jack, standing silently beside her, did the same.

Other people visited graves, but no one looked their way. Kate saw an older woman weeping, holding a white handkerchief to her mouth, as a man comforted her with an arm around her shoulders.

When the brief ceremony was finished, and people began to hurry to their cars to get out of the rain, Kate instead went to stand for a time over the graves of her parents, there beside where John was to be laid to rest.

It struck Kate how ironic it was that she was standing in a graveyard, wondering if someone wanting to kill her was watching, waiting for his chance to end her life.

The tension of it all was getting to her. She wanted the whole thing to end. But she knew that it never would.

After the brief service at the cemetery, the remaining people went to a reception hall for a simple buffet. They had meats and cheeses, along with bread if you wanted to make a sandwich. The atmosphere was considerably less grim and more lighthearted. People talked and laughed a little as they ate finger food.

The reception hall was on a busy street. Through the front windows, Kate could see a gas station and convenience store not far away on the other side of the street. The streets were busy with cars. The rain slowed everyone down, making it seem even more crowded. There were apartment buildings across the street. People were continually going in and out of the parking lot.

When the gathering ended, and she and Jack finally left and went to the car, Kate couldn't help thinking of what a hopeless task it was to know if any of the people she could see were hunting her. For all she knew, the man putting gas into a gray minivan who looked over his shoulder at her could be simply curious, or he could be stalking her. A car parked in the lot across the street, and the engine and lights were turned off, but no one got out. Because of the rain, she couldn't tell if there was someone sitting inside talking, or if they were waiting for someone, or if they were watching her.

It was an uncomfortable feeling not knowing if a killer was watching, waiting for an opportunity to strike.

CHAPTER FIFTY-TWO

So what do you want to do now?" Jack asked as she pulled out onto the busy four-lane street.

Kate looked over at him. "What do you mean?"

He shrugged. "You took today off work for the funeral. Are you going to go back to work tomorrow? Or are you going to take some time off?"

Kate thought for a moment. "I suppose I'll just go back to work. But I'm nervous about going home. I guess that for right now I'd feel better staying at a motel. I don't like the idea of sleeping all alone on the X. At work there are people around."

"Your photos have only just been posted on the Scavenger Hunt site. A lot of killers tend to be impatient, like the guy who attacked the woman where you work when he couldn't find you there. Not all of them are clear thinkers. If they go looking for you but can't find you where the information says you are but you're never there, some of these people will give up."

"Some of them," Kate said, "but not all."

"Not all," Jack agreed. "And I don't mean t create false optimism, but there is no way o knowing for sure if any killers, much less th super-predators, visit the site."

"You think that maybe no one else knows about it?"

"It's hard to say."

"Considering how many negative reviews were posted by visitors to the Scavenger Hunt site, that would indicate that a number of people go there."

"Yes," Jack said, "but there is a difference between writing a bad review to earn a few bucks and be part of a hate campaign, and being willing to murder."

"Staying away from my house is one thing, but I don't know if I can take time off work right now," she said. "I was out of town for three weeks and I have a lot of cases pending."

"Can't you give them to someone else?"

"Sure, I suppose. But I would need to make arrangements for that kind of thing, give people briefings."

Even though he didn't answer, she could almost ear him asking if it was worth her life, but he mained silent.

The windshield wipers slapped back and forth an effort to keep up with the spray from the kup in front of her. Kate finally tired of owing the lights and spray of other cars vding the four-lane road, so she turned off on e street to take a different route toward the .

you think we should stay at the motel for a "

“At the minimum,” Jack said.

“What would be more than a minimum?”

“Why don’t you come with me to New York? Take a vacation. It will give you a breather.”

Kate turned down a deserted street that she wasn’t familiar with, but that headed in the general direction she wanted to go. She noticed that a car some distance behind took the same turn.

“How long do you think you will be in New York?”

“I don’t know,” he said. “I need to see my editor, Shannon Blare. Maybe meet with the publicity department. I suppose that I only need to be there for a day or two. But we could spend as much time there as we want, see the sights. Maybe go for a ride up or down the coast without having to worry about who might be following us.”

Kate looked over. “Did you see that car that turned with us?”

Jack nodded. “I saw it get in our lane, a few cars back, and then make the turn behind us.”

Kate made another turn, into a junky industrial area with chain-link fences protecting rusting car parts, stacks of railroad ties, and piles covered with blue tarps. It was late in the evening and anyone who worked in the area had gone home. At intersections, Kate could see lights in small houses several blocks off to the side, but there was no one on the street.

The car behind them made the same turn she did, but was going slower so that the gap between them grew. One car passed them going in the other direction, but other than that, Kate didn't see anyone.

Jack wasn't saying anything. She got the distinct feeling that he was simply going to watch and see what she would do, see how she would handle the situation.

Kate made another turn down a deserted side street with empty brick buildings and messy-looking alleys. It was not the kind of neighborhood she would want to have car trouble in.

She pulled to the curb just before the corner.

"What are you doing?" Jack asked.

"We're having car trouble," she said.

"We are?"

In the distance, in the rearview mirror, Kate saw the lights of the car make the turn behind them. It was still some distance away. She reached under the dash to pop the hood.

"Now what are you doing?" Jack asked.

"I'm taking care of the situation."

"Wouldn't you rather I handle this?"

Kate thought about her brother. She thought about the man who had tried to kill her after he had just slaughtered AJ and her family.

"No."

Kate swung her door open and stepped out into the rain.

Jack ducked down to look out at her as she stood. "There could be a killer in that car."

"I know."

"So what are you planning to do about it?"

Kate rested a forearm on the window frame as she leaned down to look into the car. "He's the one on the X. He's already dead. I just need to go tell him."

She shut the car door and then opened the hood, watching the car slowing as it came up behind them. The rain made a dull drumming noise as it beat down on the roof of the car.

Kate felt like her heart had come up in her throat as the car pulled over a little, stopping behind her car. She waved an arm, to get the driver's attention. She heard the driver's window roll down. She felt like she was watching herself in a dream.

"Need some help?" came a muffled voice.

Kate was moving toward the car before she even realized it. She picked up speed, wanting to get to him before he had a chance to get out. She reached the driver's door.

When the door opened, she clicked on the flashlight, illuminating the driver's face. She was standing right over him. She didn't intend to give him a chance to get up. His right hand came up to shield his eyes, but before it did, she saw those eyes, and saw what was in them.

It wasn't murder. It wasn't anything. He was

just a guy in a sleeveless shirt. He looked mean enough and had tattoos on his meaty shoulders, but he didn't have murder in his eyes.

Kate froze. She had the flashlight in one hand and a knife in the other, an instant away from cutting his throat.

"Sorry," she said. "Sorry, it's all right."

The heavyset man made a face. "Do you need help? I saw you put the hood up. This isn't a neighborhood you would want to break down in."

"It's nothing," Kate said, her adrenaline still making her heart pound. "I just needed to check the fan belt. I thought . . . but it's fine. It's all right."

"You sure? You aren't stranded there?"

"No," Kate said, shaking her head to assure him. "I just stopped to check, that's all. Thank you for stopping, but I'm fine. Thank you."

The driver heaved a sigh and slammed his door shut. "If I were you I'd get out of here and check your car at a gas station or something."

"That's a good idea," Kate said. "I'll do that. Thank you."

Her own voice sounded foolish to her. The guy pulled away, leaving her standing there in the rain. She folded the blade of the knife and clipped it back inside the pocket of her dress as he disappeared down the street. The thin material of the dress was soaking wet. She was freezing cold.

Kate went around to the front of her car, angry at herself for letting her imagination get the best of her. She felt weak at how close she had come to killing an innocent person. She felt foolish. She could see the dark shape of Jack sitting in the car. She wondered what he was going to think of her.

As she slammed the hood of her car and turned, she saw the nose of a car just around the far side of the building at the corner. The car hadn't been there when she had stopped. At least, she didn't remember it being there.

Almost at the same time she saw the car, she saw the silhouette of a big man. With all the black shapes of buildings and poles and fences and piles of junk, the dark form blended in and was almost impossible to see.

Kate's world spun around when he backhanded her. She landed in the wet street, stunned by the shock of pain.

She gathered her wits as she sprang to her feet.

The passenger door flew open and Jack was out of the car.

The figure fired off three shots at him. The sound of the gunfire made her flinch. Kate saw Jack roll off to the side. When the man swung back around, pointing the gun at Kate, the light from a distant streetlamp caught him just right, and she saw his eyes.

The sight of those eyes shot icy fear through her veins.

"Kate Bishop," he said, "what a payday this is going—"

Before he could get another word out, Kate backhanded his gun hand with her left fist. She would have tried to slash the inside of his wrist holding the gun, but the force of her blow had surprised him enough to knock the gun from his hand. It went skittering across the wet pavement.

Before he could do anything, before he could recover from the surprise of losing his gun, before Kate could even look to see if Jack was dead or alive, in a crystal-clear instant she saw her target.

It was as if time froze, giving her that instant of clarity she needed.

In one clean thrust, she caught the side of his neck, and with all her strength she yanked the blade back, cutting through muscle and tendon.

She had cut him so deep that in addition to severing his carotid artery it partially cut open his windpipe. His breath coming out of that gash in his windpipe sprayed the blood pumping out of his artery. It made a horrible sound as he sucked in a breath through the wound.

Before his hands could make it to his throat, she struck with her left hand and cut the carotid artery on his right side.

As dark as it was, she could still see blood

pumping out in spurts and going everywhere. She could smell it.

The big man dropped to his knees, trying to speak but unable to because of the opening in his windpipe. He fell to his side, his arms flopping out onto the pavement.

Kate, too, fell to her knees. She let out a cry of anguish, and then Jack was lifting her up.

"It's all right. You're okay."

Kate let out another cry as she fell into his arms. He hugged her tight, whispering to her that it was okay, that she was fine.

It was a moment before she could speak. "Are you okay? Were you hit? I was so afraid that he shot you."

Jack put a hand to the back of her head and pressed her to his shoulder.

"No, he missed. Remember what I told you?"

She sucked back a sob of terror. "That it's hard to hit a moving target?"

"That's right," he said with a smile as he held her away and looked into her eyes. "You did good, Kate. You did everything right."

"Did you know he was there?"

Jack shook his head. "I hate to admit it, but I didn't see him until you did. It was over before I could get out of the car and make it to you. By then, you had already handled it."

Kate nodded, overwhelmed by a flood of emotions—terror, surprise, and a rush of triumphant joy that she and Jack were alive and unhurt.

"Go wait in the car," Jack said as he bent down beside the guy, immediately starting to go through his pockets, taking his phone, wallet, and anything else he could find.

"Are we going to call the police?"

"Hell no, we're not going to call the police." He looked around briefly. "There aren't likely to be any cameras in this area, but even if there are they won't show much in the rain. The last thing you need is to get tangled up in this. How would that help? The guy was trying to kill you. You defended yourself. End of story."

"I guess you're right." Her instinct was to call the authorities, but she knew Jack was right.

"Go on, wait in the car," he said. "I'll be right there."

Kate nodded, but she didn't move. She didn't want to leave Jack there alone. Maybe she didn't want to be alone herself.

Jack finished and ushered her to the passenger side of the car. He held her arm as he sat her down, and then he shut the door. When he got in, he started the engine, then looked over at her.

"Kate, you need to be clear about this. I know that individual cops would be happy that you put down a killer, but their political bosses don't care about your life as much as their careers. You could prove your innocence this time, but if it happens again they will call it vigilantism. They will say that you are looking for these people so you can 'take the law into your own hands,' as if your life is less important than their notion of law and order. Do you understand what I'm telling you?"

Kate was finally gathering her wits. "It's hard for me to think of things that way, but I understand. My life depends on me now, not the law."

He put a hand over hers. "It's hard, I know. You did the right thing. You defended your life. That's all that matters."

Kate turned the rearview mirror and looked at herself.

She saw the eyes of a killer looking back.

Not the eyes of a murderer like the man she had just killed, but eyes like Mike's had been, eyes like Jack's were.

It was so strange to see that look in her eyes looking back at her that she had trouble recognizing herself. Her hair was wet and matted. She saw that blood was running down her chin from where the guy had clobbered her. It made her angry at herself that he had managed to get in those three shots. He could have killed Jack. He could have shot her. She needed to be faster the next time, or she might not be so lucky.

But she had survived, and he was the one who was dead. That was what mattered.

"He knew my name," Kate said. "He said my name and that this was going to be his big payday."

"Like you said, you intended to put him on the X. You succeeded," Jack said. "He must have followed us. I didn't even realize it until I saw his car parked on the other side of that building."

"He knew my name," Kate said again with emphasis.

"I know," Jack said as he pulled away from the curb, taking care to drive around the corpse. "He undoubtedly knew it from the Scavenger Hunt site."

Kate picked up her phone from the center console, unlocked it, and pressed a speed-dial number. She pointed, directing Jack to take the next left.

She wiped her nose with the back of her hand as she listened to the phone ring.

"Hello?" a man's voice said.

"Theo, it's me, Kate."

"Kate . . . are you all right? You sound . . . I don't know. Are you all right?"

"Yes. I'm fine. It's just that it's been an emotional day for me with the funeral and all."

"I understand. You gave John a beautiful ceremony."

Kate put her elbow on the armrest and rubbed her fingertips on her forehead as she held the phone up to her ear.

"Listen, Theo, if you think you could do without me for a little while, I think I'd like to take your advice and take some time off."

"Of course," he said immediately. "All the time you need, Kate." He thought a moment. "Have you ever even taken a vacation?"

"No," she said, trying her best to control her voice.

"Then you have one coming. Take all the time you need."

"Thanks, Theo, you're the best. I'll be in touch."

"Okay. Please take care of yourself and you call me if there's anything I can do for you."

"I will. Good night."

She sat for a moment after ending the call, staring at her trembling hands. Finally, she looked over at Jack.

"Can I come to New York with you?"

Jack smiled as he reached over and touched her chin.

"Sure."

That made Kate smile.

CHAPTER FIFTY-THREE

Kate walked at a brisk pace beside Jack, both of them pulling their carry-on bags behind as they made their way through the clots of people in the sprawling airport. They were both dressed casually. They had to alter their course constantly, weaving among people crowding into gates, walking slowly, looking in store windows, or not paying any attention to where they were going. For midweek, O'Hare was unusually busy.

Terminal 5, post-security, was as elegant a shopping experience as just about anywhere in the city. The wood and glass design elements of retail spaces were graceful and modern. It was a strange juxtaposition to see some disheveled flyers in flip-flops shuffling past such stylish shops.

Kate never looked forward to flying. It was time-consuming and wearying to have to deal with the bureaucracy and all the security restrictions and regulations that seemed to grow day by day. But this time she felt better about it, because at least they were getting out of Chicago and away from where people were actively hunting her. They were getting off the X.

More than that, though, she couldn't help

feeling good to be going with Jack. It was going to be a needed respite from the duties of her job and a chance to decompress from the terrible grief over the deaths of John and AJ's family.

Kate wasn't carrying the small knives Jack had given her. She felt naked and vulnerable without them. She had never felt that way before. But of course no one had been trying to kill her before, at least not that she knew about.

Now her photos and personal information were posted on the darknet. There was a reward for her life. She was relieved to be leaving town for a while to vanish into New York City, where no one would know her.

They had both put their knives in their checked baggage. Being in security herself, Kate knew that the results of tests conducted by any number of agencies had shown that between ninety and ninety-five percent of testers had been able to get guns, knives, and even bombs past airport security with no problem. Jeff Steele had warned her not to be lulled into complacency by airport security and to remain vigilant.

Security was mostly a show for the public to make them feel safe, to make them feel like the government was protecting them, when it really wasn't. Most people believed in the show and felt safer for it. And to some degree a show of security did tend to discourage people who meant harm. Still, Kate knew from her own work that not everyone was discouraged by a show of security.

The chances of security finding their knives in a carry-on bag were slim, and since they were so small, the most they were likely to do would be to confiscate them. Jack didn't want to take that risk for no good reason. He said that she already knew how to fight, and just about anything could be used as a weapon, even a rolled-up magazine. He said it was better to remain unnoticed by authorities. Besides, there was a lot of security in airports, both security you could see and security you couldn't see.

Kate had gotten used to having the knives on her. Jack had given them to her to help keep her safe. Because of that they had taken on a meaning of their own. They were symbolic as well as defensive. Especially after the time he spent teaching her to use them, and especially after they had saved her life the day of her brother's funeral.

As they walked past a gate for Air France, a man on crutches was being allowed to board before anyone else. He was in a tan jacket and had a dark blue backpack. As he went past the boarding kiosk he looked back, scanning the crowd.

His gaze briefly met Kate's.

When she looked into the man's dark eyes Kate stopped dead in her tracks.

He obviously didn't recognize her ability by looking into her eyes, because he didn't show any reaction to seeing her, but she certainly reacted to him.

Jack stopped beside her and glanced in the direction she was staring.

"Kate. Kate." Transfixed, she hardly heard him. Her mind filled with images. His grip tightened on her arm and he kept his voice low. "Kate. Look at me."

She blinked and looked into his eyes.

"Do you see something?" he asked.

In the chilling grip of fear that that kind of eyes always gave her, she struggled to find her voice.

"Yes."

"Then walk."

"What?"

"Walk." He squeezed her arm harder. "Kate. You need to walk." Once they started away, he leaned closer. "What did you see?"

"A man on crutches, in the tan jacket, just going into the jetway," she said, looking back over her shoulder as Jack dragged her farther away. "He's planning to kill the people on that plane."

Jack paused. "Are you sure?" He pulled her to the side, out of the way of the churning rivers of people. "Kate, are you sure?"

She looked back at him. "Dead sure. He is

planning to kill all the people on that plane." When he continued to stare at her, she tilted her head toward him. "I'm positive, Jack."

Jack stared at her for a few brief seconds longer. He glanced back toward the Air France gate and then pulled out a cell phone. He pushed the number at the top of the speed-dial list. Someone answered after the first ring.

"Get me Dvora Artzi—this is an emergency."

Jack gave his name and then rattled off a series of numbers and letters, obviously a code. Almost immediately someone else got on the line.

"Dvora, it's Jack Raines. I have an emergency. I'm at O'Hare Airport in Chicago, terminal five. I'm with a subject. She just identified a man getting on an Air France plane"—Jack looked over the heads of people moving through the busy aisle, to the gate number diagonally across the concourse—"gate M twelve."

He listened and then tipped the phone down away from his mouth to speak to Kate. "Describe him."

Kate leaned in, putting her mouth close to the phone. "Five-ten, on aluminum crutches, tan jacket, dark blue backpack, short black hair, clean-shaven, silver bracelet on his right wrist."

As Kate leaned back Jack listened to the woman ask something.

He looked up. "She wants to know how sure you are."

Kate twitched a frown. "I'm positive."

"She says she's positive," Jack told the woman on the phone.

Kate leaned in to speak into the phone. "He has a bomb that was surgically implanted in his abdomen. It doesn't use metal for shrapnel so that it wouldn't be easily detected. He intends to explode it once they are midway over the Atlantic Ocean."

Jack's face lost some of its color as he stared at her.

He listened to the woman on the phone for a moment and then asked Kate, "Anything else?"

"The bomb has a deadman switch."

"Dvora, did you hear that?" he asked the woman on the phone. "The bomb has a deadman switch."

The voice asked something laced with brief hesitation.

"Do you remember Jemina?" Jack asked. "Yes, that's the one. On her very best day, Jemina couldn't begin to be the equal of the subject I'm with right now." There was a pause as Jack listened, and then he said, "All right. Hurry."

He slipped the phone back into his pocket. "I'm afraid that we're going to have to catch a later flight to New York. All hell is about to break loose and the airport is going to be evacuated."

Kate looked around. Everything looked so normal.

"I'm a subject?" she asked without looking at him. "Is that what I am to you? A subject?"

Jack grasped her by her upper arm and turned her back to face him. "That's what the Mossad call the people I work with, that's all. They know what I mean when I say it."

Kate nodded. It seemed a hollow explanation.

"You're more than that to me, Kate," he finally said. "It's not you. It's just that I'm not . . . I can't be."

Kate understood. Rita, and who knew how many others before her, had been too painful an experience. Kate vividly remembered him telling her about the videos of her being tortured, of her calling out his name and begging for him to save her. Of her dying.

He was too afraid of exposing himself to that kind of heartache again, so he had walled himself off.

That was why he had told her that he would never have the chance to hear a woman say that she loved him.

Two men dressed casually raced up through the terminal, pushing their way through the throngs of people. They looked like any of the ordinary passengers in the airport, except they had chains hanging from their necks with some kind of ID. Kate could tell from their demeanor that they were anything but ordinary. Holding out their IDs, they ran past the two women at the check-in desk without slowing. Both of the women, along with most of the passengers waiting at the gate, looked startled.

"I hope they can stop him," Kate said. "Maybe it will be okay."

"I hope so," he agreed.

Jack's brow drew down as he turned his attention back to her. He looked more than a little agitated.

"You said that man has a bomb. What makes you think he has a bomb?"

Kate blinked at the question. "Because he does."

"You said it was surgically implanted in his abdomen. How in the world could you possibly know that?"

Kate's brow tightened. "You're the expert." Kate was concerned by how upset he had become. "You tell me."

"You could tell by his eyes that he was a killer?"

"Yes."

Jack held a finger up, as if for emphasis. "Okay, you saw in his eyes that he is a killer—I get that . . . but what could possibly make you think he has a bomb?"

Kate wasn't sure what he was getting at, what was upsetting him. "By looking in his eyes. I just know. It's all there."

"Knowing a killer by looking into their eyes is one thing," Jack said, "but telling anything else about them, like that they have a bomb, is something else entirely. Have you ever done anything like that before?"

"Yes. I picked a couple out of a bunch of photos AJ showed me. I told her they were killers. I told her that the man wasn't very bright and that he had raped a girl and that it was the wife's idea to kill her, but they both took part in the murder. I told her that they used knives."

"Did you ever find out if you were corrcct?"

"Yes, AJ told me that when they brought them in, they found out that everything was exactly as I had told her."

Jack stared at her briefly. "You can't do that."

Kate was alarmed by the concern in his eyes. "What do you mean, I can't do it? I just told you I did. You're the one who came to find me because I can identify murderers by looking at their eyes."

"Know that they are a murderer, yes, but that's all. You can only tell that they're a killer. You can't tell anything else by looking into their eyes."

"Yes I can," she insisted.

Just then, two muffled shots rang out in quick succession, almost together.

Jack put his hand behind her head and protectively pulled her toward him. "That's air marshals."

An instant later, another shot.

Jack looked toward the Air France gate.

Kate looked back, too. Stewards ran out of the jetway, the pilots and flight crew right on their heels.

Before they were clear of the jetway, an explosion ripped a hole the size of a truck in the side of the plane back near the tail. Flying debris from the plane blew out all the windows of the Air France gate and several the next gate over.

Pandemonium erupted as glass flew through the crowds of screaming people.

A human head attached to the upper portion of a bloody spinal cord landed on the rows of blue chairs in the waiting area.

Chunks of debris skated and skipped across the floor, knocking a few people down as smoke rolled in through the broken windows. It seemed like everyone was screaming and running. The tail of the plane, lifted a little by the explosion, settled down at a crooked angle.

The two air marshals stumbled out of the jetway, both covered in blood.

Men with long guns forced their way upstream as most people parted to make way. Other men ran in with dogs on leashes. Police appeared, directing panicked people back away from the area. The passengers who had been waiting to board scattered. Everyone in the terminal started running, a good many of them screaming.

Jack circled his arm around Kate's waist and

started her walking back the way they had come, moving her into the river of people going the way they were being directed by police.

"Like I told you," he said, "the place is going to be evacuated."

"Like I told you," Kate said, "the guy had a bomb."

He looked down at her. His face hadn't regained its color. "You just saved several hundred lives."

Kate frowned at his odd expression. "Did I just also do something that you didn't think I should be able to do?"

"You sure as hell did."

CHAPTER FIFTY-FOUR

Jack pointed. "There."

Kate craned her neck and saw an older, lanky man in a black suit, standing in a line with other men of every size, shape, and color dressed in similar black suits and white shirts, all holding up a piece of paper or an iPad with a name on it. The lanky man's iPad said "Raines."

They followed the limo driver through the airport outside to a shiny black SUV standing at a curb in a limousine-only area. The streets and parking looked like they were all too small to accommodate the volume of modern life. After hours of looking out at an empty sky and soft layers of clouds, it felt strange to be hemmed in by the hard shapes of buildings and congested streets packed with traffic.

Shannon Blare, Jack's editor, had arranged for the limo to pick them up. She had told Jack that she was eager to see him the following day. In the meantime, she said that she insisted on getting them a beautiful suite near Gramercy Park, which she said was one of the most lovely spots in the city. Kate was just relieved to be away from places where she was being hunted.

Shannon Blare told Jack she was looking forward to meeting the young lady he brought with him, having been at least somewhat responsible for them meeting since she had been the one who put AJ in contact with Jack.

It felt good to sit at last in the relative quiet of the back seat. It was nice to have someone else drive and negotiate the heavy traffic. The hours of jet engine noise had been tiring, leaving Kate with a dull headache. Fortunately, the flight had been routine.

It had taken two days before O'Hare Airport was cleared to reopen. Airline schedules were struggling to get back to normal, and they had been fortunate to catch another flight. Kate had been relieved to finally make it out of Chicago.

While waiting for a flight, they had stayed in a hotel near the airport. Jack hadn't wanted to take any chances, so he had used another fake ID. They had killed the time with hours of practice lipstick fights, room service, and a few long conversations. It felt good to talk with him about nothing of any particular importance.

The hotel, being near the airport, was noisy. In a way Kate longed for the quiet of her job at KDEX. It was nerve-racking not knowing how long her "vacation" was going to last.

The almost continual news about the bombing at the airport had been filled with inaccuracies. Most of it was the usual careless reporting spiced with speculation, but Kate suspected that some of it was wrong for security reasons. The bomb, for instance, was reported to have been in the bomber's backpack. No mention was ever made of it being surgically implanted in the man's abdomen.

Kate had no doubt about that part of it. Jack's contact in the Mossad had confirmed that she was right. They were very interested in this new "subject" he had located. Jack had promised that one day he would introduce them.

Excuses and explanations for the failure in security were continually being given out. Congressmen were outraged. The president spoke on the "tragedy." He announced the formation of an investigative committee and called for Congress to act to increase the TSA budget. There was very little actual information in any of the reports. They watched almost no TV after the initial reports.

The two air marshals were both hospitalized in serious condition. One had lost an eye; both were expected to live. There were numerous stories about how, because of the "placement" of the bomb, the plane's hydraulic and electrical systems were compromised in a way that, had the plane been airborne, would have resulted in a crash, killing all on board. Kate knew by what she saw that had it happened in the air, the plane would have lost the entire tail section. Had it happened over the ocean, it was possible that wreckage wouldn't be found and no one would have known the reason the plane went down.

News accounts said that authorities had been alerted by a "tip," and that was all that had prevented a horrific tragedy.

Kate had trouble reconciling the fact that because of her, that crash had never happened, and all those lives had not been lost. While the whole thing in a way didn't seem real, it did help make up for how her ability had turned her life upside down. A lot of good people were still alive. A killer was dead.

An Islamic terror group claimed responsibility and promised more such attacks against aircraft. In those promises Kate saw the inexorable movement of the pendulum.

During those two days waiting in the hotel to get another flight, Jack had questioned her in detail. Kate had thought that what she had done at the airport, just like what she had done with the photos of the husband-and-wife killers AJ had shown her, was simply part of the same ability she had to recognize a killer by seeing his eyes.

Jack had assured her that it most certainly was not.

At least, it was not a part of her ability as far as his experience with others had taught him. He said that what she had done was a complete unknown as far as he was concerned. Kate had no useful answers as to how she did it except that she just could.

When she had looked into the man's eyes, in that instant she had seen it all in his eyes. She didn't know how, but with that single look she simply knew. It wasn't something separate, like a scene from a movie streaming into her, it was simply something she knew in totality, like looking out of a window and taking in everything all at once.

The only reference to such an ability Jack knew of was in an eleventh-century text about a monk believed at the time to be a prophet. It was said that he identified murderers and at the same time revealed their crimes. Jack said that it was hard to know how much truth there was in such accounts, since so much of it involved superstition.

As their limo made its way through the crowded streets, Kate couldn't help but marvel at the endless, tightly packed buildings. The enormity of the city made Chicago seem like a small town. Even though it was getting dark, the city was awash with light. Windows filled with light rose all around. The city had a distinctive aroma, not unpleasant, but different from any other place she had been.

It was rather amazing to see so many people, and to know that this was their home, the only home they knew, and that many of them had never seen anything else of America except on TV. In a way, the neighborhoods with stores and traffic and alive with crowds were exciting. They were life. They were civilization.

"That's Gramercy Park," the limo driver said over his shoulder. "We will be to your hotel shortly."

Off to the left was a beautifully manicured park bordered by a black wrought-iron fence. Kate could see a statue standing in a circle in the center of the park. It was surrounded by wide paths and inviting green benches.

"Can we go for a walk there?" Kate asked.

"It's a private park," Jack said. "People who live around it pay an annual fee to be able to get in. Our hotel's not far from here. They may have a key to allow guests to visit the park. If they do, we'll go there tomorrow. All right?"

Kate smiled as she nodded, looking out the window at all the people strolling along the sidewalk outside the wrought-iron fence and the green world within.

Without thinking about it, Kate took hold of Jack's hand as she gazed out the window at the city going endlessly past outside the limo window. Jack squeezed her hand.

For the first time, a vacation was beginning to feel pretty good.

CHAPTER FIFTY-FIVE

That's really nice of you, Shannon," Jack said on the phone as they stood near the check-in desk waiting for another couple to finish registering.

"No, really, it's all right. I understand. To tell you the truth we're both pretty tired, anyway. It's been a long day. I think we'd both rather get some sleep. Thanks again, Shannon. . . . All right, we will. . . . Yes. See you tomorrow, then.

"She wanted to take us to a nice place for dinner," Jack said as he returned the phone to his pocket, "but she has an appointment she can't break."

Kate yawned. "Good. Honestly, I wasn't really looking forward to going out to dinner and having to smile. It's already getting late, especially on East Coast time."

Jack nodded his agreement. "To make up for it, she said she is having a special dinner sent up to our suite."

"Dinner in our room rather than a knife fight would be nice," Kate said. Jack laughed.

The lobby had a lot of white Carrara marble and frosted glass, warmed by the dark wood of the registration area. A young woman in a crisp gray uniform, her dark hair pulled back into a ponytail, took Jack's information. For once he gave his correct name and ID.

The receptionist said that their two-bedroom suite had already been reserved for one week and it had already been paid for. Kate envisioned flopping down on the bed on her back and letting out a weary sigh.

The bellhop brought their bags in from the limo, and put them on a cart. Jack let the man lead them up to the fifth floor. The bellhop told them about the hotel restaurant and several others in the area.

The suite was less spacious than suites in other cities, but it looked cozy enough. There was a small central sitting area with two tufted wing-back chairs at a small table near a window with floor-to-ceiling white sheers and gray drapes. The room was painted a strong but pleasant green. There were framed black-and-white photos of dancers on the walls.

Jack suggested that Kate take the larger of the two bedrooms. It had mellow rose-colored walls, a bright blue velvet headboard, and a red throw on the white bedspread. The bellhop put her suitcase on the stand for her, and put Jack's in the other bedroom. After Jack gave the man a tip, they were alone at last.

Kate had been in her share of hotels, but this one was different. Spaces were smaller. It felt old. The noise of the city was a presence in the room, part of the feel of the place. Still, it was attractive and quite lovely. Mostly, Kate was tired of being in crowds, so it felt good to be alone. As tired as she was, she hoped Jack didn't want to practice knife fighting.

Jack appeared in the doorway to her bedroom. He had one of the phones they had bought at the electronics store.

"Why don't you keep one of these so that we have a backup with the same numbers. When we go out, we shouldn't leave these in the room."

Kate put the phone in the back pocket of her jeans, then took out her two knives and clipped one inside each front pocket. She felt better having them on her.

Before she had a chance to unpack anything, there was a knock at the door.

It was a waiter with a white towel draped over one arm. He pushed a table into the room. It was set with silver-rimmed plates and oval dishes with silver covers.

"Compliments of Ms. Blare," the man said as he arranged the wingback chairs at the food cart.

He lifted the lids, showing them a chicken casserole with baby potatoes around the edge and another serving dish with asparagus. He pointed out sherbet for dessert. He held a hand out toward two bottles of water.

"Still, or sparkling?"

Both Jack and Kate said still.

"I'm so dry from being on the plane I think I could drink the whole bottle myself," Kate said.

The waiter smiled and bowed slightly. "If the lady would like more, there are extra bottles under the table." He lifted the side of the white tablecloth to show her. He uncorked a bottle of wine and replaced it in the bucket with ice.

"Will there be anything else at the moment?"

"No, it's more than enough and it looks delicious," Jack said, handing the man a tip. "Thank you."

Once he was gone, the two of them both flopped down in the wingback chairs, opposite each other at the table.

"I wish I was more hungry," Kate said. "Mostly I'm just worn out."

Jack agreed. "Some food will give you some energy."

They both downed their glasses of water and Jack poured more. He also poured them each a little bit of wine.

He held up his wineglass in a toast. "To the rest of your life."

Kate smiled and tapped his wineglass with hers. She took a sip and sat back. "Are you going to tell your editor everything about your new book? Everything you told me?"

Jack shrugged. "I'll tell her as much as I need to in order to make sure she's interested enough. I'd rather have her read the manuscript when

I'm done, but she needs a certain amount of information to do her job. Just kind of depends on how it goes. She knows that the central theme is how murder is part of our nature, and that already has her interest. She said that she loved the first book and they're looking forward to publishing the second."

Jack poured himself another glass of water. Kate held hers out for a refill. As she drank it down, Jack put some chicken and a couple of little potatoes on a plate for her.

Kate leaned back as she let out a heavy sigh, not realizing how tired she was from the long day. She didn't know if she had the energy to pick up her fork.

She saw Jack slump back in his wingback chair. She was having difficulty focusing her vision. Her head rolled to the side.

She saw her glass slip from her hand to the floor. It didn't seem to matter.

The room closed in around her as she felt herself slipping away. A distant sense of terror tried to get her attention but dimmed to little more than a thick, incomprehensible whisper. She strained to remain conscious, but she could feel it fading away from her.

Everything was getting fuzzy. She blinked, trying to make her eyes focus. Something cast a shadow over her.

A big hand slipped under her arm, lifting her.

She was a rag doll, unable to react. She saw shapes ghosting into the room.

"Good evening," a gravelly voice said into her ear. "I'm Victor. My, my, but you're a pretty one. You're going to be the perfect star for my next show."

As her eyes rolled back, she briefly saw his eyes. They were the ice cold eyes of a killer.

Kate's world evaporated into nothingness.

CHAPTER FIFTY-SIX

Kate became dimly aware of light. Nothing made sense. A shadow passed over her. Her mind felt as if it were immersed in a deep, thick darkness. She made an effort to force herself to think. It didn't produce much of anything, other than that she recognized the taste of blood in her mouth.

Someone slapped her. It was hard enough to nearly knock her over. The shock of pain startled her. Her immediate reaction was to yell at them to stop it, but no yell would come out.

The sting of the slap started to sharpen her senses back into focus a little. She realized that she was sitting, but for some reason she couldn't move her arms. Her shoulders hurt.

Her first thought was that she was paralyzed. She tried and was relieved to at least be able to move her fingers. But her arms remained trapped behind her. She couldn't move them even a little.

A second slap came out of nowhere. The force of it was hard enough to knock her and the chair over. Her head banged the floor, instantly giving her a headache.

Someone leaned down and tipped the chair, with her attached to it, back up and planted it on the floor with a hard thump.

"Wakey wakey. Sweet dream time is over."

She had heard that gravelly voice before, but couldn't remember where.

Kate squinted against the harsh light. Wherever she was, it was mostly dark all around her. The only light in the place was the one shining on her.

Smelly hands reached in and squeezed her cheeks. "Smile for the camera."

The man squeezing her cheeks shook her face. "Come on. Smile. It's showtime."

He had a stocking mask over his head, with holes cut out for the eyes and his mouth. He leaned down and put his face close in front of hers. "Feel free to scream for the camera. After all, you're the star, and the star always screams."

Kate was momentarily confused as to whether or not she was awake or asleep in some kind of bizarre dream.

And then he twisted her left nipple until she did scream, an involuntary, helpless cry of pain that felt like it was shrieking up from her soul. The more she screamed, the more he twisted.

The shock of pain brought her wide awake and brought tears to the scream. The sharp agony of it radiated through her entire chest as he kept at it until she was sure he intended to rip it off her breast.

The man finally let go and stepped away from

her. Kate shivered, panting under the agony of lingering pain, wanting nothing so much as to be able to put a comforting hand over it.

As her wits came back into focus, she realized that she was in trouble, but she was having a hard time making sense of how she came to be in the dark room.

There was a camera on a tripod not far off in front of her. The red light was blinking. She was being recorded.

Beyond the camera was a dark metal table with a collection of items on it, but she couldn't tell what any of them were. She looked around and could see little more than a few glimpses of dark walls. There was a closed metal door she could just see over her left shoulder.

"Who are you?" she asked. Her voice sounded strange, hoarse and dry. "Where am I?"

The man turned back. He grinned. His two middle teeth on the bottom were missing. The rest were a dark yellow. He looked like nothing so much as a homeless derelict.

Something told her he was something else entirely.

"I'm Victor," he said in a cheerful tone, as if happy to make her acquaintance.

Kate vaguely remembered someone saying that name in their hotel room. She couldn't understand why she wasn't in the hotel. She could only remember being there.

"Where's Jack? I need to see him. What have you done with him?"

"Me? Nothing. He is for someone else. You are for me."

Kate spit blood to the side. It still didn't seem real. With the way her mind was swimming it felt like some kind of drug-induced hallucination.

"What are you talking about?"

He cocked his head as if she were dense. "Jack Raines is meant for someone else. You, Miss Bishop, are here to entertain me and my audience."

A wave of dread washed through her when he gestured at the camera.

"Where's Jack!" Kate screamed at him.

He looked amused. "The founder of our little website has taken him somewhere for a private conversation."

Website. She realized who Victor was. He was the one who provided date-rape drugs for Sid. It all came rushing in. He was the one who had tortured and killed Rita.

"What are they doing with him?"

She knew it was foolish to ask the question, but she couldn't help herself, as if it would somehow slow events from their headlong rush.

"Probably pulling his intestines out a foot at a time," Victor said with a wicked grin, "wrapping them around a stick." He shrugged again and cocked his head. "Maybe something else just as fun. That's not up to me. You are the one up to me. You belong to me, now."

"Why are you doing this to us?"

He shook a finger at her face. "Jack Raines is a dangerous man. You're nobody. You're only here to entertain me and my fans. But Jack Raines has outlived his usefulness."

"What usefulness?" she asked as Victor started toward the camera.

He turned back and smiled. "He thinks he's so smart. But he has been finding those like you for us without even knowing it." He cocked his head to the side. "He finds them, just like he found you and your brother, and those before. He finds them, we snatch them."

Kate suddenly understood. It all came into sharp resolution as all the connections registered.

Now that she was more awake, she tried again to move, but she was helplessly restrained. Kate remembered AJ's stories of killers and what they had done to their captives. She remembered AJ lying there on the floor with duct tape wrapped around her head, blinding her. Kate's frantic sense of panic at being so helpless, at what was to come, began to build.

As Victor turned back toward the camera, she remembered what the sifu had said to her that day. *If you are attacked, it is because they have the advantage. For you, they will always be bigger, stronger. No one is going to help you, so don't expect any. You must do everything you can with the bad intention of hurting your enemy.*

She didn't see how she could do that. It seemed like meaningless words.

She knew, though, that if she wanted to live, if she was going to help Jack, then her only chance was to think. No one was going to come to help her.

She looked around again, trying to take everything in, trying to find something helpful. Her vision was still a bit blurred, but starting to clear. It felt like someone was pushing on her eyeballs.

She knew that her arms were tightly bound behind her. By the way her skin pulled, they were probably wrapped with duct tape. It felt like that tape must be wound around the back of the chair. When she had been drugged and limp, Victor had an easy time of restraining her just the way he wanted.

Victor suddenly returned with a pair of pliers. He put a grimy hand on her head and tilted it back.

She tried to twist her face away from him. "What are you doing? Stop it!"

"I'm going to have to take out your teeth."

Take out her teeth? It sounded insane. Kate twisted her head from side to side.

"No! Stop it!" she yelled.

He slapped her hard and shook the pliers at her face. "I had a girl bite me once when I was in her mouth enjoying myself. That was a bad experience. So now, I always take their teeth out first." He grinned. "Feels better for me without the teeth. You know? You'll see how much I enjoy it."

He came back from the table with a small metal bucket, rattling something in it. He tipped it toward her so she could see inside. It was half full of bloody and broken teeth.

It dawned on her what he was talking about.

After putting the bucket back, he grabbed her hair to hold her head still. He pushed a filthy thumb in her mouth, feeling all of her teeth as if taking inventory. The hand with the thumb in her mouth was holding the pliers. She knew that if she didn't think, if she didn't do something, he was going to use that pliers to rip out her teeth. The thought terrified her.

Kate bit down as hard as she could.

Victor cried out in pain. "Let go!"

When she didn't, he pressed a knuckle of his other hand against the rear of her jawbone. The pain was blinding. She tried to keep biting down on his thumb, knowing that if she let go he would go to work on her teeth with the pliers, but the intense pressure against the back of her jaw was more than she could endure, and it finally forced her mouth open.

"You will pay for that," he growled, comforting his thumb.

He went to the camera, checking the settings.

While he did, Kate frantically looked around for

something, anything, to help her. There was nothing, and besides, she wouldn't be able to grab it if there was. There could have been a gun in her lap and she wouldn't be able to use it.

She realized that her left leg ached something fierce. She looked down and saw that she still had her panties on but her legs were bare. There was a tourniquet wrapped tightly around her left leg at midthigh. Below the tourniquet her skin was going purple.

Her arms were duct-taped behind her, but her legs were free. She realized why. With a sickening sense of dread, she remembered Jack describing what had happened to Rita. Kate remembered that it was Victor who had done it, and that he had videoed it for the Scavenger Hunt site.

Kate saw her jeans thrown off to the side. Her knives were in her jeans. They couldn't do her any good.

Victor tipped the light above her to the side. "See? This is my collection of pretty ladies, like you. They all brought me great satisfaction. Like you will."

She could just make out half a dozen bags of some kind hanging against the wall. As she squinted, she realized that they were the naked, bloody torsos of women tightly wrapped in plastic. Dismembered limbs were laid against the bodies under the tight plastic wrapping.

Victor let go of the light, letting it swing over

her. “After I finish my time with you, you will join my collection. But that’s still days away. We will have plenty of time together. My fans enjoy my shows so much. I want it to last.”

At the thought of what was in store for her, she couldn’t stop her trembling.

Kate could see the red light on the camera blinking. Victor went to the table and threw the pliers down.

He picked up a handsaw.

He returned and knelt down beside her. She could see his murderous eyes through the holes cut in the stocking cap.

“Since you are going to be difficult, I’ll wait to pull your teeth until later, once you’re more cooperative and don’t thrash around as much. Your mouth will be more useful, then.”

His grin was as evil as anything she had ever seen.

Victor gripped her knee in a powerful hand. Try as she might to pull away, he held it still enough for what he wanted. He brought the handsaw up and laid the teeth down against her flesh between her knee and the tourniquet.

He looked up at her with those murderous eyes.

“Drug cartels and the like use a chainsaw for this, but I think that’s silly. That way it’s over so quickly. What fun is that? Better when it goes slow. Better for you to feel every saw cut, one cut at a time. One scream for each.”

Kate could tell by his voice how excited he was getting.

She remembered Jack telling her how Victor had sawed off Rita's legs just above the knee as she had screamed.

Kate started crying in helpless panic.

"No. Please, no."

He paused to look up at her. "But I have to."

"No," Kate wept, "you don't have to. Please."

"Yes, I do," he said as he turned a grin toward the camera. "Having sex with you will be so much better once your legs are off, and I pull your teeth."

He laid the teeth of the saw back on her leg and cocked his arm back.

Kate screamed.

CHAPTER FIFTY-SEVEN

Kate panted so hard as she screamed in panic that she was choking on her own spit.

Through her panic, some part of her that wanted to live forced her to think. Begging a killer was what all victims did. They always begged. Always. It never helped. Killers wanted their victims to beg, to scream, to cry in terror.

If there was something she could do that might save her, it wasn't going to be begging. If she didn't do something, she and Jack were both going to die.

As hard as it was, she forced herself to stop begging.

"Your camera just went off," she said.

Victor paused before taking the first saw cut and frowned up at her. "What?"

"Your camera just shut off," Kate said through gasping tears. "The battery must be dead. Your audience is going to miss this."

Victor shielded his eyes from the overhead light as he tried to see the camera. Kate could just make out the red light flickering, but for some reason he couldn't see it, or maybe her suggestion was enough to make him fear she was right.

He rose up and walked across the room to the camera.

Kate's arms were taped tightly behind her back, taped to the old wooden chair, but her bare legs were free. He wanted them free so he could saw them off. He wanted her to struggle and kick while he cut them off. He liked his victim to struggle.

As Victor fiddled with the camera, cursing to himself, trying to check if it was working, Kate swung her legs, rocking the chair onto its front two legs. She took one more big rock and rolled forward until she was standing on her feet. She was bent over at the waist, with the chair taped to her back, but she was standing. All the sharp grit was painful under her bare feet.

She remembered what Jack had done.

Without a moment's hesitation, and with every ounce of her strength, she raced across the room toward the camera. At the last instant she sprang up, throwing her right leg around Victor's head as she violently spun her body around.

The momentum yanked his head around. The collision and her weight drove him to the ground as she twisted herself in a circle with her leg still locked around his head. She felt his neck snap just before they crashed to the floor.

Kate lay on her side a moment catching her breath, right leg locked around his neck, triumphant.

Not wanting to waste any time, she extricated herself and struggled to her feet again, then raced backwards, smashing the chair into the wall. The wood splintered. She hit the wall twice again until the chair broke. The bottom of the chair came off, but her arms were still taped together to the remainder of the chair back.

Kate ran across the room, dropped to her knees, and slid to a stop by the saw next to Victor. After three tries with her fingertips, she managed to tip the saw so that the teeth faced up. She held the end of the saw tight between her bare knees, straddling the saw blade, and raked the duct tape around her wrists against the teeth, tearing it apart. Once she had enough of it cut through, she was able to wrench her arms in a way that tore the tape. In a few minutes more she had the tape off her arms.

Kate removed the tourniquet, pulled on her jeans and socks, and quickly put on her shoes. She didn't waste a second to congratulate herself. Instead, she opened the door on the side of the camera and pulled out the SD card. She put it in her pocket. As she crossed the room she pulled the little flashlight Jack had given her out of her back pocket.

Opening the door just a crack, she carefully peeked out. She didn't see anyone, so she slipped through. There were no lights on, leaving the mysterious place in the dark. By the looks of everything revealed by the flashlight, she was in a basement. As she came upon rolling steel doors, she pulled them aside. She pushed chain-link gates open as she frantically moved through the basement, searching all the grimy rooms and storage areas, looking for Jack, all the while her sense of dread rising by the moment.

Even as she ran through the empty basement, she began to realize that he wasn't in the same building. This was Victor's slaughterhouse. Jack would have been taken somewhere else.

The place was an immense, filthy, confusing maze. Plastic sectioned off portions, making it more confusing. She couldn't find a stairway up or a way out.

Kate eventually found a window covered in bars up high. Outside she could see only a dark alley and the corner of a Dumpster. The window was too high to reach. She cast about, looking for something she could drag closer, but there wasn't anything she could use to stand on.

She didn't know what to do. She was growing more frantic by the moment. She put her back against a wall and slid down, putting her head in her hands as she started to cry in fright for Jack. How was she going to find him? How was she going to help him?

Stricken with a sudden idea, she pulled out the burner phone Jack had given her. She stared at it a moment, crying, trying to think. She pushed the first speed-dial number. She wiped her tears with the back of her other wrist as she listened to the phone ring once, twice. Then someone answered.

"Yes?" a voice asked.

"Please! I need help! I need to talk to, to, Dvora! I need to talk to Dvora! It's an emergency!"

"Code in."

Kate made a fist as she screamed. "I don't know the code! I don't know it! Jack Raines is in trouble! They're going to kill him! I need help!"

"Code in."

"I don't know any code! I only heard Jack say the name Dvora Art-something!"

"Who is this?"

"Kate Bishop! I'm Kate Bishop! I'm the one who saw the guy with the bomb at O'Hare Airport! He called this number to get help! Please, they're going to kill him. I need help. Please help me . . . please . . ."

"Hold."

As Kate held the phone to her ear, she gave in to weeping as she waited, not knowing if they were going to help her or not, not knowing if they could.

"This is Dvora Artzi," a woman abruptly said.

Kate jumped to her feet. "I'm Kate Bishop! Help me! They're going to kill Jack! I need help! Please!"

"Jack?"

"Jack Raines!"

"You are the one who said that you saw someone with a bomb at O'Hare Airport?"

"Yes! A man went on an Air France plane. I'm the one who saw him and told Jack. He called you."

"What kind of bomb did he have?"

Kate grabbed a fistful of hair, hardly able to control her rage. "It was surgically implanted in him. The bomb was inside his abdomen. When you were on the phone with Jack I described the bomber and told you he had a bomb inside him."

"I remember you, Kate. What's wrong? Tell me."

Kate momentarily gave in to a cry of relief. She wiped her nose on her hand as she composed herself in order to talk.

"Jack and I came to New York City. We went to the hotel. We were drugged. I woke up in a basement duct-taped to a chair with a killer who was going to saw off my legs."

"How did you get away?"

"I broke the bastard's neck. I managed to get free but I don't know where I am. I don't know where they're holding Jack. The guy who had me said that they were going to kill him."

"Who is 'they'? Do you know?"

"I think it's a woman named Shannon Blare. She's the editor for his book. We came here to see her about his new book."

There was a brief pause. "All right, I want you to listen carefully to me, Kate. Can you do that?"

"Yes." Kate sucked back a sob. "Just please help me find him before they kill him. Please."

"I'm going to do that. Stay on the line with me."

"Do something! Don't just talk to me! You need to do something!"

"I already am, Kate. You need to trust me."

The woman's voice sounded calm and controlled. Tears running down her face, Kate nodded. "All right. What do you want me to do?"

"Do you have any idea of where you are?"

"No. It's a basement of a big building. They had me duct-taped to a chair."

"Okay, you need to stay on the phone so we can find you."

"This phone doesn't have GPS."

"That doesn't matter. We're already on it. Can you see if you can find a door for me? See if you can find a way out of the basement?"

Kate nodded as she looked around in the darkness. "I'll try."

"Just don't hang up. Even if you say something and I don't answer, I will still be here on the line. I'm trying to get you some help. Just don't hang up."

"I won't," Kate said with a sob of relief as she started down a hallway. There were pipes high up along one wall. She followed them through the darkness, her small flashlight showing her the way. Jack's flashlight showing her the way.

He had to be all right. He just had to.

CHAPTER FIFTY-EIGHT

Kate pushed open the heavy door. It scraped against dirt and rubble. Before her was a cement stairway filled with papers and garbage. It led up to an alley. At the top she stopped and carefully looked around.

"Dvora, I'm out. I'm outside. I'm in an alley."

"Can you see anything noteworthy?"

Kate looked around. "No. I can tell you that it's not the kind of neighborhood you'd want to be lost in at night."

"I understand," Dvora said, sounding distracted as she also whispered something off to the side Kate couldn't hear.

"There's a lot of scaffolding all along the street side of the building I was in. At the curb there are a couple of burned-out cars with no wheels up on blocks. There are coils of razor wire on the tops of some of the fences and walls."

"Do me a favor, Kate."

"What's that?" Kate asked as she looked out of the alley up and down the dark street. There were gangs of men on the corners to either end of the block. Their body language told her she was right about the neighborhood.

"Kate, I want you to step back in the alley and stay out of sight. Can you do that?"

"Why?" Kate asked as she moved back into the dark alley.

"Because I see your location and you were right about the area. We don't need any complications right now. I want you to stay out of sight. Help is on the way."

"It is?" Kate was a bit surprised. Her hopes soared. "Thank you, Dvora. Please tell them to hurry. Do you know where Jack is?"

"Not yet. Just stay back out of sight. We almost have you."

Almost had her? Those words nearly made Kate break down, but she held it together.

All of a sudden, a black SUV squealed around the corner, nosed partway into the alley, and slammed on the brakes. The passenger door popped open.

"Kate, he's there. Get in the vehicle."

Kate leaped up and jumped into the front seat. Even as she was pulling the door closed, the driver was backing out of the alley. As the men standing on the corners to either side started swarming in toward them, he put the truck in drive and shot away.

"He's got you," Dvora said. "You're in safe hands now."

"Thank you," Kate said.

"Shalom." The line went dead.

Kate looked over at the driver. He gave her a brave kind of smile and extended a hand across the armrest.

"I am Gilad Ben-Ami," he said. He was middle-aged and had neat salt-and-pepper hair, a goatee, and a perfectly tailored gray suit. The knot of his dark red tie had a collar pin under it.

Kate took his hand. "Kate Bishop."

"I know," he said. "We are grateful to you and Jack."

"Are you the police?"

"No," he said with a kind of knowing smile. "I am a diplomat. At the UN. Here in the city."

"Diplomat." Kate had been around security long enough to know what that meant. "Mossad."

He shrugged, noncommittally.

"Better than the police," she said.

He smiled at that. By the way he looked her up and down, at what a bloody mess she was, she knew that he was concerned for her health. She didn't care about that.

"Do you know where he is? Have you found him yet?"

"Not yet. We're pinging his phone. You told Dvora that you and Jack were drugged?"

"Yes. A killer named Victor that Jack had seen before had me down in that basement. He told me that someone else was going to kill Jack."

"How did you get away?"

"My arms were taped to a chair. The guy likes to saw off women's legs, so my legs weren't tied down. He films it and posts the videos." Kate pulled the SD card from her pocket, held it up for him for a second and then dropped it in a tray in the center console.

"When he had his back turned, fiddling with the camera, I was able to run up behind him and throw a leg around his head, twist it, and break his neck."

Gilad arched an eyebrow. "Smart thinking."

Kate looked down at her trembling hands. They were bloody. "I saw Jack do that before. That's what gave me the idea. He did that to kill a man who was trying to kill me."

Gilad nodded as he raced down a street, going through a red light. "We taught him that. Do you have any idea who could have him, or where?"

"I think this woman, Shannon Blare, has him. She's his editor, and I think she was using him without his knowledge to find people like me. He told me one time that he couldn't figure out how these killers were getting to people he found with my ability before he could help them. I think she was the way they were doing it."

He nodded as he let out an unhappy sigh. "This is bad business."

The phone rang. He pushed a button on the steering wheel to answer it.

A voice said "The phone he made the call on from the airport is in your car."

Gilad cursed in Hebrew, then said "Okay" and hung up.

"Jack split up our phones," Kate said, her heart

sinking. “He gave me one to carry. It must have been the one he used at O’Hare.”

“What can you tell me about this woman, this Shannon Blare? Can you tell me anything?”

Kate recognized an investigator asking critical questions, even if this one did have a thick accent.

They raced past little markets, liquor stores, bars, and crowds of people hanging around on street corners, smoking. Blocky brick buildings rose up to either side.

“She’s an editor,” Kate said, trying to focus. “But Jack said the job is just a hobby for her. I think her job was an excuse, a way to use him. He said she’s wealthy, travels in a limo all the time, and she likes to buy buildings. I think he mentioned high-rises. She must be some kind of property owner for her main business.”

Kate’s mind was already racing to put all the pieces together.

She looked over at him. “Can you find out what buildings she owns and if any of them are empty, like maybe they’re being remodeled?”

Gilad pressed a button on the steering wheel for the phone. When someone answered, they spoke to each other in Hebrew, so Kate didn’t know what they were saying, but she recognized the names Jack Raines and Shannon Blare, and she heard the urgency in the voices and the clipped clarity.

After a brief wait, the person on the other end of the line came back with two addresses.

Gilad cut around a corner, squealing the tires. "We're lucky," he said as they picked up speed. "They aren't too far and the traffic is light this time of night. This woman owns and rents out property. She purchased two buildings late last year. They are near one another and both being renovated."

Gilad checked his mirrors and stepped on the gas.

As they raced down the street, cutting through the traffic, sometimes taking to an empty oncoming lane, he looked over at her. "How well do you know Jack Raines?"

Kate's brow wrinkled. She was hardly able to keep it together enough to get the words out.

"I'm in love with him."

She loved him and had never told him.

"Ah" was all Gilad said, but that said it all.

Gilad made another call. He gave brief instructions and the two addresses. Kate couldn't understand the words but she recognized that he was calling for backup.

The drive seemed to take forever, but he finally skidded to a stop at the curb in front of a brick building. A dented Dumpster sat on the sidewalk outside and plastic covered the dark windows. Gilad turned to her and pointed a finger up at the place. "This is one of the buildings." He pointed a thumb back across the street. “That’s the other one.”

Kate already had her hand on the door handle. “Let’s go.”

“No,” he said. “You wait here. I’m going to go in and search this one. Help is on the way. It will be here any moment. After I look in here, I will go check the other one. You wait here, please.”

“Like hell,” Kate said as she opened the door and jumped out. She looked back in. “While you check this building I’ll go across the street to look in the other one.”

It was obvious that he knew he wasn’t going to be able to talk her out of it. He tried anyway.

“Wait—I have backup on the way.”

“Good,” she said as she started running. “If you don’t find him, come find me.”

Across the street, the second building looked in bad shape. The outside was encased in a web of scaffolding pipe and a lot of plastic. Planks among the pipes made levels of walkways high up in the air. The sidewalk was boarded off to keep people from being killed by falling rubble.

She didn’t see anyone on the street.

Kate ran along the wooden fence to the alley. It was dark, wet, and lined with dumpsters.

She ran into the alley, looking for a way to get into the building. She found two steel doors but they were both locked. She stumbled to a stop when she saw a low window with the corner broken out. She carefully reached in, unlatched the lock, then pushed the rusty window open.

She shined her flashlight in and saw that it was about a six-foot drop to a floor littered with dirt and crumbled debris.

Kate slipped her feet through first and jumped in.

CHAPTER FIFTY-NINE

Kate landed on her feet as lightly and quietly as possible. The flashlight revealed square, concrete support columns at regular intervals. Overhead were webs of pipes and ductwork draped with filthy cobwebs. She made her way across the room, trying to rush, trying to do it quietly. Crumbled debris crunched under her feet, echoing through the darkness.

She paused, listening for voices, but it was dead quiet.

On the far side of the room she found a broad opening into another section of the basement. Once through the opening, she thought she heard something to the left. She followed the sounds deeper into the dark wasteland.

After going for quite some distance, she rounded a corner to abruptly find herself beside the driver's side of a stretch limo parked in the near darkness. Ahead of it a ramp rose quite a ways up to the street level, where there was a closed metal garage door. A single fluorescent fixture high up near the door provided weak light in the sea of darkness below.

It was too late to be careful. The driver had already seen her.

"Hey!" he yelled as he bounded out of the car,

reaching under his suit jacket for a knife in a sheath on his belt. He hesitated for an instant. "You?"

He obviously recognized her. Kate certainly recognized the murderous look in his eyes.

He was probably one of the men who had carried her and Jack out of the hotel, no doubt out of a service elevator and back-alley entrance. Kate was sure that Shannon Blare, who got them that particular room, had it all planned out and prearranged. They walked right into her trap.

The driver was a burly man with greasy black hair combed over to one side. Before he was fully standing, before he had fully drawn the knife, Kate was already in the kill zone. A lightning-quick strike sliced open the side of his neck. By the jet of blood she knew she'd hit the carotid artery, but she rapidly slashed it again for good measure.

His killer eyes widened as shock and panic froze him in place. Blood erupted from under his hand at his throat. In mere seconds she could see in his eyes that he was rapidly losing consciousness.

Kate kicked him over. He slammed heavily to the floor beside the car. She leaned into the limo and quickly searched around inside. She opened the center armrest and glove box, looking for a gun, but didn't find one. She saw a garage-door opener on the visor.

She knew that if she pressed the button, the metal door would make a racket as it opened, but maybe no one was close enough to hear it, or they might think the driver had opened it for something.

If the door was open, not only would Gilad have a way in, it would give him a good idea of where she was. The body beside the limo at the bottom of the ramp would certainly confirm that they were in the right place.

Kate pressed the button. The metal door clattered as it began to open, but it wasn't as loud as she had feared.

As she turned, her flashlight revealed footprints in the dirt and debris all around the car. She spotted drag marks leading away from the back door of the limo.

A sense of desperate hope flashed through her at knowing that those drag marks would be from them pulling Jack out of the car and dragging him to the place where they likely intended to torture information out of him before they slaughtered him.

Kate followed the swerving tracks of the drag marks and footprints back into the depths of the basement. They led to a concrete stairwell on the far side of the room. She hurried down the steps into the bowels of the decrepit building. It stank of mildew and rancid oil.

At the bottom she leaned out and saw light

ahead among the support columns, ductwork, and the building systems equipment layered with dirt. The drag marks wove their way among the machinery toward the light.

With her vision adjusted to the darkness, Kate switched off her light, put it in her back pocket, and took out her second knife. The blade snapped open with a soft metallic *snick*.

As she came around a large, square support column, she suddenly spotted Jack. She gasped.

He was hanging on a rope by his wrists. The rope went up through a pulley at the ceiling and then to a cleat on the wall, where it was tied off.

Jack was without a shirt and covered in blood and angry red wounds. His feet swayed a few inches off the floor.

Kate's heart was beating so hard she could feel herself rock back and forth.

She quickly peered around but didn't see anyone. She knew, though, that there had to be people around. Either they were back in the shadows, or maybe they had gone off for some reason. If they were gone, this was her best chance. She might not get another.

She ran for the rope tied to the wall.

"Kate! Behind you!" Jack shouted.

Kate spun in time to see a big man reaching out to grab her. She hammered her knives into his eyes with a one-two punch. As he screamed with an ear-piercing shriek and his hands came up to cover his face, Kate swept her blade across his abdomen. His intestines spilled partway out and then began unfolding down toward his feet.

Kate immediately turned back to Jack, dangling helpless at the end of the rope.

"Move!" Jack screamed.

Kate instantly understood and dove to the side as a woman in a dark pantsuit across the room fired a gun. The sound of the gun going off in the basement was deafening. Kate heard the bullet hit the floor right beside her. She immediately rolled the other way as the woman fired again. The sound of the gunshots echoed through the basement, but the shot missed.

Kate rolled back to her feet and frantically ran in a zigzag as fast as she could, back and forth, denying the woman a clear shot, all the time racing closer.

As she dodged to the side, running past a square column for cover, an arm reached out and lifted her from her feet. It was a sweaty man in a black sleeveless undershirt. Kate stabbed a knife down in each side of the man's bull neck several times, as fast as she could. She knew that it wasn't a fatal strike, but it cut muscle and surprised him enough to drop her. As she fell toward the floor, she stuck a blade in his thigh and dragged it down with her, laying his thigh muscle open.

When the woman fired at Kate again, the shot instead hit the man in the center of his back. By the way he immediately went down, the bullet must have hit his heart and killed him instantly.

Kate sprang over the man, using her foot on his body to help her push into a dead run. As Kate raced in to close the distance in time, the woman urgently turned the gun toward Jack.

"Enough of this."

She fired four quick shots into Jack as Kate screamed, "NO!"

Shannon Blare swung the gun back toward Kate, but Kate was already there. She snatched the woman's gun hand as she raced in, twisted violently under it, breaking the woman's wrist. She spun the arm around behind and used her leverage to flip the woman through the air.

Shannon Blare slammed down hard on her back with a grunt. Kate's full weight came down on a knee to the center of the woman's chest, driving the rest of the wind from her lungs.

Kate had stripped the gun from Shannon Blare's hand when she flipped her over. She gripped the gun in both hands, pointing it down at the center of the woman's face.

The defiant eyes of a killer looked up at her.

Kate pulled the trigger four times.

With the cement floor right under her head, the bullets fragmented and blew out the back of the skull, spraying blood and brain matter across the floor. The sound of the shots echoed through the basement.

As Kate scrambled to her feet she heard shots, but these were different. It was a burst of full-auto fire, three shots in the span of a fraction of a second.

When she turned to the sound, bringing her gun up, she saw red mist spray from the head of another one of Shannon Blare's men. His gun clattered across the floor as he went down.

Kate saw two men way back across the room running in out of the darkness. One of the men was dressed in a gray suit, the other in dark clothes and carrying a small submachine gun. He had taken out the gunman with that precise, brief burst.

Kate turned and raced to the wall. Her fingers clawed at the rope laced tightly around the cleat. She was finally able to undo it and free the rope. Using her weight to counterbalance Jack's weight, she lowered him to the floor. As she was doing so, she heard two more bursts of automatic gunfire in the distance. The threat was being handled by Gilad and his men.

Once she had Jack down on his back, a pool of blood immediately started to spread under him.

Kate cut his wrists free and then took his face in both hands. "Jack—Jack. It's all right now. I'm here. We're all right."

Even as she said it, she knew it wasn't true.

He stared at her, unable to take his eyes off her.

"Lie still," Kate said, smoothing a hand down

his face. “Don’t talk. Help is on the way.”

“Too late,” he whispered. “She fooled me. I couldn’t see what you can. She fooled me.”

“No, Jack, it’s not too late.” Kate took one of his hands in hers. “Don’t say that. It’s going to be all right.”

He smiled a little.

“Jack—I love you. Do you hear me? I love you. Please hang on, please. I love you so much.”

His smile widened and his grip on her hand tightened. “You made my wish come true.”

“I love you, Jack—I do. Hold on, please hold on. I need you so much.”

“I love you, too, Kate. . . . I was going to tell you at dinner. You taught me what living really means. Life is too precious to let the past steal it away. I was going to tell you. . . . I was going to ask you to spend the night with me . . . to spend every night with me.”

“Yes.” She kissed his lips as she squeezed his hand. “Forever yes.”

He smiled.

“It doesn’t hurt anymore,” he said. “I want you to know . . . I don’t hurt anymore. You made all my pain go away.”

“Me too. I love you, Jack.”

He smiled again. “Live, Kate. Live.”

And then the light of his soul began to fade away from his beautiful eyes. His hand went slack. His last breath left his body.

Kate screamed. "*No!* Jack no!"

She lay across his chest, listening for a heartbeat. There was none.

"Don't leave me. Please Jack," she wept, "I love you. Don't leave me."

Kate looked back over her shoulder and saw men in dark clothes coming at a dead run. "Hurry!" she screamed. "Help him!"

As they rushed in, Gilad's gentle hands lifted her out of the way as the men crowded down around Jack. Gilad sheltered her in his arms as she wept in helpless agony.

One of the men gathered around Jack checked him and immediately started giving him CPR, counting each compression out loud. Another man put a mask over Jack's face and started squeezing the bag attached to it to get air into his lungs.

A third man pulled packs from the cargo pockets of his vest. He put a needle in Jack's arm and held up a bag of fluid. A man who'd been carrying a case in each hand set them down and started pulling out equipment. He lifted out defibrillator paddles and squeezed gel onto them as another man switched on the machine.

Kate watched in a daze as he used the paddles, trying to start Jack's heart. Each time he called "Clear" and hit the button, Jack's body flinched, but each time they had to go back to doing CPR as the defibrillator charged. She lost count of how many times they tried to restart his heart. Each attempt felt as if it jolted her heart.

Gilad, seeing how grave the situation truly was, started pulling Kate away. She stretched an arm back toward Jack. "No! No! Let me stay."

The man with the paddles sat back on his heels, looking at Gilad, and shook his head.

Kate heard a truck engine in the distance, rumbling though the basement, and then more of the men in black ran in pulling a gurney. They never stopped giving Jack CPR even as they lifted him onto the gurney. Once he was on the gurney, the man with the paddles tried again. Jack's body jumped, but she knew by the men's reaction that it hadn't worked.

Kate thought she might faint when she heard one of the men say that when they got him in the van they were going to have to crack open his chest to get at his heart.

She clutched Gilad's sleeve. "I want to go with him."

Gilad's arm around her shoulders squeezed her tight as he pulled her away. "You don't need to see that. Please, Kate. You must remember him for his words to you. That would be what he would want the most."

Kate looked up at him. "I have to go with him."

Gilad finally relented and gave her a nod. "Let them do their job. We will follow in my car."

She could tell that he believed Jack was beyond help.

CHAPTER SIXTY

Kate saw the impeccably dressed figure of Gilad Ben-Ami coming across the expanse of grass. He was holding a bouquet of flowers.

Kate, lying on her side on Jack's grave, didn't get up when Gilad came to a stop over her. He stood for a moment, gazing down at her, and then he lowered himself down to sit on the grass beside her.

"I brought some flowers," he said. He lifted them out to show her briefly before he placed them in the small metal vase above Jack's gravestone.

"Thank you," Kate said. "They're beautiful."

After that terrible night, it seemed like the world had slowed to a stop, leaving Kate feeling empty and numb. John's death and the deaths of AJ and her family seemed like they had all happened in a dream.

But Jack's death was a nightmare.

Kate knew that the sight of them loading him into that van in the basement while working on his unresponsive, blood-slick body was something that would haunt her forever.

Gilad and Kate had followed the specially equipped van on the way to a trauma center while what he assured her was an elite Israeli combat medical team worked on Jack. When Gilad received a call from the van as they followed behind, he told her that they had opened Jack's chest and were massaging his heart to try to keep him alive.

Much later that awful night, as she sat beside Gilad on a bench in the cold hallway of a private medical facility, doctors continued to try everything humanly possible to save Jack. But in the end there was nothing more they could do.

Gilad had been invaluable after Jack's death. He had handled everything, including taking care of all the arrangements as well as helping her in a strange city.

If there were any police involved, Kate never knew of it. She suspected that diplomatic immunity had been involved and everything had been kept under the radar in order to protect her. Gilad had taken her to a secluded hotel and made sure that no one bothered her. He had meals delivered. She ate few of them.

His country had given Jack a beautiful funeral in a private, exclusive cemetery protected with towering, old trees. A lot of people attended. She hadn't known any of them, but they all knew Jack and they knew of her. Most all of them wept.

Kate was appreciative of those who came, who shook her hand or hugged her and told her how sorry they were, and how much Jack had done for them all.

A woman with wavy black hair had given Kate a hug and introduced herself. It was Dvora Artzi. She had come from Israel for the funeral, as had a number of others. She told Kate that she was the bravest woman she had ever had the honor to know. Kate remembered begging for help on the phone and didn't feel the least bit brave.

Dvora had stayed until just the previous day, spending the time with Kate so she wouldn't be alone. It was comforting to have her there. She confided in Kate that her husband had been killed in a bombing. That bonded them in a kind of silent sisterhood, the living left behind by evil, both having been in love with men who fought to protect life.

Gilad had given the eulogy. He said to the solemn audience that they were all his countrymen, and they all lived every day with what Jack Raines had told them about, that the world was coming to dark times, and that in the fight against evil, Israel was the tip of the spear. Jack, he said, was the sharp point of that spear.

In that effort, Jack Raines, a man from another country, a man not of their religion or heritage, had been a true friend to them all, for he fought for something universal. He fought so that others might have the chance to live their lives. He said that Jack's tireless work had saved a great many people, more than any of them would ever know.

Gilad said that while darkness had taken him,

it did not defeat him, because he had brought light to them all, and in each of them there would always be a piece of Jack Raines, lighting the way for them.

Kate told Gilad that it was the most beautiful thing she had ever heard. He said it was because it was from his heart, and the hearts of all those who knew Jack.

Jack had no living relatives that anyone knew of. Gilad insisted that everything he had should to go to her.

Among Jack's possessions, besides the bank accounts, was the thumb drive that he had used to take her to the underworld of the darknet. She also had his burner phones with all the numbers he had, like the one he had used to call for help when Kate saw a killer boarding the Air France plane, the same one she had used to call Dvora for help.

Jack's laptop had a lot of information on people he was trying to contact. Gilad said that he hoped she would get in touch with them, because they were like her, they had the vision she had, and maybe she could help them come to understand that vision and the gift of life they had been born with.

He told her that they had worked with Jack for years, and while Jack had found a number of people who could see evil, none of them had ever been able to do what she could do.

What Kate could do, Gilad said, was something beyond exceptional, beyond what any other had ever been able to do. He had no idea how to explain the ability, he only knew she possessed it. Kate didn't know what to think of that.

He also delivered an open invitation to come to Israel anytime she wanted, for as long as she wanted, as their guest.

In the days after Jack's death, Gilad and his people had managed to go through Shannon Blare's effects and found passwords, credentials, and other information that allowed them to take control of the Scavenger Hunt site.

Gilad told Kate that their investigation revealed that Shannon Blare had been a rare, and ruthless, female serial killer, a black widow, linked to fourteen murders they knew of so far, but he was certain there were many more. Apparently, she started out killing homeless men she found living in the buildings she bought. There was no way to tell how many more of those men she killed, or what she did with the bodies. From what they learned in her effects, she was obsessed with the act of killing.

By chance, from Jack's book, Shannon Blare learned of those special people like Kate. It was one of those connections Jack spoke of wherein predators crossed paths with those able to see them. As a result of that connection, she had formed a nest of killers dedicated to eliminating those who could see them for who they were. Because he was blind to what Kate had easily seen in her eyes, Jack had unwittingly helped Shannon Blare find some of those people with that rare vision.

Like a black widow, she drew them into her nest.

Gilad said that they had cleaned everything off the site. Kate's photos were gone. The rewards were gone. There were no longer any active scavenger hunts. The torture videos were gone. The review section was gone.

The only thing left of the site was the home page. There, the Mossad had posted a photo and some text. They had lined up over a dozen dead who had been a part of the Scavenger Hunt nest, with Shannon Blare lying in the center, the back half of her head gone, and taken a photo of the collected bodies in all their bleeding glory. They put it up on the home page, saying only that these were killers who had been dealt with. They then locked down the site so that no one could add anything, alter anything, or take it down.

All of the killers or want-to-be killers who had visited the site before would now find only a photo of their dead idols.

The remains of Rita and others killed by Victor and other members of the nest had finally been laid to rest.

Rights to *A Brief History of Evil* went to Kate, as did the royalties. But with the numbered account Jack had given her and his considerable wealth, the royalties hardly mattered.

Besides the information on others like herself that Kate had found on Jack's computer, she had also found the manuscript of his new book. Jack had told her that he had work to do on it, but he wasn't exactly telling her the truth. She discovered that it was actually mostly finished except for the last important connection he was trying to make.

He had notes having to do with a rare kind of super-visionary who could see more than merely a killer by looking into their eyes. Jack theorized that as a result of evolution such a person would have to exist and they would be able to see evil itself, and the shape it would take.

In his notes he said that he was still looking for that rare individual who could see those things that no one else could.

Kate knew that she was the one he had been searching for.

She now knew enough to complete the manuscript, but she decided not to. She had it, and that was enough. Jack believed that mankind would ultimately survive or not. He couldn't save the world.

She couldn't save the world.

She knew from Jack that it was up to each of

them to live the life they had to its fullest in the world they were born into. Only in that way could they make their world better.

"How are you doing, Kate?" Gilad asked.

"My life is over," she said as she sat up.

Gilad smiled as he touched her cheek. "Jack would not like to hear you say that. He fought so that you might live."

Kate felt a flash of shame. She nodded. "You're right."

He handed her something. She saw that it was an SD card.

"What's this?"

"It's the card out of the camera that Victor was using to record what he was doing to you. The one from the camera filming Jack has been destroyed. No one will ever see it.

"I am returning this one to you because it is you on the video. It was difficult to watch. I was going to destroy it, but I thought that maybe you should be the one to do that if you wish. I think that someday, if you ever decide to watch it, you will see a woman who is brave, a woman who is inspiring."

Kate closed her hand around it and held her fist to her chin. "Thank you. You are a very thoughtful man, Gilad."

He huffed a brief laugh.

He turned serious then as he gazed at her.

"When there is great trouble in the world, God

sends us angels. You never know what form those angels will take. You are one of those angels."

Kate shook her head. "The only angel I ever knew was Angel Janek. She was an avenging angel. She protected lives. She died in this struggle. It was because of her that I met Jack."

He gave her an admonishing look. "You saved the lives of hundreds of people about to board that plane. None of them will ever know of the angel watching over them, the angel who saved their lives from evil that day."

"You saved me."

"We all save each other, Kate Bishop."

She smiled a sad smile. "I guess we do."

Gilad reached into the inside breast pocket of his suit jacket. "Speaking of which, I have a problem. I hate to do this to you. Honestly, I do, Kate," he said, looking quite guilty. "I am hoping that you might be willing to help me . . ."

"It's all right," she said, laying a hand on his. "I understand."

Kate took the stack of photos from him. She shuffled through the whole stack, then pulled one photo out of the rest and tossed it on the grass before him. It was a smiling, intelligent-looking young man. But he had the terrifying eyes of a killer. She saw that in his eyes, and so much more.

"This one," she said.

"You are sure?"

Kate nodded. "You have twelve hours."

"Twelve hours?"

"He has a bomb in a moped, or scooter, or whatever they're called. It's a faded red and has some rust. It's a big bomb, in the hollowed-out seat. He intends to set it off just over twelve hours from now."

Gilad frowned. "Where is he? Where is he going to use this bomb? Do you know?"

"The Israeli embassy in Sweden."

He stared at her. "You're serious?" When he saw that she was, he asked, "How can you know this just from looking at his photo?"

Kate arched an eyebrow. "You're the one who said I was an angel. You tell me."

She thought about what Jack had said in the manuscript about believing that there was someone who possessed the ability to do just such a thing. He had written that before he met her.

Gilad hastily stuffed the photos back in his breast pocket as he clambered back to his feet. "I must go and tend to this. Thank you, Kate. Thank you for all the people who will not die in twelve hours."

He reached down to touch her cheek. "Shalom."

Kate looked up at him. "What does that mean? 'Shalom'?"

"It means peace," he said.

Kate smiled. "I like that. Shalom, Gilad."

He turned back as he was leaving and waved. “I will call you. I would like to take you to dinner. Someplace nice.”

“I’d like that,” Kate called after him.

When he was gone, Kate went back to her silent vigil at Jack’s grave. She touched the headstone with his name. He was part of the history of mankind now, the long history he spoke so passionately about.

She knew that someday she would move on, but for the time being she felt that it was important to come every day to tell him that she loved him. She had been able to tell him that when he was alive, and she knew what it had meant to him. He had told her that he loved her, and she knew what it meant to her.

It would last her a lifetime.

By the time it was dark the other visitors had long since gone.

Kate didn’t want to leave. It felt like she would be deserting him, leaving him all alone in the night. But she could see the caretaker waiting by the door of the reception area, a finger flicking the keys at his belt. He obviously didn’t want to be rude and ask her to leave, but it was past closing time.

In the gathering darkness Kate made her way across the grass and then the asphalt path to where the caretaker stood, waiting to let her out so he could lock up.

She was staring off into her thoughts of Jack as she walked past the caretaker. He reached out and gripped her upper arm to stop her. Beyond the man's filthy tan shirtsleeve, she saw the sign on the door marked EXIT.

Something had been handwritten under the EXIT sign with a grease pen.

It said *Not any more*.

Kate looked over into his eyes. They were the eyes of a stone cold killer. The eyes of the devil.

"We don't often get visited by an angel here," he said with a wicked grin. The grin faded as he leaned closer, peering into her eyes. "Do I know you? You look . . . familiar, somehow."

Kate's thumb on the assist button snapped the blade of her knife open.

"I should look familiar," she said, "especially in this place."

"Yeah? Why's that?"

"Because I'm the angel of death."

CHAPTER SIXTY-ONE

"It's for you," the flight attendant said, holding out the handset of one of the three phones on the bulkhead.

Seeing that it was the secure line, Dvora sprang up from the thick leather chair and took the handset.

"This is Dvora."

"It's Gilad," the voice on the other end said.

"Gilad." She was suddenly tense. "How did it go?"

"Kate Bishop was right. We caught the man before he could get to our embassy in Sweden. He had a bomb in the hollowed-out seat of his rusted, red moped, just as she said he would."

Dvora let out a sigh. "Kate Bishop just saved yet more lives. Jack never before found a subject quite like her."

"Yes," he agreed, "she is for sure a remarkable woman."

"I'm glad I had some time to get to know her a little better."

"Me too," Gilad said. "She has a warrior's heart."

Dvora knew why he was calling. She wished she had better news. She waited, listening to the constant, muffled roar of jet engines. The monitor on the bulkhead said they were at an altitude of forty-two thousand feet with a time to destination of just over five hours. Out the window, the setting sun behind them was mostly hidden by a haze of clouds far below. The surface of the ocean glowed golden in the late-day light.

"So how is he doing?" Gilad finally asked. "Any change?"

Dvora looked over at the bed locked down along the side of the cabin. An assortment of equipment stood clustered at the head of the bed, near the bulkhead, all of it alive with a steady stream of information. Lights blinked, green lines blipped in spikes, numbers flashed. Every once in a while, the blood pressure cuff inflated. She looked at the slow, steady rhythm of the heart monitor.

"I think the same."

"No better?"

Dvora appraised the collection of tubes coming out of the side of his chest, the PICC line in his upper arm, the bags of fluids hanging over him with lines running to both wrists, all the information on the monitors, and the ventilator helping him breathe. Two nurses sat below the equipment, monitoring it continually and hanging full bags of fluid when needed. The doctor was resting in one of the jet's plush, tan leather seats opposite the bed.

The doctor looked up at her. She lifted out the

handset as if to say Gilad wanted a report. The doctor shook his head.

"No, I'm afraid not," Dvora told Gilad. "His condition is the same."

"But he is still alive," Gilad said, sounding as if he insisted on it.

"Still alive," Dvora confirmed. "Jack Raines is a hard man to kill."

"This is good news," Gilad decided. "They did not expect him to live even this long. So this is good news."

Dvora didn't want to let him read too much into it. "Listen, Gilad, Dr. Lewin warned me again that Jack will likely never come out of the coma, and even if he does, there is no telling how long his brain was deprived of oxygen so there is no way to know if Jack Raines is still Jack Raines, or if he ever will be again. Dr. Lewin knows full well how important Jack Raines is, and he's keeping a constant watch, but he doesn't sound optimistic."

"But Jack is still alive," Gilad said again, the insistence still in his tone.

Dvora smiled. "Yes, my friend, he is still alive."

"When you get him to Tel Aviv, maybe the doctors there will be able to do more. They are remarkable. You will see. They will be able to do something."

Dvora knew that while Jack might in fact live,

it was likely that he would always be in a coma and on life support. From what Dr. Lewin had told her, people simply didn't recover from the kind of injuries he had sustained, or from having their heart stop for as long as his had.

"Maybe," she said, not wanting to crush his hopes. She changed the subject. "Have you told Kate Bishop that Jack is still alive?"

The jet engines droned on as she waited for him to answer. Out the window Dvora saw only what looked to be an endless expanse of ocean.

"No, I have not told her," Gilad finally said. "I don't have the heart to give her hope when there is so little."

Dvora let out a sorrowful sigh. "I suppose it's for the best."

"For now, I think it is," Gilad said. "We will get him back to Tel Aviv and let the best people we have see what can be done. They have a team standing by, waiting for you to get there."

"I don't think Dr. Lewin has slept for more than ten minutes at a time," she said, looking down at the man. "He's been by Jack's side continually. He's worried, Gilad—something about the fluid drainage. Even though the opening down the center of Jack's chest does seem to be healing, Dr. Lewin says that as soon as we land he thinks they may have to open up his chest again and go back in."

"If it is possible to save Jack, I know our people will do it."

Dvora twisted the phone cord around her hand. "From your lips to God's ear."

"With the funeral and all those who attended," Gilad said, "everyone believes Jack Raines is dead. That is what we need. Now, if we plant some seeds in the right places, word will leak out, then those who hunt him will also believe he is dead and buried. Having everyone believe Jack Raines is dead is the best way to protect him."

Dvora nodded. "You're right. He's too important not to do everything we can. Having the funeral to make people believe Jack died was the best thing to do. But if he recovers, he's too important to let anything happen to him."

"We won't let anything happen to him," Gilad assured her. "Jack Raines is again a ghost. He was always good at that. We will help keep it that way. He will once more be off the grid, so even if he lives, no one will know anything about him. As far as anyone is concerned, as far as anyone but us knows, Jack Raines no longer exists."

Dvora laid a hand on Jack's arm as she looked down at him. It would be good to have him be safe. She didn't know if he would ever come out of the coma, if he had brain damage, or if he would ever be himself again, but if they had to, they would care for him in return for all he had done for them.

He would be safe from those who hunted him.

And if he did recover . . .

"Agreed," Dvora said. "Jack Raines will once again be a ghost."

Center Point Large Print
600 Brooks Road / PO Box 1
Thorndike, ME 04986-0001 USA

(207) 568-3717

US & Canada:
1 800 929-9108
www.centerpointlargeprint.com